GOING
PLACES

GOING PLACES

BY BERTRAND BLIER

TRANSLATED BY PATSY SOUTHGATE

J. B. LIPPINCOTT COMPANY
PHILADELPHIA AND NEW YORK

This book is a translation of *Les Valseuses* by Bertrand Blier,
which has been published in France and is © Editions Robert
Laffont, S.A., 1972.

U.S. Library of Congress Cataloging in Publication Data

Blier, Bertrand.
    Going places.

    Translation of Les valseuses.
    I. Title.
PZ4.B6492Go [PQ2662.L47]   843'.9'14   74–13135
ISBN–0–397–01013–3
ISBN–0–397–01042–7 (pbk.)

TRANSLATOR'S NOTE

I would like to thank Robert Barker for his technical advice on cars, and express deep gratitude to Alan Martell for his invaluable assistance with slang.

PATSY SOUTHGATE

GOING
PLACES

We're real fuckheads.

For openers we copped some wheels. Just to take a little spin. Because we didn't know what to do. Saturdays we never know what to do. Sundays either. The flicks are a drag, broads are a pain, and you need bread, which we ain't got.

A Citroën 21, fuel-injected, brand new, parked in a deserted street—too good to pass up. A honey of a little four-door sedan. I put my hand on the hood: the engine was still warm.

All that shiny metal and leather in that alley full of funky family cars and tarnished chrome! A high-priced swinger from a classy neighborhood lost in the outskirts of town. A stray thoroughbred. Naturally we did a double take.

Nine o'clock. I scanned all the dark corners, doorways and balconies. Behind each cozy window glowed a bluish TV screen. A soap opera murmured reassuringly. Not a soul outside. It was then or never. In life you have to know when to make the play.

A Citroën D.S. is a sitting duck. I showed Pierrot the gimmick in a flash. At the ass end of the rear fender you've got this bolt. All you need is the right wrench, a twelve, which I always happen to have on me. You remove the bolt, pull on the fender and it comes right off. It's made that way for when you get a flat. Turns the customer into a body-and-fender artist. Those engineers in their little white coats must have worked for years to come up with that one. Thanks, you guys, now we can help ourselves to a D.S. with no hassle.

Once the fender's off, the back-door locking mechanism swings into view. A slight twist of the pliers and it's open.

At this point Pierrot said, "Watch this," and opened the front door. It hadn't even been locked.

"Never mind," I told him. "You'll know how next time."

I replaced the fender, bolt and everything, and we slid our butts onto those sensuous seats. The car sighed with pleasure. All we had to do was start her up. And that's just what she'd been waiting for, the bitch. We'd have been better off if she'd stalled, or flooded, or if her nozzle had gotten clogged.

Jumping a 21 is like jumping any other car. Just cross the wires, no sweat.

"Check your watch," I told Pierrot. "Start timing."

It took me three minutes, not a second more. Pierrot was fucking impressed when he saw that red ignition light come on. Of course it helps to have worked in a garage, even if only for a couple of weeks.

The engine caught on the first try. Quick glance at the gas gauge: full. Shit! When I think that we could have made it all the way to Paris! With an engine like that, at night, nobody on the roads, we'd have gotten there before daylight easy.

Paris—Christ we'd been wanting to get our asses there for a hell of a long time. Seems the scene's cool all night long in Saint-Michel. That's what we should have gone for—the big trip. The capital or bust. And then hitched back, no hassles, waiting for a good trailer, preferably one with a bunk. That would have shook the Toulouse shit right off our shoes.

Only, you see, we're fuckheads. We were chicken and we just took a little spin to Narbonne Beach. Talk about playing it safe—we hardly got around the corner.

Pierrot felt like a swim and so did I. We always agree, especially about doing dumb things. So we took the road to Narbonne.

Ten minutes later we got a flat. Back wheel, of course. So I got out my number-twelve wrench again and wrestled with that bitch of a fender. Chucked the flat into the weeds.

After that I really floored her. I wanted to take it out on her, wanted her to beg for mercy. But a 21 never begs. Unless you drive like a prick. And it so happens I drive like a master.

Toulouse–Narbonne in an hour and a half. Driving like public enemies. Pierrot kept his mouth shut—scared shitless, but kept his mouth shut. I was really putting on a show for him, too, trying to blow his mind. Flying around unbanked curves, giving her a little more gas when the tires were already screeching, tearing ass through villages full of blind intersections with my brights on, giving the kid quite a ride. Heel-and-toe, synchronized acceleration and braking, optimum utilization of the gears, 6,000 rpm in third, pure poetry. A dream car. The only one in the world, I explained to Pierrot, you can blast down a country road at 100 mph hugging the right bank, because the chassis will always stay level, no matter what.

I showed him how to leave so-called sports cars behind on tricky curves. We wiped out an Alfa. Left it standing still on a series of hairpin turns. I must say the cat didn't look like such a cool driver. I watched him, in my rear-view mirror, clutching his steering wheel. He wanted to look good because of the chick. He was an old fart with pigskin gloves, the type who dresses like he's in his twenties. He spun out to the left coming out of every curve—you could see what he was heading for. After a while he dropped out of sight. Probably came to a sticky end. Wrapped around a tree. The chick with her mouth hanging open, terrified, in the arms of the old jerk who would be making googoo eyes at her, very dead. I'm sure there are plenty of accidents like that, that are never explained. A new car, an empty road, and not even a sign of a raindrop!

Narbonne Beach was closed up tighter than a clam's ass. Ten thirty: the few families out for the weekend were already in the sack. We were alone on the deserted boardwalk, in front of concrete buildings exactly like at home, with an added bonus —the sea. But you still had to cross an enormous stretch of beach to get to it. I'm telling you, the joint was dead as a doornail. The wind was rising, too, damp and penetrating. Really too cold to make asses of ourselves running around on the sand. So we looked for a spot where we could grab a drink. There was one snack bar open. A huge empty dump with pinball machines and a greasy chick behind the bar.

"I'm closing in five minutes," she announced.

I blew her a kiss. "Just enough time to serve us a couple of beers."

We started playing pinball. Pierrot won a free game right off the bat.

"Drink your beers," the broad said, and she turned off half the neon lights. Right away it seemed more intimate.

We eased over to the bar, grinning, and began sipping the lousy beer and eyeing the fox.

A dog. Twenty, tops, big flabby tits, wet rings under her armpits and a filthy apron.

"That'll be six francs," she said, drumming on the Formica countertop with her dishpan hands.

I told her that was too much, she would be lucky to get half.

"I said six francs," she repeated.

"Well," said Pierrot very calmly, slowly letting his beer dribble onto the counter she had just wiped, "I say that you're ugly, you're a mess and you look like a whore."

"An ugly whore," I added. "A six-franc whore."

She didn't look too pleased.

I don't know how she pulled it off, but suddenly her old man was there, not looking too friendly.

"You're going to pay for your drinks," he told us, "and then get the hell outa here."

"We'll leave when we feel like it," Pierrot said. "We're customers here, and the customer is king."

The dude started to shove us outside, and I don't dig getting pushed. Then the broad got into the act—she started to shove too. Pierrot, to cool her out, grabbed one of her tits and gave it a twist.

"Quit pushing!" he yelled, "or I'll trash your fucking tits for good, you cunt!"

That knocked the wind out of her for a moment and she stopped pushing, like we asked. But her old man started shoving twice as hard, threatening to call the fuzz.

The chick had to sit down from the pain and started rubbing her left boob. She was bawling like a baby.

Finally we split, laughing our heads off, and the dude started locking up his rotten shack. As he was rolling down his iron shutter, we let him have it from the street. We told him his chick was ugly, his flippers were fucked up, and his beer was piss. We told him all that and lots more, and then we took a long leak on his shutter as it was still coming down.

12

"Here, big daddy! You can have your beer back—nice and foamy!"

We hit the road, busting our guts.

I let Pierrot take the wheel on the way back, asking him to take it nice and easy, since he didn't exactly have the hang of it yet.

He drove like a smoothie, no problem. Of course I was clueing him in on all the tricks as we went along: "Cut out, step on it, fall back! Cut that corner, pass that jerk, flash your headlights in his kisser!"

I tried on the safety belt just to see what it felt like. It made me feel like an ass so I tore it off. Seems they eliminate 80 percent of the serious injuries in accidents, but you've got to be some kind of idiot to hook yourself up in a contraption like that. And what if the car flips, huh? And catches fire? You'd be french-fried!

Personally I always like to feel that I can split. I have a hang-up about getting tied down, locked into one place. Like I was in prison. And when I think about prison, real panic sets in, chills up and down my spine, icicles. I'm sure I couldn't handle it. I'd rather have my head sliced off by a windshield. Besides, in the slams you're exposed to all that bad influence, rubbed by tough dudes who school you in their bad habits, disgraceful, a hood's training camp. How to pull a real job, for example, a big rip-off, carefully planned, commando-style, with synchronized watches, supporting artillery and inevitable deaths. Which means that we'd scarcely get out of the hole when we'd be sent up again, and for longer and longer stretches, our hair getting shorter and shorter, thinner, grayer. What they call a vicious circle in the papers. Had to avoid that at all costs. That's where my head was at the time and that's how I missed the play for Paris.

I even said to Pierrot, "We'll put the D.S. right back where we got it. The guy won't file a complaint."

Might as well have turned myself in. Because when we got the wheels back the schmuck was waiting for us.

You gotta admit we had lousy luck.

Midnight: not even a cat in the streets, especially since we flattened one on the way into Toulouse, a black motherfucker who flung himself right under our wheels.

Pierrot, who's an animal freak, wrenched the wheel around to try and avoid him, and we jumped the sidewalk.

"You crazy?" I asked him.

"You think we got him?"

He searched the rear-view mirror, looking really bothered.

"Watch the road, you jerk!"

"A black cat, I don't like that . . ."

"O.K., all right then, you got him, I felt the hit, he's dead. Let's cut out!"

"Shit."

"You couldn't help it, he ran right under the wheels! Anyhow, I'd rather have a black cat laid out."

"Do you think some of them commit suicide like that, by jumping in front of headlights?"

He was starting to bring me down with this heavy pussycat number! I had to relieve him at the wheel, he was so shook up.

Anyhow, we were getting close to the neighborhood. La Croix-Blanche, it was called. I killed the headlights, the dims, everything. Even my cigarette.

"Let's just ditch her here!" Pierrot said.

"No," I answered. "We're putting her back where we got her!"

He cooled it and we drove on. Allée des Séquoias, there it was. I made a right. I crept forward silently.

"Spot anyone? Keep your eyes peeled."

Pierrot looked. No one. Not one light. Total hush. The natives were in the sack, boob tubes all dark, lights out. It felt like we were inside a prison camp prowling around between those gray concrete cubes. A very quiet camp, nothing going on, not the slightest hint of a breakout. All the inmates just snoozing. You could smell their jailbird breath all the way out in the street. All clear.

We found exactly the same parking place, in front of the hairdresser's shop. I flipped her into reverse, parked. Turned the wheel with two fingers. Power steering. A honey.

14

I cut the ignition and breathed a sigh of relief.

"That's what I call borrowing a car—not to be confused with stealing!"

I don't know where the dude came from, how he'd managed to hide, but if you ask me, he must have been hanging out inside his shop, peeking between the slats of his venetian blinds. Anyway, we didn't see him coming—suddenly there he was, enormous, standing in front of the hood, a gun in his hand and a sneer on his puss. The only guy awake in Croix-Blanche, and he was out to get us.

We froze for a couple of seconds and then I muttered to Pierrot, "For Chrissake, play it cool. We'll try to make a deal."

We hauled our asses out of the car, looking like a couple of real dumdums. The dude eyed us. He was obviously crowing. A turkey about thirty, a clothes horse. Blue suit, flowered tie. The sporty type. With a sunlamp tan, like he was wearing makeup. If I'd been a chick I wouldn't have wasted my time telling him he was cute. He already knew it.

"Well . . ." he said. "And what have we here? Don't you think you look sort of stupid?"

At that moment the chick appeared. She came out of the hairdressing shop. She looked chilly, all bundled up in a fur. She was dragging her feet, tired-like, and stopped beside the guy, who made the introductions: "Will you look at these two creeps!"

We said nothing, just waited, checking out the broad. A blond beanpole, very skinny and caked with makeup. Little gusts of wind blew her coat open. We could see her naked thigh.

The guy caught our glance. "Not bad, huh? Can you afford this type of merchandise?" He generously held her coat open so that we could get a better look at her treasures. "You'd love to get your filthy paws on that, wouldn't you?"

Bothered, the broad pulled back.

"But right now," he went on, waving his rod at us, "you're going to put those filthy paws of yours up over your heads, that's what! Up, now! Reach!"

We lifted our hands a little, limply, not really getting into it. As high as our shoulders, let's say. To make him happy. To make him feel tough and everything.

He wasn't exactly jiving, the conceited ass.

"You've hit on the wrong guy, boys. I'm breaking in this gun. A brand new gun to teach pricks like you a lesson. Would you believe this is the third D.S. I've had stolen in less than a year—it's starting to give me a real pain."

"We didn't cop it," said Pierrot, his voice rising. "We *borrowed* it. And we just finished bringing it back. There it is! Safe and sound. Parked in the same spot. It hasn't moved!"

"You can tell that to the cops." He turned to the fox. "You can go get them."

The chick didn't move, looking put out. The bastard beamed at us, almost lovingly, and then started dishing it out again.

"The cops are really going to be tickled, having two long-haired weirdos like you handed over on a silver platter."

I caught the picture: Christmas in the clink. They'd treat us like two little Jesuses. Shower us with gifts.

Pierrot must have been thinking the same thing as me because he got the shakes.

"Listen," he shouted, up against the wall, "don't do that! No, not the fuzz! Shit. All this just for some wheels, it's too dumb! We didn't burn anyone. We just took a little spin because we didn't have any bread and we were bored. Just killing a Saturday night. It's like we'd been hitchhiking—same thing! Like you'd picked us up beside the road, except you weren't there, that's the only difference!"

It was my turn to give my spiel. I tried to smooth things over, still friendly.

"There's really no reason to pop your cork," I told him. "Now come off it. All we did was use a little gas. We didn't hurt anything, not even a scratch, nothing. There's just the idle that needs adjusting, but that's not serious—if you like I can do it for you right now, I've got a screwdriver on me, it'll only take a minute . . ."

"Get going," the guy told the broad. "Don't listen, you might start feeling sorry for them."

16

She stepped back, hesitated, then stopped. I pinned all my hopes on her. She was the same age as us, that could help make the difference.

I regained my cool. "Hey, man, please, listen, I have to explain. You don't dig what you're about to do."

Instinctively, rapping, I stepped forward and lowered my hands. Your hands can help when you're trying to persuade someone. I would have loved to use them. But he moved back, the piece of shit, rod raised, cowardly and menacing, both at the same time.

"The first to move gets a slug in the leg!"

And when the chick didn't budge, he shouted at her, "Well, what the hell are you waiting for? Get the cops!"

He was blowing it.

"Miss!" I called to the chick. "Wait! You can't give us to the fuzz. No way! Because, you see, my buddy and I, we already had a little run-in, in a dime store. It was really sort of a drag. So, you see, it's like we're on parole. This caper here would throw us in the slams for sure, they told us that. And we don't want to go into the hole. We couldn't hack it, really couldn't swing it . . ."

And here's what the fart answered, with his usual snottiness: "Poor little assholes . . ."

That was just the wrong thing to say.

Pierrot, I'd felt for a couple of secs, was getting too scared to stand still. Panic was crawling down his legs like armies of ants. All of a sudden he lit out for the corner. The guy wheeled around. He fired, the bastard! I grabbed the chance to give him a swift kick in the balls. Groan. He doubled up. That gave me a shot at his kisser, still going at him with my foot. He started pissing blood. I landed another blow somewhere near his liver. He sank down, dropped to his knees. The fox lunged for the gun. I was faster. I grabbed her by the hair and picked it up out of the gutter. The guy was puking on the sidewalk, totally out of it. Lights started going on in windows.

"Pierrot!"

I saw him staggering, leaning against the cars.

Holy shit! My head started to click. First, find another set of

17

wheels. The broad would be useful. I shoved her into the D.S., the gun up her ass, and tore off. At the end of the street I picked up Pierrot and yanked him by the arm onto the back seat. We floored it out of there.

"I'm in pain," Pierrot groaned.

Just from his voice I knew it was serious. He called out like a kid: "Jean-Claude!"

"What?"

"There's blood all over me!"

The chick turned around. "Quick," she said. "We've got to find a doctor!"

"Shut your hole! Nobody asked you!"

Pierrot couldn't even say where his wound was. "I don't know," he whimpered. "In my thigh . . . but my balls hurt . . ."

"Open your drawers! Check it out!"

He unbuckled his belt. "Jean-Claude!"

"What?"

"There's blood all over my balls!"

I raced off through the suburbs, a right, a left, covering my tracks as best I could. No one was tailing us yet.

"Where you heading?" Pierrot asked.

"To Carnot's. We'll change cars, because this one's cooked. The pigs will have our description out in five minutes."

"Hurry! I'm bleeding more and more!"

His voice quavered like an old man's.

Carnot, a buddy, was a night watchman in a garage. Not really a garage, exactly. Just a car storage dump that had a lift for tinkering with the engines. A corrugated iron shed stuck out in a vacant lot, with a rusty sign attached to the fence: USED CARS BOUGHT AND SOLD, MAISON PLOMBE.

The joint was deserted. I blew the horn three times to wake Carnot. A two-toned siren echoed horribly in the night. Enough to scare off the three mutts that were sniffing through the contents of an overturned garbage can.

The light went on. Carnot showed in his T-shirt. He was buttoning up his greasy jeans.

"Keep down," I told Pierrot. "He can't hack the sight of blood."

18

Then I pushed the chick to make her get out. At the sight of the German shepherd she stifled a scream. I led her by the arm over to Carnot, who was starting to squawk.

"What the fuck's going on?" he bawled.

I opened the fur coat so that he could dig the goods.

"You'll have to keep an eye on this for a while," I told him.

He didn't say yes, he didn't say no. The German shepherd came to sniff between the fox's legs.

Then I added, "You'll also have to stash the D.S. and hand us another buggy."

Still he said nothing. He was eyeing the chick's legs.

"You're not going to leave me alone with that guy, are you?" she asked.

"Why not?" Carnot answered. "Don't I turn you on?"

A lot of buildings around there had doctors' nameplates on them, so I told Pierrot, "Stay cool, we'll find one in a sec."

But Pierrot was really freaking. It wasn't that he was afraid of croaking, that would be pushing it. No, he was just in a panic about his balls, really going bananas about his nuts. He kept shouting things like: "If they have to cut them off, I'll find him, the motherfucker, and I'll make him eat his." Suddenly his voice would break, then he'd start in again, moaning and groaning. He was laying it on a bit, there wasn't that much blood on his pants. But it was a downer, all right. Especially since he was flopping against my shoulder and hassling my gear-shifting. I kept saying, "Move over, you shithead, how do you expect me to drive?" But it was no use, he didn't move over, he kept leaning more and more heavily on me. I had to shrug him off with my shoulder, and his head banged against the door. It was a bitch because the poor jerk did look like he was suffering, but I had no choice. It was like a cat who's drowning and tries to take you down with him, you have to cool him out.

"Hurry up!" he kept repeating every five minutes, hunched over his crotch like a miser guarding his pile. Easier said than done. Carnot had stuck us with a rotten old Dauphine with four shot shocks, and the least little bump made Pierrot moan.

"Can't you go any faster?" he asked.

"Take your pick," I answered. "I don't mind flooring it if you won't holler at every bump. Or else I'll take it slow."

He stifled a cry.

"There!" I said. "See?"

I headed for a residential area, going slow so as not to miss the doctors' nameplates. It was full of them. On almost every building. You'd think everyone in La Croix-Blanche was sick.

Every thirty feet or so I'd get out and look. Kinesitherapist, endocrinologist, otorhinolaryngologist: my mouth was hanging open! I would go back and consult Pierrot, who didn't understand all those fucking words any better than I did.

"How the hell you expect me to know?" he'd say. "What's the difference? They're all MDs. Why should I give a shit about their specialty? I'm pissing blood, that's all I know! Soon there won't be a drop left in my veins. We don't have to buy a dictionary, do we?"

"You're a real gas," I told him. "If you wind up with some dude who's only interested in ass holes or breast cancer, the joke's going to be on you!"

But Pierrot had a one-track mind. "What I need is a man who takes care of balls!"

"No, dummy, you need a surgeon!"

No luck: dentist, radiologist, veterinarian, everything except a plain surgeon. I began to feel like throwing in the towel.

Finally I hit on one. At last. Loraga, he called himself. Doctor J. P. Loraga, general surgeon.

We went in. Not exactly a breeze. I played nurse. Pierrot was getting worse, his legs were giving out, he had a death grip on me with his icy hands, and moving him was no small job— felt like his shoes were nailed to the sidewalk. I was fighting dead weight. I had to drag him, holding him up, to the door of the building, then into the hall, and prop him up in a corner of the elevator. Some rat race. To top it off, he was giving out hoarse groans that echoed something awful in the silence.

"Look, will ya cool it?"

It was turning into a real Calvary. Luckily everyone was asleep. No night owls in the building—or early birds either.

Fifth floor. We made it to Loraga's. A polished wood door with another copper nameplate, all shined up. And a peephole. I let Pierrot slump to the floor and bent down to check out the lock.

Shit. A real security system. Two bolts: one up high, one

down low. A suspicious jerk, the doc. He must have some bread stashed away, or else jewels, valuables, maybe in a safe. In any case there was no way to force the door quietly. Even if I did know something about locks, it wasn't worth getting out my pick or anything. No way to bust the door down with my shoulder either, because the neighbors would come to life like a fucking barnyard. Only one solution remained, dangerous and not very smart, a solution based on the fundamental goodness of human beings, Christian charity and all that jazz, and a ploy that could whip the fuzz there in two shakes. But it was worth a try, we had no choice.

So I knelt down next to Pierrot to see if he was still alive enough to play a part in the action. With his eyes at half-mast, he looked like he'd passed out.

I shook him, slapped his puss a little. "Hey, Pierrot!"

He rolled his feverish eyes at me.

"You think you can talk?"

He gasped out "yes" weakly.

I took him by the chin. "Now dig, man. Here's the pitch . . ."

He started ringing the doorbell. Or let's say he was leaning on it so as not to fall flat on his face.

The Loraga family was really zonked. Maybe they were sleeping one off. Or else they'd split for the weekend. To Narbonne Beach.

Pierrot kept on ringing. I watched him nervously, wondering if he'd be able to stay on his feet.

"You O.K.?"

He nodded yes.

Finally there was a little action in the apartment. A door opened, steps came closer. Light filtered through the peephole.

A long silence. The light disappeared. I imagined the doc, eye glued to the hole, checking out the hallway. He could only see one thing: Pierrot, leaning against the wall, having trouble breathing. Because I was stashed in the stairway, in the dark, just sneaking peeks around the corner.

"What is it?" the doc asked. Seemed to be pissed, not exactly a warm voice. My idea began to seem like a bummer.

Pierrot, following my instructions, began to gasp, "Doctor ... Doc-tor," clutching at the wall to keep from falling.

"What's the matter? Are you ill?"

Pierrot gave him the general idea by letting himself slide down the wall in slow motion and slumping to the floor with a sinister death rattle. Remarkable. Guaranteed to blow your mind.

Then came the payoff. I heard the top bolt slide back, then the bottom, and finally the key turned in the lock, the door opened and a shape rushed out, in a bathrobe.

"Are you hurt?"

Obviously, you asshole! He ain't inviting you to no stag party! Finally the man of science saw the hole, the bloody pants. "Shit!" he said. The action speeded up, whipped into a frenzy by his sense of duty.

He grabbed Pierrot under the arms and dragged him inside, opening doors and turning on lights as he backed, ass first, all the way into a tiled room, where the wounded could leak all over without messing up the joint.

I took advantage of the action. I snuck in, hugging the walls, and holed up in his waiting room full of slick magazines. The doc hadn't spotted me. I heard him go back to lock his door, the bolts, the whole snappy arrangement. During that time I checked out his pad, made tracks through his high-class digs to see what the layout was, number of rooms, population.

Luckily it wasn't big. The pad of a guy who's just getting started, making his first pile. Two bedrooms: one with kids in bunks, the other with a mop of bushy hair, a broad all curled up trying to hide her face from the light. What little I could see didn't exactly turn me on. An ugly mama. And it stank in there. Window closed, it reeked like hell.

"Who was it?" she asked, taking me for her old man, the father of her kids, her better half.

Since I didn't feel like stretching the rap or slipping between the sheets and getting hit with her stinking breath, I split.

Two kids, the old lady and no back door—that's all I needed to know. It was time for me to go introduce myself to Dr. Loraga.

Should have seen his face when he saw me come into his

office, leading with my piece! He dropped Pierrot on the spot and stood there like a puppet, arms dangling, eyes bugging out of his head, zonked, half asleep, not even the strength to get uptight. Even in his sporty bathrobe, frayed red terry cloth, you could tell he was going soft. And yet he was a young dude. Thirty-five at most. But already paunchy, half bald and with a wasted face. Wasted by food, in my opinion. Food and booze. The puss of a guy who's about to croak, who'll never make forty. Who'll kick off on some holiday highway, too much red wine in his veins and lousy tires. I was starting to dig him, his bummed-out look.

"Who are you?" he asked.

I pointed to Pierrot, stiff on the floor, looking at us upside down.

"He's my buddy," I explained. "He's been hurt. He's already lost quite a lot of blood and it keeps coming. He needs to be patched up."

He kept mum, the douche, but his eyes never left me. He stared at me like he was eyeing a cobra. I fascinated him, the turd. I was something else, a change from his regular visits at a hundred francs a throw. Meanwhile, the seconds were ticking by and he still wasn't making a move. He was eyeing me, unable to budge, totally wiped out, crushed, paralyzed like a guy in shock, almost like amnesia. Gone was the man of action, the tough surgeon giving spunky orders to be brave before laying his patients out on the table. Now he was letting his hands shake shamelessly, still stunned at finding himself in the front lines, called out one night with just a bathrobe over his ass, to face the enemy. But if you ask me, it wasn't so much fear that was making his hands shake as it was high living, lack of sleep, nicotine, the effects of those asshole trips called the vibes of the modern world.

"What have you done?" he stuttered.

He didn't seem to dig that we were for real. Since I had no desire to get into a pissing contest with him—he probably would have won hands down—I decided to fill him in.

"My buddy got a slug somewhere in the thigh and if you just stand there with your face hanging out he's going to start

24

running a fever and I'm going to bust your puss and all your teeth and everything in your fucking joint and your kids will never forget the sight of their old man crawling around on his hands and knees begging for mercy and as for their old lady snoring in there bare-assed in that big sack, no telling what I'll do to her in front of them and you. Now I don't know if you can dig the generation gap that might cause . . ."

All this was said in a whisper, like at confession, so as not to wake the little fuckers. I already had enough on my hands that I didn't need any brats crawling over my shoes.

The doc finally seemed to catch on. "All right," he said, "I'll extract the bullet for you. Give me a hand."

Things started to move. We lifted Pierrot onto the table. Being supercareful, we peeled his bloody pants off. And there he lay, bare-assed on the white rubber, really a mess. A crotch can be pretty heavy anyhow, from certain angles—like a cesspool, a horror show, etc.—but this, forget it! Enough to freak you out, clots and shit sprinkled with ketchup, could have been a snack for a vampire, a wedding-night bloodbath or some horrible abortion. The medic frowned: impossible to localize the wound. As for me, with my delicate stomach, I instinctively turned away. Felt sort of like I might blow my breakfast. To take my mind off things, I ripped the phone wires out of the wall.

Pierrot's moans were slacking off. But when the doc started cleaning him up with alcohol on wads of cotton, he really cut loose. Had to strap him down to keep him on the table.

Gradually, as the mop-up continued, his skin began to show and on the upper part of his thigh, fringed with hairs, a little red hole that dripped, a fucking crater.

"He needs a transfusion," the doc declared, staring gloomily at the wound. "We'll have to get some blood."

"O.K.," I answered. "Your wife can go."

Glass slide and dropper: he got the blood type.

"A," he announced. "You're in luck, it's the most common."

Bet your buns we were in luck! Having a real night out on the town!

Poor slob. Might as well milk it for chuckles.

I tailed him into the bedroom. Even from the doorway I could catch his old lady's dog breath. I took in their little wake-up act. He shook her, she grunted, he turned her over, she cooed. She thought there was a little humping in the air. No dice. I switched on the overhead light. She sat up in the bed and rubbed her eyes. She had hair under her arms. I could feel that the doc was put out because I was staring at his old lady's boobs. Even though they weren't exactly winners. They were heavy mothers, hitting her knees. Especially the left one, which was lower than the right. With huge nipples, as big as saucers, all purplish.

"Already?" she asked. "I didn't hear the alarm."

He patted her cheeks. "Solange, wake up, there's been an accident, I need your help. There's a wounded man in my office, you'll have to go and get some blood."

It was at this point that she caught the gun and then me holding it, aiming it right at her chest. And I must say she really blew my mind. She didn't squawk. No screaming or dumb-assed questions. Strictly businesslike. An outasight woman. Suddenly she was wide awake. She threw back the sheets and jumped up.

"My clothes," she said. "In the bathroom."

And while her old man went to get them she stood in front of me, stark naked and not giving a shit, in the same way she didn't give a shit about my gun. She looked at me as though I were her son and the most embarrassed of us was me.

"Be a good boy," she said. "Try not to wake the children."

"Don't bug me with your snotty kids!" I answered.

And I felt like a shit for having said that. If she had run her fingers through my hair I really think I would have started to bawl. From sheer rage.

Luckily she didn't. Her husband came back, his arms full of clothes, which he passed her one by one. She got dressed very fast, but without rushing, without awkwardness, with calm, efficient motions. She just put on her underpants, her sweater and slacks. She pushed aside the bra and stockings. I didn't know a woman getting dressed could be so beautiful. She slipped her bare feet into her shoes, ran a brush through her hair, took a pair of glasses off the bureau and stuck them on her nose. That changed her completely. Suddenly she looked like a prof, serious as hell.

The doc, during this time, was spelling out what to do: "Dutoit's on duty, ask him for A-positive, three pints, there's some in the refrigerator."

When she opened the door to the hall, I grabbed her by the arm.

"Of course," I explained, "you could tip off the police. But then I could beat it with one of your brats as hostage, the littlest one, preferably."

She split, shrugging her shoulders.

She must have really made tracks because she was back in fifteen minutes. An interesting fifteen minutes spent in confab with the good doctor, during which he begged me three times, for Chrissake, not to wake his kids, getting out his instrument case, putting rubber gloves on his soft hands, but also during which I got my shit together enough to relieve him of his bread and, as a result, give him back his cool. Because no more bread, no more worries—you can leave the door unlocked.

It was his trapped look when he opened the white cabinet to get his equipment that tipped me off. Of course he had to show his bunch of keys, the tight-ass! Then I suddenly remembered the security lock with the two bolts. I really thought about it very hard, crazy how hard I was able to think about it. And then I thought about us, too, Pierrot and me, about where we were headed, how, with what, that we'd have to crash somewhere, Pierrot would have to rest—all the problems of survival. Then I asked the doc, as a matter of information, what he had in the way of bread around the joint—with the rod in plain sight, threatening to scare the shit out of his kids and everything. And in cash, I added.

He was a fuckhead, that Loraga. He made a dumb play.

"You're out of luck," he told me, looking about as innocent as a pregnant nun. "Not a cent left in the house."

Something went click in my head, and I asked him if by chance, just a guess, he might possibly be trying to hand me a line of bull.

Incredible—he plunged right on, the asshole, getting in deeper and deeper! "I assure you," he said, "I only cashed enough for the weekend and we spent it all last night with some friends in a restaurant that just opened—a new black place, a real dump, and overpriced too!" All he needed was to fill me in on the menu and what dirty jokes they told! I could just picture them with their wives dripping mascara and puffing on Pall Malls.

Then I started very quietly heading in the direction of the kids' room.

"Wait!"

I turned around: done in, freaking out, he lunged for his desk, reached for a drawer.

My finger was tickling the trigger just in case he tried something, had a piece, an alarm bell or a Mace canister. Next I noticed with horror that I was totally capable of squeezing the trigger, of killing a man, just like that. Not in cold blood, of course, but out of fear of the slams, just out of that fear.

All he did was fish up a wallet and take out, a little too fast to be for real, two one-hundred-franc bills, which he threw down on the desk.

"There! That's all I've got."

"Hold it!" I said as he tried to stash the wallet.

What did he take me for, born yesterday? I had to go help myself. There were three more bills that size left, and a five. That came to one thou, and he was really put out.

"You little shit!" he screeched, gnashing his teeth. "You little shit!"

I pocketed all but a one, which I dangled in front of his nose. "Here! Your fee! Tax-free."

He even got down on his knees to pick it up. What a money-grubber! I'd have to watch it with him. He was the type that would stoop to anything. But maybe only where bread was involved.

When his old lady got back with the bottles of blood in her arms, the first thing she asked was, "Are the children still asleep?" I had to work to keep myself from going and getting the little monsters, kicking their butts out of bed and showing them my buddy's bloody crotch, a thing they'd never caught on TV. But I cooled it—the carving session was about to begin.

They hung a bottle above the table, with a tube leading into Pierrot's arm. Then she gave him a shot to keep him quiet and the doc started cutting in to find the bullet, with his old lady handing him the instruments. Pierrot was sailing by then, out cold, but I wasn't feeling any too hot. The smell of blood, maybe, which I've never been able to take. The desire to barf everything onto the floor—or perhaps right into Madame Loraga's kisser—gripped me again. She kept giving me looks I didn't like, too cool for my taste.

"There's some whiskey in the kitchen," she suggested.

"No thanks," I answered.

The doc extracted the bullet. I took it and stuffed it into my pocket.

"His balls?" I asked. "He was afraid for his balls."

"They're perfectly fine. Just the right one was grazed a little. A simple superficial laceration. I'll put three sutures in it. The bullet entered the fleshy part of the thigh. A hell of a lucky thing—half an inch more and it would have burst the testicle. Lucky, too, that the femoral artery wasn't severed!"

To listen to him you'd think that Pierrot had gotten all the breaks. A real golden kid, with a guardian angel saving his sweet balls.

He had to sew him up, then bandage him. When it was all over I noticed that dawn had come.

"There," said the doc. "As soon as he wakes up, you two get out of here."

His wife lit a cigarette and announced, "I'll make some coffee."

Through the kitchen window we listened to cars starting up and doors slamming. The coffee was watery and mixed with chicory. Then laughs came bursting out of the next bedroom.

"The children," their mother said. "They're coming!" She eyed me anxiously.

I stashed the pistol in my pocket and she handed me a piece of bread smeared with jam.

The kids came in and blinked at me, their eyes swollen with sleep. "Say good morning to the gentleman," their mother ordered, and they said good morning to me. I even shook the hands that they had been taught to hold out.

"What's your name?" asked the little girl, who must have been about five.

My bread and jam was stuck in my throat and I felt pretty asinine.

The old lady answered for me. "He's a gangster," she said.

The girl's face really lit up with amazement. But that was hardly the case with the boy, a kid of seven. He wasn't having any. He checked me out, skeptically, like an old man who knows where it's at.

"A gangster," he stated, "doesn't look like that."

"What does a gangster look like?" his mama asked.

"Big and scary. Besides, they have guns."

"He has a gun."

I was torn between an urge to bust out laughing and, just as strong, a need to smash my fist into the little brat's snout, and then again, more far out, a desire to stay there, in that kitchen, forever, with a napkin ring of my own with my name on it.

"Lemme see your gun!" the kid said.

I obliged. It really knocked him out, the little snot, when I popped it out of my jacket, especially when I poked the barrel into his gut.

His old lady just kept on smiling. It was starting to get to me, her smile, her goodness, her fucking sweetness and the whole cruddy family scene. I jerked the kid's pajama top up and stuck the cold steel against his skin.

"Hands up! One move and you're dead!"

He raised his hands, chuckling away—you might have thought he was a retard. Mama was chuckling too.

"Why do you smile all the time like that?" I asked her. "You got a screw loose or something?"

She answered by shaking her head and asking me how old I was.

I was about to answer, "What the fuck is it to you?" but didn't, because just then the doc showed. He got quite a jolt when he took in the barrel of my piece aimed at his darling son's little belly! Too much!

He stopped in the doorway, white as a sheet, and nodded me toward his office. "Your friend's asking for you. He just woke up."

The kid said, "Hey, I've got a Colt."

"Go get it," I answered. "You can scare your old man."

I gulped down the rest of my coffee and followed the medic into his office.

Pierrot was looking at me weirdly.

"Everything's O.K.," I told him. "Stay loose."

But he didn't seem too relaxed. Probably having all those strange faces around was getting him uptight. Especially when the little monster decided it would be a gas to aim his dime-store plastic Colt at him.

"Is he a gangster too?" the kid asked.

Pierrot sat up, winced, and tossed aside the blanket they'd thrown over him. The first thing he checked out, as you might guess, was his balls. He groped at the huge bandage that hid everything. Not knowing what was going on underneath it panicked him.

"My balls?" he asked.

I told him that they were fine, he had no problem in that department.

Since the kid was catching Pierrot's prick, which drooped bloodily down over the gauze, his mother decided to take him into the next room, especially as Sis was now heading our way too.

I felt the time had come to cut out. I gave Pierrot my hand, and he got to his feet as best he could, leaning on my shoulder.

"My head's spinning," he said.

"A blast of fresh air will fix you up."

I helped him into his pants and we started for the exit, arm in arm. He was walking on the outer edges of his shoes like a drunk cowboy, and I had to hold him up. The whole damn Loraga family was following us—the old man, the old lady, the cute little cherubs.

We all stopped in front of the door. Time for the good-byes, heartbreaking, pathetic. For two bits we'd have all gotten out our hankies.

"You going to call the cops?" I asked.

"You bet your life!" the doc answered.

What a shit, that Loraga. Now that we were cutting out, he was tipping his hand!

I grabbed him hard by the collar of his filthy bathrobe and talked to him very softly.

"Watch out," I advised him. "We might come back someday when we've got time on our hands, when we can take care of you permanently. You and your next of kin."

His wife split us up.

"We have to phone the police," she told me, "but we'll wait an hour. We won't do anything for an hour."

It was crazy, I don't know why, but I believed her. I liked that dame pretty well, I guess. I would have liked to tell her lots of things, that she should change guys, change scenes, go and get it on somewhere else, but I didn't have time to rap because suddenly, flash, I realized that that turd of a doctor, who at that very moment was edging down the hall dragging his kids with him, was about to lay us a classic egg.

"And the antibiotics?" I shot. "Are you forgetting them or are you trying to screw us? You want my buddy to slowly rot away?"

He handed me three bottles of penicillin without a peep, and off we hobbled. I could hear the kid behind me asking, "Hey, Mom, why are the gangsters leaving?"

I turned around to wave at him with my free hand. To tell the truth, we really didn't much feel like splitting, but we had to keep moving. We always had to keep moving.

"**W**hat kind of a chick is this? You can do whatever you like to her and she don't give a fuck! She don't scratch, she don't bite, she just opens up and waits, real cool, counting the flies! Holy shit! Not a murmur, not a tear! Nothing gets to her! You call that a woman? Might as well get yourself a piece of meat! And besides, she ain't got no tits! Talk about an intellectual . . ."

That's how Carnot greeted us when we got back to his slum. We'd scarcely gotten the door open, hadn't even had time to park our asses, get out a butt, zap! he starts giving us a hard time. And really sincere about it. He was genuinely pissed! He thought we'd double-crossed him.

"So what else is new?" the chick asked, not even batting an eyelash. "Didn't you get what you wanted? What are you squawking about? Aren't you satisfied?"

No kidding, she really gave the impression of not giving a flying fuck. Sprawled on the filthy cot, bare-assed under the grimy sheets, she was filing her nails, insultingly relaxed. In fact, relaxed was not the word. Indifferent, that's what she was—indifferent and somewhere else, like nowhere. Lying at her feet on the bed, the German shepherd, panting, tongue hanging out, looked like a smug john.

"Move your ass," I told the fox, "my buddy's got to rest. Give him the sack."

Poor Pierrot, he wasn't in such hot shape. He had collapsed onto a jerrican near the door, white as a sheet, with hollow cheeks and rings around his eyes like some fucking skull, plus one day's beard, which didn't exactly help the picture. With empty, stricken eyes, he gazed at the chick.

Taking her time, she got up. She slouched across the shack toward her duds, which were draped over a pile of old tires. Totally ignoring the scene, she started to get dressed, as if no one was there, not giving a shit that we were watching.

I took Pierrot by the arm and laid him out on the bed, with the pillow carefully propped behind his head. Then I turned back to Carnot.

I'd been checking him out of the corner of my eye anyhow, and I'd noticed his head, which had been turning all around, suddenly stop, like he'd seen a ghost. His anger faded in a flash, he forgot about his bitching and all that, and suddenly realized that we might be up to our necks in shit. Because he'd finally caught the blood-soaked pants. And he couldn't take his eyes off them—the pants, the blood—and his fear grew, doubled, tripled, you could see it in his eyes, which started bugging out of his head, and his wide-open yap, slack with surprise.

"What's all that blood?" he finally blurted, his voice shaking.

"Just blood," I answered. "A-positive. You haven't seen a thing."

"Maybe I haven't, but I don't need it."

Then his rage came back, full tilt. "You get the hell outa here. I don't want any hassles with the man."

"Right, Carnot, O.K. . . ."

We had a little taste of what was in his flask, and then I tried to reassure him.

"We haven't left a trail of stiffs behind us, so stay cool. We just borrowed some wheels and happened to hit on this shithead, the chick's little friend."

Pierrot's eyelids were drooping. The sleepless night, the wound, the panic, the knife—it had all been too much for his boyish heart. He was signing off. Even the naked broad didn't interest him. Even though she was taking her sweet time getting dressed, the slut, as though it amused her to wave her ass around in front of us. What an act! She had just pulled up her long boots and was slipping on her black pullover. I felt uncomfortable. Very uncomfortable. It bugged me to be eyeing her snatch, but I didn't dare look over at Carnot either. Because I could feel that he was looking at me and putting me down for sure, since I couldn't help peeking at that round little ass, like some minister's son. Finally she put her tiny skirt on, but that's all, nothing under it.

"Will you get that broad," Carnot said, disgusted. "She don't even wear pants!"

She picked up her fur and asked if she could go.

"Why don't you wear any pants?"

It was Pierrot who said that. He had opened one eye to ask the question.

The babe sighed and insisted on leaving. She was fed to the teeth, we were all fed to the teeth.

"Not yet," I answered. "We're not quite through with you."

"Answer my question!" Pierrot bawled, sitting up suddenly.

"Lie down," I told him. "Don't be an ass and wear yourself out."

He wasn't having any. All at once, mad as hell, he jumped to his feet to show the chick.

"Here! Look what he did to me, your prick friend! Look!"

He started unbuttoning his blood-caked fly. I forced him to sit back down, tried to make him lie down. No deal, he wanted me off him, yelling at the top of his lungs, "And what if I can't screw anymore! Never again! She's got to look, the whore!"

Impossible to cool him out. "Stop acting like an asshole," I kept saying. "There's nothing wrong with you at all!"

Then the fox chimed in with, "Shut up! I wasn't in on it, after all! It wasn't me who pulled the trigger! What was it to me if you took his D.S.!"

"Who was that bastard anyhow?"

"My boss."

"You make it with him?"

"If you think *that* turns me on . . ."

"Is that why you don't have anything on under your skirt?"

"Of course! He always wants me to go around like this. Even in the street. It gets him hot."

"What a prick."

She shrugged her shoulders as if she didn't give two shits. About that or about anything else.

I asked the chick what kind of trade she did.

35

"Shampooist," she answered.

"For that asshole?"

"Sure. Didn't you spot the shop? You were right in front of it."

Still had the feeling she was talking with her mouth full. Like there was a peanut-butter sandwich stuck in her throat that wouldn't go down. I imagined her whipping up shampoos like egg whites over hairsprayed heads. Going through her act with the marshmallow lather. And her twat spreading under her uniform all day—the haircutter's secret, the wind-blown look.

"I want to go home," she said, "and catch a nap before work."

It was Pierrot who shot back, "No!" A "no" that fell like a guillotine. Carnot and I looked at him, puzzled. What was he up to, wearing that weird expression like he was hearing voices? He looked like a dude with an obsession on his one-track mind. I could tell it was going to be a lulu, a real knee-slapper, because he was all smiles. And it gave him the strength of the miraculously healed. He jumped up and bounced across the room, hardly limping, as if he'd forgotten all about his wound. No more wincing—his smile just twitched a little with each step, gave a slight twinge, but that's all.

Cloaked in mystery, he paused at the door and turned back to us, his lowly disciples. "Follow me," he said, and on that he exited, an invalid who'd tossed away his crutches. I rushed to help him down the five wooden steps, so narrow and rickety. Carnot was right on my heels.

"O.K. to leave her alone?" I asked him, meaning the chick.

He gave a broad grin. "With Ringo, no sweat." Ringo was the name of the German shepherd. He stayed behind in the pad to keep her covered.

Pierrot led us across the garage. We followed, intrigued as hell. I kept hold of his arm, so that he wouldn't fall and bust his ass. He halted beside the D.S.

"Guess what we're going to lay on that haircutter!" he asked me, a wild light in his eyes.

"You got me," I answered.

His hand clutching my shoulder, he began very softly, sensuously, to lay out his plan. "Since the cocksucker seems to be more than a little fond of this heap, even to the point of using his piece to keep us from laying our filthy hands on her, well, we're just going to hand her back to him. Mustn't be grabby. We'll leave her off for him beside some road, like good guys. The fuzz will pick her up and he'll come to claim her at the station. He'll see that she's O.K., just a few drops of blood on the back seat, that's all. He'll drive away, tickled pink, whistling Dixie. Only what the asshole won't know is that we'll have tinkered with his precious jalopy, almost sawed through one of the front axles!"

He was sailing, it was a gas to see.

"One wheel hanging by a hair, you dig? Just waiting to fly off on a curve! So one day there he'll be, out on the highway, doing ninety, with the radio blasting, just grooving along . . . and suddenly—oops! the wheel flies off! Isn't that beautiful?"

"You're right," I answered. "That's just what he deserves, the faggot. Sit down, buddy, before you fall down."

He took a seat in the D.S., chuckling to himself. I gotta admit, I was getting a kick out of it too. Carnot, on the other hand, wasn't. He was getting pissed at the idea that we might hang around too long.

"You ain't gonna do that now? Here? Get the fuck out, for Crissake! The cops could show!"

"By the time you opened up the gate for them, we'd be gone out the back way in the Dauphine."

"And the broad? What do I do with her? Forcible detention, does that get to you?"

"We'll take her along."

"And the D.S.? And receiving stolen goods? And what do I tell the fuzz when they've just caught the Dauphine driving off?"

"That we had a gun, we were waving it at you, we were off our rockers!"

"No! Shit! No way! Get the fuck out right now!"

Panic. Total refusal. So I grabbed him by the shoulders and talked to him like a brother, very calmly.

"Now get this straight," I explained, "you're in the same boat. If we ever get busted, we'll spill all the shit we know about a certain Carnot and his little business. The chicks guys bring him in return for copping wheels, what he does to them, the whole scene. We'll even supply the names of the poor victims, the ones who didn't dare squeal because they'd been scared shitless. The cops will be a lot more interested in you than us, if I know them. When you get right down to it, Pierrot and I are just a couple of small-time bums. We pick a few pockets here and there, take things at the dime store, but we'd never rape a defenseless minor terrorized by a vicious dog! You dig what I'm saying?"

He wasn't about to answer. He just nodded yeah and rolled his eyes. I twisted the knife a little more.

"For example, the chick who wasn't even fifteen yet, remember? The one the Arab brought you! That wouldn't go over so big with the fuzz, that story."

"Stop."

"So, don't give us shit, man, and lend a hand cutting that axle. If you know where it's at, you'll give us all the help you can."

"Grab the wheel," he said. "We'll stick her on the lift."

I could congratulate myself on that little exchange. It sure cleared the air. We immediately felt much less strung out. Carnot kept his yap shut after that and knocked himself out to please us. He was a real gem of a mechanic.

Where to start the cut? I discussed it with Carnot, we searched for the perfect place. What we wanted was for the bastard to be able to drive around for about a month before it gave. Just enough time for him to get his jollies back. That was what broke us up. The beautiful look of surprise in his eyes, the three-wheeled coffin . . .

We got down to business, working with a droplight. It took us a good hour. Not an hour of sweat, no. An hour of intense pleasure. The all-time high, the joy of creativity. Nestled at the bottom of the pit, under the D.S., comfortably settled on an old car seat, Pierrot grooved on the scene, smiling as he watched us work, lulled by the gentle grating of the hacksaw on the axle.

We went back to Carnot's pad. Found the fox asleep on the bed, wrapped in her fur, the mutt at her feet guarding her. She must have really been wasted, didn't budge an inch when we came in. She was really zonked! Funny, she looked much younger in her sleep, with the tip of her thumb stuck between her lips. Like I said, a real cocksucker mentality. Which didn't exclude the little-girl part. She was breathing oddly, whistling through her nostrils. We couldn't get over it, her being so calm under the circumstances.

I picked up her purse, it was empty. Just some makeup, a few coins and a key. And her worn ID card, patched with tape. In the photo she looked like a kid. She was wearing pigtails. Her name was Marie-Ange, Marie-Ange Bretêche. She was twenty-five, lived in Croix-Blanche, 16 allée des Erables, building D7. I made a note of all the info. Name and address. Then I woke her.

I used a cute trick that got her up fast—a finger up her ass right to the hilt! Zap! Scream! She was sitting cross-legged on the bed. Gasping. And us doubled up.

"What's the matter?" I asked, puzzled. "Did you have a bad dream?"

"You poor bastards," she answered.

That called for a couple of belts. I let her have it on the spot.

"Watch it, you little slut! I got your address! Even if you move, crash somewhere else, we'll find you! And if it's not us, it'll be our buddies. We've got loads of 'em—in Croix-Blanche and all over. If you blab to the cops we'll hear about it for sure. And we'll pay you a little visit. And you won't be looking twenty-five when we're finished with you, more like sixty! You won't be needing rouge or eye shadow anymore! We'll turn you into a toothless old hag! Got it?"

She started to cry softly. A touch of the blues, maybe.

It was at least ten when we cut out in the wrecked-up Dauphine.

Carnot, it was agreed, would take care of the D.S. on the spot—that is, abandon it discreetly at the edge of a road, like some guy had stopped to take a piss and never come back, so that it would be picked up fast by the cops and its satisfied owner could once again groove on its far-out mechanics in complete safety.

We dropped the fox at a crossroads, near a bus stop. Before letting her off, we asked to touch her crotch hairs for good luck. She said O.K. We slid our paws up her thighs.

She giggled like a dumb cunt. "I never heard that brought good luck!"

"Oh sure!" I answered. "Touching something dirty always brings good luck. Like stepping in shit!"

She wasn't too happy when she got out. But we were having a ball, and that was the main thing. We dumped her off in the suburbs, at the mercy of the Arabs, the snow and sleet, and we took off.

Where to head? The problem was urgent. Home? No way. The fuzz would make the rounds, ring doorbells, go through the building with a fine-toothed comb, shoot their mouths off on every floor. No way to show in that neighborhood—some responsible citizen would always turn us in. Hairy freaks like us are frowned upon, even in a joint like ours, more or less a working-class dump. The workers aren't exactly mad about us longhairs.

"Hey, Jesus!" they call out when our paths cross. You see, they work like dogs and we don't do a fucking thing. We stay out all night, sleep all day, do sleazy things, get it on with broads, sometimes even with guys if they're cute enough. In a way this must hurt our reputation . . . But take it from me, no matter what we do, it's still shit. Even when we work, serious and all, try to make good and go straight, there's always some red-necked thug who gets smart and starts looking for trouble. "Don't wear yourself out, cutie! Don't ruin those soft white hands!" and snotty digs on that order. They take us for chicks. But then, when the so-called chick—surprise, surprise!—gives them a good kick in the balls and pulls a knife, then they see they missed the play and get back by getting us thrown off the job. What would you do in our shoes? We'd have to get cleaned up, get a haircut, put on work clothes, boots and caps—shit! For bastards like that, no way!

"Suppose for starters we get some bread?" Pierrot came up with.

A remark with common sense. Can't go far on empty pockets. We needed at least a little bread, if only to give our heap something to drink.

Pierrot started rapping about cash registers, isolated grocery stores, or, better still, a nice defenseless little old lady like we'd knocked off a couple of times already, an old bag with a pension, trucking unsuspecting down a quiet street, coming home from the post office, when suddenly— What an asshole I was! I remembered the doc's nine hundred francs sitting in my jacket, and a great wave of love for the human race swept over me. I'd forgotten the Loraga loot. That shows you how green I was to the whole idea of robbing people. Back then, I mean.

"Wait a sec," I told Pierrot. The idea of surprising him was really getting to me. "I think I'll just look and see if I have a little change left . . ."

Then zap! I dumped the whole roll into his lap. And parked the Dauphine to dig his expression.

It was worth it. He didn't believe it. He looked at the bills without daring to touch them.

"Count!" I told him.

He started laughing like a blind man who's just seen the light. Especially when he learned where the bread came from.

All of a sudden we realized we were starving. The mirage of a hash house loomed up on the horizon.

"No way," Pierrot said. "I can't go in anywhere with these bloody pants on!"

"I'll buy you a new pair," I answered. "Right now!"

"Where?"

"At the new shopping center. They don't know us."

Five minutes later I entered the giant parking area.

"Tell me what you want," I asked Pierrot.

"Some pants," he said. "Some shorts, chocolate, smokes."

Before getting out, I passed him the gun, then half the bread. "For Chrissake, don't move an inch from here. Except if you see some tail. The fuzz or some local dipshit might recognize you. In that case make tracks. I'll make out O.K."

The idea didn't exactly turn him on. "But how will I find you again?"

"Sniff me out, man . . . Maybe in Paris, under the Eiffel Tower!"

I left him and headed for the shopping center.

No sooner in the door than this jerk cut me off. I eyed him with all the affection I could muster. I'll never forget that mug. He was about forty, with a puny mustache and the reddish glow of a dude who hangs out at the corner bar. Electric-blue suit, suede shoes, groovy tie. Crew-cut yellow hair, pint-sized. At the barber's every Saturday, judging from the way his ears were exposed, two magnificent appendages. His badge was no news, since you could spot him a hundred yards away, or at least smell him, the way he reeked of brilliantine and self-satisfaction and smug assholeness. He gave me a big toothy grin, his hands in his pockets, pleased with himself, contentedly scratching his balls. A square kind of optimist who figures he better keep smiling, otherwise he might as well put a bullet through his head.

The fact is he was getting his kicks checking out my filthy hair and two-day beard. And no matter what gave, he'd never put a piece of lead through his head. The worst that could happen was that I might give him a knuckle sandwich, God knows I had the urge . . . Bastards fascinate me. I want to touch them, they're so beautiful. So there's this constant threat of total disaster in my life. This time, luckily, fatigue saved me. I just amused myself goofing on his life for fifteen wicked seconds.

I imagined him a bachelor shacking up with his mother, wearing darned socks. Or pawing a salesgirl he'd snagged copping a bunch of bikini panties. I stuck him on a pedestal wearing an Eminence jockstrap, farting with his buddies. I could really dig him in the army—as a sergeant, for example, a great connoisseur of beer. Also possible to see him as a football fan, following every play, screaming all the louder because he'd never even held a football. It was crazy how well I knew him, my private dick, to the point of feeling like his oldest buddy, or even his cousin. But we were no soul brothers, him and me, because me, when I get the chance, I lift from the five-and-ten—just junk, I don't do any harm, I don't pinch food out of their mouths—while him, his dream, his ideal, is to shaft some poor dame who's copping a few Christmas balls for her kids. That's worse than being a fuzz, worse than anything else, that's nothing but guarding the goods.

It wasn't the first time it had happened to me, a fucking rent-a-cop blocking my way. They think they've got my number and they're right. But this time I was put out. I'd come to make a legit buy, fingering the four C-notes in my pocket. I felt really put down. Much more so, even, than the time at Primix, when they'd carted me off in front of everyone, my jacket crammed with cans. A craving for crab meat had hit me . . . This has got to end, I told myself, not flinching under the two-bit cop's stare. Never let an asshole like this block your path again!

"You sure this is really where you want to be?" he said casually.

"Why not?" I answered.

He didn't move an inch. He simply started shifting from one hoof to the other, not taking his eyes off me, and finally coughed up another of his cute remarks, his specialty.

"People buy things here. You need money."

Moment of bliss: I fanned out four bills right under his schnoz, no comment.

What a chuckle! He busted out laughing. Me too! We were

both splitting our guts. Gotta admit it was fabulous—another upper-class snot disguised as a filthy weirdo!

Far out to be pushing a cart that didn't squeak and loading up with goods that I could pay for! I strolled like the last of the big spenders between the walls of food, the soft Muzak playing my tune. Please, lady, go to it! I dig catching you rummage through those bins of undies. I recommend Coeur-croisé. Go ahead and throw me a dirty look, what the hell! Step aside if you like, I need plenty of elbow room. Clear the aisles, clear the aisles! Let the customer through. I'm helping myself to everything and it's really bugging the shit out of you! I'm cleaning out the shelves, compliments of the management! If it hits me I'll stay all day. I'll go swig a glass of juice at the bar. Tough shit for Pierrot if he's getting uptight! He'll dig me even more when I buzz back.

At the checkout I met up with Dick Tracy again, eyeing the people in and out. I smiled back at him.

My dream would have been to invite him out to a fancy chop house, watch him loosen his tie, buy him a Calvados, groove on his every word.

The chick started adding up my tab. The cash box cut loose for a while under her fingers. A black fox in bloom, a sad-eyed gazelle with three-inch lashes and outasight black hair. Boobs practically busting out of her blouse, reaching for air and sunshine.

The dick couldn't resist the subtle comment that naturally leapt to his lips. "Too bad," he muttered, "she's not for sale."

No point answering. We cut him dead. The chick didn't even turn a hair. Reaction zilch. It's a cinch she was giving him a tumble, I know only too well how these things work. They usually fuck in the stockroom. A hunk of mattress laid out in the middle of the cartons—which means that the checkout girl can always amuse herself reading the labels while the owner, manager or guard gets off on top of her. Drop your illusions, that's how it works all over, or else the chicks don't last the week, they get the brush-off.

"One-eighteen forty-seven," the sweet thing announced.

44

I laid my bread on the counter. The rent-a-cop scanned my pile of goods. "Do you have anything to carry all that in, sir?"

He called me sir, the ass-kisser!

I answered no, I had nothing.

"Are you in a car?"

I love it when people stew about me. When he found out I had wheels, joy spread over his good-guy puss! He beamed!

"Take the cart," he told me. "You can leave it in the parking lot."

I thanked him a bunch.

The doors opened automatically for me and my cart. Not because of their photoelectric cells but because a new life was in the cards for us ex-fuckups. We weren't going to let ourselves be had anymore!

For openers, I shoved the cart in the Dauphine. On the fifth try, the engine shot off. And us too, flat out. A beautiful unching pad, that parking lot.

So long, Toulouse! We were zipping through the countryside. Item number one: Pierrot had to change his pants. I split the highway and headed down a bumpy road, aiming for a clump of trees. It was starting to get hot. The Dauphine was was twitching like a bitch, dragging her tail through the grape-vines, creaking and groaning in every joint. We finally jolted into the clump of trees in question and stopped under them, in the shade, hidden from the highway.

I hauled the cart out and then watched as Pierrot, really flipping, spread all the goods out on the grass. It was a riot to see. Like Christmas. All we needed was a tree, some lights and wreaths.

"Get your ass moving," I ordered. "Don't forget all the great eats waiting."

So he stripped, tossed all his old threads to the wind and took a long leak on the grapes, bare-assed in the bright sunshine. He pissed out his panic, the pentothal and quite a few cusses.

"What if I never get it up again?" he asked, groping at his wad of bandages.

"Get dressed," I told him. "You'll get it up soon enough."

He slipped on a new pair of pants and a shirt no one had ever worn before. I told him he was boss, he was tough. He wolfed a chocolate bar while I stowed the rest of the shit in the trunk. Then we hit the highway again. We left the nickel-plated shopping cart under the trees. It looked lost, standing there on its little wheels in the middle of the vineyard.

46

Pierrot was whistling a hit tune. We still didn't know where we were heading. But we were going anyhow, cruising at 50, flooring it. All we knew was that the sun was really beating down. Ideal for a little outing. In the villages we rolled through, the churches were spilling out hordes of people in their Sunday duds.

"Looks like we're home free," Pierrot said.

"Yeah," I answered. "Looks like it . . ."

Deep down inside, I was thinking, As long as we play it cool. We'll have to be fucking together.

We pulled off the road. For some time we'd been sniffing around for a sweet little bar, not too crowded, our kind of joint. Which was the case with this one, an old-time place.

We went in. No one, not even a dude behind the bar to guard the smokes. Not even a dog. Total desertion. And not a sound, except for the cars ripping by on the highway, full of kids, cakes and straw hats for the weekend. At the other end of the room was a little terraced garden. Beyond, trees alongside a river. It was a mind-blower. We went out and sat down, immediately refreshed, rejuvenated, fantastically loose. The shade, the leaves, the dampness, the soft gurgling—it was a far-out combo.

Then the owner showed, behind a huge gut that flopped out over his belt. Scanning our not exactly conformist threads, he tensed up. I laid a hundred francs on the tablecloth and he relaxed at once. He treated us like salesmen, that is to say royally. Cheeses, sausages, bread, butter, red wine—we did it all in. It was almost noon, and we hadn't eaten for a hell of a stretch.

Sorry if I pour you all the facts, it could be a drag, though in my opinion food is a basic, but I'm spilling all this so you understand that, when you don't mess around with us, Pierrot and I are also capable of digging the simple pleasures without hassling anyone. The hitch is that we're always running into shits like the turkey with the D.S. or the dick at the shopping center who rub us the wrong way and put us in a rotten mood. Unfortunately, you run into pricks like that on every street corner, and every day there are more of them around.

So I want to ask you one little favor. From now on, as I tell you the most painful episodes of our story, always keep this cozy picture in mind: two buddies sitting out under the trees, resting their butts on an empty terrace, silently chowing down, their only music the murmur of the running water. It was the greatest, no joke, we didn't ask for anything more, only that it would continue like that—especially with no one else around.

Only, the world is always there, right on top of you, no two ways about it, it surounds you, tracks your steps, your scent, it runs after you at top speed as though it couldn't do without you, as if you were indispensable, as though, if you disappeared, zap! everything would crumble. Even fuckheads like us, long-haired nothings, real weirdos you'd think they'd be glad to kiss off. Dig it, they still won't back off.

An example.
We were starting to nod a little, the calories having taken their toll, when suddenly two motorcycle cops pulled up outside the bar. The muffled backfire of powerful BMWs. A token sound. I could picture them bopping out of their fat saddles.

They strutted in, birds of ill omen, sinister black crows. Pierrot woke with a jolt. He turned white as a sheet, jumped to his feet.

"Let's split!"

I grabbed him by the arm, gently led him out to take a walk along the river, down below. Had to hold him back, he could only think of one thing—getting his ass out of there on the double.

"Cool it," I told him, braking hard. "Try not to limp, walk slow, we're out for a stroll . . ."

He didn't see that the more he hustled, the more he limped, and the less normal it looked. No dice: he couldn't slow himself down, that's how scared he was. He was dragging me along like a laundry bag, his hand clutching my arm, his grip hurting. And fear is catching. I could feel the cops' eyeballs riddle my shoulder blades. No way could I have turned around. There are certain sights I don't want to see: the man on my tail, for example, getting out the cuffs. Unless they took us for lovers . . . I could picture their subtle remarks: "Which one is the girl? The one on the left or the right?"

Down on the riverbank we were out of sight, unless they cropped up on the terrace.

"Let's split!" Pierrot repeated.

"Don't panic," I told him. "They just came to have a drink, that's all. It gets hot under those helmets, you know."

"Move!" he answered.

My spiel wasn't working, it was having the opposite effect. I couldn't even get with it myself anymore. My optimism was fading, becoming completely unreal. Especially since across the river, on the other side of the bridge, was a farm just waiting for us, with an old jalopy in the barnyard.

The old lady was alone in the middle of her barnyard when I stuck the gun in her ribs. She shrieked, dropping all her chicken feed. Rush of chickens to the feast.

"The keys to the car! Fast!"

Pierrot was already getting into the front seat.

"In the kitchen," the woman spluttered.

I pushed her over to the farmhouse, we went in. Inside it reeked of cabbage soup. I sent the kids around my feet flying. One snotty little bastard started to bawl, he'd hit his head on a dresser. I grabbed the keys off the hook, ran to the car and we roared off, which didn't mean much in that old heap. We blasted out of the barnyard zigzagging around the puddles, shaving the nose of a barking mutt. Stampede among the geese, chickens and ducks. Even almost managed to skewer a pig on the bumper. I could see the old lady glued to the phone: "Marie-Claude, quick, get me the police!" I dodged in and out of wagons, then plunged down a road full of mud that splattered in our faces—windshield wipers, for Chrissake! We came out onto a highway, then another, done, home free again, except that we'd lost the Dauphine full of groceries, plus a C-note stuck under a plate—a little too high, to my mind, for what we'd scarfed. It's crazy what allergies will drive you to! It made me sick to think that most likely the motorcycle cops would quietly finish their beers, spend five minutes telling the owner accident stories, take a walk through the garden, then swing their butts into their saddles again and buzz off into the dust, not giving us another thought!

Talk about fucking up! There we were in the public eye again: "Farmer's wife accosted on farm!" Life is heavy enough as it is, but when you're scared shitless it doesn't help. One fuckup leads to another, and you end up doing only that, one fuckup on top of another. Stranger than fiction.

"This is a piece of shit," I said, meaning the car.

"Have to swipe something else," Pierrot answered. "And fast. We'll be spotted any minute."

Meanwhile we buzzed down the road, putting as much space as possible between us and the farm. Or trying to, because with the peasants' heap it wasn't exactly a fair race, not with trouble making hills and dudes passing us, even trucks. Our only chance, we told ourselves, was that the fuzz would come after us on bicycles, like in the old days of Bonnot and his gang. I never took my foot off the floor.

It wasn't a valve job that was needed but a good junk dealer with a strong stomach. It reeked like hell inside that mother, and when we turned around we dug why. It seemed our peasants had had a sick cow and a vet too lazy to make a house call. A thick carpet of cow shit covered the floor. And Pierrot, who knows a thing or two about cows, after a close take on the shit, made a quick diagnosis. "You're right, man, that cow was sick."

We started scouting for our next hit.

A good piece of advice: forget about ripping off wheels in broad daylight. It's much tougher than at night.

You can be sure that the man is watching you. You can't see him, but he's watching you, take it from me. Especially if you have long hair. He has piercing eyesight, the ever-present mister nobody. And when he can't see you, he can hear you.

Take it from me, don't hit a car in broad daylight, it's really looking for trouble. Of course, there are a couple of deals worth a try: isolated campers, for example, but you've got to find them. It's getting harder and harder, they just love to clump together in camps.

The parking lot of a country inn at chow time. Now there's where you can find some cool rip-offs from salesmen, in good shape, that start right up. But you have to do some spying, watch for a real gourmet—it's a risky burn, and even if you pull it off, the fuzz get into the act fast. No chance of getting very far. Net result zero.

Then there's the gimmick of thumbing it on a deserted road and hog-tying the first stupid asshole who stops, then zipping off at the wheel of his heap. But you can't be in a rush because people don't stop anymore. They read the papers, two longhairs on the road give them the creeps.

Calling a mechanic for a fake breakdown and lifting his tow truck is completely crazy. You see, you can wind up with some stretched-out head trips when you think about scoring in broad daylight. It's so fucked up, forget it. That's why we jumped the train.

Now there's a slant that might not hit you: the train. And yet it's a gas. The cops, those Sherlock Holmeses, have just one idea in their noggins: stolen car, stolen car, they figure it's got to drive somewhere, you don't hit a car to move a hundred yards. So they fix their formula: stolen car equals roadblocks, and they launch an operation they code with the name of a flower, like Operation Lilac. That's the law for you, it will never change, along with all the routine and red tape. We had a laugh, in our cozy little compartment, watching the cops stopping cars, checking registrations, bugging the shit out of miles of Sunday drivers. They really did a number on the kids, the poor longhairs, wedged inside their old wrecks. They really searched them, hands up and legs spread. Heavy traffic jam on the highways! It was too much! Since the object of the whole number was sitting waiting for them, parked right under their noses, in front of a railway station in a charming little village, about twenty yards from the police station!

We were glad about messing up all those jerks. Glad but worried. We hadn't killed anyone but they were tracking us like bloodhounds.

An empty compartment, with just a young mama nursing her little baby: gotta admit, that's really beautiful!

We went in. We closed the door carefully and sat down side by side across from the good woman. We were as quiet as mice so as not to louse up the tender scene. Of course, I thought the sight of our pusses would probably be enough to make her milk turn. And the madonna did begin to twitch. So much that she finally pulled the kid off her tit and stuffed it back inside her blouse. That's one way to freak a nursing infant. He started howling.

"He's still thirsty!" I shouted, pissed. "You have no right to do that!"

Terrified, she rolled her eyes and began to show signs of getting her shit together to split.

"Don't leave!" I begged, stretching my legs out across the seats. "We just want the baby Jesus to get his share, that's all."

Pierrot took her by the shoulders and made her sit back down.

"Don't be afraid of my buddy," he told her gently. "He's only taking on because he thinks you look like his old lady."

And the brat was screaming. What a squawk box!

I took a bill out of my pocket and handed it to the broad. A hundred.

"Here," I told her. "Take this, be a doll, and give the kid another taste."

She looked back and forth between our mugs and the

bread, then back at our kissers. I crackled the bill right under her schnoz. Tears sprang to her eyes. That meant yes.

"Why are you offering me this money?" she asked. "I can't take it . . ."

"My ass!" said Pierrot. "Go on, don't make a scene."

He got up, took the bread, stuck it in the broad's purse and stroked the little shaver's cheek with his finger.

"Now, chow time!"

Completely freaked out, the poor mama! It was a dirty trick, really, because she didn't look any too well heeled. You can buy anything with bread. She took her tit back out and the kid fell on it, head down. He sucked and sucked. We just watched, grinning, digging her white boob sticking out of her blouse and the brat's toothless mouth sucking on her spit-wet tit. The Adoration of the Magi in a second-class car. But the chick didn't dare look at us. She was dabbing her eyes with a huge hankie.

At the end of the feeding she patted the little shaver on the back and he launched a lusty belch, a salesman's belch, with a little dribble of slobber to boot. That gave us a good laugh, and the mama laughed with us. She was starting to loosen up.

We rapped. Sweetly. Back and forth. She told us she was going to meet the kid's old man, who was in the army. The train rolled along through the heat. The kid nodded out, like most of the passengers, I figured. No one came down the hall, no danger of us being disturbed. Behind our lowered shades the darkness looked fucking opportune.

I drew a second bill from my pocket, same as the first. Another hundred. When she flashed on it, the chick paled. I cracked the bread between my fingers, grooving on it.

"What do you want?" she asked, getting uptight.

"Nothing! Can't I even dig my own bread now?"

I quietly made a cute little boat out of the bill. Pierrot really dug that. He sensed that something was going to click, something new and exciting. She felt it too. But she didn't know what. She was on her toes.

"Your old man, he's got a pass?"

"Yes . . ."

53

"How long?"

"Six hours. It's his first. From one to seven."

She was relaxing again.

"He's in boot camp?"

"Yes . . ."

"Must be some time since you've seen each other?"

"Two months."

"You're going to have quite a ball!"

She turned scarlet. And at the same time she grinned, the fox.

"Where will you go?"

"I don't know . . . To a hotel . . ."

There was a short silence. My boat was finished. It was a beautiful boat, a real prize. A hundred-franc boat.

"It's really O.K. if I play with my own bread?"

"But of course . . . sure . . ."

I laid the little boat on her thigh. "There . . . It's for you."

She didn't dare touch it. Her red face turned white. She stared at me, petrified. Didn't move a muscle.

"What for?" she asked, choking.

"What we'd like," I explained, "is for you to hump a few hours in the best hotel, in the most ritzy room, the classiest room with a bath where you can scrape the crud off your old man, who's sure to reek, and for you to get your rocks off on a huge bed! For them to bring you up champagne on a silver tray! For you to guzzle in the sack! Does that grab you?"

She giggled "sure" and blushed.

"Good," I said. "Only you'll have to earn your bread!"

More agony.

"How?" she asked.

"Well, what I'd really dig is for you to let my buddy here have a little taste. He just loves milk, and I'm sure he'd get off on it. Right, Pierrot?"

"Yeah."

"Well, do it, man!"

He got up. Not looking especially proud. The chick even less, shrinking back on the seat like a snake was about to bite her. He went down on his knees, moved in between her legs. Attacked her blouse. Under the material, her bosom was heaving.

54

He undid the buttons one by one. Some lace appeared. A very special bra that hooked in front. Pierrot fumbled in back and got all tangled up. Luckily the broad helped him out. It opened. Both their hands were shaking. They freed her bosom, the two breasts swollen with milk. Very gently, Pierrot bent over one grainy nipple and sniffed it greedily. He started to suck, the long-haired baby. He sucked and swallowed, harder and harder. The chick freaked a bit, murmured, "No, no, no," to him, then buried two frantic hands in his hair. And Pierrot started messing around under her skirt! And she started helping him out!

But then he flopped, drew back, froze head down, as though done in.

"What's the hitch?" I asked.

He turned to me, his face twisted. "Jean-Claude! I can't get it up anymore!"

"Well I can!" I answered. "For both of us!"

I was laughing like a maniac.

The chick didn't get it at all. Tits bared, legs waving in the air, she was hot for the next scene, her tongue hanging out. But suddenly it was curtains. The train was slowing down for a station!

"My God!" Mama cried, "this is where I get off!"

She jammed her boobs back inside her blouse, buttoned it up all crooked, grabbed her gear and the snoozing brat, who woke up and started bawling, and the whole act split, banging against the walls, getting stuck in the sliding doors, zap! just as the train stopped.

What a scene! We watched her fall out onto the platform and throw herself into the arms of a four-eyed army schmuck.

"Now there's a lucky bastard!" I said. "What a ball he's going to have! We really got that little nookie steaming for him . . ."

But Pierrot was still wrecked out on his knees in front of the empty seat.

"Don't worry," I tipped him. "You just got the jitters. It'll come back."

The train pulled out again. We yanked our boots off and stretched out, each on his own seat, full length, resting our lonely butts in the empty compartment. The wheels rocked us as we stared at our feet.

"With bread," I told Pierrot, "you can get them to do anything."

"Talk about a find!"

"Wait—I'm not rapping about the chick with the brat. That was really too smooth. You could tell she didn't have a pot to piss in. Did you catch her sweater, how worn it was at the elbows?"

"No."

"Elementary! The two C-notes we laid on her, you better believe it was pretty fantastic for her. Besides, we turned her on, she was getting pretty revved up."

"We should have hung onto her!"

"But her old man? His pass?"

"Not our problem! And how do we know she wouldn't rather have stayed and messed around with us, instead of going to get the schmuck's rocks off? One word from me, most likely, and she would have stuck with us forever!"

"Forget it! With that brat?"

"A groovier case would be a broad who doesn't need any bread," I went on. "For example, picture on this train some well-heeled snatch in fancy duds, jewels, a crocodile purse, the kind who has everything, who runs to the beauty parlor whenever it rains . . . You dig the type?"

"Yeah."

"Good . . . Well, we truck in. A first-class compartment, natch. We roost, no sweat. With butts going, open beer cans, a total turn-off. The chick checks us out, our filthy kissers, our greasy hair, our bulging crotches. She starts saying "shit" to herself, sniffing how we stink all over, we really reek! All she thinks about is splitting, changing compartments—fast. You follow?"

"Yeah."

"Good. Then real cool, I flip a one-grand wad out of my pocket, dig it, one grand! Which I start leafing through casually, right under her powdered schnoz. Immediately she stops shifting around, riveted. She eyes the bread, tries to figure it.

First thing she catches: the stuff ain't where it belongs. There must be some mistake. What can it mean, so much establishment bread in the hands of a no-good dropout? It disgusts her, intrigues her. There's been a crime, she tells herself, it's stolen money for sure. Unconsciously, she starts thinking about the law. At that moment, I hand her the roll. 'This must belong to you,' I say to her, very sweetly. 'I just found it on the floor.' She stares at us, stunned, eyes bugging out of her head. 'Oh!' she stammers, 'I don't think so . . . Are you sure?' And the whore peeks in her crocodile bag, she's checking it out! Even though she *never* trips out with more than a hundred francs—precisely because bums like us might rip her off! You dig the character of the bitch?"

"Yeah. They're all over."

"They're all like that! Then she adds, shaking her head, 'No . . . Really . . . I'm not missing anything. Is it a large amount?' 'A thousand,' I answer. 'It's yours, if you like.' She bursts out laughing, amused. Anyhow, she's starting to think we're pretty great. But don't forget—she's got a fat checkbook in her bag, joint account with her old man, and fifty thou in the bank!"

"Then she doesn't give a shit about our bread?"

"Theoretically, no! But that's not how it works. A little something under the table is always O.K., doesn't hurt anybody . . . But wait! I insist, grinning. I grab her bag. The cunt doesn't stop me, even though she's getting jumpy, wondering if it might be a trick for copping her hundred francs. I open the bag and toss the roll in. Can you picture her face, her shit-eating grin when I close her bag again? Now there's only one idea in her pig head: That does it, I don't understand why, but the money is mine. She breaks up. We break up with her, as if it was a far-out joke. Only then she goofs—instead of being straight, just saying thanks, she asks why. Why the handout when we don't even know her? 'Because we want a fuck,' I answer. 'We want your cunt. We want to do a take on it, nosh on it till we hit Bordeaux.'"

Pierrot gave a crazy laugh. "What next? What does she do?"

"Well, she plays along with us, man! And not only does she goof with us, but she gets fucking hot! She comes on like some whore! Wallowing in smut with two filthy bums who stink! The wildest time of her life!"

"We screw her?"

"And how!"

"Fill me in! It might launch a hard-on . . ."

"O.K. Obviously her first reaction is to return the bread and split. Normal. Of course she's pissed. So we beg her pardon, real polite and all, we give her a hand getting her suitcase down, we play embarrassed, creeps who are sorry, we lay it on. It doesn't go over. She splits, nose in the air, miffed and huffy. O.K. I pick up the bread. After half an hour she shows again. 'The other compartments are all full,' she hands us. 'I hope you're going to act like gentlemen!' We swallow the excuse, even though we find it far out. We toss her suitcase back up, still polite, still laying it on. She sits down across from us, not peeping. Doesn't dare raise her lids, knees pressed together, skirt pulled down. She takes out a cigarette, lights it nervously. You and me, we don't bat an eyelash, we twiddle our fingers. Only, I haul out the ten C-notes again and lay them nice and flat on the little table near the window. And then I gaze out at the countryside. Can you dig the vibes? Not a word said. A loud silence, deafening. We're all hot as billy goats, especially the dame, who doesn't know where to put her legs. She crosses and uncrosses them, her stockings squeaking, her Chanel suit heaving with sighs, with impatience . . . the whore. Finally she gets up, climbs up on the seat, opens her suitcase. She gropes through her undies. I get up too, offer to help her, fingering the bread. 'I'm just looking for my book. It's right on top.' I get up beside her. I dive into the suitcase, plunge into silks, woolens, jars of cold cream. I feel the book. I take it out, bring it down, open it under her nose. Dig: I lay the one thou between the pages. She pales. Her blood rushes to her secret parts. She waits, petrified, knowing that this is it, that it's going to happen, that we're settling down to business. 'Don't move,' I tell her. 'Hang onto the luggage rack.' I get down. I spread her legs. Then I go to the door and lock it. The cunt has her back to you, standing on the seat, gripping the luggage rack, legs braced apart. Got it?"

"Got it!"

"It's your move. You get up, go over, roll up your sleeves. At this point you have several choices. If you like, you can sit down quietly on the seat between her legs, with your head up under her skirt, and take a big gulp of pussy air, the finest kind. You don't move, you hold your fire and wait for her to start going crazy. Or else—a faster play—you feel around under her jacket and fetch out her two hefty numbers. I come up behind and flip up her skirt. Her big establishment ass takes a bow, with you filling your nose right under it—" Shit! Someone was knocking on the door! A metal object rapping against the glass pane. A dude in a conductor's suit.

"Tickets!"

When he saw that we had them, what a letdown showed on his prison-guard kisser! He gave them a filthy look. But he had to punch them, no way out of it.

"Do you put your feet up on the chairs at home?"

"Sure!" Pierrot shot back. "Sometimes on the table!"

The conductor moved forward. Very touchy moment: Pierrot wanted to get up, I hung onto him as best I could. Finally we took our feet down and the conductor split, giving us the hairy eyeball over his shoulder.

"He was asking for both my feet right in the chops!"

"Cut it!" I told him. "Where was I?"

"Oh, you're not going to start that again, are you? Those lame stories of yours don't turn me on."

I decided to cool it, wait until he calmed down . . .

"Pierrot?"

"Huh?"

"I thought you were asleep."

"No. My balls hurt."

"It's all in your mind."

I reached in my pocket and brought out the piece of lead that had messed him up. "Here—this is what you had in your leg."

That got him. He grabbed the bullet, held it between two fingers, eyed it lovingly, like it was a fucking diamond. It must have slammed against a bone, it was all twisted.

"The bastard," Pierrot said. "I really hope he croaks . . . You think he's gotten his heap back yet?"

"You kidding? Not yet!"

"Well, what're the cops waiting for?"

"What's the rush?"

"It's *my* rush! I want to read his name in the obits column!"

"You should never wish another person dead."

"Damn right. Since nothing I wish for ever comes true, it just might protect the mother. And I want him to croak at the wheel of his fucking car. If I never get it up again, it'll be because of that prick!"

The train pulled into the Agen station. A fifteen-minute stop. I went out onto the platform, clipped some stuff from the newsstands: a pile of mags, comics and tons of pornos, in the hope of sparking Pierrot's little dingdong so he'd give me some peace. Not to mention beer, sandwiches and smokes, enough to last us till the end of the line.

We'd decided to ride on to Bordeaux and crash somewhere around there, away from the heat. Wouldn't you know it, our train was a local. It stopped at every haystack. Abandoned stations came to life for it. It sometimes even stopped for no reason, in the middle of a field, as if the engineer wanted to take a piss on the poppies. Getting nowhere fast.

So we read, butts hanging from our lips, beer cans handy. Pierrot was feasting his eyes on the bare-assed chicks sprawled all over the glossy pages. I read the papers, the real ones, that give you the news. We weren't mentioned yet, we'd have to wait till Monday. However, in a weekly, I zeroed in on one piece that really hit me. I started to read it, but got so shook I had to stop. "The Scandal of the Prisons," it was called. I could feel the cold sweat running down my back. For some kooky reason, I tore the page out and kept it for later, folded up in the bottom of my pocket, my snot rag on top of it. Then I plunged into a comic, trying to clear my head out. But it was no go, nothing clicked, the cartoons just didn't grab me. I couldn't stop thinking about that piece on the prisons, couldn't get out of it.

"It begins," the article said, more or less, "with a welcoming committee of guards: blue-serge uniforms, silver stars . . . Identification, fingerprints, mug shots—the formalities of registration, it's called. You empty your pockets, hand them your watch, turn in your bread for an identification number and go into the dressing room. Clothes off, you bums! They frisk you: open your mouth, spread your legs, bend over, cough. You exit with a bundle in your arms: your blankets, mess kit and your monkey suit. When you reach the hallway, the stench immediately hits you: mold, disinfectant, rotten food. You hear whispers, the sound of keys, the doors clanging. Now you're a lost soul, alone in the world. You're in the clink, my friend."

Nothing much happened till we got to Bordeaux. Except that we got fed to the eyeballs with the fucking train. We dozed some, headachy. The porter kept eyeing us.

No visit from our buddy the conductor. No sign of him. Too bad—we'd decided to shove something into his fat gut. A knife, maybe, or the gun, his choice. Just to put a little action into his boring life, give him something to remember. We waited, he didn't show.

Just the two of us. Didn't see a soul. No one came to keep us company. But of course our compartment wasn't that inviting with all the shit we'd spread out in it, the cunt shots, the wrinkled newspapers on the floor, and us two filthy bums stretched out on the seats with our feet up. Our smelly feet plus the stink of the boots we'd taken off made eight distinct stenches, rising in great waves and mixing with the stale cigarette smoke. And the whole mess was cooking in the sun. Quite a melting pot. We'd spilled some beer on the floor, and an empty can was rolling back and forth, banging from left to right. But that fuck-off Pierrot wasn't even with it enough to bend down to pick it up and toss it out the window at some railway bum!

I miss it today, that good old compartment—it stank, but we were comfortable. It was cozy as a little nest. I think we could have gone to the top of the world in that second-class car, crossing endless frontiers, mountains, bridges and tunnels, seeing snow and then the sun again, rolling day and night with long stops in foreign stations to change engines and buy sandwiches on the platform, followed by a slug of beer and black tobacco.

Instead, like fuckheads, we got off in Bordeaux! O.K., so we were at the end of the line, but still . . . We lacked smarts, that's all. Should have just laid low in the compartment, cooled it till all the cars were empty. They would have hauled us onto an abandoned siding for the night. We would have had breakfast in the sunshine, with a squadron of ancient cleaning women come to wash the windows. They would have given us a little coffee out of their Thermoses, like they'd found two lost children after a war, would have brushed our hair, patted us, called us beautiful . . . and Pierrot would have started to bawl just as the train shoved off suddenly, pulled by a huge diesel toward an unknown destination. Paris, Amsterdam, Vienna, Moscow, Athens . . . Still hidden, we'd roll at night across moon-drenched plains, sleep days in switching yards or under tunnels, slip from the customs officers and be saved by a young chick in blue denims, a blonde with pigtails, sixteen, covered with soot, who'd snatch us from between two freights, make us scramble up into a cattle car and give herself to us in the hay, cooing in Czechoslovakian while they searched the train for us.

Suddenly I'm tired of laying all this on you. It bores and disgusts me. We were hitting the end of the road, I could feel it. Where were we heading? I didn't have a clue. As for the chick on the train, the cows and the whole bit, it was all pure bullshit, only a riff. What really happened was zilch! Just pulling into Bordeaux, an endless crawl into the station, brats, suitcases ricocheting down the corridors, then lurching to a stop, with the mob spilling onto the platform, and us, no need to hail a porter, trucking along hands in pockets, 10 percent juiced and 100 percent lost.

Two men in blue blocked our path, without so much as a howdy-do.

"Papers."

We were in France, all right.

They eagle-eyed our ID cards. I had trouble standing still. One in a thousand we'll clear this, I told myself. If Pierrot doesn't blow it and try to run . . .

It was the first time I had been face to face with the fuzz and had a gun on me. They're carrying too, I thought. Their rods are neatly stashed in pretty leather holsters, under their left arms. As for my piece, it was in my coat pocket weighing a ton and probably making a huge bulge.

Naturally some of the passengers stopped to gawk at us. They ate it up, two long-haired bums being fucked over by the fuzz. They really dug the scene. They felt protected. They congratulated themselves on paying their taxes.

Lucky day: our two dicks hadn't caught the news. No sweat, they tossed us back our papers. We slunk off, getting the hairy eyeball from the crowd. They opened a path for us, mamas clutching their brats against their skirts as though we might give them some dirty disease.

Found ourselves smack in the middle of the city.

Where to head? The eternal hassle. We wandered from street to street and, like everywhere if you wait long enough, it started to get dark.

Pierrot's balls were hurting from walking so long. He landed against a tree, white as a ghost. He was totally fed with dragging his ass around Bordeaux.

"Let's score some wheels."

"No way."

"Then what?"

"Ya got me."

We were really drifting. And drifters always float in the same direction. In any decent city there's a hangout for bums, whores and faggots, like a sewer grate to herd them together. If you're wasted, bummed out, a total orphan with the man on your tail, then let yourself go, you won't need a map, just sniff the curb till you reach the gutter. You'll make it no sweat, it's the end of the road when you've had it, when you can't play it their way anymore. Open your eyes and you'll be there. You'll see, it's cozier than the so-called chic neighborhoods, if you've got a strong stomach. In Bordeaux it was the port, and we waltzed right into the middle of it. The scent guided us.

At first, Pierrot could only think about one thing: crashing. There were plenty of hotels, all right, each more scummy than the next, and he whined for a room to sack out in. He'd had it with limping through the fog.

"My crotch hurts!" he kept saying.

I was thinking, Fuck your crotch! but instead told him, "Come park your ass for a sec. No one's making you drag around like that!"

Only, he'd get cold sitting down. "Let's flake out," he'd moan. "With all the bread we got, why can't we get a room?" He was out of his skull.

I would shrug my shoulders, pissed. "Don't you know a room clerk is always a stoolie? And what if he sees our mugs in the papers tomorrow morning? The two hoods in number seven! What would he do? Use your head, man! Who would he ring up? You forget we're wanted!"

An idea, I admit, that's tough to grasp. Twenty years old and already got a record: "Theft, assault, believed to be armed and dangerous, use caution." That's hard to swallow. Pierrot didn't quite dig that we were condemned to travel underground. I had to fend for both of us.

We jolted ourselves awake with big gulps of black coffee in a smoky whore bar. Warmth and good vibes. Pierrot felt in such good shape that he fixed his head to ball one of the chicks. Under the stairwell, a fox was checking him out with her big cocker-spaniel eyes. The douche, I bet she'd hump him free. He turned her on. I must say that old curly-locks Pierrot really knocks chicks out. That poor broad looked bowled over. And cute, too. Fucking young. Pierrot's age. A real beginner—her minishorts and little black stockings gave her away.

"Slip me a hundred," Pierrot said. "I'm going up."

He didn't give a shit about the fox. What he wanted was to settle once and for all the question that was bugging him: would he ever get it up again.

I got a firm grip on my chair. Stay cool.

"Good idea," I told him. "Let her spot your bandages and your stitched-up ball. Make her a first-class witness!"

I felt his hand snake into my pocket and close over the pistol.

"Give me a hundred and no shit!"

I didn't dig the way he was whispering in my ear. It sounded like he'd made up his mind.

"O.K. Go to it."

I forked him a bill under the table. He whipped his hand out of my pocket.

"Thanks, man."

The girl was already grinning at him.

"Don't split, I won't be five minutes."

He leaned on the chair back to get up. I held him by the shoulder.

"Just a minute!" I said. Better take this too . . ."

I winged him the rest of the bread, down to the last cent. He picked it up and stuffed it under his shirt, completely freaked.

"Why you throwing me all this?"

I also dragged out the gun and parked it on his knees.

"Here, since you're itching for it . . . Take the mother! It'll keep you company, 'cause now you can cut me out! Dig? Cut me out!"

And I stomped out of the bar.

A lame bluff, piss-ass poker. If Pierrot had had any sense at all, he'd have had a good laugh at me: a tough son of a bitch making a scene like a lousy chick! I was in fine shape now! Had to turn my collar up, the damp cold gave me the shakes. Stewing on the docks, my eyes fixed on the steamy barroom door, I waited, hands in my pockets, frozen to the spot. What if Pierrot, real cool, went and did it! I could picture him whanging his dong while I froze my ass in the port. If he's not here in five minutes, I told myself, I'm going in. The three of us will spend the night together, all fucking each other, waiting for the cops to come and cart us away!

But the bar door opened. And in the blue light, his curly head poked out.

"Jean-Claude!"

What an asshole,, to holler like that! A real stereo blast. I waved at him to knock it off. He spotted me. Immediately he broke into a run, and I laughed like a madman at his limp.

66

I started to run myself, doing a gimpy sprint number for him, really laying it on. He tore after me hollering insult upon insult, pissed that I was imitating him. From the bar door the whore watched us horsing around in front of the ships. I bet she damn near joined us for an few laughs. But we didn't wait for her to make up her mind, since a sinister echo suddenly hit us: the eerie sound of a police siren tearing through the city at top speed, a thing you usually hear in the movies. You never think that someday it may be screaming for *your* ass . . . I jerked Pierrot by the arm and hauled him out onto a dark jetty.

Flat on our bellies on the damp stones, we watched the cops pass. They weren't hounding us. We weren't stars yet, not at that point—those were the days. The car went its way and we relaxed. And then the night rolled on, soft and endless. Pierrot was making faces, following me silently, dragging his leg. I could have led him anywhere, even into a cop station, and he wouldn't have given a shit. It was like being hitched to a con with a ball and chain.

We studied the tide rising and pissed in it, saw freighters full of cars and sailors who called us faggots in every language. Some wanted to ball us, offering us bread. We felt Turkish, Irish, Argentinian hands groping our asses. Had to hold back from pushing their faces in. And I couldn't take my eyes off Pierrot: I knew he was itching to use the gun.

We scarfed some french fries and downed a beer in a giant café full of back rooms and sculptures. Pierrot crashed on a bench, all curled up. I retrieved the gun and all the loot from his pocket, then set myself up in front of the pinball machines and played till I could hardly stand. I kept firing the balls, not even digging the hits anymore, completely groggy, and couldn't stop winning. It's always when you don't give a shit that things pan out. I got tons of free games and the bell kept ringing. It took a bum hoofing in with the morning papers in his arms for me to connect: outside, the sky was getting light.

I opened to page 3. I freaked on the spot. And yet I was expecting it—it was Monday. All at once I was totally awake.

No point in busting Pierrot's sleep. I opted to savor this

first moment of glory in peace. Anyway, it just might have gone to his head. Because the story had broken, we had become stars: there were our big mugs in black and white, along with five columns about us.

There was also a photo of the doc and his wife—scads of pics, a whole portrait gallery. All our buddies from the day before. All smiling, too, the meatballs, like they were at a wedding. Pierrot and me, the new heroes, we were the only ones who looked pissed. They'd used our old photomat ID pics.

The chick also looked pissed, but she knocked me out! Marie-Ange, the bare-assed beautician. I thought she looked fucking beautiful in the photo, really humpy, probably because of her sad look. It was a great shot. I automatically sniffed my fingers. They just stank of tobacco. But I remembered that sweet rub between her legs. A cool fox, not too bright. Not the kind to brew a national incident every time she spread her legs. I know we'd get along just fine, no sweat.

The winner was the shot of the turkey with the D.S., the hairdresser. He was smiling, the shithead, like he was in front of a mirror. I'd swear he'd snapped himself in the bathroom. It would have slayed me to see his puss the way I'd fixed it for him, his features rearranged, teeth busted and mouth swollen, on his hospital bed, since according to the newspaper he was under observation. I would have given anything to have paid him a little visit, with a cement cake for his stubby teeth to chomp down on.

When you think about it, it's a drag to be famous. It gives you the willies. I looked around the café: there were a few sailors reading the papers, but no one showed any signs of hitting us for autographs. And Pierrot was still sacked out, sleeping like a corpse. I ordered a large coffee to whip my gray matter into shape and then launched into the story of our exploits.

From line one I was wowed. A suspense story. With blood, violence and sex. And the guy who wrote it hadn't filled his pen with Pepsi. He was a real pro at cutting to the heart of the news. A master at run-over dogs and cruelty to children. He used tough words like "banditry," "irresponsibility," "mo-

68

tivation," and heavy expressions like "the thin line between good and evil." According to him we were really going downhill, but that wasn't any news to me. On the other hand, and here *was* news, it seems that we were part of a new generation of hoodlums. Make way for youth, the hope of tomorrow! Move your ass, Pierrot! The country is banking on us! Our call to duty has sounded!

What a great tool the papers are when you know how to use 'em. I'm not talking about classifieds, employment opportunities and other ball-busters. What gets me is the news items. That's where I score my great ideas—after my imagination shows signs of copping out. A trick I discovered in Bordeaux that morning. Before that I only read the sports page and the comic strips! Think what I was missing!

Thanks to the paper—that good old rag I bought down by the waterfront just at dawn—I got the idea about the fancy villa. A dinky little article tucked away in the corner of page 3. You dig that our new-found glory was splashed over the whole page, not leaving much room. But finally the harmless little headline caught my eye: "Gangsters on Vacation."

Tilt! Suddenly I was hooked.

Gangsters, I said to myself, that's like Pierrot and me. Now, overnight, we're gangsters, have to get used to the idea. Two brand new gangsters, full of promise.

But it was especially the word "vacation" that hit me, because we sure needed one, even though we weren't big-time murderers yet. We were out of work, Pierrot and I—all the more reason to take a break. We were tired of that fucked-up life. It was vital to rest our butts. Loosen the collar. Take a real vacation, while everyone else worked their balls off.

So as I lit into my second coffee I looked over the story about the gangsters on vacation. It was a pitiful story. Three jerks who'd fucked up over and over till they got pinched like sitting ducks. And yet, in the beginning, their idea wasn't too bad. It deserved looking into. I told myself that we might be able to use it later, in our own style, and stashed the paper in my pocket, neatly folded.

Pierrot was still zonked. I shouted a volley of hell-raisers into his ear: "Police! Hands up! We've got you covered!" But forget it, he refused to come to life. So, sad to say, I had to grab the bench from underneath, lift it off the floor, and then —crash! Pierrot found his ass on the floor.

"Hey!" he said, opening his bleary eyes. "What's going on?"

"A train wreck, man. Everyone out."

He wasn't too pleased. Especially when I told him to slug his coffee down.

"Shake your ass!" I said.

"My lips are burning," he answered. "You're a real pain! Where we going anyhow? Where's the fire?"

"Don't ask questions, one-ball! It's time to hit the road."

He'd forgotten all about his balls. He groped at the bandage very gingerly.

"You'd better check," I told him. "Maybe you've got three this morning . . ."

He didn't appreciate the dig.

We said "so long" to the waiter and went out onto the sidewalk. It was damn fine weather, vacation weather, and I could picture it already.

I started walking at a good clip. Pierrot followed, completely in the dark.

"What's the story? Where we going? Why you going so fast?"

I answered, not turning around, "Don't get uptight, man! Just move it! We're going to be late."

"Late for what?"

I was doing a mystery number on him, playing the enigmatic kind who follows his own plan with fierce determination, who's come up with something so big he can't talk to anyone, even his best buddy. Things were really rolling. I was in a terrific mood. But I'd have to keep an eye on him, make sure he didn't shoot his mouth off again like the night before, making an ass of himself and giving me lip. Unbelievable! Never again!

71

To have a smooth team you need a captain, and I was the man for the job. Shit, after all, I was the oldest—and the only one whose balls were together!

"We going back to the station?"

"You'll see when we get there."

We walked and walked, looking like two yoyos who're afraid to be late for work. Which proves you can't go by appearances.

After half a mile Pierrot stopped asking questions. He was busy tagging along, just trying to hang in there. Having trouble keeping up, huh, man? Slowing down? Like to know why I'm breaking our butts like this? Sorry, pal, I can't tell, your nerves ain't strong enough, you might panic. No point both of us being in a sweat. Just think about your balls for now, consider me a shit if you want, but I gotta keep you in the dark. You'll get your kicks soon enough. Pretty soon you'll be spotting cops all over the place. Too bad they're not all dummies or weak in the head. Some of them have memories—radars on legs, monsters who want to do you in, fanatics for promotion, blending into the walls like putty, lurking in the shadows or prowling through the crowd, invisible. Some of them are longhairs in filthy jeans they call plain clothes. They could spot us at any moment. Better you don't know the pitch. Best way to cross a mine field is to think you're in a bed of clover. Not to give a shit. Or you bump right into a staked-out dick or accidentally step on the chief's toes. Anyhow, I was so uptight that every street and intersection, each step we took, made me feel like puking. Fucked by a filthy hairdresser. That's where it started. All it takes is running into one real shit. I thought about him all the time, dreamed about him zipping along in his fancy limo. Go, daddy! Do it! Two fingers on the wheel, the car does the rest. Reliable, that's what they told you. Why don't you light up a Marlboro while the suspension swallows all the bumps? What aroma! Rich, flavorful. Go! A beautiful downhill race with the sun in your puss! You don't give a shit, you've got your shades! Pass that jerk, the wise-ass in the Capri! All you gotta do is make a sharp turn, power steering, slow up for the curve, power brakes. Ain't you got confidence in me? I'm there, beside you, in the suicide seat, in my black cassock and my golden stole. I'll use my little Caltex can for the holy oil,

72

it'll be O.K., don't worry! I know all about last rites, I used to be a choirboy. Amazing, right? Go! Pass! Now, floor it! Listen to the beautiful crash. It's sweet to die in a squeal of rubber. It's manly, it's modern. It's better than growing old in chains or in a cell that smells like shit! Anyway, we all gotta go sometime, you're going early, that's all—an advance man, you oughta be proud.

"End of the line!"

The bus full of Portuguese threw us off in the suburbs, at the intersection of two national highways: N 10–Bayonne 170 and N 650–Arcachon 60. We'd bought a Michelin map.

We went and stood under the sign for Arcachon and started raising our thumbs for the benefit of truck drivers. Unobtrusive hitchhiking, very cool. We kept a lookout for a possible squad car in the mob of bikes all heading one way, like the start of a race, except that the contestants looked as if they'd been hitting downers, like ads for some drug company. Coming at us in slow motion. But the fakers could still get it up to give us the finger as they passed, or blow us a kiss. Jealousy. But I didn't envy them at all. I answered them with a half-assed obscene gesture, like my hand under my cap in front of my fly or a finger sucked and then waved around.

Pierrot, white as a sheet, kept elbowing me.

"Don't be an ass!" he said. "Dig those monsters!"

But the turds, all too beat, didn't even react. Even though you could spot something like blood in their eyes. Pierrot must have thought the whole pack was going to stop and get off their bikes to jump us, sleeves rolled up. He was totally shook.

And yet he'd been feeling spunky back there on the bus when I'd laid my vacation plans on him, keeping my voice down in the middle of all those Portuguese. Some of them were reading their morning papers—must say I've been more relaxed in my life. But nobody crossed themselves at the sight of us. So, for the whole ride, both to pass the time and to cool my nerves, I whispered my story about "Gangsters on Vacation" into Pierrot's ear.

"I read it in the papers last year. It was somewhere in

73

Brittany, I don't remember the name of the town. A modest family seaside resort. The kind of joint that's deserted from October to May. You dig the scene? Two hundred houses and not even a cat on the streets."

"That's cool."

"You know it! The four of them went there, three guys and one broad, to crash after a hit. All they had to do was force the door on an empty house, settle in comfortably and calmly count their loot until the heat was off."

"And that's what they did?"

"Yeah, but right on the beach!"

"So?"

"Think, man—that was their second mistake."

"And the first?"

"The broad! You never take chicks on a job! Broad plus beach equals jail! A fatal combo."

I often think about the chick and the three dudes. I picture them as being fucking O.K., all four of them. They didn't deserve that lousy end. Where are they today? Separated, that's for sure, each rotting in his own corner, and not even able to visit each other.

They'd been there two weeks, taking it easy, like real gentry, the fuzz starting to cool off. They killed time playing cards with their bread, a huge pile they kept losing and winning back, which finally evened it out. Also, I suppose, though the paper said zilch about this, the three guys would fuck the chick between deals, all together or taking turns, because she looked more or less wasted in the photo. Not bad, but sort of bushed, and no spring chicken. The guys were starting to show their age too. Well over forty. You get careless at that age, you make mistakes.

They got caught, I'll lay you ten to one, because the broad took it into her head one fine morning to go soak her ass in the waves. A weird idea on April 15 in Brittany! She really must have been hot, or else she'd read in a magazine that icy water tones your muscles. No one had seen her swimming, but there were footprints in the sand leading straight from the sea to the cottage. The only tracks on the virgin beach. You can guess the rest . . .

At that moment a Portuguese across from us folded his

paper so that our two photos came into plain view, eight inches from Pierrot's schnoz. What a scene! Pierrot almost passed out!

We didn't have to wait long till a truck stopped. A brand new blue Stradair, a truck driver's D.S.: air-cushioned suspension, radio turned low, air-conditioned. Almost seemed like you didn't need the guy to drive it.

"Help yourself to some fruit," he told us. "A few vitamins can't hurt you."

All he had to do was tell us if we looked that bad. There are plenty of things that can't hurt you—a good kick in the ass, for one.

Pierrot, in the back, reached out and came up with a basket of enormous strawberries.

"Sorry," said the driver, "I don't have any cream to go with them."

"We'll make out."

Those strawberries had no taste at all, they smelled like water, like all big berries.

"They good?"

"Fantastic!"

He was a decent prick but not too bright. We intrigued him.

"I like young people," he said. "Where you two heading?"

"Arcachon."

"Vacation?"

"Yeah."

"Funny time for a vacation."

"Midterm break."

"You got friends in Arcachon?"

"No, an aunt, a schoolteacher. She has a little cottage by the sea. She's going to chef up meals for us."

"You really oughta take care of your health."

"No joke! The sea air's just what we need. We're going to take long walks on the sand in our bare feet. Suck in the oxygen."

We rolled along at better than 70, smooth as glass, a fine atmosphere for rapping.

"You brothers?"

"Not exactly, but it feels like it."

Doubt suddenly gripped the guy. He turned around fast to sneak a peek at Pierrot sleeping under all that hair, then let me in on his confusion.

"Say . . . Is that a boy or a girl?"

"A girl."

"Funny kind of girl."

"Oh, well, right now she's not quite herself because she just had an abortion. In Denmark."

"You've come from Denmark?"

"Yes, we hitched back. She's a little tired. Besides, she really wanted the kid."

He shut his trap, worried. I took a limp old Gauloise out of my pocket and offered it to him. Unbelievable! He thought it was a joint, the jerk. But he didn't dare refuse. Afraid I'd take him for a square. He had a strange look on his face as he smoked. Sure as shit he'd get home and tell his old lady, "You know, marijuana doesn't do a thing, it's just a gimmick for commies."

He let us off on the waterfront in Arcachon, a big open space surrounded by large buildings. Sinister. I checked the map and we hoofed it, avoiding the shore so as not to leave any memories with the natives. We took back alleys, relying on the edge of the pine trees to keep parallel to the sea. The farther we got from the city, the less people there were, and we began to see those cottages with closed shutters—one, then two, then lots of them.

In Pyla-by-the-Sea there were still some signs of life. In Pyla Beach there was nothing. It was empty. Stores, houses, cafés, restaurants, hotels, all shut tight, double-locked. Our dream. Closed shutters everywhere, padlocks, grilles, iron gates. We were moving in on a dead town, like after an atomic war. Not a cat in the streets, no one, only sand and stubble, and the dark pine trees waving above our heads.

"Now here's what I call a ghost town," I said.

No one would come to bug us here. If there had been people, we would have pushed on, to Biscarrosse, Mimizan,

Vieux-Boucau, there was no shortage of dumb beach resorts. We would have gotten there with our thumbs, on our hands and knees, any old way. We really needed that vacation.

Using my head, I chose a cottage outside the village. A beautiful white one with red shutters, all by itself at the edge of the moors and forest. A prime location.

I showed Pierrot the map.

"Look—we're here. Behind us, nothing but pine forest for twenty miles. So you dig, in case of a bust, trying to find us in those trees . . ."

Breaking in was like taking candy from a baby. The lock gave at the first twitch of my screwdriver. Just sprang open. All we had to do then was look the joint over.

The door opened onto a hall laid in black and white tiles, with an iron lantern, rattan coatracks, an oval mirror framed in rattan and, on a rattan stand, a phone and phone book. The dumbest house in the world. You could tell just from the front hall.

Limp white sheets were draped in every room. Chairs piled on the dining table, like in a bar. The cracks in the shutters let in a feeble light, and the walls, bare as a hospital, looked sickly pale. The whole joint smelled of newness and mothballs. We wandered around, more or less depressed, like we were part of some sort of glossy travel folder. We lifted dust sheets as we went, uncovering the corny furniture. We had the feeling no one had ever sat on the modern sofa, the flowered armchairs. Or else they put newspapers under their asses so as not to dirty anything. It all was empty, sterile, dead, in a freakish state of cleanliness and order. A real maniacs' pad: not even one crotch hair left around.

"Let's split," said Pierrot, "it's too creepy. No one ever sets foot in this morgue!"

"That's just it! We couldn't have hit a better joint. They only come for the summer, we won't be bugged on weekends."

In the garage we found a few signs of human life. A shrimp net, some rubber boots, a snorkel, three tennis rackets and a motorbike. A brand new little machine with a snappy wicker

77

basket lined in flowered material attached to the carrying rack.

"It's a chick's bike," said Pierrot.

"Yeah . . ."

There was a little gas left in the tank.

"The daughter of the house."

"Could be . . ."

"Sure! Look, there are three rackets—the old folks' and the chick's."

Then I noticed that we had stopped rapping and were staring at the bike seat, riveted. The bare, cold seat. Suddenly I felt like I couldn't move, couldn't take my eyes off that stiff piece of leather made to fit between tender young thighs. I could see a little girl's ass on it, all hot, in the middle of August when the sidewalks melt. Pierrot was thinking the same thing.

"What do you think they wear under those tennis skirts?" he asked.

"Special pants."

"Transparent?"

"You crazy? Picture the mob scene when the chick plays! A tennis skirt is always flapping up, it's fucking short! The chick would bend down to pick up a ball and zap! You could see her twat! You O.K., man?"

He'd sniffed the seat and, when it hadn't smelled of anything, looked sort of down.

"Come on," I said, "let's get settled. We need some rest."

We turned the gas and water on. I started the hot-water heater with my lighter.

But when Pierrot stepped up to the fuse box, I said, "No. No electricity! No lights, you could see them from the outside. Tomorrow I'll buy us some candles."

"Terrific."

"Jail's much less terrific."

We went back into the house. The sun was setting, it was getting more and more sinister. We took the dust sheets out of the living room. Tried out the sofa and the armchairs: hard as rocks. Rummaged around a little to see if we could dig up anything interesting. Zilch.

"She can't have too many laughs."

"Who?"

"The chick."

There were a few old *Jours de France*, a set of gilt-edged books, some plates hung up on the walls and a dark boob tube.

"We going to watch it?" Pierrot asked.

"Yeah."

"Then I'll have to turn on the juice?"

"Yeah, but just for the tube. O.K.?"

"O.K."

In the sideboard we found some plastic dishes, jelly glasses and three napkin rings with names taped on: Papa, Mama, Jacqueline . . .

"Poor Jacqueline," said Pierrot. "Alone at the table with those two old farts."

In the ultramodern kitchen, done in rustic Formica, it was the same story. The cabinets, lined in washable contact paper, were empty. They hadn't even left a lump of sugar, the pigs! they'd figured their last shopping trip so there'd be just enough to eat and taken the leftovers with them. The only thing they'd forgotten was a roll of ass-wipe. Scented Scott.

The electric clock on the wall had stopped at seven.

"She must have been really beat, poor Jacqueline. Leaving at seven—they'd have had to get up by at least five to get everything all cleaned up, give it the last vacuuming."

"What if it was seven at night?"

"No difference. In either case, they were uptight about the trip. They knew all the statistics by heart. Only one thought in their heads—beating the rush hour. So they left either very early in the morning or late enough to drive at night."

"Depends where they were going."

"Far. I figured that to be such sanitary freaks they must come from the north."

"Poor Jacqueline. Can you see her in Maubeuge?"

The same gaiety reigned in the bedrooms: beds covered with dust sheets, blankets folded neatly, mothballs, pillows in the closets. In the parents' room: twin beds on high legs, separated by an aluminum crucifix. The chick's little room was as bare as the rest. The pillow, in the closet, hadn't even kept the smell of her hair. Except, in one of her bureau drawers, in a cute black cardboard box, carefully wrapped in tissue paper, guess what we found . . .

Three bathing suits faded by the sun. Two-piece. Tiny pieces, not much to fill. Little girl's bikinis.

"How old?" asked Pierrot.

We checked out the bras.

"Twelve-thirteen, tops . . ."

Suddenly—don't know why—there I was sniffing the inside of the panties.

"Oh shit! Much older, Pierrot, much older! At least sixteen! Dig that aroma!"

He sniffed it too, and I took another bottom. Same thing.

Jacqueline . . . Already a real little lady . . . I knew why she'd wrapped her bikinis in tissue paper: for us. The odor, miraculously preserved, had survived the test of time, of loneliness and the cold. It was treasured up for us, intact, almost still warm, and we filled our nostrils with it, sniffed and sniffed, our eyes closed. Dynamite mixture of suntan oil, sweat and seaweed, very spicy. We almost fainted, it smelled so good.

"It's like she's just taken them off, like she's in the next room. Hey! Jacqueline!"

She didn't answer, the bitch.

After nineteen straight hours in the sack, Pierrot woke up in a panic.

"My cock's limp!" he shouted.

He stared down at his blood-smeared crotch like a chick who hadn't been clued in about getting her periods.

"Hey! Jean-Claude! My cock's limp!"

"So what? So's mine! Why should they be hard? I don't see Brigitte Bardot around anywhere!"

"But usually in the morning I get hard-ons."

"It's all that crap that's keeping you from getting it up. There's so much crud on your ass it would take a bulldozer to get it off."

I threw off my covers and headed for the can.

Beautiful! Plenty of hot water! Shaking with impatience, I ducked under the shower. Ahhh. Unbelievable how great the heat felt on my poor old rusty joints, stiff from all that sitting on trains and car seats and barstools. I felt my muscles coming to life one by one. They all answered the roll call. Shoulders, back, ass—present! It felt like I was taking off a plaster cast, like I was being reborn.

Pierrot, sitting on the bowl, was trying to take a shit and looking droopy.

"You prick," he muttered.

I really had one on.

He was freaking, and like a jerk I couldn't keep from laughing.

"There's a stud for you!" I howled, waving my cock around. "Dig that!"

He didn't say anything, didn't move. It really hurt me to look at him, and yet I kept breaking up. It was awful, but it was bigger than I was.

Finally I stopped horsing around and turned the shower off.

"Hey, man," I said, going over to him. "Let's have a look at that thing."

I sat him down on the bidet, like a girl, with his legs spread. "Hang on."

He yelled like a banshee when I pulled off the tape, which was stuck to his crotch hairs. And when I took off the gauze pad he really let loose. It sounded like he was giving birth to twins.

"Shut up! You'll have every tomcat in the neighborhood here."

His wound really wasn't too bad.

"Well, so you've got two holes now, man."

Wrong tactics. No way to get him out of it. He just sat there on the bidet, head hanging, staring at his limp prick, really down. Oh, Pierrot! I pushed his hair aside. Shit! His eyes were full of tears. I can't stand to look at such things. I leaned over to check out the situation.

"Do you know that you stink, man?"

"But if I take a shower it'll start bleeding!"

"Your feet, for Chrissake!" I told him. "They're not going to bleed. We could get some of the crud off them."

I sat him down on the edge of the bathtub, his feet under the faucet, and started scrubbing. The water turned black.

"Don't sweat it," I said. "It'll come back. It's just a lousy head trip. It's all you can think about, that's obvious!"

I also washed his hair with a big piece of laundry soap. I dried him, rubbed him down, combed his hair. Then I dragged him toward the bedroom.

"Come on," I said. "Let me have a go at it, you'll see."

He lay down in the dark, like a good kid, on one of the twin beds, and I started taking care of business. Gently, patiently, I did everything he likes, I knocked myself out, I think my hands must have been shaking, that's how much I wanted the miracle to happen. But the fucker didn't move. Might as well have been working on a newborn baby. Would have been better off dragging him to Lourdes. And then the bastard started cutting me!

"You don't think I'm going to get turned on by the likes of you, you faggot! What I need is a good piece of ass! A foxy mama with sweaty tits, that's what! Not your stupid fag number!"

The little turd! That called for a response! A couple of punches knocked him out of bed, and I fell on top of him. He struggled, yelling that I was hurting him. Tough shit! I blocked him with a hold I knew, twisting his arm behind his back, and shot him a series of jabs from behind.

"You'll see if I'm a faggot or not!"

He howled all the louder when I treated him to a dry fuck, the poor kid. He moaned into the carpet as I whispered sweetly into his ear. "You'll see," I murmured, "your prick will get huge, like mine, like that, can you feel it! And your woman will go crazy, you'll hump her for hours, she'll shout, she'll cry, she won't be able to thank you enough."

"I'm bleeding!" he hissed. "Look at my hand—can't you see I'm bleeding?"

"Sit tight. I'll fix your bandage in a few minutes."

I came out of the garage with Jacqueline's motorbike.

"Where you going?" Pierrot asked.

"Shopping."

I gave him some money, then the gun.

"There. If I'm not back by noon I've been strung up somewhere, and you better get your ass out of here and try to make out somehow. Try to stay with it, cross the mountains into Spain or something."

"I'd never make it without you."

"We could get together again after they spring me. They can't hold me forever—I haven't killed anyone."

"But why can't I go do the shopping?"

"Because you're too young. There are two things you just can't resist. One, your need to fuck things up. Two, the slams. And all the guys would screw you, you're so cute. Including the guards and maybe even the warden."

I started the motorbike.

"Don't move from here, Pierrot, please. We still have everything going for us."

And just so he'd have something to think about while I was gone, I gave him the old article I'd cut out on the train, the item about prisons I hadn't had the guts to finish, it brought me down so much. I told myself that maybe it would keep him cool.

I rode back to Arcachon the back way, like an old man, not speeding or anything. You can always crack up, especially when the roads are deserted. Fatheads who have accidents always think they're alone in the world. It's easy to skid on sand, and there was sand all over the place around there. I was scared. I rolled along haunted by cop cars and army Land-Rovers that might crop up any moment, and I thought about poor Pierrot lost in his reading.

"The moment you're in the gate they do everything they can to humiliate you, bring you down, make you dig you have to fly right. You're no longer a man but a number, and a number has to shut up and above all not ask for anything. 'Hey, you over there, you going to shut your yap? You going to shake your ass or not?' That's how they talk to you. Not to mention the nickname they automatically hang on you. If you sing in your cell, you're Caruso. If you take your time getting out of the sack: Loverboy. If you don't wash: Shitface. And if you don't act happy, they beat you over the head with the argument: nobody asked you here!"

That wasn't the last of the prison lit. I'd scarcely set foot in the Arcachon Maison de la Presse when a red-lettered title jumped out at me: "The Misery of French Prisons."

A weekly. I flipped through it. There were four pages on the subject, with photographs and everything, depressing. It was starting to make me dizzy, but I caught the owner getting blips from my long hair and high-heeled boots. He was a yellow-skinned Algerian, in full costume. Both hands were on the counter, near the phone, near the cash box. The store was empty, and since it was big, it looked even emptier. I smiled at him as if he were a long-lost cousin—he probably took me for a fag.

I started wandering down the racks, looking relaxed, making my little purchases: newspapers, weeklies, sports mags—and pornos, of course, for Pierrot.

"Seventy-five forty-five!" the old man belched, like a challenge.

I let a five-hundred-franc note fall gently on the counter. A dynamite dead leaf.

He looked at it, then at my puss, then all around, to make sure he wasn't dreaming, then checked his pocket for his snot rag, checked that his mutt was still napping behind the counter —like my bread was a gun and I was pointing it at him. They're afraid you're going to rip them off, and when you shell out, they're even more afraid. He fingered the bill like a maniac, not really daring to hold it up to the light in case I got pissed and started slapping him around.

"Do you have anything more . . . interesting?" I asked, leering at the pornos.

It was like I'd given him an electric shock.

"What?"

I looked around: no one else was in the store. Then I leaned toward him, like an accomplice in the underground, and came to the point.

"You wouldn't have anything Danish . . . in the spicy line? I'm willing to pay . . ."

"Well . . ." He hesitated, couldn't quite get started.

"It's not for me, it's for my father. He's resting at the Grand Hotel. He's very tired. I was told you were the only store in town that . . . The doorman told me . . ."

He looked reassured and took a grimy paperback out from under the counter.

"Good?" I asked.

"Very good," he said. "Very, very good."

"I can take your word?"

"Oh, yes! You'll see. It's very popular."

"I'll take everything."

"Then that'll come to two hundred francs."

Pierrot was going to flip!

But Pierrot could only see one thing: the red title about the prisons. He damn near started to scream.

"Not more!"

The other article had destroyed him, no doubt about it, he had a crazy gleam in his eye. He lunged for the magazine.

"Six o'clock: the bell rings, rattle of locks being opened by the guards. You get up, you wash, you clean your cell, you fold your sheets and blankets, corners squared. From the time you get up until the time you go to bed, your sheets and blankets must be kept folded at the head of your bed. It is forbidden, during the day, to lie down on your mattress, even if you have nothing to do, even if you're tired; because the less you do, the more tired you get. And if you're shivering, if there's no heat, you are forbidden to wrap yourself in your blanket, even standing up or walking up and down."

We moved closer together on the couch, because the cold was getting to us. I was reading top speed over Pierrot's shoulder.

"You march out to the exercise yard in a line; no talk in the halls, no singing or whistling in the yard, even if the sun's shining. First you get fat, then you get thin. You go blind, your hair falls out, the days never end, one just like the next, forever. You have heartburn, your intestines are ruined by the chow. You wait, you're always waiting, nerves on edge, for the sound of the bell: the rising bell, the dinner bell, the bell to go outside. For ten to twelve years. Until the day you don't even wait anymore. Then your teeth rot and start to fall out."

I decided to close the magazine. No point in overdoing that kind of reading. Pierrot seemed to agree—he was white as a sheet.

"Here," I said to shake him out of it, "I brought you some vitamins." And I showed him the pornos. He opened the first one.

"Shit!" he said, all choked up. "Have you ever seen a chick do that?"

"No. I never knew one that filthy."

"The whore! You can practically see her molars!"

He raced through them, really charged up.

"You hungry?" I asked.

No answer.

86

"I bought some hamburger."

By the time I'd gotten everything put away in the kitchen, he'd disappeared into Jacqueline's room with his reading matter. And I didn't see him again for some time.

When I went to get him for chow I found him bare-assed on the chick's bed. The pornos had been thrown all over the room. Just from his face, I knew what had happened.

"Come eat," I told him as gently as possible. "It'll do you good."

Instead of getting up, he started to holler, "I don't want him to croak, that piece of shit! What he deserves is to spend his life in a wheelchair, paralyzed from the waist down!"

He paced back and forth like a crazy man.

"Don't worry," I said, holding out his pants, "that's what's gonna happen. He'll be trapped in the car wreck, they'll have to cut him loose with a blowtorch and when they get him out, he'll be paralyzed down below till the end of his days."

"And I'll push his wheelchair!" Pierrot added. "I'll be his little nurse, I'll take him for walks on La Croisette, I'll show him the chicks in bikinis, I'll keep rapping to him about asses and tits, and I'll whisper softly in his ear, 'It's all over, big boy! That stuff's not for you anymore. Now it's me who screws your broad!' And I'll get enough for both of us. Right Jean-Claude?"

His morale was rising.

A weird vacation . . . I don't know how I kept Pierrot in that fucking cottage for eight days without his losing his marbles or doing something crazy, and still staying good buddies. Some trip!

It took constant surveillance. During the day I had to keep him from opening the shutters, he was sick of the dark, he wanted to let the sun in. I had to stop him from leaving the village, heading out for the beach. I took him in the woods out back. You have to get some fresh air, stretch your legs a bit. But he didn't dig the woods too much, too deserted for him. He would toss a few pinecones around and then want to go back inside right away. He was afraid we might get lost.

Then we went to the dunes on the point, crawling through

the underbrush. We slid down the soft slopes, took off our clothes and tanned ourselves bare-assed, looking at the ocean waves in the distance. But I was in a panic that a helicopter might buzz over, and that sort of took the joy out of it. But Pierrot had it bad. He dragged around looking so dark and obsessed that it finally got to me. All that talk about his wilted dick being only temporary . . . We didn't discuss it anymore, but that just made it worse. The ghost of Pierrot's cock was hovering over us, not giving us a moment's peace. Pierrot wore his tragedy on his face. He had the eyes of a guy who's being eaten away by cancer. "Only temporary . . ." I practically got down on my knees and prayed that he'd get it up, *soon*, or else I might have a fucking dangerous type on my hands. I was beginning to get a reading on him and it gave me the creeps. That's how you become a murderer—you have it in for everyone and you feel like hurting people, wounding the flesh, until the cries of a chick sound like cries of pleasure. That's what I caught in Pierrot's eyes.

"What are you thinking about?" I asked him.

"Jacqueline," he answered, not moving a muscle.

I watched him more and more closely, ready for anything, even for putting a slug in his leg if he freaked.

He paced around the house, went from one room to another in total silence, like a cat, barefoot. I couldn't hear him walking on the tiles so I never knew where he was. I would rap to him, to place him, but he didn't always answer. He spent hours stretched out on Jacqueline's bed, bare-assed, cigarette in his mouth, watching the smoke curl up to the ceiling. He was waiting for it to happen. He kept sniffing the bikinis. He would throw himself down flat on his belly, nose buried in the faded crotches, and wouldn't budge.

"If you take them out all the time," I told him, "the smell's going to evaporate."

He was beautiful, I felt sorry for him and I wished like hell I could bring him up. But all my jokes fell flat, I didn't dare go near him, much less touch him, he was so jumpy and uptight. Sometimes he weakened, came to me like a whipped dog and sat for hours at my feet, gazing at my prick, which seemed to double in size daily. Inevitably, like the survivor of an accident, I felt terrifically lucky—and it showed, especially when Pierrot put his head on my knee and stared at me with his sad eyes. Time would pass and we wouldn't move, riveted to each other without touching, me always just as stiff, he always just as sad. I would try to read, we would share a cigarette . . .

"You'd better think about something else," I advised him, "or you're going to turn into a flaming queer."

"You're right," he'd say, and he'd go back to his bikinis.

One morning as I was cutting out to go shopping, he asked me to score some things to help pass the time: scissors, felt-tip pens, glue.

"I feel like drawing," he told me.

"O.K.," I said. "If that'll take your mind off things."

I bought him a whole set of markers, fat ones that made thick lines, little ones that wrote thin, every color in the rainbow. I was glad to be able to give him some pleasure.

I handed them to him. Not saying a word, not even thanks, nothing, he went and shut himself up in Jacqueline's room. I left him alone, relieved to have some peace and not feel him prowling barefoot around the joint. He didn't show his puss all day, which gave me a chance to read all my mags and relax. But at six o'clock, being nosy, I went to the room.

Wham! It hit me in the face! The room was unrecognizable. Pierrot was quite the artist. He had drawn all over the walls, in every color. Nothing but porno stuff! Tits with purplish nipples, thighs spreading around black and bloody scribbles, asses of every description, some of them farting—but mainly pricks, enormous pink cocks, balls with crimson dongs aimed at blue-eyed little girls with their lips parted as though about to take communion. He'd glued dirty shots from the Danish mags to the walls, along with the three bikinis, which he'd made into life-size drawings and stuffed with paper so they'd look more natural. There was a girl tennis player in a microminiskirt bending over to pick up a ball—no panties. Farther on, you saw the same chick on her motorbike, with a big cock for a seat. And the whole place was filled with passionate declarations: "Jacqueline, how do you dig my magic wand, Pierrot-the-Prick stuffs it in you, one for Papa, one for Mama, one for little Jesus, right up your ass."

He beamed at me, proud as a peacock. "Beautiful, huh?"

"Dynamite."

"Just think of the chick's face, and her parents' faces, when they catch this on August first!"

He decided to do all the other rooms in the house too. That kept him busy during the day, but at night, when the tube went black, he would start bullshitting again. He could only think about one thing: hitting the streets.

"In the dark," he kept repeating, "what the hell could happen?"

"Nix," I'd answer, "we're O.K. like this."

He would have liked to pay a little visit to all the cottages around, to have a look and cop things.

"I don't know," he'd tell me, "chicks' clothes, some new bikinis to sniff, shirts, see-through numbers . . ."

But I always said, "Nix." It was tough, I'm telling you, because I would have dug those things too. Pierrot bare-assed in transparent nylon would have given me a real kick. But I had to be together for both of us. He made me play cop, and I don't dig that. Every day I had to scream at him. And on top of that, he'd shit on me: "Don't yell so loud!" he'd whisper. "You'll get the riot squad out." Or he'd stand at attention and call me Sarge.

Worse than a broad. A chick, a couple of smacks and she'll clam up. If necessary, you can always lock her up in the can. While with a fucker like Pierrot, watch out! You gotta be fast. Once or twice, I felt he needed a belt. Well, I had trouble connecting and he got me. He's the kind who slips through your fingers and hits you from behind. Luckily my gray matter works faster than his, and more often.

My best weapon for cooling him out was fear. I did all I could to scare him shitless, and that was a cinch for me, since I was shaking myself. Besides, the more sane you are, the jumpier you feel about life, that's a known fact.

I kept a constant watch near the shutters for the man, the uniform that inevitably would come poke its nose into the premises. At night I slept with the gun under my pillow, the safety off. I woke up at the slightest sound. That got to Pierrot. And as soon as I felt he was getting too soft, I would casually bring up the subject of prison. Guards, solitary, mail call, chow, lineup, yard, march, lights out: we knew it all by heart.

That's pretty much how we lived for a week—woods, dunes, bike, shopping, house, candles, bandage, chow, and every night in front of the tube, like an old married couple. All we needed were slippers and a faithful dog. We ate raw hamburger in huge amounts, with raw onions dipped in salt and fresh garlic. We ate that every day on loaves of bread, washing it down with milk. Pierrot kept on with his cock mural, going from room to room. He drew portraits of the parents at the heads of their beds, two enormous mugs that stared at us, pissed. Mama, a bag of bones with a mouth like a chicken's asshole and hands folded in prayer. Papa, bald and paunchy, looking like he had ulcers. A road sign ran along the walls, a mixture of arrows and messages that pointed from every room in the house to his masterpiece in the can, a giant multicolored fuck-in where you couldn't tell who the hell was screwing who.

We hit the sack early. Pierrot thought that was a drag, bitched every night and then finally conked out right in the middle of a sentence: "Hey, Jean-Claude, did it ever happen to you, with a chick, that you got to stick your . . ." And zap! Just a sound like potatoes boiling over a low flame. He snored so much that I had to sack out in the other room. We got plenty of rest, all right. We were breathing fire at the end of a few days, except that Pierrot still couldn't get it up. That was the only flaw in his Olympic form. And he wouldn't stop whining, "A chick, Jean-Claude, I gotta have a chick!" It was like a disc that's climbing the charts. "Nix," I would answer for a change. "We're giving them time to forget us, no point diving back into the shit. Chicks mean trouble, you oughta know that. If we hold our hand out to society, it'll never let go till it's put us away. Does that grab you? Personally, I don't dig it."

That didn't mean I wasn't flashing the same thing nonstop. Chicks, fucking, that's all that was in my head. Especially mornings. And all I wanted was to share my terrific jollies. "What are we, joining a monastery?" Pierrot would ask. It was starting to hit home. We would have to change scenes sooner or later, not to mention our bread, which was fading out.

"With a chick it would come back."

"Sure, but what chick?"

Obviously there was some snatch out there just waiting for us. The problem was to make the hit without sounding the alarm.

"A whore," Pierrot suggested. "A dance-hall slut. We'll drag her here blindfolded and jump her in Jacqueline's room."

"No way," I told him. "You really go for broke. As if you were just crying to get sent up! I wouldn't let you near a whore!"

"Then who?"

We thought and thought, and we started to lose control. At night, after chow, we'd sneak out for a little stroll through the village, jumping at everything that moved.

One time, flat on our bellies in the pine trees, we were watching a squad car drive by when suddenly, somewhere in my head, something went click.

"Pierrot!"

"Yeah."

"I've got it!"

"What?"

"Everything!"

He turned me over on my back like a lover, his face right on top of mine. I broke up, I couldn't help it.

"What do you mean, everything?"

I took his head in my hands.

"Everything, Pierrot. We're searching for a piece of ass—I've got us a piece of ass. We're out of bread—I've got us some bread."

"Who?"

"Marie-Ange."

"The beauty operator?"

"Right! *Think*. Everything points to her! She's holding out her hand to us! She's jumping up and down! She's just dying for us!"

92

"Why?"

"For three reasons. First, we fuck her. Right?"

"Right."

"Next we rip off the haircutter's bread, in his shop, with the chick's help! Right?"

"Right."

"Finally, and this is the most important, she cuts our hair!"

"You're crazy!"

"I'm a genius! A crew cut, man! And then no sweat, we'll be able to go anywhere, right under the man's nose, out in front of anybody! We'll be squares, you dig, real assholes!"

Pierrot started to laugh. We both broke up.

But hang in!

We headed back to the cottage in stitches, making plans for the future, when suddenly, what did we spot parked in front of a fancy house with all its lights shining, windows wide open?

A beautiful Porsche with German plates. We snuck over. The keys were in the ignition. We crept closer. The Kraut was in the house, with a broad.

"Four hundred thousand," she was saying to him. "That's a good deal."

He was ogling her, his eyes misty. "I'll buy the house if you'll live in it with me!"

She busted out laughing. The Nazi pig, a fast operator, made a grab for her. The chick, a shrewd businesswoman, let him unbutton her. Tits in the air, she just kept laughing.

What would you have done in our shoes?

We tipped back to the Porsche, released the hand brake and pushed her very quietly toward the road that led down to the sea. On the fine sand covering the asphalt she didn't make a sound. We picked up speed and hopped in, like acrobats.

"The way they're heading," I said, "they won't catch a thing till tomorrow morning."

And I threw her into second, real easy. After that motorbike, it did me good, it cleared my head. A real mind-sweeper.

I made terrific time, gunning her all the way to Toulouse. The faster you go the less afraid you are—a simple question of setting the pace, after that you're home free. Fear is like a muscle: you just have to warm it up enough and it hardens into courage. Of course, we were in a car whose owner was getting his rocks off. That gets you moving. We charged ahead, aware only of the roar of the open throttle and the real estate agent's tits swinging into view around every curve, busting out of her dress into the Kraut's mitts, superdazzling. A good deal, like she said. I kept flooring it to try and catch them.

We didn't see a soul, though, no cops, only butterflies and toads and Marie-Ange when she opened up her door for us. But that was in Toulouse. We'd made it.

It was midnight but she wasn't in the sack. It was hot but she wasn't bare-assed. It was Saturday but she wasn't making out. She was alone, plain and simple.

She opened the door in a half-assed way, as if she'd been waiting for someone. But she was wearing a wrinkled skirt, an old sweater and the faded makeup of a chick who's not expecting anyone, except maybe us, and she didn't have to go to any trouble for us.

"Oh, it's you . . ." That's all she came up with. Then she turned back to her ironing board.

At that I started to get jumpy. She was pressing a white blouse with a steam iron that smoked and whistled in our face. "Get the fuck out," it hissed. "Don't come to me with your panic and tears, I don't have anything to do with freaks like you!" She was listening to any old station on her chipped transistor, any old pop tune, not batting a lash at us. She even had her back to us. She was so cool, calm and collected it gave me the creeps. Because she was getting with it, dig? She was onto the situation as if it was normal for us to be there.

Think about all the people who've popped into your life, just like that, not making waves. It always happens quietly, like nothing was up. The guy or chick simply takes his place, no big deal, like a familiar object. A few words are all you need to click with each other, no need to raise a flag. Example: Pierrot and me . . .

"You doing anything tomorrow?"

"No."

"Me neither."

"Same time?"

And we never left each other's side. Short but sure. Anyway, there aren't that many things to say, just "Hi," "See you tomorrow," or "Want a drink?" or even, "Oh, it's you . . ."

Everyday things, harmless yet tough. Good or bad? You only know later, when it's all over.

"Close the door," the chick said. "You coming or going?"

See, we weren't coming into her pad, she was moving into our lives, all of a sudden yet very subtly, the classic case.

Split, I kept telling myself, fast! Watch out for comfort. We're not here to move in. She's our age and we'll never come out alive. You can't kick the human-warmth habit. A cunt, yes! A chick, no!

I don't know if Pierrot was thinking the same thing as me, since we weren't rapping and both had our eyes glued to the fox's ass—or more exactly, to her skirt zipper, open or broken, I don't know which, like a fly in the back opening onto the soft skin of her ass, the whole vision swaying gently as she ironed.

But anyhow, Pierrot kicked the door shut and we both jumped, me and the chick, though she didn't miss a beat in her pressing.

Pierrot moved slowly, checking out her pad, dragging his boots across her waxed floor, then came and stood smack in front of her, very close. She was still ironing, ignoring him, her head to one side, a strand of hair over one eye.

Then Pierrot very slowly laid his hand on the iron, over the chick's hand, and leaned on it calmly. For a long time. All the steam escaped, and the broad's hand must have been hurting her because she had a funny pinched look. But she didn't say anything. It lasted a century like that, with the iron not moving. Then Pierrot let go and the blouse was burned. A big brownish spot right on the front.

"I don't care," the chick said, shrugging her shoulders. "It's old, all worn out." But she had tears in her eyes and a lot of trouble hiding them. She turned her head from side to side, using her hair as a shield, but you could see them anyhow. Crying over a blouse—shit! We must have arrived in the middle of a blues crisis.

I locked the door, closed the windows and curtains. There was only one room, with kitchenette, bath and no phone. When I got back they hadn't moved, neither the chick, who was hanging her head, nor Pierrot, who was eyeing her. I'd checked out Pierrot's fly in passing: obviously it wasn't about to bust. Nothing in the room moved, except a fly on a limp, sweaty old piece of Gruyère left out in the middle of the table near a box of crackers.

I didn't exactly feel at home. All I felt was that the situation could blow up at any moment, that our whole future was going to be played out there, between Pierrot's cock and the chick's ass, separated by the ironing board, and also that I had to be cool, fucking cool, especially not make any moves that might block Pierrot forever. All I wanted was one thing: for Pierrot's virility to bloom again in all its glory. So I did all I could to get lost, which isn't exactly easy in a joint 90 feet square. I didn't peep, didn't even cough, just pretended to dig the little things around the house, tipping on eggshells so that my buddy's nerves, so touchy and dangerous, wouldn't let us down at prime time.

Finally something moved: Pierrot's hand slowly rose up to Marie-Ange's face. To get a better take on her he lifted her head up by the chin. She let him look, her eyes still lowered, and said simply, "It's no big deal. If you want to fuck me, go ahead!"

Zap! The slap hit like lightning, immediately followed by another just like the first, zap zap! Head thrown back and hair thrown forward, the chick landed in my arms like a wet mop. My hands closed over her and I held her tight against me, calmly gripping her skinny forearms—a prisoner facing Pierrot, like a gift I was laying on him.

He came over to us, took the chick by the chin again. "I don't dig the way you talk," he told her. "We didn't come here for your ass, cunt! We'll fuck you if we feel like it and we'll be the ones to decide, dig?"

Holy shit! Pierrot was really breaking me up! I could feel the chick's ass pretty clearly, crushed against my prick, and she must have caught the effect it was having on me too. She didn't budge, I'll have to hand it to her, no rubbing around to get me more turned on, digging no doubt that I'd already made my maximum size. But there was her odor, the emanations of a hard-up broad, the smell of death that rose from her armpits, her hair, all over. I wrenched her arms back, and two tiny nipples popped out under the sweater, pointed at Pierrot.

"Well, what do you want then?" she asked.

"News about your buddy," Pierrot answered.

"What buddy?"

"Your pimp."

"He's not my buddy or my pimp. I don't give two shits about him. And I don't give a fuck about you either, you lousy faggots!"

Pierrot stayed cool. He simply took the two tits and twisted them, slowly, pinching just a little. The fox crumpled against me, screaming. I held her tighter.

"Repeat that!" Pierrot muttered through clenched teeth. "What did you say?"

"Nothing . . ."

"You don't have any tits but it hurts anyhow, doesn't it?"

She shuddered against my shoulder and I almost choked on her hair.

"You're a slut, aren't you?"

"Yes . . ."

"Repeat what I say! You're a whore, aren't you?"

"Yes, a dirty whore . . ."

"Who sucks hairdressers?"

"Who sucks hairdressers . . ."

"And doesn't wear panties?"

"And doesn't wear panties . . ."

He lifted her skirt and it just so happened that she was wearing panties, white cotton ones.

"Bitch," said Pierrot.

He ripped her skirt off. Now I had her almost bare-assed between my legs and Pierrot *had* to do something. But he did nothing. He just kept asking questions.

"Did he get his car back?"

"Yes."

"Is he happy?"

"About what?"

98

"About getting his car back?"

"Why the fuck should I care?"

"Answer my question!"

"He sold it, so . . ."

"He sold the D.S.?"

"Yeah!"

"To who?"

"I don't know anything about it. He gave it to his garage for them to sell."

"What a bastard!"

All of a sudden he let go of her and backed off toward the window, pissed.

"The piece of shit," he kept saying. "When I think that innocent people are going to be riding around in that death trap . . ."

I let go of the chick too. I couldn't hack it anymore. She headed over to the table to light a cigarette.

"O.K.," she asked after the first drag, "what do we do now? Shall I take the rest off or what?"

It was pretty tense. Pierrot didn't answer, he just stood there with his back to us, in front of the curtain covering the closed window. And the chick smoked, awaiting further instructions.

Finally, I heard Pierrot's voice. "Jean-Claude . . ."

"Yeah."

"Fuck her . . ."

Shit! The chick was looking me right in the eye. All of a sudden I didn't feel like it. Didn't feel like anything. And I was shaking, terribly jumpy. Because I kept telling myself, Pierrot's not getting it up, that does it, he's going to kill her. It'll do him in. He'll strangle her or stick his knife in her belly.

When he turned around, his expression bore out my worst fears: a real death warrant. I would have given anything to be in Australia or even farther, I would have given anything—including my balls, so Dr. Barnard could graft them onto Pierrot.

"Don't you feel like it?" he asked me, with a strange look on his puss, hands in his pockets.

"Sure," I answered. "But what about that haircut? Why don't we do that first? What do you think?"

"O.K., I don't give a shit."

"We'd feel better."

The fox didn't get it, that was obvious. "You got some scissors?" I asked her.

"Yes. Why?"

Pierrot lifted a razor out of his pocket and opened it with his fingertips as if he did it every day of his life.

"Here," he told the chick. "This does a better job, more stylish." He held the razor out to her. She took it. It looked enormous in her little manicured hand. She gawked as if it were smeared with blood.

I decided to butt in. "You're going to give us a nice little cut," I said.

"Your hair?"

"Yeah."

"Why?"

She caught less and less, and the less she caught the more scared she got. She wasn't afraid to have us jump her, but now this bit about the hair and the razor made her blood run cold. She was white as a sheet.

"Just for kicks," I said. "To make us feel better. You mind?"

"No. If that's what you want . . ."

We went into the bathroom.

Some underwear was hanging on a line dripping into the tub and more was soaking limply in the sink. Common everyday underwear, white, from the five-and-dime, barely yellowed in spots where it got raunchy during the day and got rubbed the most to get it clean. Quite a little housewife, Marie-Ange, neat and tidy.

She pulled a stool over to the tub and asked Pierrot to sit down. He sat down. He let himself be ordered around like a kid, as if it was the first time he'd been to the barber's with his old man and his old man had said, "I'll be back for you in an hour. I'll be in the bar. Wait your turn and don't wiggle. Read your comics." He did just as he was told, staring down at his feet. We told him to take his shirt off, to make it easier, and he took his shirt off. The only difference was the barber wasn't an old Niçois in a white jacket but a perfumed chick with just a pair of panties hiding her honey pot. But Pierrot wasn't at all turned on by the dainty legs twinkling around him. He stared at his feet, that's all. And I eyed him, none too reassured.

She started by giving him a shampoo under the shower. Pierrot let her work on him, not even closing his eyes. He stared off into space as she dried him. I don't know what he could have been staring at, but it can't have been too sweet judging from his down expression.

The chick started to clip him, the big razor squeaking on the wet hair.

"Short," I said. "A crew cut."

As I flash back on it, that night was really our second coming. Marie-Ange, a true mama, gave birth to us again. Wielding the razor, she brought us into the straight world. What a night!

Her hands flew from one ear to the other, light, precise, and as his curls fell to the tiled floor I couldn't recognize my old buddy anymore. I felt like hollering for the massacre to stop. But it was too late, I knew, and it was better that way.

Pierrot's looks changed, slow but sure. He got brighter, lighter, as if the sun was shining into his cell, and as his looks changed he slowly stopped staring off into space. His gaze even took on a strange intensity, focused on Marie-Ange's crotch, which he followed like radar as it swayed around the stool. He couldn't take his eyes off that dark spot under her panties with the curly hairs peeking outside the elastic and poking right through the cotton. He was counting those hairs one by one, and his eyes were starting to bug out of his head.

"Jean-Claude!" he suddenly shouted.

"What?"

"I got it up!"

A great day, as I was saying.

He slowly rose, dizzy with emotion, his eyes raised to heaven, as if he were hearing voices. He staggered over to me. "Look!" he said.

It was true! His cock was up to his waist and I heaved the sigh of relief of the century! Marie-Ange, not even waiting to be asked, had already tossed her sweater off with a resigned shrug.

"Look at that fucking whore, will you!" Pierrot said, pissed.

He sent her into the room with a couple of boots in the ass.

Taking my time, I picked up the razor, folded it, put it in

my pocket and casually trucked in to see what was going on, just in case they needed me or anything.

"What foul breath you have!" That's all she said to us, not one word more or less. Not too chatty, Marie-Ange. Restful, maybe, but as a conversationalist, zilch. No scenes, no putdowns, nothing. The same with her bed—brand new foam rubber and totally silent, not a squeak out of it.

But she let us do whatever we wanted, even kiss her on the mouth and everything, despite our stinking breath, reeking of garlic, onion and cigars. The chick wasn't really turned off, but she didn't come on to our advances either. She just let herself be had, and after a while we no longer even knew what the hell to do to her. You run out of ideas, you know, when the chick doesn't fight back, doesn't get put out, lets you do anything like that.

We'd snap her into a certain position and she'd stay that way. She didn't move, she waited, stiff as a board, with no sense of the comical or anything else. As for modesty, forget it, she couldn't have given less of a shit. It was like the shots in those Danish pornos: side-splitting, some of them . . . Having us peer into all her holes didn't get her hot or cold, no more than going to the dentist. It was a lucky thing, too, because Pierrot was coming on like Lewis and Clark, exploring Marie-Ange's deepest nooks and crannies, hooked by every little detail. "You gotta admit this tops your graffiti!" I said. He busted out laughing, but the fox didn't turn a hair. She lay there like a patient on an operating table. We could have gone out for a drink at the corner bar and found her in the same position when we got back.

If we asked her to do some specialty, she'd do it, no hassles, and wouldn't miss a beat either. A real meat grinder! An outer-space lay! A blender with a lifetime guarantee!

She didn't sweat, she didn't moan, she didn't toss her head from side to side, she didn't bite her lips. She didn't bite anything, not the pillow and not us. She didn't roll her eyes wildly. She kept her eyes open the whole time. She looked at what was right under her nose, never off to the side. We could have put anything we wanted under her nose and she wouldn't have made a scene, been put out or acted huffy. Nothing about us shook her. It was like she had been raised in a large family of boys and

102

we were all her brothers. In any case, we weren't the first dudes to have done a number on her, you could tell, nor the dirtiest, nor the sickest. We might even have been the cream of the crop, for once. That was why her machinery worked so smooth, it had been well oiled before. The most lubricated moving parts in the neighborhood, I'll bet. Two dicks more, two dicks less—no reason to lose her head. That explained her rational cool.

Rational but sad. We didn't get one smile out of her, not one cry, not one emotion. She was a hole with hair around it and no more. A lifelike doll that shit real shit but didn't say mama. And not especially pretty either. A Twiggy with a flat ass, no boobs or almost none, a little bony in places. But in good shape, not an ounce of flab. Gotta hand it to her. And very into personal hygiene. No scabs or anything.

But even so, I couldn't help remembering Carnot's dig: "Might as well be screwing a piece of meat." It wasn't really true but there was something to it, like most things people say. A real head-scratcher.

Then why, you'll ask, did we hang out for seventy-two hours —thirty-six of them in the sack—with that boring cunt?

There are a lot of reasons.

First, as you already know, we're fuckheads.

Also, let's face it, because a twat was exactly what we needed at the time. A twat with no frills. Just a view of crotch hairs. Our bodies had a phenomenal desire to fuck. They kept us glued to the mattress. So we stayed till we were wasted. Besides, it was the only twat around.

Pierrot was having a ball celebrating the return of his hard-on, and what hard-ons he got! He kept waving his groovy glistening prick at me. "Look!" He'd shove it under my nose, tap me on the shoulder with it. The sick-leave had made it double in size! A real miracle! I was the one who was wiped out this round—like I was eighty or something! I got drained, but him, the more he fucked, the more swollen it got! Only one thing was bugging me: that his skin would bust open! What a monster. A real horsecock! Hats off to the fox for not howling!

But I really got stung when he decided to let me have a personal demonstration, the mother. I caught on too late! He socked it to me, lubricated by the chick, which helped. A total shock, huge and painful as hell! A red-hot poker up my ass! I didn't want to say anything, especially not holler, since I didn't want Pierrot getting a laugh on me, or the fox either, seeing as she never peeped herself. I didn't want to be the only one to let it loose in that pad, so I just clenched my teeth. They were all I had left to clench, so I clenched them hard.

Then it dawned on me that there were a lot of fishy things about that broad, and it bugged me. Things that weren't normal at all. It made me feel like sticking around because I hate being in the dark.

Her chest, for example: a desert, a total lack of boobs, and yet it got to me. Why? I had always dug bulging bras and rubbing big balloons. I couldn't get over it. What on earth did I see in that boy-scout figure? The mark of fragility, perhaps, even poverty, that rose from her flat chest. All she had on her ribs was skin! And two brown circles, large but so delicate, almost transparent, you could damn near see her heart beat. Forever-erect nipples, short and stubby, like push buttons. Not knockers but much more than knockers! A far-out understatement, a beautiful lesson in feminine modesty! A chick who no way would have laid you out with obscene, flabby udders! With Marie-Ange, we started to hate big boobs. Her fragility made us feel like protecting her—or busting her, we didn't really know which. A kid's chest, followed by a kid's belly. And since she also had a pouty little doll's face, the whole picture was pretty juvenile.

But what was fishy about her youth, her fragility, her modesty and all that bullshit was that between her legs she had the anatomy of a mother, heavy-duty, as if she'd given birth to three fat kids—a somewhat sluttish mother, to be exact.

Her cunt opened out generously and came up high in front, on a big mound, so you could get a good view. What a scene! A banquet table. A spring tide that had left everything stranded, octopuses, seaweed, starfish. The whole world on a platter. When you think that most dudes drive hundreds of miles and more to find a vacation spot! We'd found our own picnic grounds—out of the way, charming, and great eats! Fucking Marie-Ange! What a spread!

How could she be so unsexy up top and such a whore down below? A new breed of chippie, perhaps, invading the planet. Like Martians. Trippers from outer space who mixed in soft and sweet like nothing was wrong. An army of third-sex milkmaids to blow our minds so that we no longer knew whether we were fucking a guy, a chick, or both at once.

One more thing that didn't click: Marie-Ange obviously didn't come. A fox makes noise when she comes, she convulses, she thanks you with her eyes. No, she didn't get off at all, not even for a second, and she didn't try to either. She was just an icy cunt. But then why did she get so wet—the two just don't go together!

When I say wet, that's putting it mildly. She didn't just get wet, she flooded the joint. A river of secretions poured out of her muff. And in two shakes of a lamb's tail no less, not after we'd been working on her for an hour! At the first thrust we were hit. *Drenched!* A broad who hardly knew us already dripping —gallons! And not because she was hot, or else she would have come on a little, at least gotten sort of turned on. But no, she just lay there like a life-size Barbie Doll. So what gave? What did all that cream mean? Nice, naturally, but suspicious. Suppose it was a gift from the hairdresser who'd shot his load there just before us, the filthy bastard? What a bummer of an idea! The stuff was starting to reek. We gave her a couple of smacks and told her to go clean it out, the slut, and fast! And with the rotary spray switched to high! We even went and checked out the routine.

Then we got back down to basics again, a little cooled off, you might say . . .

Unbelievable! She was starting to cream again from every pore! Far out! No need to hold our noses this time! We started scarfing in earnest, like the starving dudes we were. No need for fingerbowls! No holds barred! Just a napkin around your neck and go, man! Ah, what scavengers! You should have seen us! Our tongues were hitting the floor! A real gravy boat, our new mama! We just gorged on that little beauty operator's proteins!

And what a shampoo she gave us! A special! Superconditioned with intimate oils! Ultrasudsing! Restores your mustache to its natural sheen! It was too much! We came until our balls were busted, we even jockeyed for position. And what a rush at the box office! Sounded like pigs in a spaghetti joint! The sauce was splattering everywhere in yummy little drips! Never saw such a wet fox! Must have been making her whole building damp! Must have been giving the neighbors lumbago!

But why didn't she get in on it if she got that juicy? Didn't she give a shit? And why couldn't she get her rocks off, even if only in a small way, with all those wild thrusts we were letting her have? Dig it, man! A deformity, perhaps, independent glands gone berserk. Or a chick from outer space, that's all I could figure.

After a couple of hours, anybody in his right mind would have gotten sick of that lazy bitch, especially since we weren't even rapping or anything. Sucking sounds were all you could hear. We had planned to split before dawn, but the sun rose and nobody moved—not the chick, who was still dripping, or Pierrot, who couldn't get enough, or me, who was watching them, zonked. Pierrot looked so funny in his new haircut. His ears stuck out like an army brat's, his forehead, which I'd never caught before, stood out a mile. He seemed older, harder, like some pig kid who knows what he wants out of life and looks straight ahead, into the future (gotta admit he always did stand like he was at attention), but he also seemed younger, all shaved like that. For the first time he looked like the young kid he had never been. I felt weird looking at him, a sort of crazy feeling of not knowing him, like finding myself in the buff in bed with some little brat from the local high school. But he was still banging away, tireless. A trusty stickman, my buddy, when you don't mistake his parts for a shooting gallery. I was happy to see the old stud rise again, and didn't have the heart to bust it up. One more hour, I told myself, he looks so proud. That's why we didn't cut out.

She was a sweet kid, too, that Marie-Ange, even if she didn't dig us in bed. She was our age and as down as we were. These things count in fucking. We felt at home, sort of like a family. We'd pulled the covers up because it had started to get cold in her pad and were snuggled nice and cozy under there, all sticky and warm. That's how you blow time when you should be taking care of business, like keeping your ass out of the cage. Luckily I had stashed the Porsche way outside of town, in a parking lot where it wouldn't catch anybody's eye. What looks more normal than a car sitting in a parking lot? Of course the man was in the back of my mind as I gazed at Marie-Ange's head on my shoulder, but nothing in the world could have made me get up. She turned me on, that far-out fox, with all her hang-ups.

It's a heavy trip when you start checking yourself out, when your head starts tuning into the past. That's when it hits you, all the things you couldn't keep on top of, like traps you fell right into without even knowing it—even saying thanks, for Chrissake. Your head tells you you haven't done one thing you wanted to do and now it's too late, baby, you're going to croak whether you like it or not, no two ways, even though you're too young to die and it's a bitch because there are so many rotten pricks around who are making it, really living it up, shaking their heads as they read the papers! Like hairdressers, for example.

We crashed for three days in her comfy little pad. It just happened. Her alarm went off at eight and she said, "You want some coffee?"

We drank her coffee and ate her ham, eggs and toast, and then she cut out in a rush, asking what we wanted for dinner. As simple as that. No sweat.

Three days. We hung around while she went to work for that hairdresser. We slept late. We lolled around in her big bed and her nice hot shower. And when she got back we started messing around again.

In the morning we dressed our little Barbie Doll, washed her ourselves, chose her little panties, watched her tipping down the street through a crack in the curtains, and at night we undressed her, took off her little panties and sniffed those eight hours on the job between her legs, all those dainty little motions in the armpits of her nylon blouse. She would show up reeking of perfume and hairspray and nail polish. And then she'd do it any way we wanted, as usual. Kneeling, standing, lying down. All you had to do was ask her. But she never took the lead. You had to think for her, do all the work for her, break your ass for her.

I couldn't keep up the pace, personally. I would get off real fast and go into the kitchen. While they were still at it, I'd chef up little snacks with the groceries Marie-Ange had brought back. The smell of cooking would make Pierrot even hornier, and he'd outdo himself each night. Marie-Ange, of course, stayed true to form. She'd lie there counting the flies on the ceiling and calling out cooking hints to me, hipping me to her favorite recipes.

We ate on the bed and watched the boob tube for a while. Then Pierrot would get back into it for another hour or two and we'd pass out curled up against each other like a litter of puppies.

But, just a sec, that's not *all* we did.

I got my hair cut too! And we hashed out the details of our scheme to pay a little visit to the hairdresser . . .

It wasn't so much him we wanted to see, that faggot hair-curler, although we would have enjoyed giving him a knuckle sandwich. The point of the visit was his bread.

Marie-Ange, as usual, had no qualms about telling us what her boss's money routines were. She leaked information like a PA system. She really opened up a lot of things for us, that little Toulouse beauty operator: her legs, her haircurler's cash box, the doors to a better life. Thanks, Marie-Ange, thanks for everything! You'll get yours in your heavenly hammock, you'll see! The Man Upstairs will give you a pretty cloud all to yourself, where angels with hard-ons will come ring your chimes! Seems they have beautiful cocks—long, sweet ones, missiles with heat-seeking heads diving into your deepest crannies! And angels don't stink like we do, they smell divine! You'll catch on quick in heaven! You'll get wetter than ever! You'll zap the whole human race with white tornadoes, they won't know what hit them! Hurricane Vulvy flattens Fontainebleau! All those Mr. Cleans will think it's the end of the world!

He had brains up his ass, that hairdresser, and was a full-time shit as well. Just listen to what Marie-Ange laid on us.

We were eating on the bed. She had brought home some seafood.

"He leaves all his bread in the cash register," she told us. "He feels safe because of the dog."

"There's a dog?"

"Yes, a special attack-trained Doberman. He always sleeps in the shop at night."

"How big's the mother?"

"Big as the table."

There was what you might call a pause in the conversation, and I went to get the steamed mussels off the stove.

"He only obeys his master, but he knows the employees, of course."

"Does he know you?"

"Well, yes, slightly. We walk him, we take him out for a piss three times a day. Of course it's hard to say who's walking who."

"Would he attack you if you showed in the middle of the night?"

"I don't think so. He likes us girls pretty well, he's gotten used to us from the fuck-ins."

"Huh?"

Pierrot and I eyed each other over the mussels and suddenly lost our appetites. The mussels were starting to smell sort of rotten.

"What fuck-ins?"

"Well, with Marc . . ."

"Who the hell's he?"

"Marc's my boss!"

"The haircurler?"

"Yes."

"And he gets you into fuck-ins?"

"Well, yes . . ."

"With the mutt?"

"Well, yeah . . . It's that or no job!"

She seemed to think that was normal. Her boss, a dog, a garage mechanic, two hippies, an elephant, an infantry battalion—she thought everything was O.K.

"What does the dog do to you?"

"Oh, nothing terrible. He licks us a little. Sometimes one of the girls gets uptight and that amuses Marc, it turns him on. The girl will be running all over the place with the dog running after her."

"Does he fuck any of you?"

"It's happened five or six times, But usually the girls scream too much, so Marc stops the whole thing."

"And you? Has he screwed you?"

"Once . . . yes . . ."

"But *you* didn't scream, I'll bet."

"Me? No, I didn't give two shits."

Far out! She kept right on slurping down her mussels as though nothing was wrong. The juice was dripping down her chin.

"How does it feel to get fucked by a dog?"

"Oh, it's nothing special. It doesn't take as long as with a guy. And it's cleaner. A dog doesn't feel you up. The only trouble is his paws on your back—they scratch."

We didn't have dessert, Pierrot and me. And she'd brought us back a big napoleon, and we love napoleons, we're crazy about them. Well, we just couldn't handle it. Couldn't deal with Marie-Ange's creamy napoleon, not after that.

The Doberman looked happy to see her again, his tongue was hanging out two feet. She hadn't worn anything under her skirt on purpose, to turn him on so he wouldn't freak out, so he'd feel at home with her. He was a real sweetheart. Popeye was his tag, a beautiful beast. She let him lick her for a while and then handed him the napoleon, which she'd brought especially. Popeye really had a feast. Then we locked him in the can and that was the last we ever saw of him.

Pub-Coiffure it was called, a big English-style joint full of wood paneling, copper and red chandeliers. You could curl forty dames at one shake in there, Marie-Ange told us. It was crazy how many facts she laid on us! We couldn't shut her up. She gave us a tour with her flashlight, like a museum guide.

"And that's Monique's booth, the head manicurist, the one who's kid is in Paris along with her old man, the bastard—a lawyer. He doesn't want her to see her kid, he has the law on his side, of course, poor Monique can't even fight back, he's always getting her caught in the act, he claims she's a whore—a fallen woman, it's called—and she is! But she's hung up on her kid, I swear, even if she is a whore. You wouldn't believe the times I've caught her bawling on the sly, huddled over her stool, doing some local housewife's nails. It's a real downer seeing those things. She tells the customers everything—about her abortions, her old man, her kid, how she used to live on Boulevard Saint-Germain with servants and an English car, and play golf at Deauville—to the point where Marc's going to have to can her, even though she is a great lay! But the soap opera she keeps spilling out to the customers does make a bad impression, even though they dig the dirt and love airing everyone else's laundry. They always bust in at the end of the week, the pigs. No way to spread the work out in hairdressing—same as traffic on the highways. Sometimes you spend four days just hanging out in the empty salon . . ."

Impossible to shut Marie-Ange up! What a rapper! Like trying to stop an avalanche! No way, it had to keep coming, she had to spit it out. Must have had it all stored up for a long time.

All the same, it was a groove to see that there were still some sweet chicks left in our country who led normal, healthy lives, didn't take dope, loved their work and all that!

But that wasn't the end of her act. Then she had to drag us into the wig salon. It seems that wigs and wiglets were all the rage in those parts. Wigs and Polaroid cameras, the new rip-offs. And the old man was all for the wig—it made the mother of his kids more appetizing over the long haul. An old lady with different disguises can change the music. She comes home a blonde, a brunette, frizzy-headed like the pediatrician's wife, a redhead like the broad who just moved in next door, teased like the little beauty operator. The poor bugger has the notion he's fucking all of them. It clicks in the sack, especially with a scotch or two under your belt. Those terrific little rugs make the meat taste better, and they're a good investment, when you get right down to it. A new way to serve up the leftovers, a jiffy reheating process. That and a good Polaroid to snap dirty pics you can always get a charge out of flashing at the office, that was the big rush. And

Marie-Ange had seen scores of those photos which the mamas hustled in their purses and let her peek at. Far-out yellowed prints, all dog-eared like old driving licenses and fixed with Scotch tape. And the poses! You couldn't hawk one under your coat outside the men's can! No one would want any—you'd go broke!

Our little chickadee was really blowing her cool with these torrents of memories, and I could feel we were in for a heavy scene. It came over her in a flash. Suddenly she went bananas: she whipped up a wig in each hand and started rubbing herself with them! "Madame Cardan!" she cried, sponging her twat with a red one, "I'm styling your fall for fall! Just wait! I'll spray it for you with my little cunt! Nice and bouffant! A real mane, Madame Cardan!" And she was getting off on it, freaking . . . "It'll turn your husband on! He'll think you're out-asight! 'What an exquisite perfume, my dear! Something new? From Paris? By Dior?' You'll spend the weekend of your life at the Grande-Motte! And you'll make that baby you keep rapping about! Your tubes aren't plugged at all! No, it's never too late at forty! You look twenty in your hairpiece!" She was spitting on it now, hawking and spitting like crazy on all the wigs, stamping around on the hair-covered floor. "So long, Madame Cardan! I won't need your fat tips anymore! I'm splitting with my two stinking buddies! And I hope your little brat is born dead, too! You kept rapping to me about him when he didn't even exist yet! Bored the shit out of everyone with a kid who hasn't even been conceived, when the sperm hasn't even gotten to-gether with the egg, when there are too many fucked-up little bastards in the world already." A real space-out! She started heaving things at the mirrors. What a racket! Enough to wake the whole town! We started chasing her ass through the store. The bitch slipped between our fingers like a fish. The mirrors were crashing down off the walls!

Popeye started howling in the shithouse! Pierrot was yelling. Total panic. There was only one solution—the gun. I aimed. Monster bang: a slug in the shins. Marie-Ange dropped flat on on her face among the mirror shards. She didn't budge. She groaned. We moved her to a swivel chair, tipped way back in the shampoo position. "Sorry 'bout that," I said. She was pissing blood all over, from a million cuts. She clutched us like an octopus. No way to make her let go. We had to hog-tie her to the chair with towels that turned red right before our eyes. "Take me with you!" she begged. "Don't ditch me, take me with you! I'm not any trouble! I won't get in your way! You can fuck me forever! I'll do the cooking, the laundry, everything. We'll stop by my pad and pick up my bread! I've got five thousand francs in a Kotex box in the back of my closet!"

We cleaned out the hairdresser's cash register fast and cut out of there. Marie-Ange was bawling but we really didn't have the time to let it get to us. We barrel-assed by her joint to rip off her Kotex box loaded with tips and then made tracks to get ourselves lost in the night. We weren't playing the hero role, I swear.

We even felt a little sleazy. It wasn't the rip-off that was bringing us down, more like a case of the burnouts and too many bangs in too short a time with that crazy fox who had ended up freaking us. A clean but tough bitch. Who popped a jinx on things, I bet. The kind of chick you miss, yeah, but you're fucking glad to ditch anyhow, to have her behind you, like certain cars that hog the whole road. She was starting to sap our pity, and pity brings bad luck. It's like leaning over a canyon: you're drawn by the bottom, and if you get a little dizzy, the odds are you drop in.

Easy enough to say you'll just get lost in the night. It's cold at night. Drafty. Not to mention the dew soaking through your jacket. Even in vacant lots with no grass or trees, just cement, mud and old buggies with oil spots under them, the dew still nabs you. Especially when you're out of hair.

We didn't know where to head in that fucking night, and I didn't even dig whipping up a good idea about a place. I was just pissed, fed up with everything. I couldn't seem to get a move on. I felt like a complete wipe-out in the smarts department. My brain was fizzled, I tagged along behind Pierrot, who had no idea where he was heading.

We'd never been so rich, but even that didn't lift us. We hadn't faced toting lots of bread yet. Buying power was bulging out of our pockets, but what the fuck can you buy at two in the morning in a hole like Toulouse? Also, you have to feel like buying something. Think I would rather have puked. A foul aftertaste lingered at the back of my throat, a dirty heave, sour and suicidal. A desperate little beauty operator had stuck in our craws. No way you can dump your guts of indigestible memories, even with your finger. You gotta keep them down, live with the nausea.

We wandered like sickies through those treeless streets, on the verge of checking back to Pub-Coiffure to grab our little shampooist, waiting for some kind of signal, a kick in the butt to push us into action. We knocked about, dragging our asses, when suddenly what we were waiting for happened, the signal— a police siren wailing in from the other side of town, an obscene noise in the residential silence. It had our names on it. "Follow me," I told Pierrot.

We ran like maniacs along the lines of parked cars. I made a sharp left and a hard right, then headed off across the dried mud, skirting the streetlights on the boulevard that led nowhere. We raced through pools of darkness, coming out behind the power station. We pounded down a little street of row houses, came out in a housing development, sprinted across three court-yards, knocking over a garbage can, sending the cover spinning with a clatter. Which sent the dogs after us, snarling. We poured it on, they gave up, we lost the poor man's mutts in the night. "Where you heading?" asked Pierrot, hot on my heels. Shove it, you dummy, I know the way by heart. My guts ached from running, that insatiable female had really slowed me down. Sorry, man, I can't talk, not even to answer a buddy who's dropping back and freaking. "Hey, Jean-Claude! Where you heading?" There, relax, baby, you made it, it's this block of tenements.

"Take your boots off," I told him. He didn't ask questions. He did like me, kicked his boots off, and we dove onto the open stairway, then down the hallways full of Spanish graffiti. The drafts made the greasy wallpaper flop. Some newborn fucker started to howl like we were stomping on his head. Even though we weren't making a sound in our socks! We moved as fast as we could. I slipped my key in door 324, which was scrawled on it in chalk. Pierrot watched me, coughing his lungs out, eyes popping. We snuck in, closing the door behind us soft as possible. Outside in the hallway, someone came to have a look. The building was alive with concierges. A whole army of spies surrounded us. Those old hags have fucking sharp ears, and they wear hearing aids to boot. Besides, they spend hours checking their ears out, getting them clean as a whistle. Fingernail, pen, match stick, knitting needle, anything to scoop out the wax. They don't want to miss a trick through those thin walls. A symphony of whispers, sobs and moans. A door squeaking, bare feet in the hall, the rustle of a jacket—nothing escapes them. They stock up at night, these gossipmongers, hoarding items for winter, for the silent months when the fog cuts the sounds. Then they squeeze out their juicy tales drop by drop. What gabfests! Beats what's on the tube!

The neighbor's door closed again.

It took us a while to catch our breath and calm our racing hearts. We stood in the dark, a dark much deeper than the night, a real blackout, with grease and old tobacco stuck in a thousand layers to the walls and ceiling. In a silence so thick you could cut it with a knife.

"Who's there?" A woman's voice, straining.

I had my hand on the light switch, the one that's always hidden by the coatrack.

We needed light, so I flipped the switch.

"Jean-Claude!"

She looked like she'd seen a ghost. She wasn't just pale, she was greenish, rotting, racked by fear, shame and a million other emotions. Her makeup cut across her face in big red and black streaks.

"Jean-Claude," she repeated, dazed, blinking, "is that you?"

With a flip of her hips she pried herself out from under the two-ton turkey on top of her, his head turned to the wall in embarrassment. She steadied herself by fixing her eyes on me, got up, white and sweaty, not giving a shit about her deflated boobs, her wrinkles, folds and pathetically few pubic hairs. She came slowly toward me.

"Jean-Claude . . . What is it?"

"I'd like you to meet my mother," I said to Pierrot.

"Good evening, madame," he said, the dummy.

"He's your friend?"

116

"Yes. Pierrot, the buddy I told you about that the papers have been playing up."

"You crazy, showing up here?"

"If you ask questions, we'll split."

"No! Stay!" She cupped my face in her hands.

"Then shut up!" I told her. "And go wash your hands."

"Yes," she said. "Right away."

While she was in front of the sink I pulled the gun out and stepped over to the lump of flesh stuck on the bed.

"O.K., Pops! On your feet!"

I let him feel the cold barrel. All I could see was his back, the outline of his undershirt and his skinhead. He was all Jell-O. Didn't dare scratch his ass. I tapped him.

"On your feet, I said!"

He turned over limp as a dying cock. The puss of a pious family man, distorted by a case of the shakes.

"What do you want?" he asked.

"For you to make tracks."

"O.K., right away."

No need to tell him twice: he was already on his feet, he didn't want to hassle us.

We all watched him head to the chair where his clothes were. My old lady dried her hands with a dish towel while he dressed. She felt sorry for him.

"Give him back his bread," I told her.

"All right."

She went to get the C-note out from under the pillow and handed it to her customer. He hesitated.

"Take it," I shouted, "or I'll make you eat it."

He stashed the bill in his pocket.

"What's your name?" I asked.

That shook him. He faked not digging. He wagged his head. Didn't want to surrender his incognito. My mother had to answer for him.

"Fixecourt," she said, "Alphonse Fixecourt."

"You from around here?"

"No," she continued, "he's from Bohain, up north."

"He works where?"

"At the E.D.F."

"Address?"

"Rue Bronze, number fourteen."

"Any kids?"

"Five."

I stuck the gun in his fat paunch. "It doesn't bug you to fuck my mother?"

He started to stammer. "Excuse me . . . I couldn't have known . . ."

"That makes you sort of like my old man, when you think about it, since you sleep with my mother, right there in the family bed."

"I guess so," he answered.

"Then you should also take care of my education and everything."

"I can help you if you like, if you need a job . . . At the E.D.F. perhaps . . ."

"Thanks but no way. We're wanted by the police."

"Oh."

"And we don't drool for the can none."

"I understand . . ."

"You know shit about jail?"

"No . . . not personally . . ."

"You know that it stinks?"

"I can imagine . . . The dirt . . . everything . . ."

"No. Not the-dirt-everything! The shit!"

"Yes . . . that too . . ."

"Not that too! *Only* the shit! And you know what you got at night to help you sleep?"

"No . . ."

"Masturbation."

"Oh . . ."

"Otherwise you don't sleep. Some guys even make holes in the mattresses and put pieces of meat in them. There's no way you can get your rocks off with somebody's mother in there! All you got is your hands!"

The family man looked wobbly—even fainter after I laid my message on him. "And if we go to jail, you're to blame."

"Why?"

"Because you will have ratted!"

"I won't breathe a word, I swear."

"When we get out we'll skin you alive!"

"But I told you I won't breathe a word!"

"Get out."

"Sure . . . There, I'm leaving."

He was already opening the door.

"His glasses," said mother. "He's forgetting his glasses."

"He doesn't need them."

"That's right, I don't need them. I'm going."

I pushed him out into the night like a piece of shit, and the three of us were alone.

"Make us some coffee," I told my old lady, "and put on a bathrobe. If there's one thing my buddy's really nuts about, it's modesty."

I suddenly wondered what the hell we were doing there.

I'd wanted to see my old lady, no doubt about it. A corny idea. O.K, but now I'd done it, I'd seen plenty of her. There was nothing she could do for us. So why didn't I give the signal to leave?

All Pierrot wanted was to get back on the road, you could tell from the way his hands kept dancing in and out of his pockets, he didn't know where to park them. Also his expression, like an embarrassed idiot, making a far-out effort not to stare at his buddy's bare-assed old lady. See, a mother was a sacred thing to him because he'd never had one, he was an orphan. He didn't know where to look. He would have loved to take his eyes out and stash them in the bottom of his pockets with his hands over them. That would have been his dream. But he didn't peep, didn't breathe, that's how sacred a mother was to him, even a whore with her tits hanging out.

I tried to piece out why I felt like being there, and nowhere else. And staying there.

It wasn't because we needed her place to crash. We couldn't have scored a hotter pad with all those news hens faking sleep around us, hot lines hooked into the police station. My old lady's neighbors had plenty to yack about already because it just ain't proper to still be earning your bread with your cunt at forty-one.

But I just stood there like an asshole, not moving, watching my old lady wrestle with her sleazy peignoir, a peekaboo number trimmed with mauve nylon frills, enough to make your skin look deathly. She was all flustered, couldn't find the right sleeve, and this went on and on, with her ass still in plain view.

"Put on something else," I told her.

She turned around. "What? What do you want me to put on?"

"Something decent, for my buddy."

"Yes, you're right."

She got up on a stool to rummage in the depths of the closet, and with that Pierrot looked the other way. He couldn't handle it any longer.

I rummaged around too—through clumps of ironing scattered on the floor. I tipped over half of them but finally found it: a little flowered cotton dress, quite chic. I tossed it to my ma, who was about to climb into some dingy skirt. "Here," I said, "slip this on. Whose is it?"

"The Alzonnes' daughter. It won't look right on me."

"Try it on. I want to see you in it."

She dashed into the can and Pierrot took the chance to quiz me.

"Hey . . ."

"Yeah. Something you want to ask me?"

"Well, what I mean is . . . Is that really your ma?"

"Yeah, man. It's better than no mother at all."

"Bastard."

"Shut up. And be polite in front of her. Watch your manners and stuff. She's a lady."

Just then she came back. The dress looked great on her. She fixed her hair at the back of her neck. She looked like a different person, a million bucks. I was glad I'd stayed.

She pushed aside the laundry, the irons and clothes and set two cups on one corner of the table. Water was boiling on the stove.

"Wash your face," I told her.

"Why?"

"Wash your face, like I said. With water. Lots of water."

She went over to the sink and turned on the faucet. She scanned herself in the little mirror hanging on a pothook, reviewing her forty-one years. But there was no way, she couldn't drop her mask. It was me who had to do it.

I grabbed a rag and rubbed her face hard under the cold water. She tried to back off but I held her down by the back of the neck. I scrubbed. Gobs of makeup came off. Every color in the rainbow ran down the drain. It looked like I was cleaning a palette. Then, little by little, the original appeared.

"You want to see me like this?" she moaned.

When nothing was left but her skin, the circles under her eyes and her wrinkles, I turned off the water and dried her gently, like a fragile antique.

"Just a whim," I answered. "What's your beef, I'm your best customer. Maybe it's the last time I'll see you, here tonight, dig? At least I want to remember your real eyes, your real skin."

Pierrot and I sat down at the table to drink our coffee. Ma thought of everything she could to make us happy—drinks, eats, it was neurotic all the things she suggested that would be good for us. We nixed it all, the omelet, the sandwiches, the chocolate, the hot bath and the cheese. So then she sat down with us and poured herself a little glass of Casanis, neat. We watched her drink it. Then, when her glass was dry, we all stared at each other, not saying beans.

Ma rubbed her eyes. "Go to bed," I told her. She didn't want to. I insisted. Finally I got up, led her by the arm over to the bed and made her lie down. I kissed her on the forehead. She took both my hands.

"What are you going to do?"

"Wait for daylight. We'll leave then."

"Will you wake me at five?"

"Sure."

"Then I won't set the alarm . . ."

She picked up her old clock and turned off the alarm.

"Don't you notice anything?" I asked her.

"No. What?"

"My hair."

"What about your hair?"

"It's all gone. I got scalped."

"Oh, so you did."

"It's not noticeable?"

"No."

"I don't look different?"

"No, yes, I don't know . . ."

"Well, shit!" That wasn't exactly good news. "I'll bring you breakfast in bed," I added.

She was already asleep. I pulled a blanket over her shoulders and joined Pierrot at the table. We did a fast take on our cash situation. Our favorite haircutter had netted us ten thou and change. Plus the five thou in Marie-Ange's Kotex box, it came to a tidy sum, for kids like us.

I slipped a one-thou wad under my old lady's pillow, like the tooth fairy, and we split without waking her, making sure to hug the walls because of the local hoods who might have lifted our lovely loot. (You should never travel with a lot of cash on you in rough neighborhoods.)

"Let's drop in on Carnot," I suggested. "We'll buy a middle-class buggy off him."

A few days later, a lot had gone down.

First of all, my gray matter was steady as she goes again. You don't suddenly run out of smarts.

We'd been honored by the press, too—it was blowing up into a real chiller. "The Hoodlums' Revenge," it was called. It seems we had pounced on a hapless haircutter, having sworn his ruin. He didn't understand why, the poor devil, he didn't know shit from sheep-dip. We clipped his car, beat him, and two weeks later there we were back in his shop for an after-dinner hit! We pinched him again, tore the joint apart and took him to the cleaners! And to top it off, we raped his best employee! He hadn't been awarded the Legion of Honor yet, the poor mark, but it was just a matter of days. And our pictures had been printed larger and clearer than the first time. Real popular heroes. We made the ten-most-wanted list. But Marie-Ange had been a doll, she hadn't blabbed about our haircuts. As far as the man was concerned, we were still part of the long-haired world, the great unwashed and easy-to-spot. There had been raids on hippie hangouts. Our morale rose.

Carnot, for example, had not recognized us with our hair short. And there was a guy who really knew our kissers well! Five full minutes before he made us!

This led me to two conclusions: first, you should never bet on the takes of a mother 'cause she can always spot her own kid no matter what, even blindfolded in the dark, it's an umbilical phenomenon, it twinges in her guts; and second, if an old pro like Carnot, who always has his eyes peeled, didn't read us, some poor half-blind cop wasn't about to. No hair, no hoodlums! We looked straight, believe it or not. You have to learn to wear the enemy's mask.

So we could unwind a little. And that's what we did—for a week.

We were extra cooled out. Loose all over. Not one joint creaked, no twitches or hang-ups, we just flowed with it. We felt light in the head and around the ears, easy as never before. You should have seen us! We were unrecognizable, ten years younger! I wasn't even sure that was Pierrot draped beside me on the soft seat. I checked myself in the rear-view mirror—far fucking out! Our new description was too much: fine young men in every respect, cautiously coasting in a modest second-hand car, never flying over 70 because it was a Dyane 6, scrupulously respecting the rules of the road, the rules of society, all the rules. We stopped at crosswalks to let widows and orphans pass, we even stopped to help a poor blind man cross the street. We were regular Sir Lancelots on public thoroughfares. Ladies envied our mothers for having such well-bred sons, and lectured theirs for being slobs covered with hair and zits. We smiled at schoolchildren, and agreed that all babies looked exactly like their mothers.

We had integrated.

We had stumbled into public approval. People walked on the same sidewalk as us. Sometimes we even brushed against them. We bumped into their luxuriously perfumed persons on purpose, for pleasure, and they begged pardon, panicked at the idea of offending us, the notion that we might have gotten a bruise freaked them out. No one asked for our papers or anything. Even the fuzz gave us info in a friendly way. It was so great that we were always asking them any old half-assed questions. At every intersection we asked for directions, the time, or the way to the post office. They gave us little salutes. They let drivers stall behind us, fight and curse each other, just for the joy of a bit of conversation with us. For once we felt at home, in a large, warm family.

We could touch anything, go in anywhere. In department

124

stores we charmed the ladies, offered to carry their packages. We smiled sweetly at the sleek salesgirls so that they would pet us, cuddle us, flash their tits at us. But instead they gabbed about shoe sizes, inner seams, buttons. They stuck us with pins, marked us with chalk, circled around us, letting their hands linger a little. They smelled so good kneeling in front of our flies that we had to brace ourselves against the walls to keep from showing a lack of respect, especially when they sized our crotches with their measuring tapes. But we behaved. And little by little we comboed real man-about-town wardrobes, ditching our old duds in the trash.

We weren't too steady yet in our gray-flannel threads. We itched and staggered about. The air in the classy neighborhoods was so pure that it went to our heads, so sweet and full of good vibes for the future that we got high as kites.

We ate only rich foods, in dimly lit restaurants—quenelles, lasagna, zabaglione, kéfirs. We heaved great fat belches. We drooled on our ties.

Clean-cut kids, like I said.

At night when it got dark, we almost believed that it was time to go home, that Papa would blow his stack if we showed up late for dinner, that we'd better step on it. I pictured us pampered by a mother whose ass we'd never even glimpsed, who insisted that we knock before entering, who made artistic flower arrangements and played the piano for us, who would have a fit if by chance some man dared to proposition her, even one of Papa's friends. She would no longer allow him at her table, would refuse his apologies . . .

I only saw my mother five days a month—when she had her period.

Only one thing fucked up our new image. No matter how much we scrubbed, polished, brushed and fluffed up, hair and crud scraped off, in France there is only one thing that counts: your ID card. Carrying our old Scotch-taped papers was like laughing our way through a cocktail party with a hand grenade in our pockets. Even if we could pull it off for a time, sooner or later the thing would blow up in our faces! We couldn't exactly go register ourselves a second time at some city hall. We had to stage a clandestine birth. Illegitimate children midwived underground. We were hardly of royal descent! We had to shuck our shitty old names forever, no one would touch tags like ours with a ten-foot pole. But how could we hook into some new IDs? A real hassle, believe me.

We'd already chewed the problem with Carnot, but there wasn't one forger in his crowd. Impossible for him to cough up a name, even when we bopped him on the bean. So it was true: once you got him off cars, he was like a fish out of water. We didn't know where else to tumble. It was a fucking drag. We didn't even know a good con, a real one. We didn't keep what you might call bad company. There had never been any shady influences in our lives. We thought like hell. Till we started getting fed up—we'd been sleeping on the seats of the Dyane for over a week, on nowhere dirt roads in the surrounding woods, waiting for our suits to be stitched, the alterations to be done and all. We shaved with an electric razor hooked to the battery. Could have been worse, sure, but at night we froze. Our ears got chilly with those crew cuts. In the morning the windows would be frosted over with a dense fog. Maybe the fuzz were closing in on us. We didn't know. The first one awake —if he had the balls to crawl out from under the covers— quickly started the engine so the heat would go on. We faked sleep as long as possible. Our suits got wrinkled. As for washing, no way. We started to get raunchy again. It couldn't last. Shit, we needed papers! With any name on them! We would have even settled for Kovacs or Silverstein if that would have let us sleep in a hotel bed. We weren't into dawdling our lives away in abandoned summer resorts. And what about summers, huh? Where would we go when the season was at its peak? Not counting the fact that the game was dangerous, breaking and entering joints where the owners might show any sec! It was illegal! Perfect ticket to the shadows of the hole! No, what we wanted was to get out of the shadows, live in broad daylight, be able to run over a pedestrian without becoming fugitives for life. Finally, after beating my brains out, I latched onto a solution. It came to me like a spark from rubbing two flints together. Logic, legit logic.

126

We were going to mingle with the mob. A breeze! All we had to do was be around to welcome the real cons when they got sprung from jail, since the worst thing about prison, if you read the papers, is the corruption of youthful offenders by hardened criminals. We were going to find a way to make their acquaintance!

Opposite every pen there are cheery little bars. We recommend them if you're looking for a place to take your friends. Don't pass up the treat. A business lunch, engagement party, old-folks dinner—everything should happen there. For New Year's Eve they're ideal. There's always a guard looming around, you ask him to your table, he hands you some good laughs. Nothing beats a nice, well-fed bouncer. A real hoot. He'll tell horror stories. You'll wallow in social truths, the ladies will be turned on, you'll feel terrif. You'll eat facing an ugly building where you know the inmates are starving, which will boost your appetite. It's all a matter of proportion, you have to dig what you're missing. Stuffing yourself at home doesn't cut it, you don't know how lucky you are. But there you do. You think about their tin plates of soup with rubbery shreds of meat floating in them. You enjoy your leg of lamb more.

The first of these cozy taverns we got to know was called A la Ronde. It was raining. We arrived, looking sharp, and ordered two hot chocolates with croissants. It was morning—the cons, it seems, are always sprung in the morning. We had cut out of the woods, our asses freezing, still wrinkled and starving. We were the only customers except for two goons in painter's coveralls guzzling Pernod and chewing the fat with the owner. His old lady, in front of the smokes, had her nose buried in *Le Petit Parisien.*

A waiter brought us our breakfast.

"What's that big building over there?" we asked casually.

128

"Central," he answered. We stared at him, not digging it. "Central Prison," he specified.

Pierrot and I exchanged looks. Shit! It gave us quite a jolt, we were floored—and fucking impressed.

"No kidding!" we said. "Not a bundle of laughs as a boardinghouse."

"You bet," he answered. "Better outside than in that place."

We were making progress, having the kind of real-life rap that makes the world go round!

We ate, ordered more croissants, sat around, went to take a leak, came back, slammed some coins in the jukebox and pinball machines, goofed off, took another leak, the painters split, we played another short game and still nothing happened. Not a single solitary con on the horizon. The prison gates didn't budge, not even the door inside the gates. Closed, dead, shut for the season. We sat there alone, like dummies, watching the boob tube.

Same scene the next day and the day after that. We looked like rich kids in our new threads. We were even clean again after hitting the public baths, careful not to let the soap drop because of the Arabs.

We made A la Ronde our base camp. We dug in there, they got chummy. We said, "Good morning" and "The usual." We had our routines. We rapped. The dialogue got smooth. We were setting our trap . . .

We said that we lived in the neighborhood, we'd just moved in, a little studio two blocks away. We couldn't hack cooking, our mothers hadn't cued us, it was time we got hitched. That was why we always showed, morning, noon and night, 'cause we couldn't hack housekeeping. We munched the special on paper tablecloths. We were students cramming for important exams, we worked constantly, till three in the morning. The waiter swallowed the line of crap 'cause we looked so brilliant, we left such handsome tips. He started to really dig us, so did the owners. Christ! We were fucking cash customers! Had to be, since we were waiting on someone.

We never pumped, it was them who started dishing out

129

their prison stories, mainly to dazzle us. They were sure we couldn't take it, like all middle-class kids raised on milk and honey.

"The worst part," they explained, "is having to wipe your ass in public. You never get used to it. All you have is a toilet bowl, just sitting there in a corner of the cell with no screen, nothing. When a guy uses it, you have to open the window wide, even in winter. Sometimes they give you some Lysol, but only in small doses. So the guys all get together to build a makeshift john with a blanket tacked up."

We'd have a little taste, they'd pick it up again.

"There was a famous head guard over there whose bag was busting into a cell unannounced, pouncing on the can and tearing the blanket down. He got off gawking at guys crapping. The bit with the blanket made him furious, it cut his view. So he'd ship the guys to solitary for damaging government property!"

We goofed around, acted terrified. We couldn't believe it, we were scandalized that these things went on. So they'd pour it on more, the dopes, they really dug our horror.

"The weirdest one was the screwdriver case. This guy slammed a screwdriver in his head by banging on it with a hammer! You've really gotta want to croak to do yourself in like that!"

It's not every day you get to freak out a genius. They didn't see too many like us, who pulled up toting our books at 8 A.M., looking hassled, with bags under our eyes from burning the midnight oil. We were the real thing, intellectuals, not just little snots playing revolution.

"Our neighbor," we told them, "is some kind of odd-job nut. Hammer, saw, sanding machine, he makes a racket all day long. We work better here where it's quiet."

Our major was math. We copied pages and pages of phony equations in the notebooks we'd bought. We even went so far as to smoke ridiculous little pipes and treat ourselves to horn-rim glasses to make it more real. Just the kind of audience our bartenders had been aching for. Young, pure, untouched by evil. It was a switch from the usual low-life crowd in their shabby duds.

130

They dished out the dirt about the house across the street, whispering like it was some kind of spicy exposé. "The big hall full of benches used for movies, TV and mass—well, believe it or not, some guys work it to get themselves sucked off in there!"

The best part was they faked outrage too, claimed to be humanitarians bucking for reform with their hands tied. They put down all that sadism as a disgrace, laughing all the way to the bank! 'Cause without the illegal traffic with the prison they never could have owned that fucking joint!

Those smart-ass businessmen got a cut on everything, you'd better believe it. On letters smuggled in by their buddies the guards. On packages of clean laundry dropped off by women who could never see their men because they worked during visiting hours and Sundays there weren't any. A real racket, veiled as a service to lighten the rigors of prison life. "Thank God we're here!" they allowed, coming on like the Salvation Army.

And they kept moving up, those rake-off kings. Every year they modernized the dive, put in new lighting, Formica counters, automatic percolators—their greasy spoon was a real palace—and on Sunday, no-visitors day, they went catfishing on their branch of the river.

We should have ripped them off too one day, but the hitch was we were running out of time.

The prison gate didn't open often, and we never saw anyone come out except a few guards tagged by their badges, their big friendly smiles and the casual way they'd stroll out onto the sidewalk.

On the other hand, we did spot people going into the prison, emergency arrivals in vans, with a motorcycle cop in front, a motorcycle cop behind, and the poor fucker inside in the shadows behind the bars.

Then the little troop would stop over for a quickie, drivers and escorts, without their passenger, who waited in the dark, bare-assed, for the prison guards to frisk him, hand him his monkey suit, take mug shots and do what they pleased with him—who knew, behind those thick walls . . .

They guzzled standing at the bar, celebrating the delivery.

They bellowed long, lewd laughs. Swell people. Pierrot and I figured that the average bike baboon pissed his beer ten to fifteen minutes after downing it. A concrete statistic, we timed it. Of course there were exceptions—the sieve, the camel—but those were medical problems.

Sometimes we ran into them in the can. Pissing right next to a motorcycle cop, I assure you, is a far-out trip. They have a hard time whipping it out with all that artillery on. And they clank when they shake themselves.

How do they work it, we wondered, when they sit for hours and hours locked up in their bullet-proof vans slurping beer?

Guards, we checked it out, piss much faster than cops. And they're champs at lushing it up in a hurry. They get up early—it's first things first with the beer can.

We often saw them come in on the stroke of nine, and they'd be loaded already. They were only human, of course, and we'd be shits to hold it against them, they've got such dirty jobs. We did wonder, all the same, if a good number of accidents, escapes and suicides, might not be due to the frequent piss breaks the guards had to take all the time. The corridors are long, the surveillance relaxes along with their sphincters, and the cons make the break.

At A la Ronde there were off days and good days in terms of the population. Monday, Wednesday and Friday it was deserted and we rapped quietly with our pals. But Tuesday, Thursday and Saturday, back off! The rush was on! The joint turned customers away and bounced any roughnecks, cranks or people who took their time fixing on an order! Those were the visiting days. The bar was like a station waiting room during a railroad strike. You had to keep a tight ass on the leatherette seats waiting for the shithouse to clear. Funny thing—you never saw the cops or guards stop in for a fast one.

The families started trooping in at 7 A.M. Those with visiting privileges lined up at the entrance to the prison. They'd arrange themselves in an orderly fashion along the wall, like people who are used to being yelled at. No one was in charge of them. The line formed automatically, in the cold, in the rain, it didn't matter, even if there were pregnant women and

132

little kids shivering. The kids downed their morning toast and peed against the wall. You really wondered what the crowd was doing there so early in the morning, outside that dismal doorway.

Inside the café it was just as mobbed. People took turns on the line, like for the flicks. Friends and relatives came to keep the visitors company, mind their kids, get the latest info and cheer them up after the visit.

We would sit in the middle of the room at a tiny table, blending in to get a better take on what was being chewed over. We tried to make ourselves useful in a thousand ways, pleasant as could be. We moved over, gave up our seats, buddied up to the kids, drew swell pictures for them in our notebooks. They were delighted, and their old ladies smiled at us, touched.

Who knows? we said to ourselves, a con's wife for papers—why not?

Suddenly it happened, the door was opening.

A shudder ran through the line, everyone began to push. Not for long. Some guards took charge with hoarse yells: "Cut it out! No pushing! We'll throw you all out!"

Peace returned. The guards let everyone in. The huge door sucked in the line and then closed on the deserted square.

In the bar it was like halftime at a football game.

We waited with a few kids, relatives, friends.

One day a woman gave us her kid because he'd gotten too cold outside. Pierre-Paul was his name. A kid of five, covered with impetigo, with snot hanging between his nose and upper lip. We stuffed him with goodies. He asked us why his dad was still in the big clinic. He'll be out soon, we answered, he's almost cured.

After ten days of the student life we started to wonder what the hell we were doing there. We saw ourselves gradually guzzling our way into beer alcoholism. We pissed more often. We were sure our brains were turning to mush. The view of the pen wall began to get us down. At night, in our woods, we had nightmares about the awful din of jailhouse noises: hinges, keys, locks, tin plates, toilets flushing, yells, marching steps, beatings.

We had to buy tranquilizers in a drugstore, something made of orange blossoms. Losing our marbles would be next, not to mention the fact that we weren't any closer to scoring some IDs. "Congrats on your thinking!" Pierrot would hand me. "First-rate idea you had there! My buddy is a genius, you guys! I'm fucking proud to know him! We're sitting pretty here. It's real comfy. Safe as a church, too. We're farting through silk!" I didn't even bother to answer, since my plan was a total bust. In the flicks you always see tough cons getting out of jail, looking mean, ready to bust the world open. Well, that's all a pile of shit! They keep them all locked up! They stockpile them! Or else we'd have to kiss this beautiful society good-bye. Kids wouldn't be able to go to school. And if you chuck education, the whole fucking house of cards falls down!

Nothing in the world would have made me drop a hint about our problems to the stoolie owners of A la Ronde. Might as well cross the street and check in—with our own supply of Lysol.

Fuck it! I started telling myself. We'll keep our shitty IDs! We'll stay underground, since that's what they seem to dig! Condemned to live as outsiders. To steal, riot, break and enter, sabotage, set fires, pull off the crime of the century wherever we go. I was in a flaming rage.

It was at that moment that the assholes came up with the good news: a con was getting out! Sentence commuted. A real gangster, they claimed. And they offered to introduce us, 'cause they figured he'd interest us. A cat not to be missed! We were sort of cool about it, but since they insisted . . .

He didn't even get out early, the slob! We had to hang around till noon. Seemed he couldn't be bothered to climb out of the sack for the big day, or else he didn't give a shit about his freedom.

It was pissing rain, a real downpour, a flood! There he was, he'd finally made it! He ran across the square, zigzagging like a chicken in an earthquake. Almost crashed into a bus, the jerk, fell into three puddles and missed the curb. The guards howled, sheltered in the doorway, waving their hankies.

He finally stumbled in soaking wet, his baggy old suit dripping. He looked like he was about to drop, so we all rushed forward. The owners tried to sit him down. He slid off the seat, too wet. So they propped him on a chair, took the towel off its roller in the can and dried him with it. They took off his suede shoes and his striped socks. His feet stank like rotten eggs. We reeled back, nauseated. The waiter brought a mug of grog. "Grog's bad for the liver," the gangster said. "Bring me some beef broth." His first words as a free man. He spoke in a falsetto voice that came from the bridge of his nose. The broth arrived, he grabbed it, started lapping. Made a noise like a railway station toilet. His hands were shaking. He spilled it all over himself, dripped it down his tie. They wiped his chin. We couldn't take our eyes off him, like he was gravely ill. He fascinated us, this great criminal. We all hovered around him, a little coterie. The owner's wife stuck his feet in a basin of hot water. Shit! She got down on her knees and started washing his rotten feet! He let her do it, like he was Jesus! And kept swilling his beef juice. Pierrot and I didn't dare look at each other. What a bummer . . .

We'd never get a tip out of that creep! No point even trying. He'd never talk, never rise again. He was finished. Wiped out. Looking forward to retirement. That's what the guards did to you, after ten years of detention. A rag. A husk. Three-Churches, he was called, a train robber. There was nothing left of him except a few teeth. Forty years old. His whole life still ahead of him.

We were about to split when we heard the owner ask, "Well now, Three-Churches. Tell us. What can we do to help? Huh? What do you need?"

"A piece of ass."

"A woman?"

"A piece of ass! Fast!"

They all busted out laughing, except Three-Churches, and we made tracks, revolted.

A crazy idea came to me . . .

Pierrot dug the idea right away. He jumped with joy. "Now you're talking to me," he said. He slapped me on the back, grabbed my arm, I thought he was going to kiss me, like I'd given him an electric train. When it was just a little idea any idiot could have hatched, providing he had a taste for human distress and fallen women, real ones, for whom a kiss has no price. But it was a swell idea. The kind you don't dare dream about.

After all the time we'd blown farting around with those boring barfly guards, the weaselly waiter, the tear-stained widows and other ball-breakers, shit! We deserved a break. 'Cause when you get right down to it, wheels, sharp threads, good eats ain't everything! That's not tuned in. There was a short-circuit in the emotional department.

We hit the road after checking the oil and tire pressure, 'cause we were heading on a long trip, for a faraway country full of game birds. Pierrot jumped up and down, frisky as a setter. "I get a hard-on just thinking about it," he said. A preserve of females, does that turn you on?

Fuck those forged papers! We'd decided to nix it. Have to do without, since those hot-shit bastards didn't want us back in their two-bit society! We'd work it out later. All we had to do was stay cool and avoid any fuckups that might set a match to our explosive identities.

There were hang-ups, of course, about our forced dropout. No way to get a job, for example. No chance for honest labor. Driven to ripping people off. With the sweat of our guts!

That's what we missed the most, a nice easy job. We would have given plenty to become established model citizens. A little business, dig. A quiet street in a chic neighborhood. Nothing but private houses turned into historical monuments. A ladies' shop . . .

"Watch your right!" he yelled.

Holy shit! A fifteen-ton truck was coming right at our nose, from behind a hay wagon! Mama! I wrenched the wheel, the body lay over. Varoom! An entire factory grazed our radiator! Grille plastered with pinups and two huge mothers dressed in sweatsuits way up high, grinning down pleasantly. I swear they had the automatic pilot on, the bastards! No way to get the car back under control. I bit the ditch, spun the wheel back, hit a hole. Jolted like in dodge-'em cars, ricocheting like an eight ball on a rubber table. A tree loomed up. I squeaked

136

by. Whew! That was better, easy now, boys. Stop on the shoulder, gotta pull yourself together, you're shaking all over, like a fucking rattlesnake.

I looked at Pierrot—he wasn't much better. Looked like an old corpse someone'd just dragged up from the bottom of a lake. We felt our heads. We'd really got banged around. We checked our hands. No, no blood.

"You hurt?"

"No."

"Cigarette?"

"Cigarette."

"Why the hell were they in sweatsuits, those big Kraut creeps? Some new kind of driver? The trailer Olympics? Do you think they pull into the stops and have a little foot race?"

"They almost massacred us, the mothers, that's all I know!"

We took off again, really down. "You know, man, I think we'd better take the side roads. There'll be less of those big mothers, and less fuzz. We'll be less uptight."

We took the back roads, quaint local highways, bumpy dirt roads. We picnicked in the unfamiliar countryside, eating cheap sandwiches near streams to keep our lemonade cool. We didn't see one cop, one red light, no hassles all the way. Just the woods and underbrush, canals without a ripple on them, tunnels of sycamores, the old France. Even a trolley car on the edge of a canal. We took a thousand detours through villages ending in -ac, then in -ay, then in -ourg, and then we were in Rennes, after a swell two-day drive. It had cost us forty-five francs, tip included.

We went into ambush outside the preserve. The rallying point was called Chez Plomb, a half-decent sidewalk café overlooking a square planted with budding willow trees, a paradise for retired boccie players. We took up our positions coolly, behind a bottle of Gros-Plan. Spring had been breaking her ass while we were taking it easy on the road. The surrounding countryside was doing a number with the sun and bursting into millions of buds. We dropped our blazers so as not to miss one ray. We also rolled up our sleeves and loosened our ties, swilling down the Muscadet. We ordered another and a platter of seafood. The deal was to cool it and have a little taste while we waited for the birds.

We couldn't see or hear them, but we knew they were there, across the square, and one of them had our brand on her. We could smell them, all right. Their gamey odor hit us, brought by the wind, like on the crest of a wave. Our noses twitched with impatience. We were all sniffs and yummy expectations.

We fancied them fussing behind the bars, fluffing their buns, scratching the ground in their urge to run in this beautiful season of love, fluttering with pent-up emotions stifled over the years. We were sure that they could sniff us too, through the bars, catch our scent with flared nostrils. Standing under their high windows on their toes, scanning the horizon, looking for our pants. We sent them puffs of after-shave and cigarette smoke. We drank their health in clam broth. We sucked periwinkles like candies while they paced around their cages.

Eat your hearts out, you gamey gallows chicks! Marinate

your flesh in the piss bowl! We didn't make the trip to taste young bait—otherwise any local pen would have done the trick. What we want is a tough old jailbird with raunchy skin beaten to oblivion. Simmered through the years in bunshop broth. Permanently browned in the dark. A crust of shadows that sticks to the brown clothes. An old prison stew, chilled thousands of times by the damp stones, gelled in solitary. So we can hardly heat it up again. So it takes hours to thaw. So we have to knock ourselves out. An old criminal hen who's done time with every pore, been purged with her own blood, teeth, hair, grace and youth, who's forfeited it all as bail, so they'll finally let her out, drab, done in, washed out, a blind hag only fit for begging. But at that exact moment we show up with our velvet eyes and magic wands erect beneath the gray flannel, our musical bows. And we hold out our hands to her, guide her first steps. There's warmth in our arms. We are freedom! That was my crazy idea. Only one thing interests a con getting sprung: a cunt, an ass, rolling on acres of tits. He's obsessed, naturally. Same with a chick. When a dame gets out, what's her obsession? What's she thinking about, I ask you, after years of privation? Two well-built guys with all the charms you could ask for and superstretch flies—don't you think that might charge her up? Don't you think it was worth a try, worth the trip, the detour through Brittany to the Central Prison in Rennes, the great national dump for condemned members of the weaker sex?

A crone just off death row makes a far-out fiancée. A dug-up mole, weaving and wavering like a flame about to go out. The most beautiful resurrection! We'd feel around, fumble, turn the ashes over till we found the last ember, then we'd blow very softly on the abandoned hearth as long as it takes for the great fires of lust to burst into flame.

We knew it would be a long wait, she wouldn't be served on a silver platter. We had to cool it. Earn our reward. Stay in our seats. We made our spring headquarters at the foot of the prison walls.

We came every morning like clockwork. We had breakfast on the café terrace while training our binoculars toward the doorway at the other end.

A coed prison. It must have been worse knowing that the dudes were right next door and not being able to visit them.

We watched the retired men arrive one by one, with their boccie balls in string bags, their berets and pipes. In the afternoon we'd spread out to scout up a little nest for when our old lady got out of her hospital. We toured the whole gamut of seaside resorts, and Brittany is known for them. In other words, we took in bays, creeks, fortified lookout points. But no matter how we searched, we couldn't find the right spot, the ideal, safe hideout that fitted the occasion. We visited endless closed-up cottages on miles of beaches where not a soul came to disturb us. We mastered the art of forcing shutters and garage doors. But nothing grabbed us. Strange. We didn't know why. All those boring shacks just didn't seem right for a honeymoon. They weren't gala enough. They smelled of stale weekend vacations. The beds all seemed meant for retired mamas and papas with headaches. Or else they were in sleazy maids' rooms. There was nothing big enough for the great event, nothing beautiful enough for our miracle. They were all third-rate, and what we wanted was grandeur. We would spend the night here and there, wrapped in our steamer rugs, and go back into town at dawn, to be on time for the rendezvous, praying that she wouldn't get out quite yet, that she'd wait a little longer, until we'd found a way to treat her like a princess.

On the seventh day, or more exactly the seventh morning, we sensed a change in our boccie players. They weren't playing as usual. They bowled aimlessly, without feeling, as if their minds were elsewhere. They kept goofing, playing twice in a row, forgetting their turns, staring into space for long periods—a contagious daydream that spread for no reason from one player to the next, like some music they would suddenly pick up on, a message only they could hear, a weird halting of games all over the square. The time came when no one on the square was even bothering to play at all. The balls lay still in the dust, and the old men stood spellbound, like statues, all aimed straight at the prison front. Even the willows were numb, for the wind had dropped and not a leaf stirred. Nothing. Just one bony hand sticking out of a sleeve ten times too big for it, a hopeless victim of Parkinson's disease. "Dig!" Pierrot said. "They're all dolled up!" Sure enough, they all were sporting different outfits, their prewar Sunday specials, faded Prince-of-Wales cuts, spats, polka-dot bow ties.

A few seconds before nine, the old referee whipped out his watch. The cover sparkled in the sun as he opened it. As if on command, the tower bell rang out. At the ninth stroke the prison door squeaked open and a form crept out.

Binoculars. My heart started pounding.

"What is it?" Pierrot asked.

"A woman . . ." Red hair hanging loose, green eyes, a blood-red mouth. She was crackling with revenge. Pierrot stood up. "Don't move," I told him.

In less than five seconds we heard the rev of an engine, and a black limo braked short in front of the prison. The woman disappeared into the car, the driver holding the door for her. They sped off, tires screeching, and dropped out of sight.

They roared around the square on two wheels, and all the old men followed with their eyes. The limo grazed the front of the terrace, so close it splattered mud onto our flannels. "Filthy whore!" Pierrot shouted.

The old men, left in the dust, went back to their balls and picked them up with more effort than usual. How were they tipped off?

Pissed off, we shot down the coast road again.

On the thirteenth day, a little old man got out of the pen, no fuss, incognito. He put his hand up like a visor to shade his eyes from the sun and looked around timidly. He was wearing a brown raincoat and pants that were so big on him they were almost stylish, and he carried an orange canvas knapsack in his hand.

Two broads swept by the prison on motorbikes, brunettes in short skirts, joking and not watching the road, their thighs flashing in the wind. He smiled at them till they had disappeared, then crossed.

No one was waiting for him. He shuffled slowly across the square and then sat on the edge of a bench, like he was just visiting. His pants had hiked up: he wasn't wearing socks.

"What if we took him out for some good eats?" Pierrot asked.

"Yeah, sure . . ."

The sprung little man didn't move. He calmly checked out the boccie players, a smile on his puss. With the knapsack on his knees. And when the referee strutted in front of him, like the cock of the walk, he raised a finger to his bald head, a shy salute without a cap.

The referee, surprised, stopped and slowly half turned to the newcomer, eyed him from head to foot, then from foot to head, and finally handed him his balls.

The ex-con stood up, still wearing the same dumb grin of a screwball who doesn't know which end is up anymore, took the balls and joined the game without a word. He scored his first throw half an inch from the jack, no sweat.

The next morning, he was back—and the following days as well.

I don't know if you're familiar with the famous Breton rain that falls morning, noon and night, penetrating, for weeks on end. We are. A rain which at least in the cities has the decency to be light and more or less straight up and down—an urban drizzle, O.K.?—but in the country, takes a wild revenge on any poor bastard at the wheel.

It started on the night of the fourteenth day, and I bet it's still falling. As fate would have it, we were still scouting the area, feeling down, listening to the rhythm of the windshield wipers which, on the Dyane 6, like on all Citroëns, are a total waste. You could rip them off and never know the difference. At least you'd be rid of that whining noise that has you nodding as the miles roll on. Buckets of water gushed against our windshield, and the car just about took off in the gusts. No way to pass a truck or even get near it, what with all the shit they sadistically spewed out behind. They were going just as fast as us anyhow, and seemed to prefer the middle of the road. We took it out on maniacs that acted like they wanted to pass by hogging the middle ourselves, doing 45, deaf to their horns, blind to their headlights, body and soul lost in the downpour. We got a few laughs out of that. I remember one pissed-off MG that kept roaring up behind us, right, left, frantic to pass, the guy driving like an asshole, skidding like hell every time he slowed, accelerating and braking on the superslippery road full of bumps. "The advantage of front-wheel drive," I clued Pierrot, "is that the car holds the road, you dig?" The guy behind us was going ape-shit. He finally got us by skirting a village.

In the storm the seaside resorts looked like graveyards, the houses like coffins. To take a lady here when she got out of stir seemed like a sick idea to us, a trip that would make her hanker for her cell and give her a cold to boot. Anyhow, we felt the sea was about to swallow up the beaches in one gulp. We saw octopuses lying in the middle of the road. The wind lifted the Dyane like a feather, making a joke of the steering wheel.

One day we were finishing up our sandwiches on a rocky promontory, digging the wild sea. We were in our shirt sleeves with the heater on when suddenly the top of the Dyane blew off. We had to chase ass through the deluge after the mother, which went flapping off across the moors. We drove on, convertible-style, resigned, soaked. We finally ducked into a waterfront bar that was whipped by the rain, the Hôtel du Commerce. The sailors watched us sip hot wine, grinning behind their pipes. No one spoke, it was like a silent wake, and we felt like we were bugging them during the dead season. After a while we stopped shaking.

"We gotta go and hook that bitch of a top back on," I said.

"Fuck you," Pierrot answered.

Great. I went alone. The car was parked under a shed roof that the rain poured off of like a waterfall. I sweated with the top. No way. So I gave up and went back into the bar. It was six o'clock. "You gotta help," I said.

"Screw you, baby," he answered.

Far out. I sat down. "Pierrot," I said, "what's with you?"

"What's with me is I've had it! I'm not going a step farther! We're staying here and we're going to get some sleep. In a room."

"That's swell, here we go fucking up again. So you want to cop out. What if they ask for our papers?"

"No way. In a joint like this I bet they've forgotten what a cop is. I bet they haven't seen a paper since the Armistice."

143

I gave up. Sometimes you have to know when to quit, even with someone younger. I gave in because I felt we were in a tight spot. Pierrot was capable of doing anything. For several days he'd been freaking out. He was fed to the eyeballs. He talked more and more about going back to Marie-Ange's. He wondered what the fuck we were doing across from that prison cooling our heels.

"You saw yourself," he said, "when that redhead got out, there was a dude waiting for her. It'll be the same with the others."

"Not with an old bag."

"And supposing no one gets out before Christmas! We going to spend Christmas there?"

"One more week."

"You're full of shit. I don't know why I listen to you or follow you around. What the fuck's in it for me?"

"No one's forcing you!"

"Oh yeah? You've got all the bread!"

"Yeah. And the gun too."

It was true, why should I hide it, that's the kind of rap Pierrot and I were into, buddies, two peas in a pod . . . Not to mention that Pierrot didn't go for the celibacy bit, getting hard-ons every day on the road. "Don't it get you up," he asked, "all those vibrations while you're driving?" And the fresh sea air wasn't helping. He couldn't wait for the fantastic party I promised him every night at bedtime. I'd pushed him about as far as he would go. He wanted a slut and asked me to take him to Nantes.

"Nix," I answered, "gotta save our coins."

"Then let's cruise!" he'd say. "Let's pick up some tail! Shit, we got class!"

"Go, man," I'd answer. "Here, there's ten francs."

"What do you expect me to do with ten francs? I couldn't even treat a broad to the flicks!"

That's why I gave in. So he'd cool it. I even suggested a good meal, no hassling about the price. I was sick of sandwiches myself. We treated ourselves to a bellyful of lobster. Two apiece. With some white wine. Then we went upstairs, a little juiced. No one asked anything. Not even a form to fill out.

There were two rooms, one for us and the other, next door,

for some bitch in heat who kept us awake till dawn. What a bummer! She didn't shut her trap once! Sounded like all the sailors in port were working in shifts to make her moan and groan and scream like a banshee. Not to mention the rain beating against the windowpanes, the wind whistling under the door, lifting the rug right off the floor, and the clock in the nearby church tower that rang out every fifteen minutes like a fucking alarm clock. Just to help things along, the bottles of Muscadet had turned our skulls into echo chambers. Things reeled menacingly around us. Freezing cold, teeth chattering, we huddled together in the squeaky little bed that kept climbing dizzying waves. It would pause on the crest, wobbling, and—zap!—dive straight down into the foamy pit. Our guts had trouble catching up. We listened to the broad howling through the wall. She got off in some local dialect we couldn't dig a word of, but it was very intense. She was in a ground swell too, getting tossed all over. A nympho, I told myself, nothing but a cunt! A slut with stubby fingernails! With a pussy like an old douche bag! I bet she didn't even take her socks off! Pierrot was trembling silently on my shoulder like a frightened dog, and I patted his head. A girl, I fantasized, serious, well-bred, who'd take us into her family, and her folks would really go for us. A girl who wouldn't give it away, we'd have to swipe kisses from her on the swing. Two sisters is better, more what we need. The younger for Pierrot, foxy, with ringlets at the back of her neck, and I would have the older, or at least I'd court her, she'd be wary and nostalgic because of a bum first love, a guy who died in the mountains, a student. We would rap about him in the fields, picking mushrooms. I would end up loving that kid like a brother, Charles or Didier or whatever, who dug camping out and finding mountain goats just to watch and photograph them. She would show me his slides, sunsets on glaciers, mountain peaks and ice pinnacles, and then his handsome face, Charles's or Didier's, tanned and smiling. Why, I wondered, were we stuck with chambermaids, shady broads on the run, lost as us, beauty operators, waitresses, chicks who had to put out for the boss, got fired for nothing, slept under the stairs, and got up before everyone else to wash their undies, or had just gotten out of prison, wiped out? Why?

We were out of the sack at six. It was still raining. We pulled our boots on and went downstairs, all wrinkled. We didn't see the broad, she must have been getting a little shut-eye before heading back to work. We drank some juice and coffee, then cut out fast to fix the top. Toulouse. We were homesick for Toulouse. Life was fucked up. Shit.

The bitch! She had to go and choose *that* morning to get out! Naturally—since we hadn't found a place good enough to take her yet. What were we going to do? It was like she'd tried to trap us. A test, to see if we measured up. Fucking prison administration! They could have held her a couple of days more. What was she going to think? We were going to look like real assholes 'cause nothing was ready for her homecoming, that's for sure. She deserved to be pissed off. No kidding, I was shaking with rage.

Slow down! I told myself. Take it easy. We'll see, we'll figure something out. It was true, really, there was no reason to get uptight. We could always take her to spend the night at the shore in one of our crummy little cottages. Though it wasn't the greatest, the sea air wouldn't hurt her. After careful inspection, we'd picked out fifty-seven of them between Quiberon and Cap Fréhel. A beautiful trip, going from cottage to cottage. We'd located them all on the map, even inventoried them on index cards in an orangewood box, with all the details, just like in an agency: numbers of rooms, private cans, view, neighborhood, everything.

And it was still pouring.

The old boccie players didn't give two shits about the Breton weather. They kept playing, unshakable, under their black umbrellas. And that morning, once again, they'd dressed to the teeth.

Around nine fifteen they dropped their balls in the rain and solemnly turned to face the prison. It was the beginning of the countdown.

She slipped out about nine thirty, approximately. It's hard to say because we didn't spot her at first. Even though we were watching—with our binoculars trained right on the door! But the visibility was lousy in that downpour. The café windows were all fogged up. And we had to keep the binoculars hidden so as not to look too suspicious. She must have snuck out when Pierrot and I weren't looking, when we were blowing our noses, for example (the fact is that we'd caught a cold from driving without the top). Suddenly I said to Pierrot, "Hey, there's someone there, in front of the door! A woman!"

To tell the truth, I think the real reason we missed her was because she was almost the same color as the wall. She hardly stood out at all against the gray stones of the prison. She was gray herself, almost invisible, not far from a ghost. She was swimming in a drab, limp sleeveless dress that had never had much shape, but now in the rain it hung like a rag, getting more and more shapeless. A cloth dress. Gray. Gray like her straight hair and her faded, wiped-out face. The color of oblivion. Washed out, colorless, transparent. What gave her away was her metal army suitcase, not exactly shiny, seeing as there was no sun.

"What a dog!" Pierrot said into the binoculars.

O.K., she really wasn't the type you'd want to rest your eyes on for more than a second. Looks passed over her, blindly. No one, ever, looked back. She wasn't even ugly—just bland, like nothing at all. But I was looking at her. And the old farts were too, under their black umbrellas, staring at her, fascinated. Pierrot was making a face.

"I think she's beautiful," I answered. "Unbelievably beautiful! I can't help it!"

She didn't move. She just stood there, arms bare, letting the rain soak her, and she looked so puny in front of the enormous building, I got the impression she was floating slightly above the ground. It was love at first sight.

I put the money on the table so we could split, and when she finally stepped off the sidewalk I said to Pierrot, "Let's go. She's going to cross."

We got up and went out. She came into the square, which was planted with old men gawking at her. She suddenly became aware of them among the trees. She froze. We moved in quietly and hid behind two willows. We waited. One old guy went up to her to offer his umbrella. She didn't react. A second old guy did the same. No response. Now there were two umbrellas over her head. She seemed paralyzed. No, she started walking again. The two umbrellas followed. A third old man came up. He gestured that he would like to carry her suitcase. She refused, changed the suitcase to her other hand. She walked on, with hesitant little steps, looking like a surgery patient who's gotten up too soon. She came straight toward us, not seeing us, looking around at all those old men staring at her from every corner of the square, strange sentinels surrounding her from a distance, a present-arms of umbrellas. Suddenly she saw us. She stopped short. A real shock. Her eyes searched our faces. Seconds passed. I wondered if I might be blushing. I found the strength to smile. At that, she fled. She turned sharply and then moved away fast, almost running.

"She's flipped out," Pierrot said.

"You would be too," I answered.

She walked, constantly looking back over her shoulder. We didn't budge. We let her get a lead on us to reassure her. We buttoned up the collars of our English raincoats. "Let's go," I told Pierrot. We started after her, taking big leisurely strides, our hands in our pockets. She got scared and sped up, changing sidewalks. The whole thing began to get fucked up. I felt less and less at ease, and I was getting soaked. The rain was running off my ears and down my neck. She was going at an incredible clip.

We got closer, she went even faster, stumbled, we could hear her labored breathing. The houses thinned out, we'd soon be in the country. Fuck this! I lunged forward, caught her by the arm and felt the bone at once.

"Stop!" I told her. "You're tired. Why run? It's stupid!" She looked at us, shaking—it didn't show but I could feel it through her arm. "Besides, you're cold. You can't go on like this. You're completely drenched! You'll catch your death. Here, put on my buddy's raincoat. Pierrot?" He sneezed.

"What do you want?" she asked.

"Nothing! Just want to help you!"

"Why?"

"No reason. We saw you get out and we thought . . ."

"Who are you?"

"Nothing! Nobody! Two friends, that's all!"

"Let me go."

We could hardly hear her, her voice was so faint.

148

She sat down on a milestone that happened to be there, her suitcase between her feet in the mud. And she wouldn't take the raincoat, she pushed it away without even glancing at Pierrot. He looked hurt in spite of everything.

"Leave me alone!" It was awful, she was almost begging us.

There was a silence during which a trailer truck passed, and then she raised her head to scream, "Can't you give me some peace? Especially today!" Christ! A terrible vision of her twisted mouth, her face distorted by much more than despair or rage. Probably the sum of all her pain and bitterness that erupted like a geyser of venom. For the first time in my life I realized that I was a civilized person.

"Go get the car," I told Pierrot, who was looking at me, horrified. "Run!"

He trotted off, struggling back into his raincoat.

I was alone with her. I bent down to her knees and took her hands. She pulled them away. O.K. I tried to talk to her as gently as possible. "Madame," I said, "listen to me. You have no reason to be afraid. You can't stay here alone in the rain, nothing on your arms, no raincoat or umbrella. We can drive you. Where are you going?"

"I don't know . . ."

"Do you have any money?"

"Fifty francs . . ."

"Someone you can call?"

"No . . ."

Her eyes were resting on me absently, as if she were looking at something behind me. I felt transparent. She had big gray-green eyes, the color of dishwater, that turned down at the corners. I felt like I was diving into a stagnant, dirty pool. Her mouth was bitter and turned down too. Everything was falling down. The flesh on her face was hopelessly sagging off the bones, with wrinkles holding it up, like a net. Gray strands of hair stuck to her forehead. Her only makeup was a few freckles, blotches on her cheekbones and some dark blue veins in the transparent brown of her eyelids. And I, spellbound, kept talking, ad-libbing, stuttering, knocking myself out to try and melt her cold indifference.

"I could tell you anything," I said, "bullshit you in a million ways. Tell you that I'm, I don't know . . . A journalist, yeah, a journalist, that's a hot one. Reporting on the scandal of the prisons, or something like that. It would be easy. But I'm not going to hand you any bull. I'm nobody, see! Nothing at all!"

"Then what do you want?"

"I already told you."

"Yes, but why me? Why help me?"

"You mean I don't have the right to help who I want when I want?"

"I don't trust you."

"I swear to you my buddy's going to come back with a nice heated car that doesn't leak—good seats and everything! We're going to take care of you!"

"I'm tired of people taking care of me."

"But . . . Still . . . You have to change clothes! Do you have any in that suitcase?"

"No."

"So, you see? No money, no clothes, nothing! Not a good start."

"They gave me an address . . ."

"A rehabilitation office?"

"Something like that."

I shrugged my shoulders. "Excuse me if I laugh," I said. "All you're going to get is a bowl of soup and the addresses of three Catholic employers who will welcome you very politely. Ladies with soft voices. Middle-aged. Over a cup of tea they'll ask a whole bunch of questions, not meaning to get nosy, of course, but you'll feel obliged to give them the story anyhow, A to Z, with all the why's and how's, the whole bit. And the nice lady, sitting there in her living room with her piano, flowers everywhere, she'll be all ears, her hands folded on her lap. She'll nod slowly, understanding, well-meaning, and even slightly shocked by what they make you poor things go through. By the way, you'll get plenty of 'you poor things' at regular intervals, a real chorus. O.K., finally it's all settled, she'll take you on two weeks' trial, just enough time for you to get used to being the housekeeper, maid or whatever. You'll get into the work, scrub your fingers to the bone, knock yourself out, bust your buns, only thinking one thing—pleasing her. And then, at the end of the

150

first week, what happens? As if by chance things start disappearing from the house . . . A candlestick, a watch, some sheets, the kid's fountain pen. So Madame calls you in, she wants to have a casual little chat with you about this and that, and still very sweetly, with due respect for all you've been through, she'll try to make you understand, she'll appeal to your common sense, finally she'll explain to you as delicately as possible that no, she is awfully sorry but really there's too much talk in the neighborhood, if she were alone there wouldn't be any problem, but with her husband's position, you understand. Yes, madame, of course, madame, you understand very well. It's screwy how well you understand. Nothing ever seemed so clear to you. You understand so well you don't even plead your innocence, you know it's not worth it, wherever you go there'll always be a Jacques or a Madeleine, chauffeur or cook, who'll take advantage of your record to fill their pockets. So then the nice lady will give you some money, fast, as if it were burning her fingers. A hundred, two hundred francs even, mustn't be stingy, got to have a clear conscience. 'Here, my dear. Good luck. Be sure to come back and see us. Especially if you have a problem, don't hesitate, don't be alone if things aren't going well, it's bad for you to be alone, our home will always be open to you, we'll all miss you very much. Besides, you've had a little vacation. Did you get enough to eat? Get your strength back a little?' She gives you a reference. Very flattering even. You thank the lady: 'Thank you, madame, thanks for everything.' But it so happens you ask her if she could give you some addresses of friends who might, perhaps . . . At that she raises her eyes. She says, 'You poor thing, you poor thing, if you only knew how people react. When they find out where you've been. You must realize not everyone is like us. All my husband's friends are, well, I don't know if you know the type.' At this point she does an imitation of the type: high society, you see, terribly high society. Her husband has to see them, it's not that he likes to, but when you have a position like his . . . Well, that's it, it's all over, you tiptoe out thanking her a thousand times again, but you'll never come back and ring that doorbell because you know the door will always be closed to you, and the new housekeeper, maid or whoever succeeds you, will always give you the same line: 'Madame isn't feeling well, Madame is on vacation, Madame is in town, Madame has guests.' Sad, don't you think? All that's left, then, is tearing up the reference. All you will have gotten out of it is dishpan hands from doing their dishes and laundry, cleaning their toilet bowls!"

I was out of breath from rapping so much. The sky continued pissing all over us in that great Breton style. Our hair, hers and mine, was dripping all over us. My parolee looked at me without answering, lifeless, drenched, a wreck. Her soaked cotton dress clung to her skin. You could see the thin, pointed bones sticking out of her shoulders. Fragile veins beat in the hollows of her elbows. She wasn't wearing stockings. Her knees, almost touching me, seemed twisted in, deformed. I felt like covering them with my hands to warm them.

Finally she spoke. "I agree with what you've just said."

I beamed. "Ah, you get the picture!"

"But I'd like to know what you've got to offer instead."

"Everything! My buddy and I are completely at your service. With a car and bread. Which we really have. Look!" I took the bills out and stuck them under her nose. She scarcely glanced at them. "You've got two guys at your command, awaiting your orders."

She smiled. "Don't you think that's a bit much?" Wow! I was within an inch of putting my foot in it, spilling everything— Kiss off! Shit! What is this? Aren't we good enough? It's not every day you find two dudes like us, beautiful and all, who offer to fuck you just like that, sweetly, no hassles! How long has it been since you took a look in the mirror?—when I heard a car pull up behind me, a two-cylinder. I turned around, the Dyane, Pierrot, no, it wasn't him, there were two people, a window opened, what kind of mug was that, grinning at us?

"Troubles?" the broad asked.

I got up clumsily. She was giving me a funny look, and so was her guy behind the wheel.

"No," I answered. "Thanks. It's O.K., just a little engine trouble. It's nothing. Thanks anyway."

They looked at each other. Then they looked around at the shoulder of the road, in front, behind, they were looking for the wheels with the trouble and not spotting anything, no car. Really blew their minds, their whole way of thinking was being questioned. I felt four eyes trained on me like telescopes.

"You've got engine trouble?" they repeated.

"Yes," I said. "Really nothing."

"But the car, where is it?"

"At a garage."

They looked at each other again.

"And you? You're going to sit there . . . in the rain?"

I put my hand inside my raincoat pocket, trying to put off the inevitable as long as possible.

"Listen, thanks very much. But everything's all right, really . . ."

They made the mistake of insisting. "But the lady—doesn't she want to get out of the rain?"

Yes, she looked like she wanted to, the bitch, she even stood up with her suitcase. I held her by the arm and flashed the gun at them. "Split," I said calmly. "Hit the road!"

They took off, not waiting for further orders. The dude was so anxious to make tracks that he got his feet caught in the pedals, hit the wrong gear, the idiot stalled, started up in reverse, backfired. I couldn't help breaking up. The lady beside me started to laugh too, I could feel her arm shaking in my hand. We eyed each other. No way we could stop ourselves, we roared, and how great it felt! I gave her the revolver. "Here. Keep it and come with us." She stuck it in her shoulder bag.

"Is it loaded?"

"Yes."

I smiled at her happily. Along came another Dyane. This time it was Pierrot. I opened the front door for her to get in.

"No," she said. "I'd rather sit in back." O.K., that was fine. I held the door, she got in, I closed it softly. I got in beside Pierrot.

"Turn around," I said. "And move it! We had a little run-in." I told him about it, he broke up.

"When you need them," he said, "the bastards never stop for you!"

We were on the road again. We went through suburbs that were like all suburbs—in other words, shitty. And no one in the car spoke. Out of the corner of my eye I saw our guest take the pistol out to check if it really was loaded. Sharp crack of the clip. Pierrot jumped and turned around.

"Watch it!" I said. "You're going to run up on the sidewalk!"

"She carrying a piece?"

"No, you asshole! Don't freak like that, come on! Cool it! That's our piece!"

"Huh?" He braked from shock.

"Sure! I laid it on her to get her to trust us! And now she does trust us, she's not scared anymore." I turned back to her. "Isn't it true you trust us, you're not scared anymore?"

"I'm O.K.," she answered simply. She wasn't exactly all thawed out yet, but she was better, all hope of a cure was not lost. As for Pierrot, who was knocked out, he drew a pessimistic conclusion (he'd been seeing the dark side of things for several days).

"You're out of your mind," he told me. "I've gotten into a totally fucked-up scene with a real goon and a hardened criminal!"

"Fuck you!" I said. "And at least be polite! There's a lady in the car!"

"Big deal." (Now it was she who was talking, looking very cool, stashing the gun in her purse.) "And besides, all scenes are fucked up. The only decent scene is . . ." She didn't say what it was.

Pierrot sighed and drove on. He was bugging me. I decided to ignore him. I kept twisting around in my seat and looking back at our passenger. Her eyes avoided mine. She clutched her purse on her lap.

"Would it be O.K.," I said, "to ask you your name?"

"Seven sixty-seven," she answered. "Number seven sixty-seven."

Pierrot shot me a look like a comic strip balloon full of alarm words (Get her out! Chuck her! Dump her on the sidewalk!). I smiled at my good old buddy. No doubt about it, he was still just a kid.

"O.K., Seven sixty-seven, let's take first things first. What do you feel like doing?"

154

"Me? Nothing."

"O.K. That's fine with me, but we're not going to drive for hours on end with no goal in sight! So where are we going?"

"That's not my problem. I didn't ask you for anything. You insisted I get in, so here I am, in. You must have some idea in the back of your head. Don't ask me to make decisions for you!" She spilled all that out in one breath, in the same faint mono- tone, with total indifference, watching the suburbs flash by in the rain.

I kept calm.

"You're right," I said. "Excuse me. Don't you think the most important thing is to get you some warm clothes?"

No answer.

"Aren't you cold like that?"

"A little . . ."

"O.K."

We left the suburbs and drove into the city. Way downtown. I asked Pierrot to stop in front of a large department store with three floors of gleaming display windows. We got out. She stopped us.

"I'll go alone."

We looked at each other uncomfortably. "If you like . . ." I handed her two brand new five-hundred-franc bills. Sickened, Pierrot turned to stare at a window full of lingerie.

"Thanks," she said.

"You won't need the gun," I said. "It wouldn't be too cool. These stores are full of rent-a-cops."

I reached my hand out toward her purse. She pulled back. "I'm keeping it."

And she was already gone, that was that, she was inside the store, I hadn't had time to react.

I joined Pierrot in front of the naked mannequins.

"O.K.," he announced, "I'm heading back to Toulouse, to Marie-Ange's. I've had it, I'm starting to get the willies. I don't like that dame, I don't trust her."

I took the bread back out. "How much do you want?"

That cut him. He just stared at me, his arms dangling, stupefied.

"Come on," I said. "Let's rap in the car, where it's warm."

155

And I led him back with my arm around his shoulders.

I sat behind the wheel. We waited nervously, not rapping. As long as she didn't split with the rod and the bread to go hunt up some creepy pimp! As long as she didn't fuck up and start lifting things off the shelves! We didn't even know what the old hag had been sent up for!

My eyes zipped back and forth between my watch and the store's big double doors. I'd have sworn my trusty timepiece had broken down. The hands didn't even move. But the door never stopped opening, pushed by armies of teenyboppers playing hooky. Pierrot eyed them, put out.

"Dig that cute blonde," he moaned, murder in his heart. "Man, but she's stacked! Get a load of the ass! The bitch, did you catch her pants? Not a wrinkle! She's built like a brick shithouse! I'll bet she really gets it on, that chick, she must love it, the little slut. Twenty, at most. Hey, look! She's eyeing us. When I think of that crone of yours keeping us hanging around like this! No, miss, I'm sorry, I'd love it, don'tcha know, it's not that you don't turn me on, far from it, only my buddy here is an archaeologist, he works with antiques, chipped vases, amputated Venus de Milos! He gets off on ancient history! With Egyptian mummies!"

"Cool it!" I said. "Here she comes."

Was it her? Yes, it was. But we could hardly recognize her. She wasn't gray anymore, she'd turned black. She was dressed all in black. She'd bought herself a black suit, black shoes and stockings. They looked pretty good on her. Only her hair was still gray, and so was the skin on her face. She was carrying a big paper bag.

"Better and better!" Pierrot said. "I'm warning you, I'm not having any! Black widows just don't do it for me! She's all yours. You can hump her as much as you like! Even marry her if it hits you! What a good deed that would be! You dig? You'd be a real Christian!"

She got in the back without a word, just handed me the change. I refused. "No thanks." She put it in her purse. Two or three hundred francs, from what I could catch.

I drove off. There was a silence. Why black? I didn't dare ask. Pierrot was looking out the window.

She was the first to speak. "A good cup of coffee," she said. "I'd love a cup of real coffee. With some croissants. That would make me happy."

It would make me happy too. It warmed my heart that she was hungry and felt like eating something. I started to look for the best café in town.

It was a drugstore. A real fancy place. We went in. There was music and display cases loaded with bright-colored stuff. She stopped to gawk. I tailed her everywhere. "You want something?" She shook her head.

We sat at the bar. High stools, fake leather, brass fittings, red frosted lights. I didn't take my eyes off her during the whole time it took her to put away two pots of coffee and half a plate of croissants. Watching her eat was quite a scene. She didn't talk, didn't look around. She scarfed, period. Pierrot couldn't have given less of a shit, he was leafing through a girlie mag and comparing our starved bird, the prick, with the luscious chippies on the slick pages. I had a cappuccino.

After a while she stopped eating. She signaled the waiter for the bill. He showed. I cut in. No way, she got the bread out and insisted on paying, it was her treat. You could see the gun inside her open bag, and I thought Pierrot was going to croak. Luckily she closed it. "Let's go," she said. We slid off our stools.

So there we were back in the car, hopping down the highways of France again. Deep in the country. Needless to say, it was still pouring. We cut through the Breton woods with great sweeps of the windshield wipers. Seven sixty-seven hadn't said a word for fifteen minutes. She was digesting her breakfast in the back. She didn't ask where we were going, just looked at the countryside, waiting. As the miles rolled by, the silence thickened and turned to panic. I started hipping myself in that Pierrot was right: my idea was a bummer. The older I got the dumber my ideas got. I was getting senile. Where were all these hot-shot fuckups, crazy notions and zany brainstorms going to get us?

"I feel sick," she said.

We stopped. She got out for a breath of fresh air. She staggered, leaned against the fender. I covered her with my raincoat. She was shaking and sweating. Then whoops! she doubled over and puked in long brownish spurts. She spat, stood up, I whipped out my hankie to wipe her puss, she let me, gasping. "Feel better?" She nodded yes, looking embarrassed. I tossed my snot rag into the weeds and we moved on.

If you keep heading toward the sea, sooner or later you get there, it's an unwritten law no one's challenged yet.

The sea! It leaped into sight at the end of a blind curve. The waves were so high we felt we were going to be swept away.

I parked facing it, so she could get a good view.

"I'm hungry," she said.

We stopped in a real restaurant with white tablecloths, overlooking the little fishing port. It was noon, we were the first people there.

A groggy waiter handed us the menu.

She ordered oysters. Tons. All kinds. Four dozen. Then lobster. Plus the soufflé, since it was marked "special order."

"There," she said, beaming. "What's yours?"

"Us? O.K., why not? We'll have the same!"

The waiter split, his head spinning with orders. Been in the business twenty years and never seen anything like it! Even in the summer crush with all the American tourists doing all the Invasion beaches.

The lady in black turned to us. "What do you bet," she said, "they're going to ask us to pay in advance?"

"No bet," I answered. "We get the same vibes."

Sure enough, a heavy mass of still-firm flesh swooped down on us, more or less poured into a dark dress that didn't slim the curves. An Algerian kind of beauty. We all flashed that the owner had appeared in person. She pasted a big commercial smile over her basic anxiety.

"Good day, madame. Good day, gentlemen." She spoke in a throaty voice that seemed to come from far away. I could picture her in a slip, hot to trot, at siesta time. "Your orders are on the way. Would you care for an aperitif while you wait?

I've sent for my shucker . . . It might take a while . . . You're great oyster fanciers, that's nice."

We eyed her silently. She'd bombed out, and now clung desperately to the idea of the aperitif. "What can I bring you? A little white-wine-cassis?"

No thanks, we declined, didn't want her white-wine-cassis, no way. So she shifted her heavy gaze to the raging sea beyond the port. "You're not lucky with the weather, we're right at the height of the spring tides . . . It stirs things up . . ."

"I imagine it must be rather quiet around here this time of year?" Our friend said that, very dignified. She was playing the woman of the world.

"Yes . . . Yes . . . Fairly quiet . . . But we always have a few people passing through. The restaurant's reputation, you know."

"You're in the Michelin Guide?" Pierrot asked.

"No . . . And actually, if you must know, we prefer not to be."

"I see . . . Why is that?"

"The crowds, madame, the crowds! Dreadful! We like to serve fewer customers and take better care of them. I won't try to deny that at the height of the season, around August fifteenth, for example, well, things get quite out of hand! So what would we do with two stars?"

"I can't imagine!"

"We're under terrific pressure, and the bookkeeping gets to be a nightmare. I don't have a moment to come and chat with my customers the way I love to. I spend the day adding up checks and making change."

"That must be such a bore."

"Yes. And then, you know, the clientele . . . All right, I'm pretty lucky, generally I only get nice people, tourists, families with children, lots of foreigners. But sometimes, in the crush, things get out of hand, you can't keep your eye on everyone, and . . ."

"People get in?"

"Oh yes, madame! Of course! Like everywhere else. You know the beaches—there are all types on the beaches!"

"You're still safer than in the south," I added.

"Yes, sir, that's true. But listen to this! On Easter Sunday some people who looked perfectly all right—well dressed, polite, everything, people like yourselves—they arrived in a lovely car. American car, I think. They took a table. There were eight of them, I think. They laughed all the time. Very pleasant people, just the sort of customer a restaurateur is proud to have in his dining room, you see. Young, beautiful, elegant, full of life and gaiety . . ."

At that point our friend quietly took three hundred-franc bills out of her purse and stuck them in plain sight under a plate, nice and flat on the tablecloth.

There was a slight pause. The owner eyed the bread slyly. Matter of fact, I'm not sure she even bothered to eye it. I think the smell of it was enough for her. The good smell of cash. Fuck the proverbs—money has a subtle odor. Bread smells so terrific that we oughta perfume ourselves with it, splash it on all over before going out, nothing like it to give yourself class.

The proof: all anxiety vanished like magic from the boss-lady's face. Now she was kissing our asses, all smiles. "They were people like yourselves, utterly charming . . . But then, well . . . well, they each ate enough to feed four!"

"Eight of them, that made thirty-two," shot Pierrot.

Second pause. A syncopated rap. She didn't get it, that was obvious. Lost in an unknown world she'd never dreamed existed. The dizzying heights of my buddy's wit. Nor did she dig why we were all laughing like incurable paranoids. Luckily a passing waiter gave her a decent out. "Well, Serge, are the oysters coming along?"

"Right away, madame, right away! We put an extra man on to open them."

They brought them on three rolling tables. "Enjoy yourselves," the owner said, and she split uneasily.

We dove in. Threw ourselves on the dozen dozens, not missing a beat. We ate in silence, concentrating. When you get right down to it, forty-eight oysters are a cinch to do in. They slide right down. And they're damn tasty. More than just good. It was fascinating to see her eat like that. I stopped to dig her rediscovering the simple gestures in life. She was going at it so hard with her little fork and lemon wedges, she didn't even notice me staring. She seemed to be getting some color in her cheeks. Her skin looked less papery, glowed a little. I felt like taking her hands, kissing her fingertips. I glanced at Pierrot. He smiled. He was digging her too.

We did in the twelve dozen. Washed down with white wine. Her eyes began to sparkle. But she stayed solemn and quiet. Us too.

The lobsters met the same fate, though we were starting to slow down.

The owner hovered over us, making sure we had everything we needed, refilling our glasses. I could have ordered a foot bath, she would have been only too happy. The bread, on the table, was really getting to her. Because it was still there, in plain sight, a silent snub. She would have gladly got down on her knees, the bitch, if we'd stash those fucking bills. She was knocking herself out to get us to forgive her lack of tact, to make herself agreeable, and not succeeding. She didn't have the knack.

A few other customers showed, all men, which meant our friend was the only lady in the joint, hence the most beautiful. And from the window we could see it was clearing up outside, the sky was busting through in spots, the sun came out to brighten her face.

She looked up warmly, stuffed. "Thank you," she said, grinning at both of us. She took our hands, squeezed them gently. "They must have rooms here, don't you think?" she asked. Panic gripped me, I felt unable to answer and so did Pierrot. We gawked at her, our mouths hanging open. Then she grabbed our four hands in hers. "There's only one way I can thank you," she said without lowering her eyes, just like that, completely natural, "and that's in a bed. It's all I have to offer you. An old woman's body . . . But you can turn the lights off. But please don't think that you have to! I'd understand perfectly! It doesn't matter to me anymore. It's been such a long time, I sometimes wonder if I still know how. You'll have to teach me again—the movements, how it's done nowadays, everything. And forgive my awkwardness. All right?"

"You're beautiful," I told her.

"No . . . Not too tempting . . . How old are you?"

"Twenty," Pierrot said.

"And you?"

"Twenty-five."

"My God." Her face darkened, she was back in her gray thoughts again.

They brought the soufflé, flaming, on a big silver platter. I got the impression she was crying a little behind the flames. In any case, none of us were hungry anymore. We hardly touched the soufflé.

"You didn't like it?" the owner asked.

"Oh yes," our friend answered. "It's very good, only we're a little . . ."

"Would you care for a liqueur?"

"No, thank you. Do you have rooms?"

My heart stopped.

"Yes, of course. You'd like to stay for . . ."

I plunged in, totally freaked—no, not now, not right away! "No," I said, "just wanted to find out, in case we come back someday."

"We have magnificent rooms," the owner hastened to add. "The view of the port is breathtaking. Would you like to see one?"

"Bring me the check," the woman in black answered.

I had the feeling she was put out. Shit.

Just before leaving the restaurant, here's what she did (I think about it every day, can't get it out of my head): she stopped, right there, in front of the double door I was opening for her, and turned back to the owner, who was showing us out.

"Good-bye, madame," she said. "Thanks very much. It was excellent. You know, I just got out of prison, so it was a real treat for me. I've just spent ten years in a damp, dirty cell, you understand? I don't look it, I know, but I'm about the same age as you. I'm forty. Yes, really, only forty, if you want I can show you my papers . . . Forty, and it's been five years since I've gotten my period. It stopped because of the darkness. So you see, before leaving, I just wanted to tell you that you're lucky to bleed every month, even if it puts you in sort of a bad way, those moods aren't serious. Jumpy nerves, hot flashes, that's all nothing. Maybe you even have a particularly painful

162

ovary on one side, and one month out of two it's pure hell, you have to lie down with the shades drawn. But none of that is serious. What's serious is not bleeding anymore, you see. Being dry as an old fig!"

The owner was shocked, pale and shaking. "But," she said, "why are you telling me all this? Why me?"

"So that you'll bear it in mind . . . and tell your friends. We don't talk about these things enough . . . O.K? Good-bye, madame."

The owner, stunned, watched us leave, cross the street, and go down toward the port, and then, all of a sudden, she started hollering, "I was expatriated, *expatriated*, madame! Along with my whole family!"

Wow! A great blast of air! A hurricane! A terrible wind sweeping the beach. I leaned into it. Beautiful, though. But the roar was deafening. Those huge waves, the gulls screeching. My legs felt weak, my feet dragged and my head was spinning. But I wasn't alone reeling across this furious end of the world. Her gray hair streamed behind her. There, up ahead, far away. She walked by herself. I was walking by myself too. Pierrot was miles to my right. It was crazy. Why had we split up like that? She took off her shoes, walked on, shoes in hand. Brand new, black. Her stockings were black too. Nice against the sand. Hey! What was she up to? She'd stopped. She was holding her hands out behind her, two open hands. What was she waiting for in that ridiculous position? Christ, you dummy! She was holding her hands out to us! It was for us! I ran. He ran. We got there at the same time, out of breath, dizzy. She took us each by the arm, pulled us against her very close, and we walked together, all three heading into the wind, she tiny between us. She said something, we couldn't hear her in the din, she had to shout. "I'm not mad at you," she said. "I understand perfectly. It's me who should apologize. I just wanted to thank you, that's all." We stopped, she walked on. We eyed each other. We didn't dig.

Suddenly it hit me. No! Impossible! Not that! What a crazy fuckup! I tore off, caught up with her, cut her off, took her by the shoulders, God she was thin. "No!" I shouted.

163

"No! No way! It wasn't that at all!" She looked at me in silence, her hair flying, she was beautiful so I stammered, struggled, not a word came out. Pierrot had to come to my rescue.

"Tonight!" he bawled. "All night long! And tomorrow! All day long! My buddy and I will take turns! And maybe your period will come back! O.K.? Dig? We'll try to make it come back! We'll do everything!" Now it was her turn to be scared. She trembled, wouldn't take her eyes off us. She nodded yes like a little girl promising to be good. And then suddenly she started shouting in the wind, her voice breaking: "We're not in any rush. It's true, we have all the time in the world! And it's a beautiful day!" Then she collapsed, there, between us, breaking down right on the sand, sobbing and everything! I looked at Pierrot. I don't know if it was the same with me, but his face was all torn up. Then, like brothers, we flung ourselves on top of her, turned her over, took her in our arms, wedged her between our two bodies so she wouldn't be cold anymore, stroked her hair and face. She smiled at us pitifully through her enormous tears. She hardly dared brush our lips with her fingertips. Pierrot and I leaned over close to her mouth, which opened as her eyes closed, and didn't move. We lay like that for a long time, a very long time, waiting for the sand to bury us.

"My name is Jeanne. What're yours?"

We went back to the port and hit the beach in the opposite direction, with the wind pushing our butts.

Jeanne . . . A woman wearing mourning for her period. We sheltered her from the rain, each holding half a raincoat over her shoulders. Lowered our heads, hiding behind our upturned collars. From the back we must have looked like a six-legged raincoat, a big, funny, headless animal, a gabardine parachute. From the front it looked more like the patient's first outing, propped between two volunteer nurses. A little black-and-gray old lady, shrunken, huddled between two tall figures. A fallen star with her escort of managers gobbling up the last crumbs. But inside it was cozy, we hugged each other tight as we could. She had an arm around each of our waists, under our jackets. To help herself walk she gripped our belt buckles where our shirts, forever wrinkled, never stayed tucked in, so that suddenly I felt the icy touch of her thin fingers against my skin. Only then did I dig that soon the game would be over, that the hand on my belt belonged to a woman whose saliva I had just taken a long taste of, that it was a gentle and already possessive hand which didn't dare touch but couldn't wait, that we'd led her on and now had to get down to business. But this woman was old, she didn't turn me on, I wasn't grabbed even in a kinky way. All at once I was loaded with fear. I felt cold, miserable. I didn't dare look at that emaciated hand that surely any minute now (which was normal, she had the right) would freeze my belly like the hand of death. But the hand, luckily for me and for her, didn't budge. She seemed just to want to lean on the buckle next to my belly button. The truth, Jeanne, is you were scared too, even more than me. You didn't dare move your finger an inch. So we walked in silence, hounded by the storm. The endless wait was just beginning.

The afternoon took a hell of a long time to kill, let me tell you. We wandered around for hours, pathetically, prisoners of an enormous farce no one thought was funny. We did everything we could to put off the moment when . . . It was up to whoever was most afraid of the truth, not one of us could save the other. We never stopped touching with our hands, our arms, our shoulders, we hung onto each other like on the eve of a final split. Our affair had barely begun, but already it felt like good-bye. Get it over with, we absolutely had to get it over with. We'd softened her up, warmed her, carefully prepared her, now we had to screw her! But good! Or else we'd be worse than the guards. We had to go through with it. Not to would really be too sleazy. Who else would want our little black doll? No one else would give her a tumble—ever! She was going to show herself to us naked, all hot, counting on our talents. Your move, her body would say from every pore. Quick! I'm dying of eagerness! Our move, sure, that was easy to say. A woman always begs you like a springtime field waiting to be seeded, plowed, turned from tip to toe. But what if we weren't up to it? It would be rotten to run. What was she wearing under her suit? What kind of tastes did she have? How does it work at that age? And what if she really was too old?

165

Pierrot, you feel like it? At least one of us will have to. Pierrot! Stop looking at your fucking shoes! Jeanne, I can still see your black stockings in the damp sand, your toes, your slender ankles. No, you weren't old. And you wouldn't make us barf with your gray sex and the folds on your belly. Yes, you *would* dare touch us! How wrong you were! Oh, my God, how fucked up the three of us were. We were putting up fronts that didn't fool anybody. Sitting on the end of the breakwater, for example, faking digging the waves explode against the rocks, when we didn't give a shit about all that spray. Must have been real masochists to sit there, not moving, in the wind and rain. Some head trip! And we couldn't even rap because of the racket. It took our breath away. No matter what asinine places we went, time stood still. I got the feeling we'd have gone anywhere except to a bed, we were lost in a country where beds had just been banned. A new blue law. But no one would make the first move, get us off the hook. Because we really felt O.K. like that, in our suspense. It was comfy, like a semiserious illness that gives you a good excuse not to go to work. Our illness was stage fright. We couldn't even get it together to screw this little nobody, she had so much class! A really contagious illness —all three of us had it. We were crazy not to go to bed with such high fevers. We could have caught a hell of a chill. If one of us had been on the sickly side, he might not have survived. A medieval fever, contracted in the course of a voyage through time: prisonitis. Whose symptom is atrophy of the glands due to the lack of sunshine, and which should be treated promptly with applications of hot young skin, injections of fresh cells. But we just hung around like idiots, losing precious hours, when maybe it was already too late and we should have been doing emergency mouth-to-mouth resuscitation, starting transfusions and cardiac massage. And, above all, keeping the patient warm! Forgive us, Jeanne, we didn't know, I swear! You said, "Let's go!" so we went, got going, didn't want to cross you, get you mad or scare you off. We were still very polite to you, remember? "Would you like to drive?" I asked. "Would you dig that?" We could see it in your eyes that you would, that it would give you a tremendous boost. Even though you put on an act, faking that you didn't dare, no, really, you were too scared. "I used to have a license, yes, but so long ago, my reflexes, I must have forgotten everything, no, it's too dangerous, I'm really scared about my reflexes." Useless airs, since you were already behind the wheel going bananas, all excited, cheeks flushed, but still squawking—incredible!—while I was getting you settled, moving the seat forward and explaining everything to you. "You see that round thing, that's called the steering wheel, that's what you aim the car with." And you laughed, I got in beside you, showed you the speeds, four of them, you put the clutch in, shifted into first. Would your foot be strong enough to work that big pedal? Yes! Sure! You let the clutch out slowly, and off we went. Pretty good, the engine coughed a little, you shifted into second with my hand on yours, and there we were. Doing it! Cruising at a reasonable speed. Yes, Jeanne, keep laughing like that, it's O.K., don't think about anything, everything's cool, your reflexes are in fine shape, we'll check them all out one by one later on, you'll see, they'll all work great!

"The rear-view mirror," Pierrot piped up, "remember?"

"I sure do!"

Elbows on the front seat beside her, he was grinning at her in the rear-view mirror. She was driving like a kid at an amusement park, her tongue sticking out. And he didn't take his eyes off her, waiting till his gaze, like a lover's, drew Jeanne's eyes. I had to keep grabbing the wheel to keep us from jumping the road on curves. It was a state road that never stopped curving. "Don't look at me like that," she told him. "We might have an accident." But when he didn't obey and his eyes attracted her more and more, she turned the mirror so she couldn't see him anymore. Only now I was caught in the reflection, and I grinned at her just as much. Obviously—how else did you think we'd look at you? "Oh no!" you said. "Stop!" Then Pierrot moved in right behind you, gently lifted your hair with his fingertips, and the back of your neck appeared, long, delicate, breakable, and he planted a kiss there, in the little hollow, an endless kiss. It hit you like an alarm bell. You braked, closing your eyes, braced on the clutch and brake pedals. I was sure we were going to crash, I yanked the wheel. No, everything was O.K., we stopped smack in the middle of an intersection. But you didn't budge, as if nothing was wrong, you just sat there,

167

eyes closed, under Pierrot's kiss, which went on and on forever. Then his hands appeared at the front of your suit and very daintily and cautiously, one, two, three, undid the buttons of your black jacket. The motor kept revving. You let it, legs still strained against the pedals. Your skirt, slightly hiked up, revealed a strip of flesh above your stockings. Pierrot gently opened your jacket and then I saw—I looked, you filled me with tenderness—a slip! You really were a genius, Jeanne! To have bought the one garment I had never seen or touched! A black slip, of course. We'd dug everything else, let me tell you, from the bunched-up minislip to the sagging panty hose, including a beauty operator's bare ass, but a slip, never! Except in old Italian flicks. We'd forgotten that they existed. We didn't know they could be so beautiful. A simple old-fashioned slip with an inch of lace on your white skin. We stared, knocked out, unable to move or act, which you were probably waiting for, since your reflexes, I could tell, were starting to check in one by one, a grand show, and every one of them glad to be alive again.

A truck grazed us, blew thirty tons of obscene horns, and I pictured as many tons of cusswords in the cab. What the hell did I care! No one gave a shit inside our little crushable-eggshell Dyane! It was our turn to hog the road! Our stop sign was a piece of lace on a meager chest. For a few seconds now a far-out priority had been grabbing us, and we didn't give a fuck if the entire Automobile Club of France was honking on our ass.

"Jeanne," I said to her (it was the first time I had called her Jeanne and it made me feel like I was holding her naked skin against mine), "take the first right. There's a little cottage a few miles down. We'll be O.K."

"No," she answered, "not right away, please not right away. Let's wait till dark. I'd rather . . . You don't mind?"

"No," I said.

I didn't dare rap to her about curtains, explain that even in broad daylight it was like night with curtains and that anyhow, in this weather, the sun wasn't about to zoom in, because I knew she would have answered, "Do me a favor," and we wouldn't have insisted. She needed the night to hide in, that was all, we had to work up to it slowly. So she shifted into first

168

and we took off down the highway, straight ahead. It didn't really matter, since we had hideouts staked out everywhere.

We drove for a while, just rolling along in the car, of course it's beautiful cutting through nature like that when you can't see through the windshield because the wipers are about as efficient as greasy rags, and even if you had Mercedes wipers you'd still see the same thing, zilch, because the weather outside was getting shittier and shittier, and the words for it, in alphabetical order, were blinding, cut-it-with-a-knife, pea soup, and visibility zero. We drove through a fog that turned from Jell-O to glue. We skimmed a vague shape that looked like a bus, then three cars tailing a tractor, only too happy to have something to hang in behind, like a wagon train. We passed on the right, passed on the left, not even using guesswork; by then we were navigating with our noses, our ears, and crossing ourselves, a game of chance, like Russian roulette. Jeanne's driving skills no longer played. What counted was her jacket, which she left open, her skirt, which she didn't pull down. It never occurred to anybody to park somewhere, our aimlessness was so sweet. "Tomorrow we'll cut out of this filthy area," I told her, "and shuffle on down south. O.K.?" Yes, yes, she nodded yes as hard as she could. "You need sun, and where we're from there's always sun. A real rest, how does that grab you? We'll take care of everything, all you'll have to do is tan your bod from dawn till dusk, eat and sleep. We'll bring you food every two hours so you gain some weight back." She braked short on the edge of the road.

"Why not go there now?" she said. Far out, that was the best idea, these Bretons would wind up doing us in. A quick U-turn and off we zoomed in the opposite direction. Jeanne stepped on it, going crazy, but I thought she was driving a little too fast in that fog and laid it on her. "You're right," she answered. She stopped again on the shoulder and turned around. She took us both by the back of the neck, her hands gently stroking our heads, and we turned to mush. "I'll take care of you too," she told us. "I'll get my strength back very fast, you'll see, and I'll be able to do all sorts of things." She moved her face closer. Then she paused—so shy, I'll bet she was wondering which of us to kiss first, and what the other would think. Well, shit! I was the oldest! And besides, it had been my idea! I pulled her violently to me, her head in my hands, and crushed her mouth. She started choking, I felt her almost pull back, heard her moan. Then I brought my hands down and yanked her jacket off her shoulders. I pushed her away and looked at her. She was all breathless, her sleeves were pulled down, her chest was heaving, gasping for air. I couldn't take my eyes off the play of the black straps against her narrow, delicate shoulders, so thin you could imagine two pools of tears in their hollows under the straps. "We'll sleep on the way," she said, "as soon as night comes, that's a promise." She pulled her jacket back up.

"We'll be hitting back roads," I said.

"Why?"

"Because we're wanted by the man."

She drove on without comment.

Incredible but true: the Breton flood stopped dead at the Loire. It was still pissing on our hill as we eased down around the slippery curves, but ahead the country glowed under the setting sun with a blue sky over it. As if there were a curtain between the two riverbanks. We zipped through it, crossing a bridge. On the other side lay gentle France.

As we bopped from village to village, Jeanne regained her mastery of the wheel. She drove smooth, cool, with obvious pleasure. We let ourselves be chauffeured like kings, puffing away on cigarettes. Peace reigned in our kingdom. But also impatience. And a good case of the hots that tingled all our nerves. Because night was taking its sweet time coming. In spring, they say that's normal, the days get longer. But that day was really too stretched out. And Jeanne still hadn't buttoned her jacket. Pierrot kept walking his fingers up and down her neck, her shoulder, her throat. Naturally, from the back seat, he was in a better position than me. She was right there in front of him, defenseless. I just looked at her legs, her hands on the wheel. And my watch.

At eight I told her to switch the headlights on. "The little knob, there, on your left." We rolled along in limbo.

"We'll have to find a hotel," she said.

"Hmmm," I said. "That's too risky."

"Then where?"

"Ya got me."

"It doesn't matter," she said. "Anywhere. We can find a barn with some hay in it."

"No way!" I answered. "I'll check the map."

I checked the map, then the green guide, and finally I said to Jeanne, "O.K., take your first left."

"Where to?" Pierrot piped up.

I read them what the Michelin had to say about a spot called Fleurs-les-Bains, not far to the east.

"It was at the end of the last century," the guide said, "that Fleurs-les-Bains, a watering spa formerly used by the Romans, had its hour of glory. A direct rival of the prestigious Baden-Baden, it attracted a wealthy international clientele to its shady valley. It was fashionable to come from Moscow to drink its sulfur springs, which worked wonders on chronic respiratory ailments such as asthma, bronchitis and emphysema. But the First World War brought an end to its bright lights and gay parties. Fleurs-les-Bains slowly sank into oblivion to become, today, one of the prime examples of an architecture known as 'watering spa.' . . ."

"Don't you think it's worth a little detour?"

I'd barely closed the heavy soundproof doors when Jeanne made the first move: two little shimmies to shrug off her jacket, drop her skirt, and then there she was, waiting, straight as a pin way over on the other side of the bed. She was facing us, chin up, in her black slip. One strap had slid down onto her thin arm. A simple ten-franc slip—you know, the kind of thing you pluck out of a bin of nylon full of groping hands. But she looked dressed for a ball, and we two dashing young dudes didn't even dare ask her to dance.

She wore her white shoulders like a stole, flauntingly, as though they were framing a low-cut gown. She held her arms curved, like a dancer, with her feet placed on the carpet in a ballerina position. She was breathing hard, as if she'd just finished a pas de deux. She had the nimbleness of a Bolshoi star, and under those floods of lights I waited for her to be bravoed. But there was no one left to applaud in that abandoned resort, not one tailcoat, not one fan. Those gay blades from St. Petersburg would never come again. There was no one left under the huge chandeliers but us: three nostalgia buffs.

"What if we cut the lights?" I suggested.

"No!" she answered. "Not right away!"

I didn't get it, I was stumped, when all she'd been rapping about all day was the dark. And why was she coming closer like that, straight at me?

She stopped within reach of my mouth. I felt her short breath, she communicated her fear to me, her opening-night

172

panic. I heard the theater hush, the curtain was about to rise, I would never be able to lift her and twirl her above my head! Hey there! Two white spiders had crept in under my jacket, shucked it off, were attacking my shirt. The great star was really very little, and her face, from close up, betrayed her years.

It was amazing she could still create the illusion. Her mouth scalded my lips. She let herself slip to my feet, fell to her knees, clutched my belt buckle. An unexpected move! She was improvising. She might have warned me! Where was Pierrot? What was he waiting for? I frantically scanned the shadows in the wings, caught his petrified eyes, threw him an SOS. He was unable to act, I could feel it, he was overcome by stage fright too, only too happy to be out of reach of those white hands that slowly undid me. The thirty-bulb chandelier overhead floodlit the theater, my embarrassment, the bulge in my shorts. Alone in a great gilded hall in the hands of a pathologist in black who was mercilessly dissecting me. It's easy to get the advantage by blitzing the weakest point—the soft spot in my clothes! All you have to do is open it for the joke to explode. I was tricked, betrayed by my sleazy undies. My so-called virility took a tiny bow: my dingdong, my peepee, my dickie! I felt sick, done in. And that other idiot leering at me! Ah, big brother's a winner! Just wait your turn, you'll see! But what's with this slave at my feet? Get up, madame! All I can see is your gray hair! I'm embarrassed! She was killing me with kindness. Chiseling my slow death with a sculptor's love. She stepped back from time to time to admire her handiwork. At the moment of the final touch-up, the ultimate rub, I felt a masterpiece being born, she drank to it, it was a smash hit!

Two minutes later.

Jeanne had asked us to cut the lights. The darkness soothed me like a warm bath. I chucked my grotesque threads, felt like a new man, dug my toes into the soft carpet, what luxury! Not a peep in the ceremonial chamber. What were the others up to? My eyes got used to the dark, and I made out a motionless shape, a pale glow on my left. I wove my way through the treacherous furniture to reach it. I groped and recognized Pierrot. "Where is she?"

The light snapped on. The chandelier. All the sconces with their crystal pendants.

Jeanne was at the door, still dressed, still in black. Shock in her eyes. Bewilderment. We didn't move, just handed ourselves over. She glided closer, dazzled by the powerhouse homage Pierrot was paying her. She stopped at a slight distance and cautiously held out her hand to check its contours.

"Take your clothes off," Pierrot told her, stepping back.

No, she refused. To see without being seen, that's what she wanted. She got our shirts and made two blindfolds out of them, tied them snugly by the sleeves. We let ourselves be blinded without hassle, not resisting and not turned off.

"Promise not to peek!"

We promised. We felt incapable of back talk, we'd indulge all her whims, she could take us anywhere!

Now it was a total blackout under those torrents of electricity. And total hush. No one stirred in the Grand Suite.

"What're you doing?"

"Getting undressed," Jeanne answered.

I had no urge to rip off the blindfold, it was a hell of a lot better like that! I was led by the hand over to the edge of the bed, made to lie down, told to be good and then left hanging, at the ready from head to toe. Suddenly I heard their bodies sliding against each other and a sort of convulsion on my right! "Baby," she murmured to him, "my baby!" The pace beefed up to a crazy pitch, they were racing up a dizzy slope, collapsed howling at the top, and Jeanne burst into twisted unbearable sobs. I threw myself on top of them, held them both against me, begged her not to cry, and all she could say was "thank you"! If only she'd stop! Her lips were icy. "We'll *never* split up!" I told her. "And every day will be like this!" Then I tore off my blindfold, whipped off Pierrot's and hollered, "Look!"

She was beautiful, didn't get mad, just let herself be scanned, forcing a smile through her tears. But the moment had come to check out the details of her naked body. Pierrot and I pulled back. Then Jeanne's hands slid down between her thighs, which closed, and she said with a fatalistic air, "There . . ."

She had the saddest tits on earth. Two empty little pouches hanging from her jailbird torso. You could count her ribs. Her waist was superskinny and her belly all wrinkles. I tried to pry her hands away but she fought with all her might. Pierrot came in handy. We each pulled on a wrist. Jeanne gave up, begging us to leave her alone.

She was wrong to try and hide her gray pussy hairs. I bent down to rap to them, explain that I dug them. Jeanne, picking up on the lingo, opened like a flower finally freed, a beautiful cemetery flower. I mounted and made her come three times. Then Pierrot took over and got her off three more times. And me again, Pierrot, and so on for a long time. Not missing a beat. No way to dawdle along the way with all the years we had to catch up with! It was a desperate run in hot pursuit of a lost thirty-year-old woman named Jeanne, a terrible relay race back into time! We passed her back and forth at a wicked pace, lap after lap, stretching our stride, tearing our guts out, flooring it! We were fighters! Winners! A cinch to catch up with the young woman who sparkled with life before they snuffed her out with a prison number, the woman who shot fireworks at the sun.

I was gasping. Jeanne. Your mouth was suffocating me. The dark. I was hot. The sheets over our heads and Jeanne pouncing on me in the dark. A house, she'd said, we'll make a house under the sheets. Big hemstitched sheets with enormous initials, four letters entwined: GHCR. Grand Hôtel de la Cour de Russie. There were stacks of them in the linen closet. And two cupboards full of pillows. It was she who threw the first one, which I caught right in the puss. So I struck back, Pierrot joined in, we emptied both cupboards, pounded ourselves to death, a crazy pillow chase through the deserted palace. It was beautiful running bare-assed through all those corridors. It was pissing pillows! And that fuckhead Pierrot took a ride in the dumb-waiter! We heard an awful racket, tore down three flights like maniacs, found him in the kitchen, K.O.'d, plotzed! Shelves full of bottles! Acres of labels, like a mirage! We trotted back up with two magnums, back into our suite, Jeanne perched on the rolling table like a queen on a throne of pillows and us pushing her full speed, cutting corners on two wheels.

"It's silly to have all these lights on," she said. "You never know . . . Go shut off the fuse while I make the bed."

We hit the sack by flashlight. A huge sack meant for crowned heads, for the entertainment of empresses. What time had it gotten to be? Outside it was still dark. A truck rumbled by. The headlights swept across Jeanne's face for an instant. She said, "I'm not tired anymore."

A few hours' sack time and we had a different woman on our hands. Gone was the shaking jailbird! Gone the graying forty-year-old! "I feel ten years younger," she said. "I feel like running! I feel like fighting!" And she smiled in the dark in a freaky way. I decided it would be a good idea to wake Pierrot.

We'd caught the dynamite Jeanne! Set off the fireworks again! And won our bet hands down! Only now we had to put out. Fill the second part of the deal. There was a mess of fine print we hadn't even bothered to read! And Jeanne wasn't about to let us off, no way! She wasn't the type to roll over on her back and purr like a pussy. For who? Two dudes decked out in flannel and tweed playing with a fire they'd found in a heap of rags? Guys today have really got their nerve! Came to pick her up in front of the Big House and do a number on her. On *her!* The real McCoy the people had judged, condemned, locked up like a mad dog for their own protection! Someone they'd point at, and always fear, with or without her rabies shots. The bums thought they could screw me, take advantage of the situation. The bargain of the century, they must have figured. A January sale! Liquidating the stock. Everything's gotta go. Dirt cheap! Just a decent lunch and zap! legs in the air! But not so fast, my pets. I'm going to put a few strings on this clearance sale. It's going to cost you plenty! I'm going to turn on the big heat. Won't be much left of your pretty pricks when I'm through! The old hag can burn your candles for ten years straight! Didn't figure on that, did you, my little sparkplugs? No time off with Seven sixty-seven! Have to drill till you strike blood! Been polishing my pussy for ten long years! Ten years I've been taking care of it, fluffing it up, making little finger waves, spit curls, love locks for the Grand Liberation Ball, when I'm a free French citizen again! It shines like a new penny, glows in the dark! In my cell it was my night-light. I could read under the blankets by it after lights-out! Very handy for turning the pages, too. All my buddies used it. I can still feel their fingers, like a centipede between my legs! We had to make do because we didn't have any clean-cut young dudes around to take care of us. So we crocheted kinky little orgasms to keep us warm on winter nights.

She'd stored up anger for a tenth of a century, and here she was in the first arena she came to—a bed! 'Course it had to come out, and it had to hurt. The first blasts hit us right in the kisser, since we'd had the bright idea of leading her, sleek as a cat, right to the door of the cage!

The great freeing of the prisoner was at hand. We were heading down an endless tunnel where an unknown creature awaited us, a stranger from far away who kept coming at us over and over again, triumphantly announcing her return, sounding the brasses and rolling the drums, crying, "Here I am!" from every rooftop, on every station platform, at every airport. "It's me, Jeanne! Back from the dead! Home from a long voyage! I'm alive, present arms!" And we became her red carpet, we rolled ourselves out under her feet while she shook the hands of the officials. We'd have earned our headlines the next day: "Bums give old hag rousing welcome."

She made love like war. She'd never be able to do anything any other way. Buying bread, crossing the street, it would always be war. She charged on every front, raging, in hand-to-hand combat. She was always in the front lines, covering all the flanks. A scrappy leatherneck who never cringed from blows or wounds, it had all happened to her already. An old warrior finally back in service, getting a piece of the biggest battle of her life. She was a whole army by herself. She launched her commandos all over the map. She even crawled through the mud to hit us from behind. She stabbed us in the back, tunneled with her bare hands and bored us from within. Her nails were tough. Her tongue was a flamethrower, searing us with napalm. We became human torches running across the high plateaus. She crept up on us while we were asleep, sneakily. Taking advantage of our nightmares.

She switched from offensive to defensive tactics with a strategy that could only be tagged Asiatic. Sometimes she stalled, faked being lazy, then swiftly struck like a panzer division at a target that immediately surrendered, stunned by the surprise and sweetness of the shock. Then she'd make sport of our defeat, really rubbing it in, telling us we were piggy, making us feel guilty, and then lick us all over like a mama-wolf. She caused all our fortifications to fall. No structure, even the most imposing, impressed her. She created total chaos. We dropped like a house of cards. And she laid siege to our weak places with endless patience and a wide imagination. Her words moved mountains. She felt our most secret workings through her fingertips, then found a way to start up mechanisms that seemed broken for good, useless, ready for the trash. She stuck conquering banners in unknown parts of our brains.

She made love like a princess but fucked like a whore, both at the same time. The princess nixed doing stuff, while the whore, a second later, wanted things a hundred times worse, which she flung in our faces like a slap.

The princess got miffed, demanding apologies. The whore got pissed too, hollering for more.

She let herself be coaxed and then turned around and begged, till we no longer knew who was begging, who needed to be coaxed, the whore or the princess. Was the whore showing signs of slacking off or was the princess turning into a whore? The two blended, then split, we saw double, there were four of us, lost in trick effects, out of our skulls.

It was definitely the princess who rapped about love, made tender vows cut short by broken moans. But whorish words escaped her, making her close her eyes and hide her head in our shoulders. It was the whore who solicited in our ears, recited magic formulas, drew back to see the effects of her witchcraft, then cut loose, not shifting her eyes from us. But a panicked hush would follow, during which a tiny princess sob burst forth, like a small bell she couldn't muffle.

The princess begged pardon, always whipped, hanging her head and biting the dust. She was a vision of dainty dimples. The whore sold her body, flaunted herself, issued orders and threw out challenges, upping the ante. She was a hard-assed, tireless amazon, an acrobat.

And we were going bananas between the pair of them. It was love with teeth in it, the iron hand in the velvet glove.

The purest modesty shadowed by a huge blast of filth, like a belch at a banquet, as if the bride were at the wedding standing on a sewer grate, with gusts from the sewer blowing her white dress up, and the in-laws all taking out their hankies, about to barf right in the church.

"Fuck me so I bleed," she murmured. "I'll color you red."

She flooded us with smut that would have made a sailor blush—so much that we were helpless, our hair standing on end like a fright wig. Then she'd lean back to laugh at our plight, teeth bared, mouth wide open. She'd eject us with a snobby shrug of her hips and get up, sulky, to check herself in all the mirrors, strolling around casually. "Poor little Jeanne," she'd say, lifting her boobs like an offering. "You never have any luck. But what did you expect? Kids that age sleep a lot." She'd come back, sighing, and contemplate the scene of the disaster. "I see," she'd say, "the sandman has come." She'd slip on her stockings, her black *femme fatale* lingerie. She'd cover us up, tuck us in, and put a little night-light in the hall so we wouldn't be afraid. She'd come back to sit on the edge of the bed, kiss us on the forehead, the cheek, then the neck. We'd try to hang onto her, get her to tell us a story, just a short one. "No-no-no!" she'd answer. "I can't! I have to run and get dressed, or I'll never be ready when your father comes for me, and we'll get there after the curtain's gone up! He'll be furious! Just think—the *Swan Lake* overture! The most beautiful!"

"You smell nice, Mama! One more kiss!"

"Just one."

She'd bend over us, me dying of panic that her hand might hit on my erection. (That dummy Pierrot had had the bright idea of sticking his finger in my pajama fly!)

"Sleep well, my darlings."

And she'd move off in a cloud of perfume, a rustling of silk, leaving us alone with our night-light and our hands.

She would tiptoe into our dreams, not making a sound. And our dreams would spill over into our waking hours without the slightest break.

She would appear like daylight, bringing us joy on a tray, spoon-feeding us, patiently wiping the corners of our mouths, taking our pulses, never leaving our bedside, jotting our rising temperatures on the chart every hour, inquiring anxiously about our pain, did it sting? Or ache? Placing a cool hand on our foreheads, reassuring us in a low voice, "Don't be afraid, baby, it's nothing yet, the pain has hardly begun, you'll see, it'll get worse, it'll get unbearable, you'll scream and writhe and beg for oxygen." A head nurse, a very strict gray-haired widow, let our damp little hands seek comfort under her white uniform, groping, groping, hairs and more hairs, and then rapped us sharply on our fingers with her ruler. She watched by us all night, telling us stories about the final moments, that our case was hopeless. "Wait till dawn, you'll see. No one can do anything for you anymore. Not even your mother, by the way, who refuses to be bothered. She says it's no longer worth the trouble. Anyway, it's all over. Look—day is breaking behind the blinds. You just passed away without realizing it, you lucky stiffs! Well? How did it feel? It's not as terrible as all that! People are really wrong to make such a big thing out of it. All right, cut off the IV. You're drunk enough already. You're feeling no pain now, no regrets, no worries! No more suffering. You just feel a little chilly. Quite a comfortable stretcher, don't you think? A smooth ride. And this elevator—so cozy. I'm taking you to the third subbasement, where I live, in a little hole in the ground. End of the line! Everybody out! Just listen to that silence! All that moaning and groaning is over! Here you can get a real rest, just wait and see. You're going to go beddie-bye on the marble slab. I'll switch on a little soft neon. Now, let's clean you up. I'll have to stuff you with cotton or else you'll mess all over me. Gotta shoot you with formalin!" She whipped our shrouds onto the tiled floor. "Oh! But you're still quite appetizing, my little piggies! What a shame to croak so young! But what luck for me! Yes, you'll do just fine, ducks! You still have a little role to play. It'll be a change from all those rotten bums!" She unbuttoned her blouse, freeing herself to enjoy the cool air, then climbed out of her undies. "And no squawking! I'm the boss around here! I have total say over your meat. In the beyond, I don't have to answer to anybody. I tell all the interns and externs to fuck off, including the big boss, who locks everything up. I'm queen of the hospital! I may be old, but I'm still alive and kicking!" She vaulted onto the marble slab and squatted on my face. Oh, the

180

bitch, she was having her period! I was swallowed by an oozing wound.

We sat bolt upright in bed, drenched with sweat. Jeanne, at the bedside, was puzzled by our cadaverous stiffness. Dream or reality? It was getting hard to tell. We didn't even try anymore, just let ourselves drift, said "good morning" or "good night" any old time. Day? Night? We didn't give a shit. Except that during the day we could see each other and at night we could only feel. With the shutters closed it didn't make much difference, but still . . . In the daytime there was a grayish light, the room was a crypt, and we, the corpses, watched over by a nun with soft hands, our sister, our mother, who prayed to us, adored us, slowly losing her mind. Thinking herself alone with two statues of fallen warriors and their stone swords, she poured her heart out freely, her novenas tasting of sulfur, turning into blasphemy. She pulled herself up onto the tomb to idolize our reliefs from closer up, our lordly bulges, as if we were heroes killed in the crusades. She wept for our youth, sang our praises, said her beads for us so fervently that we revived. Then, touched by her grace, we responded to her ecstasies. Together, we prepared to receive the burning sacraments. She baptized us with pagan names, heard our confessions, confessed herself. "I've robbed robbers," she admitted, "I've lied to liars, I've sold myself to profiteers. I've laughed at freaks, despised the scum. I've done evil for the sake of evil, sabotaged the prison workshop, committed unnatural acts. When my parents died, I didn't do anything, I sent them a cheap bunch of flowers, saving my pay for the canteen." We distributed penances. Then, purified, we wrapped ourselves around each other very tightly and took communion till we were out of breath. We reeled naked through the hallways like choirboys, looking for the storeroom because we needed bread and wine. We consummated every form of marriage till we ached, till we collapsed into a refreshing coma. Jeanne fell asleep like a rock in a thunderstorm shaken by lightning and feverish tremors. "You'll see," she mumbled, "you'll see, between my legs. My jam will come, my jam made of four fruits. Only you have to wait . . . You have to wait for the right day, when the four fruits are ripe at the same time. My strawberry, my cherry, my raspberry and my red currant. The four red fruits. And I'll buy white undies, very filmy, so it will leak through like a sieve. I'll let you taste it, if you're good." She woke us up at night, an amorous sleepwalker, to go with her to the john. We were her flunkies, her slaves. She wanted us to relieve ourselves in front of her and we obeyed. When we left the bathroom, dawn was already breaking and our faces were white. Jeanne officiated in the grayness, a priestess with a thousand offerings, standing spread-eagle in a trance, eyes closed, fists clenched, nails digging into our veins, taut as a cold marble arrow. And we two faithfuls on the floor, hooked, hanging on by the teeth to every word, two dogs, two fanatics waiting for the miracle, our knees hurting, while the incantation rose octave by octave. A statue so light that we had to put our four hands around her waist like a girdle and hold her so she wouldn't fly away. A sculpture from ancient times that had come to us intact, arms and legs unbroken, so smooth, polished, worn by the touch of unknown hands that the veins stood out from the surface of the marble, a fine blue network that led to a gash of flesh between the statue's legs, an old wound that had reopened deep, very deep, but without one drop of blood. Patience, patience. We intensified our attentions, implored the faded belly and the blooming flower inside it. A purple petunia in the grayness. "You had any kids?" She no longer answered, frozen. She was skin and bones, transparent with fatigue, celestial. She broke into icy sweats that the wan light dissolved. A gray rainbow rose above the bed. She grew waxen, sweet-smelling as the hours passed, and then blurted, almost angrily, "I'm sick of champagne and all that canned junk! How about a real cup of coffee?" Yes, sure, what a great idea! We told her not to move, stay in bed, rest, take it easy, we'd bring it right away. "Very strong," she said, "it'll perk us up."

We went down to the kitchen, found everything we needed, even waiters' uniforms—room-service waiters, you know, with those big aprons flapping around our legs, and striped vests. We dressed up in them just for kicks, to put on a show for her: "Madame is served," "Madame's breakfast is here," "Did Madame sleep well?" We put the coffee on a rolling table, with piles of silverware and stuff, and started back. We pulled up smartly in front of door 14 and knocked. She didn't answer. "Madame must have dozed off," Pierrot said. Then we opened the double door.

"Jeanne!"

Her period had come back all right, nice and red. The bed was covered with it, the sheets all bloody. She was smiling with joy and aiming the revolver with all her might between her legs. Our revolver.

Those old hotels for rich dudes taking the cure were really built: you never heard your neighbors. You could fire as many shots as you liked without disturbing anyone. The padded doors must have had something to do with it.

We drove back at top speed not talking. No need to say we were heading for Toulouse or why. It was just in the cards.

She opened the door calmly. "I don't have much to eat," she said.

"We're not hungry."

It was true, I don't know why, we'd lost our appetites. And yet we hadn't eaten.

"I've got my period," she said, "but tomorrow it'll be over."

We noticed red panties through her nightgown.

There was only a hundred francs in her Kotex box. We took it.

"You can fuck me anyhow."

I let her have a hard smack. "You ever going to learn to shut your hole?"

She apologized. She asked us if we had a problem or something.

"No," I answered. "Everything's just dandy. So long as you got your health you can't bitch. You also better believe you're lucky as hell to be living in a free country."

She'd been watching the tube from her bed, and she lay back down again. "It's a new game show. Very funny."

We sat on the edge of the bed. We watched the asshole game show, the book reviews, the news, the weather, sat through the works. Then, when the screen went white and dead, we got undressed and hit the sack. On either side of her. She switched off the light and pulled the covers up high so we wouldn't be cold and then raised both her arms. We put our heads on her shoulders and she held us in her arms while we bawled like babies. She didn't say beans, just waited for it to go away, holding us very tight. And it went away. Everything goes away, always.

The alarm went off at eight.

We listened to her taking her shower. She came back in her uniform, ready for work. "I'm going to do an errand," she said, heading for the door. "Be back in five minutes."

"The smart thing to do," I answered, "is get the cops."

She came back with croissants.

She brought us coffee in bed.

We ate breakfast all alone, in her pink sheets, while she worked.

"Since all my ideas are bummers," I told Pierrot, "the best thing is for me to shut my hole forever and let you do the steering. I'm played out."

"I'll give it a whirl," he said, "but I got a feeling I won't do any better."

We went into the can. It broke our hearts to take a shower because it would wash away the smell of Jeanne.

We turned the taps on all the way.

We found Marie-Ange's little underarm razor.

There was a bloody piece of cotton in the plastic wastebasket. Too gross for the eyes.

We cleaned the pistol in the sink. The water turned red.

We took a spin around the city, not knowing where or why. We played pinball and bought a paper. Then, on the way home, guess what we found on the back seat of the Dyane. An item we'd completely forgotten—her army suitcase! Jeanne's little metal suitcase! We sped back, rushed upstairs and opened it almost before we'd got in the door.

There wasn't much inside. An old worn-out toothbrush. Three packs of Gauloises. Some pathetic undies full of mends. A washrag. A broken watch. A half-eaten piece of spice cake. Some red jam. And under all that, like a mattress, packs and packs of letters tied with heavy twine. Letters in yellowed envelopes with faded writing, addressed to Number 767, Rennes Central Prison, Ille-et-Vilaine.

They all started with "Mama," or "Dear Mama," or "Little Mama." Some wished her Merry Christmas or Happy New Year. Or Happy Birthday, Mama. Some, on notebook paper, even had a kid's drawings. The oldest ones were full of spelling mistakes, erasures and ink blots. As the years went on, the handwriting took on more style. All the letters were signed "Jacques."

We read for hours, flat on our bellies on Marie-Ange's big bed.

Her kid must have been twenty by then. The letters had been mailed in Epinal, Vesoul and Colmar. Then there were vacation letters from a camp in Gérardmer. A few from Malo-les-Bains, near Dunkirk.

The latest ones, from the past two years, came from Ensisheim, near Mulhouse.

Jacques seemed to be happy in Ensisheim. "Everything's fine," he wrote. "They gave me the librarian's job when the guy got out . . . They've rewarded me for good conduct . . . They told me that if I keep on like this I might be up for parole . . ."

"I don't know how this would grab you," Pierrot began.

"Nothing grabs me," I answered.

"But," he went on, "I think we oughta go there, to Ensisheim, now. We've gotta see Jacques, wait for him. From what he says, he hasn't got too long to go. And when he gets out, we'll take care of him."

"That's just what I was thinking."

"Because you see, Jean-Claude, the kid is the same age as us. And we have a kind of debt we owe him. Shit! We killed his old lady, didn't we?"

"I don't agree," I said. "It wasn't us who killed her. She died because of the freedom. Because she couldn't hack being free anymore. *They* killed her. One more suicide to their credit. One that won't be in the statistics."

When Marie-Ange got back with her groceries, we told her right off the bat, "No point taking off your raincoat. We're splitting for Alsace and you're coming with us."

She didn't ask why, or where, or how. She didn't ask shit. She just jumped for joy.

186

Montastruc-la-Conseillère, Saint-Sulpice-la-Pointe, Rabastens, Lisle, Gaillac, Albi, Carmaux, Rodez, Espalion, Laguiole, Chaudes-Aigues: that's when she started rapping, when we got past Chaudes-Aigues. We didn't ask her anything. Didn't feel like chewing the fat because of the constant lump in our throats that hadn't left us since Toulouse, and even before Toulouse. We were all choked up. Then suddenly we heard this voice from the back seat.

"Thanks!" she said. "Thanks, you guys, thanks a lot! No, really, I appreciate it! Thanks for everything! Especially for the conversation! No kidding, it's a pleasure to finally be able to talk to someone who understands you. I just think that's great of you! But don't get me wrong. Don't feel you have to say anything. Silence doesn't bother me, I'm used to it. When I go home at night there's never anyone waiting for me. So I flip on the tube, heat the water for my egg, check out the ads from the mailbox. It's O.K., honest! And I don't feel lonely at all. There are people all around me. Loads of big fat families to warm up the atmosphere. I can hear them screaming at each other, the brats bawling and the parents beating their bottoms, the shouts getting louder and louder, and the poor dames going out of their heads, voices coming out all twisted, shrill, like a dentist's drill in your ears. Take it from me, the soap operas restore peace. I don't even have to switch on my set—I can listen to the neighbors. One on my left, one on my right. I'm in luck—stereo. I park my ass right in the middle and slurp my little supper, my decibel dinner. At ten o'clock they turn the volume down so I don't bang on the walls. Then I hit the sack and dig the wonderful silence: toilets flushing, guys pissing standing up, like horses, leaking all the beer of the day . . . the eleven o'clock bidet. I lie there like a queen, flipping through *House and Garden*. In the morning I split early, coffee at the Mirage snack counter. I'm never bored, don't worry! I'm used to silence. You don't have to say anything! You already kept your traps shut for a hundred and twenty-five miles. I personally don't give a shit except I'm bored and I'm not sleepy. You dig? If it was daylight, it would be O.K. At least I could look at the countryside and the other cars. But really, there must be better scenic tours than this! I've counted a hundred and seventy-two squashed toads in the headlights since we left Toulouse! Fascinating. No, I assure you, it's a fantastic trip! Don't worry about old Marie! And shit, after all, what's a chick to you? Huh? Just think about it a little! A piece of meat and that's all! Just a hunk of white meat! Something to munch on! Well, you give me a pain all of a sudden, I don't know why . . . I think you're fucked up and deranged. You show up whenever you feel like it. Take my ass for a meat grinder. Cop my bread. And then you disappear into the blue. No news, nothing! Not even a postcard! No address, I don't even know where to reach you! Suppose something happened to me, huh? What if I got sick? Who would come to take care of me?"

"Your haircutter."

"Oh no! I mean, shit! That would be a pain in the boobs I ain't even got! I'm an amputee! No haircutters in my pad! He doesn't even get through the door. No way, you dig? I won't have it! Out! He can do his thing somewhere else. In the bushes, a railroad station shithouse, anywhere, but not at my place. Swell in his buggy with the reclining seats! Groovy! I just listen to the radio! In his kids' room? Right on! On the floor in the middle of the dolls? Do it! In their bunk beds? Go, man! The little shampooist doesn't give a shit as long as it's not her place. Anywhere and any style! In the maid's room, when she's off in Barcelona visiting her old lady? Perfect! It reeks? There's no heat? The wallpaper's peeling? Drafty and your feet get cold? So what! That's nothing. Not choosey, Marie-Ange, at six hundred francs a month including tips she'll do anything! The boss is always right. *Always.* On his wife's sheets while she's skiing in

Barèges? Far out! No problem—I just spread out in the middle of her big bed. Right where they made their three brats. Her nightgowns look swell on me. I look like Grace Kelly, my feet waving in the air above the white piqué. Hurray for French bedding! Innerspring mattresses! I hook my feet up on the headboard and let her roll! No rush, dad! Take it slow, I got time. Just wake me when it's over, that's all I ask. Meanwhile, I drink in the decor . . . Three thousand francs, the Toile de Jouy walls. Six hundred, the antique opaline. One thou, the frilly dressing table. Two thou, the guaranteed pure-wool pastel carpeting at eighty francs a square yard, not including installation and felt padding. 'Watch your butts,' he tells me. I do his dishes in a baby-doll gown in his ultrachic kitchen. No two ways about it—his double sink is terrif! I go for interior decoration. Buy all the mags about it. I'm bananas about them, it's all I read. I never miss an issue of *La Maison de Marie-Claire!* I have the complete collection, ever since it first came out! I measure off space at home. I have a carpenter's rule, a folding one. I draw little plans on graph paper—to scale! You oughta see me! I price things. Study estimates. And when I go to other people's homes, it's to swipe ideas. The hairdresser's apartment is in exquisite taste! They called in a famous decorator. And the bathroom is something else! There are rotating douches, and then there are *rotating douches*—not to be confused! That one's like a carwash! A real service-station model! Sweeps you clean for twenty-eight days! A superduper jet spray! His wife must gleam like the Moscow subway! Must have a cunt like a mirror! Not to mention her perfumes. With all those bottles, no reason she should ever stink—anywhere! And no way she could have dry skin with that supply of creams. A lump of butter wrapped in silk, that's the way I picture her. Poke her anywhere and your finger'd sink right in, she's so fat. And the warm towels, so thick they almost seem padded. No, I'm not putting you on, wiping your ass with one is an experience! You feel like a kid again with all that wadding between your legs. Beats a cruise to Greece! Obviously, my little room can't measure up, it's modest as hell. But it's home! And the hairdresser doesn't get in. *Out!* Anyway, I like it better when he fucks me at the beauty parlor, after hours. Standing up behind the cash register or on a shampoo chair, I don't care. Just have to roll down the iron shutter. Remember, never cross the boss. He doesn't want me to wear panties? I don't wear panties! So it turns Popeye on . . . affectionate big slob . . . Tonight we're going to get ready for Christmas! We're decorating! Decorating! A cute display in the window. 'We'll be working late, girls! I advise you to make yourselves comfortable. Marie! You know all about decorating . . .' Point is he'd like to stick my ass in his window, if he could! Eight, nine at night, a pile of LP's on the hi-fi, us all puttering, arranging, decorating—a regular beehive. 'My wife's probably treating herself to a ski instructor right now!' The bitch! Screwing in Barèges while we string up lights. She doesn't give a shit; they hold out, and she just buys them with her dowry. 'Véronique! The green crepe paper!' 'Yes sir!' (She's the new girl.) 'Oh no! Hell! You frighten me, Véro. Call me Marc. No one's boss around here. Say, you can do my feet, I've got an ingrown toenail.' No two ways, Marc has a knack for creating intimacy . . . Ten o'clock, eleven, the ice has melted in the glasses. 'Well, Monique? That spot on the silver paper? Highlight the wig tree for me.' Véronique, Monique, names ending in -nique. Big Monique is getting sleepy, that uterine infection must be dragging her. 'Marc, be a doll, advance me fifty, for my kid's present. I want to send him something sharp, see, that won't look sleazy next to his father's gift.' He rolls his eyes. 'You're really nuts to knock yourself out, my dear. Besides, I'm sure your kid already has everything a kid could want. God knows what you could be sending him that costs that much!' A piece of shit like him at my place? I'd rather croak! Leave his puss at the parlor, that's what I say. His boots will never dirty *my* doormat. He'd do better to lick it. Yes! That's it! Lick it! On his knees! The little operator with her bare ass under her uniform won't open up. Private property! Nobody gets through the door. Never! Dig? I had my housewarming all by myself. And same for my holidays now. I spend them all alone. At home. Nice and cozy. Just me and the boob tube."

"Stop, you're going to make us cry."

"On the level! In solitary! I make up some excuse and turn down all invitations. Every one. It's very simple, I just couldn't hack catching a whiff of their stinking breath on Christmas Eve.

And I couldn't stand being pawed by their clammy mitts. Even just dancing. So it's better if I hole up in my pad. It wouldn't do to eat their paté de foie gras, drink their Mercier, loll in their Roche and Bobois chairs to watch their flashy tubes, and then nix all the rest, the logical outcome—the slow numbers, the increasing closeness, the sweat breaking out under the strange blazer, the knee starting to make itself felt, then moving in more and more seriously, wedging right between my legs like a ham. The hands you feel flexing up your back, hot through the crepe, then sticking right on your skin, near your neck, on your shoulders . . . The feeling of slowly sinking in a swamp. The buddies who cut half the lights. The mouth that suddenly thinks it can do anything—and rightly so, after all, since you don't even have the balls to react either pro or con. The mouth you put up with, which at least has the advantage of being alive, warm, and doing all the work. You let yourself slide into a room. Out of nowhere some chick shows up to see if you need anything. Sweet of her. The old lady of the dude who's throwing the party—the host, I guess you'd call him. 'Got your pill?' she chimes. 'Yeah,' I answer, 'everything's set, thanks.' I flip out my pill box. She hands me the bathroom glass full of water, with traces of toothpaste on it. 'If you barf, pop another one. Play it smart!' Not a bad chick. Big bouncing knockers. I try to dig myself with all that up front. 'Don't worry,' I tell her, 'I've hardly had anything to drink.' My shirt-sleeve Romeo tries to hold her back: 'Stay! You won't bug us!' The big mama shoves him off and splits, very carefully not closing the door . . . It's too hot, my head is spinning, I toss my shoes in a corner. We hear moans from the next room. A chick soloing on the first chorus. That's why the doors are open . . . Let's get it on, sugar! I let myself be stripped by fat sausagelike fingers with close-clipped, tobacco-stained nails. He's going to rip my dress, the clutz! O.K., there, my fancy outfit hits the floor. All my filmy petals on the rug. Plop! Nothing left but the stem, standing in the middle of the room, swaying, looking sort of dopey. Just the same, the old humper is quite stunned to pick up that the chick, the bitch, hasn't even got a hint of tits! Zilch! A choirboy's chest! 'Shit!' he says to himself, instead of taking me in his arms and helping me forget about it. 'I hope she's no transvestite!' And zap! He checks it out. Whips down my undies. Everything! Fumbles around as if he'd lost something, his key, maybe, or his watch. Whew! Now he's reassured. I'm happy for the bastard. I dive in the sack. It's O.K., the sheets are bearable. Now I get treated to the dude's striptease. He puts on a relaxed show, a man without hang-ups, the sporty type. He flexes all his muscles so he can hardly breathe, undresses painfully, let me tell you, like a war-wounded in a field hospital come to get his bandages changed. I smile and hold my arms out to him, let's get moving, let's get it on. The broad next door is still wailing. Then a second one hits a refrain. A warm atmosphere, as they say . . . But I feel cold, my premenstrual chills. Why couldn't I have gotten the curse for the holidays and copped out on all these parties? 'Cause, I gotta admit, it's best to stay home when you're in that state. O.K., I'll lay the mounting-pleasure number on him, building and building, flashing him signals. Get his rocks off fast! My eyes roll back, I'm panting, my hands clawing. I give him my phony act. The asshole think he's driving me crazy! I let my howls loose in the pad, like an SOS. The others are all ears. Total hush. I'm sure everyone's picking up on it, so I give them a short recital. I'm bent on waking every brat in the building! They'll think Santa's screwing his reindeer! They'll pray for their toys! Because I have a colossal reputation to live up to. An affair with Marie-Ange! They pass the word, my fine friends: 'She's not shy, you can let loose! And man, what an iron constitution! You have a hard time keeping up! She really puts her all into it!' So I do my bit, it's a question of my rating, have to fight for your place at the box office. Get the feeling my rough rider's about to bite the dust! His seat is getting the shakes. I bounce him like a filly. Toss him buck after buck, still whinnying wildly. Unbroken Marie-Ange! The poor bastard clutches the pommel. I go into start after start, racing for the Triple Crown! Trot-gallop! Trot-gallop! Whoa! I rear! That does it, the jockey shoots his wad! Now I can grab a moment's peace. Cheers from the other rooms and a death rattle in my left ear. Why always the left ear? Strange . . . No dude ever drops on the other side. His beard is starting to prick me. I shove the big lug off me a little. With that he sits up, his forearms trembling. Looks at me all humble, my cowboy. Doesn't know what to say to me. You'd think I was the first chick he'd ever laid. 'Course I try to look bowled over. Put on the ecstasy mask laced with gratitude. Zonked, don'tcha know. I even stroke his stubbly cheek a bit. I'll bet it was the best ride of his life. All the bad-mouthing about me faded. 'You happy?' he asks. A serious, pathetic good-looker. Now he's started to respect me. I interest him a lot from the human point of view. 'Very,' I answer. 'The best ever . . .' The poor slob, he beams! 'Me too,' he says. 'It was great. You know . . .' I can feel him hesitating, sprouting a swelled head. Time to pull the rug out from under him. 'Come on, you're not going to pitch me any crap about love?' 'Hell no!' he says. Forces himself to laugh gaily. 'No, not that! But listen, Marie-Ange . . . My parents have a chalet, near Font-Romeu . . . It would be great if you could come spend a couple of days there with me . . . We could ski . . . We can leave tomorrow, if you like—or right now!' 'Impossible,' I explain. 'Can't take off from my job. This is our busiest time. During the holidays we work till nine. Dames have one thing in their heads—hairdos.' 'But what if you quit for good? Wouldn't you like to walk out?' 'Quit what? My job?' 'Yes! Drop the whole thing! Hairdressing's no job for you! Besides, I think we could really get it on together, you and I. When it clicks in the sack, it clicks everywhere!' I ask him his age, just for the record. 'Thirty, just. In November. Next year I'm opening my own office!' 'What's your specialty?' Gastroenterology. And I'll be doing my own X-rays!' When I think that most chicks dream about marrying a doctor! Always running around for consultations. Thumbing through the yellow pages, A to Z. Dreaming up illnesses and making appointments all over town. Stretching out six days a week on white rubber sheets, bare-assed, purring like pussycats, hoping to hook one! Just one little MD. Doesn't do a thing for me! You can have the whole fucking medical corps! But there's one angle you don't dig, doc, a gimmick they never laid on you in med school, and that's that a woman fakes. And I'm the queen of actresses! Been playing the part for ten years!"

"But you didn't fake it with us."

" 'Course not!"

"Why?"

"No danger of its getting around, we don't run in the same

crowd. So, 'Awfully sorry,' I tell him. 'I love hairdressing! Curling is my career! Besides, I can't just sit around. I'm a worker at heart. Also, I have to admit something else. It's like I'm already engaged!' Aha! Gee whiz! That nails his trap shut. He lights a butt, to look more masculine. 'You don't say!' he hands me through the smoke. 'You're sort of a slut, aren't you? Your man in the army or something?' Oh, you big smartass! I haven't even met my fiancé! He hasn't even started taking me out! No idea what the hell he looks like! White hair, yellow, black? He hasn't even showed me the color yet. All I know is I'm waiting for him. Me! Bretêche! Nice young girl in every way! Sports model! Velvet interior! Cleanliness guaranteed! Second-class virginity! Seeks developer. Photographers need not apply. As soon as he shows, I'm his! I'll hang onto him! I won't let go! No demands. Life-style, purchasing power, I don't give a shit about all that. I just ask one thing, just one. You follow me? A specific need! Couldn't be more localized. For years I've been waiting for my little Christmas present. Dying for it. Sometimes wondering if I still believe in it. And yet you can't say I haven't been hanging my ass by the chimney! Maybe I ain't been a good enough girl. Now you dig why I go for spending Christmas Eve alone. I've had my fill of gastroenterologists, future otorhinologists and other PR men, businessmen, lawyers' sons. You can stick your brilliant future up your ass! I'm not for sale, just yours for the taking. I want to be kidnaped. Raped very, very slowly. Awakened! Unlocked! I want to feel shivers! See stars! Pass out! Pant with desire! I hear it's like a plane taking off, and the older you get the longer it lasts. According to Monique, you feel like you're dying. Well, this little beanpole wants to feel that. I can't say no to creeps, can't stop trying, you see, because you never know . . . In the meantime I stay home, away from germs. And decorate a little frosted tree. 'Have a nice evening!' my neighbors say when I get home from work at nine, not a hair out of place. 'Merry Christmas!' They climb up from the cellar with armloads of wine bottles, and the whole building reeks of turkey. 'Thanks! Same to you!' They picture me spending a wild night, bopping around some dance floor in a backless dress. Then I lock myself in with my tube. Nothing but high-class shows. I catch the greatest stars of stage and screen. Slip into my old nylon bathrobe to greet them, minus my makeup! Then hop into bed with my ten-franc jar of caviar and a big bottle of mineral water. At the stroke of midnight I pop a sleeping pill. And go blissfully to sleep, listening to them toting off their huge packages that crackle in the stairway. And the morning after is just another morning. I'm fresh as a daisy and they all have hangovers. In my pad the ashtrays are all empty. It's very exclusive, Marie-Ange's! Quite a joint! Not big, not chic, but she picks up the tab herself. Five hundred and forty-two francs per month, including utilities, for the right to privacy. No use knocking at her door. I don't ask people in. I'm not home for anybody."

"Except us."

"Just a good deed. You looked so lost. But that's an exception, you dig? The only time it's ever happened. Don't talk about other guys to me. My door's locked tighter than a jail. What's more, I'm single in my concrete cocoon. It's not that my husband's on a business trip or my kids away at school. Not at all! I'm what's called a loner. All alone. And plan to stay that way. No kids. No old man. I don't cheat on anyone. I sleep with everybody, and that way no one's jealous! I promise nothing and give everything. But not at my place! I fuck on the outside, on dates, at parties. And I'm not the type to do a number like chicks who pretend not to remember how many guys have laid them! I'm horrified by those bitches who play the whore. I don't believe them. It's impossible! You remember very well, I assure you! Unforgettable, all those drooling mouths, groping hands and the filthy words they whisper in your left ear, especially the old geezers. Memories that won't quit. I have an elphant's head for those things. Like I was still at it. And I know the exact number! Three hundred and forty-seven dudes I've had inside me! Now what? Don't pull those faces! From age fifteen to twenty-five, that's nothing to scream about! It doesn't even add up to one dude a week, I figured it out."

"Did you count us in the total?"

" 'Course not!"

"Wow! You mean you don't remember we screwed you?"

"I don't call that screwing."

"Then what do you call it? Spearfishing?"

"No. Making love a little, that's all. Trying to make a girl happy."

"And we succeeded?"

"Sorry to say, no. But I gotta admit you didn't goof off on the job. 'A' for effort!"

"And the other three hundred and forty-seven?"

"Batting zero. Struck out. All flunked . . . Say, I'll bet you'd have dug me when I was knocked up. There was something to feel up then! You wouldn't have known me! Had to buy a bra! My tits hurt when I ran. None of my pants fit. And I barfed all day. During shampoos—you dig the trouble it caused. Within two shakes of flashing everything. They could've had egg shampoos, burger shampoos, spaghetti shampoos . . . Oh, I was no bargain, except for the boobs."

"You got a kid?"

"Five! But I've lost track of them. They're all a little pissed at me because I chucked them down the sewer . . . barely formed. At three months you can't tell the sex yet. Plop! they go. A dinky little plop in the sewer water. If they'd somehow survived, they'd have wriggled out of their newspaper and crossed the Mediterranean. Very early swimmers—at that age they're like tadpoles. They'd have gotten past snorkelers, outboards, paddle boats. Riding the waves onto the beach in Tunisia. Hey, I was dumb, I should have put them in bottles. Little SOS's with their eyes glued shut, transparent, in watertight jars. But at those times you can't think of everything. You goof, especially at the street corner when a squad car shows. 'Hey, lady, what was in that package?' 'A close relative . . .' But I'm pretty lucky! Never needed to go to the hospital! Two days of probing and they were gone, just like an enema. I didn't even feel the fifth one come out! I woke up and there the little bastard was."

Suddenly she clammed up. Just as we drove through Le Puy. It was weird. Then, as we left the city, got out into the country, she started up again. "My parents live in Le Puy and I haven't seen them for five years. I'm glad I'm out of that hole."

"You dig them, don't you?"

196

"Oh, yeah! We get along O.K. We're always helping each other out."

"What do they do?"

"Nothing. They sold their store and live off the income. They used to be jewelers."

"They old?"

"Fifty. They've always been fifty. When I was born they were fifty."

"You the only daughter?"

"Shit yes! Can't you tell I'm an only child? Seems I hurt my mother so much coming out that she swore, 'Never again! I'd rather adopt one!' She was narrow in the hips, in her mind, everywhere. And I came early. There was a misunderstanding about the date. We weren't reading each other then, Ma and I. We didn't communicate. The cord was full of static. I showed up two months early! Took the woman completely by surprise. She was in labor a whole day and night. What a scene. You'd think I was clawing my way out. Deliberately. With my fingernails. Cured her of fucking, the poor thing. She clutched the bedposts. 'Never mind the baby!' she was hollering. I can still hear her. After that, you can tack on fifteen more years of agony. Years packed with pain. Like a jail term! Fifteen years of hard labor, sniffing, inspecting, popping in, checking on me every second. Weeding out my bad habits, nasty ways, lousy manners and dirty tricks. She'd disown me: 'You take care of her! I give up!' Pa'd look at me all flabbergasted while she went up to lock herself in her room. 'My little Marie-Ange,' he'd say to me, 'you're a terrible disappointment.' We'd eat together in the kitchen, separated by the newspaper he'd hold up to his nose, carefully folded in four. All I could see was his bald head, wrinkles and constantly raised eyebrows. Then he'd take me to the store, to keep an eye on me while I did my homework, since it took me hours. I couldn't do it fast like all the other kids. I followed him under the streetlights, lugging my school bag. Sometimes he took my hand. Then I felt I was leading him to his overtime, like a trained animal . . . We went in by the back way and sat silently, face to face. I'd unpack my pitiful notebooks in the middle of all the watches and clocks.

197

I'd try on a few wristwatches to see how they looked. He'd get right to work, doing repair after repair while I watched him under the lamp without moving. His suspenders, his visor and his special glasses made him look like a fly, and all those tiny tools, like so many insect legs, stingers, probes, tongues dipping into the weird flowerlike movements. A funny world with the iron shutter as its horizon and clocks ticking in the shadows. We never bugged each other. One night, around midnight—which always rang out fifteen times at different intervals—he said, 'Come on, it's time to go to bed.' As we went out he took my hand. Only instead of heading home he dragged me off in the opposite direction. 'Where we going?' I asked. No answer. It was foggy, I remember, and I couldn't see at all where we were going. Suddenly we stopped in front of a big café with steamy windows and he pushed me in a revolving door. I found myself inside. Lots of noise, light, heat and smoke. He took me by the arm over to a corner table and we sat down, the school-bag between us on the seat. 'Two beers,' he told the waiter. There were tons of people there, but he didn't know them. We were served two huge mugs that spewed with foam. We drank silently. We felt good. He put a hand on my arm abruptly and, without looking at me, said, 'You know, Marie-Ange . . . You're almost a young lady now . . . It's time for you to know about certain things . . .'

" 'Yes, Pa.'

" 'For example, take your mother. Well, I don't give two shits about her! You understand?'

"At that moment he turned, took me by the shoulders and squeezed me very hard with his little watchmaker's hands used to fiddling with the most delicate mechanisms. 'And you don't give a barrel of shit about her either! Am I right, honey? Neither of us gives a shit about her! Not one shit!' His voice was full of tears. We started to laugh like a couple of fools, we were in stitches. But when we got home, he wasn't laughing anymore. He saw the light through the window and dropped my hand . . ."

"And now?" Pierrot asked.

"Well, he's in a wheelchair and they never adopted another kid."

Yssingeaux, Monistrol-sur-Loire, autoroute, Saint-Etienne bypass, toll, Lyon, Mâcon, Chalon, autoroute exit, five francs, we took N. 83 A, heading for Dole.

"The conversation's dragging," Marie-Ange announced. "I get the feeling you're losing me again. Hey, boys! There's someone in the back seat! You'd better check your rear-view mirror, it's a chick! You dig? A woman! Who's dropped everything to follow you two bums in fag's clothing! I bet you don't even wonder why! You think it's perfectly normal. Of course! Good God, what could be more natural? She's quit her job, her apartment, just like that, without telling a soul, not even taking a change of clothes. Nothing odd about that! In a week another little shampooist will replace her, a brunette, for a change, with hairy legs. What's the diff? Now, let's see . . . She's young. And thinks it's a gas. She's going underground just for the head trip, to see what it's like to have the man on your tail. So she should shut up! When they need her, they'll just whistle! Only they won't turn and smile at me, these guys. No way. They won't stop to buy me a lemonade or anything. Not a word. Just the soft purr of their sumptuous limo. But I can't complain, I'm parking my ass in it, aren't I?"

At that I stopped at the entrance to a forest road. Mainly because I couldn't see anymore, I was bushed, but also because our passenger was making my head spin.

"What is a woman, huh? You got any ideas on the subject? I'm asking you! How are they made, in your opinion? And how do they work? What goes on inside their heads? Is it hollow? Liquid? The thousand-franc question, you got thirty seconds . . . Ah! That did it! The gentlemen have stopped to look at me! Dig my chick head! Thanks! I'm flattered to have scored the attention of such connoisseurs. Me, a poor girl, just a miserable female. It's attaching too much importance to me. Excuse me for wasting your precious time. Well, what do you think of the slut, the piece of ass, the fucking twat, the cunt, the slit, the bloody gash? To your taste? She talks a bit too much, for a retard. The dumb cunt's boring you. But let me tell you one thing—a woman is made to be gawked at, or else she fades away. Gets old. It's like being in jail. I need your eyes devouring all of me! Your eyes do me good, they warm me. I feel them on my skin like little puppy noses. That's what a woman is! Here! Here are two hands. Two hands of a woman. No wedding ring. Feel how soft they are! Manicured regularly with cream so they don't get chapped. Lemon to make them white. Look at the fingertips, the fine skin, the delicate oval nails! Carefully filed, covered with colorless polish. See how pale the moons are! Bend my fingers! Rest your cheeks in my palms! Did you dig my lifeline? Sliced right in the middle—sudden death in the bloom of youth! Enjoy my hands before they get cold! Jean-Claude! Pierrot! No kidding, squeeze hard! That's what a woman is! The blond fuzz. The fragile wrist. The tiny muscles. Take them! They're yours! I came on this trip so you could have them! What? You don't want them? They smell bad? They disgust you? You think I've fluffed too many buns?"

A slap! That was all she deserved. "We don't give a shit about your rap!"

"That ain't so! You *do* care! I have to tell you everything, absolutely everything! Marc used to lend me to his friends too. He'd send me to people who were supposed to put up bread to modernize his salon. And I got my little rake-off. Then, one day . . ."

"You going to shut up or not?"

We both shook her like an apple tree. "We don't give a shit who the hell you are or what the fuck you've done! We love you like you are, that's all! You've been great to us! And now we can't hack it without you! You dig? So cut the tears! Sit up, Marie-Ange, look at us and give us your hands. There are three of us! You understand what that means? Three!"

"Oh yes, hold me tight. When you showed up at my place last night . . . You can't imagine . . . When I saw you there, outside my door, so lost, I said to myself, Thank you, thank you. I'll be able to take care of them. And then, at night, when I held you in my arms and felt my shoulders getting wet . . . What did you do? Did you kill someone?"

"Yes and no . . ."

"I don't want to know. To me, you're absolutely straight. You're the first totally straight people I've ever met."

We drove on. And Marie-Ange started to snooze, totally wasted, in the back seat.

"Marie, Marie. Wake up!"

"Huh? What? What's happening?"

"Refreshment stop. We're going to get some lemonade."

"No kidding! Shit! How nice you are! I'm so lucky!"

"Then hop out!"

"I can't, I've lost my shoes."

"Will you two step on it? It's cold!"

"Creep! You'd better remember how to act with a lady. You help her on with her shoes. You hold the door for her. Help her on with her raincoat. O.K.? Some manners, please!"

"What's that music? A dance?"

"Any objections?"

"I look too grubby!"

Nobody home at the ticket office. We all went in together, arm in arm, Marie-Ange in the middle, looking outasight, nose in the air. The band was playing some hard rock. Not bad, these locals. The electric guitars were working out. Between the banks of speakers there wasn't room for a whisper or a sigh. You'd have to talk in sign language, but no one felt like rapping. All you could think was one thing: how to save your eardrums.

We bopped our way through the bursts of decibels to a table at the edge of the dance floor. The basses rumbled in our guts. The high notes cut us in half. We sat down and trained our eyes on the noble assembly.

No one was dancing. The floor was empty under the Chinese lanterns. So why the musical frenzy? The drummer, by himself, could have passed for a wrecking company, beating the stage to bits with his riffs. The only one who moved, by the way. Because his buddy guitarists stood like limp statues melting in the heat, really wasted. Only their ringed fingers flashed from time to time. But when they hit a chord, we were blasted right out of our seats. Who were they playing for? Why get into such a sweat—perspiration on their mauve T-shirts—when no one was dancing?

No one was dancing but everyone was eyeing each other across the dance floor. The joint was packed. Short on oxygen.

On the left, an army of guys and dolls, filthy, long-haired, on drugs for sure.

In the middle, behind his bar, the owner, white as a sheet.

On the right, a group of rich types, clean-cut dudes, with blazers, ties, and short haircuts.

We were on the right, in the front row.

And everyone was gawking at us.

Especially the gang across the way, the longhairs, the trash, the trouble-makers. They were digging our jackets, our moccasins, creased pants, and Marie's legs.

And just waiting for us to start something.

There was one big joker across the way who was giving Marie-Ange a lewd smile. A dipshit with an Afro. He laid his red boots out in the middle of the dance floor. His boots and spurs. All you could see was his fly.

He made a come-on to Marie-Ange. Obscene. With his finger. I felt her hand clutch mine, icy.

Someone tapped me on the shoulder from behind. I turned around. He flashed his brass knuckles, a nice family boy, perfumed, with a polka-dot bow tie. I declined. Politely.

The ugly frizzed goon made a second pass at Marie-Ange. With a beer can in his crotch. Inviting her to have a taste. His buddies thought he was so funny.

The band was still wailing full tilt.

We traded insults like deaf-mutes.

I saluted the enemy, third finger raised. The crowd behind us snickered.

Then the joker lifted one arm high and, with the flat of his hand, gave me a tactful signal to cool it.

That brought me to my feet. Marie-Ange held me back. I pushed her aside. Pierrot looked pale. Tight as a bowstring. With his hand in his pocket. Who had the gun? Me. He had the razor.

Red-Boots beckoned me over with his dirty finger.

I went over. To beat him to a pulp, bash his big honky-nigger kisser.

I stopped two feet short. Out of range of his boots.

He grinned, the faggot. He pointed at his fly. He showed a milky glob of spit, between his teeth, and played with it.

Not for long . . . Holy shit! Who heaved that bottle? He started pissing blood, it was all over his hands, he was blinded

202

and didn't look so smart-ass anymore. He just looked surprised.

I turned around: a stampede. They charged forward, whipped blackjacks out from under their blazers, everyone got to their feet, what a scene, chicks screaming, scattering in every direction, one there, right in front of me, her cheek exploded under the black leather, she crumpled at my feet, I picked her up under the arms, dragged her across the floor. Where was Pierrot? There was Marie-Ange coming to help. Where was the can in this fucking ballroom? The chick had passed out. We laid her out on the tiles under the sink, a bag of bones, a nothing groupie, her stockings ripped. I grabbed the grimy hand towel, jammed it under the faucet. "No!" Marie-Ange shrieked. "It's too filthy!" She opened her bag, got out a small cardboard tube —what the hell was it?—tugged on it, and pulled out a piece of cotton she held by a string. She gently dabbed the chick's face, who slowly revived, looked at us whimpering, then recognized us.

"Bunch of shits!" she screamed. "Slut, whore!" she spat at Marie-Ange, spit mixed with blood. At that moment I heard the siren.

"The fuzz!" hollered Pierrot, charging into the can. "Let's split!"

"No way!" I answered. "Too late! Put your tie on and comb your hair!"

They busted in, pistols drawn. "Nobody move! Hands up!"

We strolled out calmly, impeccably dressed, looking scared. The band played on. "Can't you shut those monkeys up?" the inspector barked, a young dude with a mustache, blue suit and authority. At a sign from the owner, the music stopped. Not a peep out of them. The cops dragged the bums off, Red-Boots and company, no sweat. We yanked the bloody groupie out of the can and headed for the paddy wagon, my foot up her ass. She was clutching Marie-Ange's cotton against her cheek. Polka-dot Tie stepped up to the inspector and opened his crocodile wallet. "O.K., O.K.," the slick dick said. "You'll be called as a witness." They quickly checked our IDs. Pierrot and I didn't ring any bells. Style is everything—we looked rich. They were in a rush and took off. We found ourselves with the good guys. The band started something slow. Music to heal your wounds.

They couldn't hear it at the station house. I let go of the revolver and took my hand out of my pocket.

Marie-Ange came to rub against me, nice and easy. We were surrounded by dancers, more and more of them, local dudes and chicks, all relieved and flashing one thing: getting laid. Mouth to mouth, to make up for lost time, like the newly liberated. The cops had come just in time . . . My hands were still shaking. But Marie-Ange smiled. "Don't worry, it's all over." An angel. She glued herself to me, buried her face in my shoulder to reassure me. That's how a woman protects you. Plus she made herself very small. Slipped her hand in under my jacket, placed it over my heart. "You're not going to have a heart attack, are you?" Female fragility, the best remedy. I felt my pulse slow down.

"I'm scared," I said, "scared of going to jail." Visibility limited. Hair, backs of necks, shoulders. Steam bath of local sweat billowing out at me through Marie-Ange's perfume, my oxygen. One big family of Siamese twins attached by the mouth, devouring one another. It must have been Saturday, I figured. "Did Pierrot throw the bottle?"

"No," she answered. "It came from behind."

I knew it. He wouldn't have done that. I spotted him through the forest of heads. He was twiddling his thumbs, moody, sitting in front of his lemonade among the empty chairs. "You going to dance with him?"

"All night! He's prettier than you!" She squeezed me even tighter. "But you're stronger! And smart!"

The fuckhead, the sweet fuckhead. She fit against me so nicely. It worked well, her not having any tits, we could glue ourselves closer, more intimately. There wasn't room for a flea between us, unless he was very cramped, his stinger squashed. The buttons on her dress were hurting me. A very slow number with a lot of riffs. Just made for an impromptu couple. Marie-Ange and Jean-Claude. What the fuck were we doing there anyhow? Reeling at the center of a mass of people, a human herd sensually swaying in place, with us stuck in the middle. Dancing butt to butt. One in your arms and one at your ass. In front, a clinging vine. Behind, some ham bones. Both sides rubbing hard. I spotted Polka-dot Tie at the bar. He was buying drinks for his

204

buddies, while Marie-Ange, the sneak, jabbed me with her pubic bone.

"You could at least get a little hard-on," she said, "out of politeness!"

"Sorry," I answered, "something happened. Maybe someday I'll tell you about it . . ."

"A woman?" She held her face up to mine, her crinkled blue eyelids, her mouth—a fruitful invitation.

"Yes, a woman."

I kissed her, my Siamese twin, my hard-luck kid sister. Her moist sympathy comforted me. Taste of strawberry, taste of cherry. Red currant and raspberry . . . A strange lady had moved all the way to the graveyard. A ghostly lady of ill repute. I knew what you were mourning. Impossible to find flowers, off-season everything's closed. So I thought of a few fruits . . . Thank you, mademoiselle, I'm very touched. Your lips do me good. I'd like you to meet my brother. The youngest, unfortunately, was unable to be here. Forcibly detained. He was her favorite. She shares our grief, our distant relative . . . She moved closer and closer. Commiserated with her eyes closed, her tongue indulgent, warm and wet between her nibbling teeth. Our tongues touched, she taught me her language, had a gift for special dialects. A slow funeral. A procession under the Chinese lanterns. In the heart of a useless city, the shadows of a palace, under the moldings of an abandoned bedroom, red and black carnivorous flowers grew on a bed soaked with blood, reaching their stems up toward the headlights of a truck on the cciling, cracked Russian leather, odor of greenhouse, a bouquet of emphysemas, faded for the opening of the season. A gust of wind and it all blows away, to the amazement of the valet . . . Now I was watching them, she was dancing with my brother, playing an active part in his pain, hanging on his neck, clinging to his lips, red tears between her legs on a wad of pure white cotton. Polka-dot Tie and his buddies, jeering, zeroed in on her. I saw them at the bar elbowing each other, laughing their heads off, glass in hand. I went to join the comedians, couldn't miss out on that one.

"Well, guys? Having fun?"

They handed me a glass. "A drink?"

"No thanks, I'm not thirsty."

"Not like your girl friend! With you two guys filling her cup, she ain't about to run dry!"

"And your mother," I shot back. "How many dudes did it take to make a creep like you?"

The gun was already in my hand, well-balanced, nice and heavy, nice and black, my faithful toy, and I aimed it right at their guts.

Pierrot handed out the punches from behind, like a bad guy. I dug that. One on each ear at the same time, like swatting mosquitoes. Polka-dot Tie didn't feel too good. He'd be deaf for a while, wouldn't hear his old lady nagging at him.

We copped their wallets, blackjacks and brass knuckles. The owner, white as a sheet again, watched us back out of the joint. Running a dance hall is no easy job these days.

We were out in the cold again. Quick, the car. To nix any desire they might have to get our license number I emptied my piece in the general direction of the ticket office. Terrif *bang-bang-bang.*

We tore off, no lights. Stroke of luck, it was foggy. That's the advantage of the Jura. Besançon twenty miles.

Rundown of the haul: nine blackjacks, five brass knuckles, not quite five hundred francs and three membership cards in a mysterious political party. We tossed the empty wallets out the window.

A dump called Baume-les-Dames. A hotel, Hôtel de la Gâre, looming in the fog. In the silence of the pissing night, an engine approaches. A two-cylinder engine. A car—or let's say, the lights of a car, or, even better, the haloes of the lights—stops. A screech of wet brakes in front of the hotel. A door opens. Someone gets out. The door slams. A pale silhouette climbs the steps of the hotel. Dainty ankles, blond curls: it's a woman. Bundled up in a raincoat with the collar turned up. Young and pretty. Perhaps even a virgin, who knows, although these days you only meet sluts.

("Just the facts, please.")

She enters. It reeks. She heads for the desk. Behind this desk—labeled RECEPTION—what does the mysterious traveler see? An orange night-light, a ticking alarm clock and a pitiful night clerk, asleep in his chair, his head resting on the pages of a phone book. "My good man?"

("No! Not 'my good man'! I shake him, that's all!")

A slender hand on the old man's shoulder. The woman shakes him with her fingertips, a little disgusted by his greasy vest. Nothing doing: the night clerk is out like a light. Copping Zs. Your typical alert concierge. The poor woman finds herself in the distasteful position of having to take a firmer grip on the shoulder, clasping the flabby flesh, shaking harder. The clerk slowly comes to life.

("We'd have been smarter to let him sleep in peace and rip off his cash box.")

"Good evening, sir," says the mysterious lady. "By any chance, by some miracle, do you have a room left?"

"For when?"

"Right now."

"Oh dear, oh dear!" He rolls his eyes, swamped in advance at the thought. "What time is it, anyway?" He squints at the clock. "Three o'clock! Do you realize? Three o'clock!" Then the traveler opens her purse and takes out—guess what!

("A pear?")

A hundred smackers! "Here," she says. "Awfully sorry to wake you . . ." The bread promptly vanishes.

"Fine, fine, that's all right," says the old geezer. "We'll see what we can do . . . Three o'clock!" He studies the register. "Number seven, would that suit you?"

The young woman is not sure. "Does it have a double bed?"

"Ah, madame, it's all we have left! Bathroom and W.C. Our most expensive room!"

"Perfect. Then it must have a double bed."

Suspicious look from the night man. "Why a double bed? How many is it for?"

"Just me, but I'm very tired. I've driven all the way from Florence. And I love to spread out. You have better dreams that way."

"But, madame, think about it! Would we put a single bed in a room with a bath? Now really!"

Fine, good, deal made, fifty francs for the night. The woman fills out the form: Bretêche, Marie-Ange, bust zero, sex feminine anyhow, check it out if you like! Single, born in Puy, in '47, of watchmaker parents, tightwads, forgotten . . . Nationality French, with all the chic, bitchiness and racy savoir faire that implies.

"Here, this is your key. Second floor. The elevator's not working."

She goes upstairs. Rug worn down to the nub, dying rubber plants, chocolate-brown halls, shoes outside the doors, yawning salesmen's clodhoppers. She looks for her number, finds it, goes in, switches on the lights, funeral-parlor furniture, restaurant light fixtures. She tosses her raincoat over a chair and goes back downstairs.

The night clerk is just dozing off again.

"Please," she asks, "would it be possible to get a bottle of water, mineral water? To drink during the night? I always get very hot at night. And also—this would be terrific—a few sandwiches, I don't know, a plate of cold cuts, anything, some leftover pie, some cheese, some pickles? Haven't eaten since Florence, you realize? Driving like a maniac."

"Oh dear, oh dear." The night man limps off and disappears inside the kitchen door, a double door to avoid waiters' collisions. The perfect opportunity. She rushes for the exit, races down the steps, there she is outside, beside the car, a beat-up Dyane 6, she opens the door. "Hurry! Second floor, room seven!" Two jokers, who'd been hiding between the seats, spring out, disappear into the hotel like rats. It's us, Jean-Claude and Pierrot! We tiptoe fast down the hall. Room 7, we enter, God but it's ugly! We strip, big laugh, we hide under the sheets, with just our chins sticking out, warming up her spot.

She arrives, the little darling, with a big round tray. Set it on the bed, please. Delightful. You been working here long? We fall to. Sausages, cold meats, bread, butter and cheese. Always so pleasant, these little moments. Gotta admit, France has the eats. What bouquet, the Badoit! A great year! And just the right temperature, room temperature. A little midnight snack. This is the life, the palace life! And we're no strangers to it! "No talking or laughing, I'm supposed to be alone." We scarf in silence. Terrific sausage. Stupid fight over it. Someone passing in the hall. A poor slob without a private can. We don't have to go out. We have the best room in the joint, all the modern conveniences. A Jacob Delafon shit bowl on a pedestal. We all give it a try. What comfort! What a seat! Beautiful instrument to work with, very reliable. A throne for Marie-Ange. The tart sits down. Piss-piss. Trickle of water like a leaky faucet. Paper. She really is dainty. Wash-up. Little laundry. My period's all over. Peace for the next twenty-eight days. The panty hose will dry overnight on that big radiator. We hit the sack. Turn out the lights. Find her shoulders again, her arms around our necks. We fall asleep not a peep, snuggled against her skin . . .

("But I kept waking up. Trucks kept passing, shifting down in the fog. You both twitched like fleas, moving from nightmare to nightmare. I caught knee jabs. Around five o'clock someone climbed on top of me blindly, looking for my hole with his white cane. I guided him, did my thing. Hardly in position when he started snoring! No good, boys! You'll have to go see a shrink! I fell asleep at dawn with the first trains, all cramped . . .")

The next morning we wake up late, like actors on tour. Marie-Ange rings for room service. "A huge breakfast," she orders, "send me everything." We hide in the can with Jacob and Delafon. And give it a good workout.

Ensisheim wasn't far, only a hundred more miles. We'd be there by lunchtime.

Trice to the information obtained by Maître Jumeau, his court-appointed lawyer of the Strasbourg bar, Jacques was set free on May 18, at 8:30 A.M. exactly.

Pierrot and I were there, outside the Ensisheim prison.

We'd been waiting almost a month, living like paupers. No matter how miraculously Marie-Ange scrimped on food, our funds were dwindling dangerously close to zero. And yet we'd eat the same stew three days running. She'd reheat it, stretch it out, and each time it would be better. Then she'd stick the remains in the mashed potatoes. "Easy!" she'd tell us. "Easy! Or there won't be any left for tonight." And it started getting to us, especially coming from a chick who didn't know her place. "One more lick, Marie-Ange! Don't be hard on us." But the little bitch did have a knack for cooking. An artist! We stuffed ourselves with her sauces. "Hey, you pigs! Take it easy! If this keeps up there won't be any left for me!" She crammed us with pancakes, out of charity. "You're getting fat!" she'd rib us. "Look at those stomachs!" Classic ploy, typically female. "Wrong!" we'd snap. "More like we're getting skinny!" "Then why are your belts unbuckled?" "For comfort. O.K.?" Come on! We couldn't let our egos be done in like that. "With us the woman eats standing up—when she eats!"

At night we'd get up on the sly, stomachs rumbling, weak in the knees, looking for a little piece of ass. While she worked feverishly on one of us, the other would sneak off to the pantry. With a pointed knife, we'd carve rat nibbles in the leftovers.

210

At dawn, always up with the sun, she'd start her hollering: "No, you guys, no! That's going too far! I'm turning my apron in!" Her buns would shake with rage. We'd wake up all surprised, fall out of bed at attention. A terrible urge to piss. "Shit!" we'd shout. "Those fucking rats again!" "Couldn't be the fucking boys, by any chance?" Morning hard-ons . . . "Well," she'd announce, "it's quite simple—I'm quitting! The little housewife is through! You can keep house yourselves!" And she'd start grinding the coffee. "But look, honey, no wonder! This wire netting is all ripped off! A fox could have made it into this larder! Pierrot, get me the hammer, I'll nail it back down." Sitting there dismayed, she'd just keep grinding and grinding, holding the old coffee mill between her legs. "This is really a great marriage! It's got everything! Eating and fucking! That's all you think about!" We'd truck over, eyeing her. "Get dressed," we'd say. "You'll catch cold. Give us the coffee, we'll do the grinding." She'd smile, like a good kid. "You dummies," she'd answer. "You might hurt yourselves."

We'd stroll out into the sunshine, take a leak in the canal, the first pleasure of the day.

It was an old hauler's house, tiny, with the date over the door: 1883. "Something quiet and isolated," Marie-Ange had explained to the real estate agent. "I adore solitude. And picturesque, if possible. You see, I'm also a Sunday painter." A student writing her thesis and a Sunday painter! "Well, if you're an artist . . ." the real estate agent had answered.

A terrific idea. So quiet and isolated that we could sunbathe bare-assed all day. Not a house or road in sight. Nothing. Just the weed-choked towpath, barely wide enough for the Dyane.

The canal, from what we could tell, led from the Rhône to the Rhine. A hell of a long way. It must have been true, too, from the number of barges that passed lazily by between the poplars. German, Dutch, a little of everything. Europe parading by under our noses, always with the same rolled-up sleeves and the same laundry on the clotheslines. The underwear of the Common Market drying. We busted our guts guessing the country of origin from the bulge of the bra cups and the width of the undies. When it came to size, the Belgians took the cake.

211

Sometimes a woman hanging out her laundry would float past Marie-Ange hanging out ours, and they would wave at each other. None of those folks were put out at seeing our asses, but then we were tanned, done to a turn. The guys ogled Marie-Ange, and the chicks examined our credentials. Red-faced old mamas called to us in their dialects. We tipped our straw hats back. And the same at siesta time, when Marie-Ange gave herself to us in the shade of the willow trees. The barges passed silently, idling their engines. The papa, in his suspenders, would put his arm around his old lady, or the mama, suddenly serious, would bend down and whisper in her daughter's ear.

A few of them stopped. We had a little chat. We accepted the invitation to go aboard, and drank to it with a glass of white wine, schnapps, or slivovitz in a dark cabin. We'd have to back down some narrow steps, watching our heads. We'd drink at water level in the coolness. *Santé, prosit,* for once it was the real stuff, you knew by the taste! We'd munch on leftover eel, country-style, beef braised in beer, or herring. Snacks on the house. Got it all figured out, these bargemen. And far from fucked up! No one to hassle them. No neighbors. Traveling with their houses like snails. Wall fridge, butane gas, boob tube. Drifting along far from highways, cars and cops. Must be a cool way to lay low. Good dodge for crossing frontiers. Buddy up to them, that's what we should've done. River-hitchhiked. Headed for Antwerp, Amsterdam or Hamburg, circling from lock to lock forever, making love to Marie on the upper bunk, in the middle of a sluice gate, while tulip fields rose into view outside the portholes. A clothesline full of T-shirts against a background of whirling windmills.

It was Marie who managed our budget. She did the shopping herself, never wasting a cent. She followed the food-price guide in the papers. Tomatoes were dropping: we'd have *pipérade*. We fed our faces with stuff on sale.

She'd lucked into a little market not far away, in a village with an unpronounceable name. Hoofing there, so as not to burn up gas. And as late as possible, at closing time, to catch the sales of leftover produce, three heads of lettuce for the cost of one, Camembert at half price, which had to be eaten right away. Sometimes even flowers that were starting to droop, which they gave her for a song or just laid on her because she was pretty.

Twice a week, while the Dyane slept under the trees, battery disconnected, she put in two miles going, two miles back, singing, happy. "Walking's good for you," she said to reassure us, "it melts away your spare tire and firms up your calves, stomach and buns. Nothing better for a chick. Besides, the country is so beautiful."

We'd watch her bop off along the canal, perky, a blade of grass in her teeth, her basket on her arm. We'd settle in for a little fishing, hats over our noses. We caught a few fish, which Marie fixed for supper, with a squeeze of lemon and a glass of white wine.

She'd come back to us all red and sweaty, a perspiring lobster, perfumed with the odors of her market basket: Muenster, onions, chives. We'd take her smart little housewife's things —her basket, shoes, dress and everything else—and give her something to drink. We checked her calves, stomach and buns. They were getting firmer, like a farmer's wife's. At first she complained of stiffness, and we massaged her. "You'll get over it," we told her, "it's just the first few days. Everything's tough at first, you have to know how to push yourself." As the weeks passed she got hardened, became a real pro at long-distance walking. "You're clocking the miles on your pedometer, we're going to have to give you a little tune-up." We popped her tiny blisters with a burnt needle, laid her down so she could rest. "Put your legs up," we advised, "the blood circulates better." Then we treated ourselves to romps on her flesh, like country dances, with the smells of the market, the dust of the roads and the rustling of the bushes. It was all there. We'd start to whoop, "My lettuce! Buy my lettuce! My onions! Look at my beautiful leeks! Who's going to buy my watercress?" We wouldn't let her wash so she'd keep all those good sweaty odors baked by the sun. Gone was the perfect little shampooist! Her hair was straight and her hands rough from doing laundry.

In view of the slow but sure drop in our buying power, she decided—plucky as ever—to go look for some paid work. We would have looked for jobs ourselves but couldn't because of our fucked-up IDs. She made the rounds of all the hairdressers in Mulhouse, listing her qualifications. No one needed a shampooist, their staffs were full. But they took down her address just in case. You never know when someone's going to quit.

Pierrot and I didn't budge. We didn't go to town or indulge in any extras. No eating out, dances or flicks. Just the bare essentials, like old folks living off their pensions. Our only extra was the newspaper, which Marie brought us from the market so we could keep up with the news, see if by chance we were being mentioned in some scary or insulting way. But for the time being, we'd hit oblivion, dropped off the hit parade. Had to admit we'd totally neglected our PR. On the other hand, we did note a big increase in the crime rate, with all sorts of violent acts. The good weather, the heat perhaps, fanning the flames of lust.

Our only treat was Marie-Ange, who gave us some high moments. Marie-Ange and her problem. Because no matter how regularly, passionately and sincerely we fucked her, there was no way to shake her out of her frigidity. Might as well be trying to get blood from a turnip. But we went into the matter—deep into it. Night and day we attacked the question. Slugging away, stubborn bastards, prospecting for gold. But above all, pissed. Math majors who couldn't figure the answer to a simple problem. A first-grade problem about pipes and faucets which we hassled with like dunces, sure the answer was right under our noses. It became a point of honor. We really put our hearts into unlocking the little chick. Worst of all, she'd apologize, afraid she was a drag. A pitiful sight, when she smelled so good. "Forget it," she'd say, "that's just the way I am, there's nothing you can do about it, I wasn't made right. I must be short some chromosome." She had the sad air of a broken watch. Her parents, those watchmakers, hadn't even left her with a working wind-up. Awful feeling of failure. Our tools started to look too small, outdated, pathetic. Depression set in.

Pierrot and I consulted each other when she was away. We haggled about the diagnosis, one eye on our fishing lines. We dreamed up new treatments.

"Let me tell you something about that chick—no one's ever

courted her, I mean really wooed her. That's what she needs. We have to stop thinking of her as a hole."

"You break me up! Shit, we're nice enough to her."

"Maybe not."

So we agreed to pour on the sweet nothings. We handed out compliments, tender words, little attentions. At first Marie-Ange looked at us like we'd lost our marbles, then smiled, touched, but in fact she was wounded, because too much kindness, when you're not used to it, can hurt, like all good things you've never experienced—champagne, for example, or the sun. She'd take us by the arms and stand there, leaning against us not saying beans, as if catching her breath after a shock. We'd found the chink in her armor, now all we had to do was plunge in, make a forced entry, lay siege till she surrendered.

At night we'd chat with her for hours—softly and very gently, as if we were talking to a kid who gets nightmares—smoking in the dark, sharing a pitcher of water, till she fell into a peaceful sleep. "You're not alone anymore," we'd tell her, "you'll never be frightened again or have cold feet or be wakened by a bad dream. Now you're with two brothers, two buddies, two old-time friends. We'll wipe out everything and start over again. A clean slate." Heavy raps close to her pillow so she'd finally melt, tremble and shake like a leaf.

We wanted to anticipate her every desire, but she didn't have any. She didn't interrupt us, didn't argue, she always said, "Yes," or "O.K.," or "If it turns you on." We would have liked her to be possessive, demanding, even bitch a little, as a healthy sign. But all she wanted was the sun, and for us to scratch her back, following very precise directions: "Up higher. More to the right. A little more . . . Stop! There! Ahhh . . ." She adored that.

We didn't leave her alone for a second. We watched her cook, went bananas over her recipes, her way with eggs, which she cracked, separated and whipped at a dizzying speed, turning out mayonnaise in a jiffy, floating island, chopped egg for decoration. Sitting there like we were at the theater, entranced, we dug every little detail—like when she'd knead dough, her hair in her face, a dish towel for an apron, a dab of flour under her nose where she'd scratched herself. We'd help out by giving advice, suggestions about the menu. "Suppose you made us a Paris-Brest?" we'd say. We kept our star scrimper company while she peeled potatoes or cried over the onions. We'd sharpen her knives for her. Whenever she washed the dishes we'd hang around so she wouldn't feel alone. We'd eye her, sipping our coffee. "You know you're beautiful?" we'd ask. It was so true—especially when she trudged up from the cellar all sweaty and grimy, with her bucket full of coal—that as she passed we'd block her, sit her on our laps and bounce her up and down.

We'd do justice to all her meals, piling on the compliments. We'd roll on the floor like dogs, begging for a little extra. We'd ask for seconds. Especially her sauces, so natural and spontaneous. And her wonderful gravies. Respectfully, we'd tuck her skirt up, lovingly fuck her, handling her with kid gloves, daytime, nighttime, inside, outside, in the shade, in the sun, under the trees by the canal, on the grass and in the flowers. She'd smile, happy. But her lust wasn't aroused, her flesh stayed lifeless, like it was disconnected. None of our cures worked.

"You really don't feel a thing?" we'd ask.

"Yes . . . Like a swelling . . . And then the rubbing . . ."

"Concentrate, for Chrissake!"

"But that's all I've been doing, concentrating! I'm zeroed in on that swelling, the rubbing, that's all I think about!"

"Then don't think about anything! Think about something else!"

"What?"

"How should I know? Count sheep! Relax!"

"But I couldn't be more relaxed!"

So we'd vary the treatment. Double the doses. Before and after each meal. Then once every two hours. We tried violence, slaps, stinging twigs. They all brought the same result: zilch, fiasco, total flood. She cried, hanging onto us with all her might, swearing that never, but never, had she been so happy. Some progress . . . Except for her back, she didn't get hot anywhere. "On the left. The shoulder blade. Down further. There! There! Ahhh!" It was too much.

One day we played a dirty trick on her. We thought that maybe a great tragedy, a crushing blow dealt to the heart, a sudden revelation during heartbreak . . .

She got back from the market, charming, pigtailed, flushed, a cauliflower in her basket, and there we were by the Dyane, trunk open, in the act of loading up our things and sneaking off.

"We're leaving?" she asked anxiously.

"Us, yes," I answered. "But you're staying."

"I'll wait for you here?"

"Wait if you like, but we're not planning to come back."

"You're dumping me?"

"You got the picture. We're getting fed up with banging a corpse. We're going to find us a real woman for a change!"

She didn't say beans. She just stood there in the sunshine bare-legged, holding her basket, watching us close the trunk, get in the car and drive off. We left without even saying good-bye. We bumped off down the towpath. We could see her in the rear-view mirror: she didn't budge. She just got smaller and smaller, then disappeared.

"You think she might have begged us! Shit! Now what? Where we heading? Now we've really fucked up."

We hung around Mulhouse all day, like dopey tourists, hitting the bars, and at sundown we came back.

"You think she's still there?"

"Shut up."

We left the Dyane beside the highway and took off across the fields, Vietnam-style, through the poppies.

She wasn't outside, but smoke was rising gently from the chimney. We waited till night fell, flat on our bellies in the alfalfa, then crept up to the darkened windows.

"I hope she didn't do anything dumb!"

"Shut up."

We didn't dare go in right away. First we pressed our noses to the windowpanes. We couldn't see a thing inside. But we could hear her sobbing.

Eight thirty: blinding sun full on the façade.

Weird resort, the Ensisheim prison. Not exactly a palace.

A big dude showed, looking like an asshole, but a harmless one.

"Jacques Pirolle?"

"Yes?"

No suitcase, arms dangling, a three-quarter slicker and a good head taller than us.

"Your mother sent us."

"Why didn't she come herself? She got out, didn't she?"

"Yes . . . She went abroad . . ."

"Where?"

"Portugal."

"That's not far, she could at least write! I haven't heard from her in a month! What the fuck's she doing in Portugal?"

"Don't be down on her. She split with a buddy of ours, a terrific guy, an agricultural engineer. We met her through him. Before leaving she told us, 'Go get Jacques and take care of him. Tell him I'm very happy and I'll be back soon.'"

"Shake."

He held out a clammy hand.

We rolled through the countryside.

Jeanne's son's face in the rear-view mirror. It wasn't possible he was only twenty, he looked thirty. He seemed like the boss now.

"Let me take the wheel," he said.

We pulled over.

"First is there."

"I know. I saw."

He drove off smoothly.

"Take a right at the next intersection."

The hair was getting thin on the top of his head. He probably didn't even know it. No mirrors in the hole. Like a fucking monastery. Hence the hairs were few and far between.

"Who's this agricultural engineer?" Jacques asked.

"A good man, don't worry. He's just spent two years in Cuba as a technical advisor, and now he's working on a contract for Sierra Leone."

"Why don't this great guy work in France?"

"He's got a record."

"How many busts?"

"One served and two suspended."

218

"Not bad."

He seemed satisfied.

We bumped down the towpath.

The tiny house got closer in the sunshine. The table was set outside, white tablecloth and flowers from the market, bowls and a tub of butter, jam and an enormous round loaf of bread waiting for us in the shade.

Marie came out like a country hostess in the bright light, steaming blue-enamel coffeepot in hand. She paused, waiting for us to stop, get out and slam the doors. We trucked over, dragging Jacques along behind us. She didn't put the pot down. She was checking out the newcomer, who was heading right for her, liberated only twenty minutes ago.

She'd gotten all dolled up in his honor, pulled herself together, following our suggestions. Fresh dress, washed the night before and pressed that morning at dawn. Ditto for her hair, fluffy from the recent shampoo, a purple shampoo pellet she'd ripped open with her teeth. Fresh makeup chosen for the occasion, blue, black, pink, all the brushes and pencils. Doused herself with lavender water. And just when she was smelling good, right before we left, all of a sudden we flashed; Shit, man! What if the Dyane won't start? What if it refuses to go to Ensisheim? The pits—Jacques sprung and no one waiting for him! Having to make out for himself. And us stuck here, eyes half closed, sniffing that far-out aroma, our lavender old lady!

For the moment she kept her mouth shut, didn't smile, waiting for the vibes to settle. It was tense. Time for intros.

"Her name's Marie-Ange," I told Jacques. "She puts out for both of us . . . and now all three of us. She knows the score and she's cool. You'll see she's nothing special in the sack—but no dog, either. The only hitch is she can't ever come. On the other hand, she'll do anything you want, no hassle."

"Coffee?" Marie-Ange asked.

"Sure," Jacques answered. "Just a drop."

He took off his slicker and rolled up his khaki shirt sleeves. Marie poured the coffee, then sliced the bread thick. We all sat down. Pierrot and I dug right in, no shyness, happily dunking and devouring like some morning orgy, slobbering coffee all over. But Jacques didn't eat, it was like his appetite was cut, he just wet his whistle and gawked at Marie-Ange, who lowered her eyes.

Pierrot and I both picked up on the action. Didn't take a genius to dig what was eating our uncaged ex-con. He was hot to trot. No need to ask, "Ain'tcha hungry? Don't like the grub? You sick or something?" No. All we had to do was to cue Marie: "Maybe our friend would like to check out the house, you oughta show him around." And without saying beans she up and disappeared inside, already unbuttoning her dress.

Jacques did a double take. Then stared at us like a kid who'd taken that Kris Kringle business as a lot of crap but got a big surprise at dawn. Santa'd laid something dynamite on him: a woman. A humpy broad. All ready and willing.

"We share everything here," I said.

He stood up slowly, wanting to say something but unable to get it out. Meanwhile, Marie-Ange was closing the shutters.

"It's a pleasure," I added. "Your mother was . . . she was something special."

He turned and headed for the house.

"She's great from behind!" Pierrot shouted. "Check it out."

Jacques forced a smile. Count on me, he seemed to say, and trucked right in.

We guzzled some more coffee and ate bread, spreading butter as thick as the slice. While thanks to us, a good deed was cooking. Fuck, we weren't always doing the wrong thing in our lives! You gotta look at the positive side too. For example, here was a kid just out of the slams, sent up for whatever sleazy thing he'd pulled, in other words, a normal dude of twenty with everything to look forward to. Going straight, working hard, finding his place in society. And it so happened we were in a terrific position to help with this kind of problem (delinquency, petty larceny, etc.). We met him at the gate with open arms, offered him our friendship, set him up in a beautiful spot in the country. Nice and cozy in the bed of a suntanned chick, an experienced swinger, a kid who understood hard knocks from having had some herself. No two ways, it was a good turn that

220

we had a right to be proud of, and with a certain satisfaction we lit our first butt of the day. The after-breakfast smoke— the best one—that hits you just right, puts your mouth back in shape, cuts the sugary coffee taste.

It was going to be a swell day. The canal was like a mirror. We sat back, consciences clear in the total hush, just a few gutsy birds pecking at the crumbs on the tablecloth.

But why couldn't we hear anything behind the shutters? It wasn't normal! No matter how we strained our ears, not the slightest squeak, nothing! What was going down? We got up and tipped over, glued ourselves against the wooden shutters. Still nothing . . . I'd swear they were sleeping. Perhaps a sort of murmur, very faint. Yes. Marie-Ange talking in a low voice. What the fuck was she gabbing about? Her old lady giving birth? Her thing with Dobermans? We couldn't catch it. Shit! Just then a barge cruised by, so loaded it had to be scraping the bottom, with the bargeman trying to figure out what the hell we were up to. We had to back off from the shutter and look natural. The barge chugged on, disappearing down the tunnel of poplars, and we got back to our post.

Marie-Ange wasn't rapping anymore. Or else she was whispering in his ear, so low that even if you were in the sack you couldn't hear it. We waited. Finally we picked up a little noise, a kind of squishing sound. Pierrot and I grinned at each other: good, A-O.K., things were moving along! We could head back to the food, maybe even eat a piece of fruit. Or see if the fish were biting.

Something stopped us dead. We eyed each other, stunned. "Hey, Pierrot, did you hear that?" He blanched under his dark tan. We shot back to the shutter, slammed our ears against it. Unbelievable! It was starting up again. A sigh! A real sensual sigh! A woman's sigh mixed with squishing sounds! Now she was moaning! She was digging it, the bitch! It was unbearable! And we weren't in on it! Not invited to the christening! Shit! The moans were mounting, shifting from groans to gasps. She was growling and gnashing her teeth. The bitch was really letting loose! Never heard the likes before! So gross! Jeanne wouldn't have dared. With her it was like music . . . Even the maid in

221

Brittany didn't howl like that getting it on! I never had such a bitter taste in my mouth or such clammy mitts as that morning. We felt fucked over, that's what Pierrot and I felt, picking up on that triumph tune our lady was belting. And she was calling for us, the whore! "Jean-Claude! Pierrot! I did it! I got off!" On top of everything she wanted us to share her luck! "Jean-Claude! Pierrot! Come here!" Well, O.K., we'd share her success. We'd hold her head or something. It wasn't enough for her to be climbing the curtains, she had to have witnesses for the miracle! Hearing it wasn't enough. Call your ma, slut, and your old man in his wheelchair! They'll be glad to come, one pushing the other, thanking the Lord for giving them such a musical daughter! Don't get mad, but we're going to split. We don't dig what's happening, so we better hit the road. We got a crazy urge to make tracks fast and avoid a double murder! Come on, let's go, Pierrot! Enough of this shit! When I think how we knocked ourselves out over her hang-ups, fucking night and day!

We took off through the fields, charging like caged beasts. Two fuckheads of the plains, in a wicked mood! The first dog that came around wagging his tail got both my boots in the chops. Up yours, too, crows! We threw rocks at them. Some big Alsatian lard-ass leaning on his wagon gave us a dirty look. We asked him if by any chance he'd like a photo of us. We had some great ones we'd be glad to autograph for him and his whole fucking family. Then the big beer-belly bastard got pissed, rolled up his sleeves and came at us with his pitchfork! We had to beat it, dodging among the cows.

We finally ditched him and dropped on the bank of the canal. Flat on our bellies in the grass, we did a take on our kissers reflected in the water, two freaky fuckheads lost between the Rhône and the Rhine. Then suddenly we heard a familiar voice. *Her* voice. Wailing her lungs out: "Hey! Jean-Claude! Pierrot! Where are you?"

She spotted us and tore off in our direction, her faded blue-linen dress a speck at the other end of the canal, growing bigger, hitting us at top speed, legs, thighs and pubes flying. She dove between us, red in the face, threw her arms around our necks, held us tight against her windblown hair and started to grin, gasping, at our three images in the water.

"Everything turned purple!" she told us, all shakes. "With white lights! My hair was burning, standing straight on end! My fingernails were on fire! I felt like a volcano starting to erupt!"

"You're a real drag," we answered. Kerplonk! We dumped her in the water. "That oughta cool you off!"

Our Ophelia-in-heat laughed as best she could. "I'm heading back!" she cried, and swam off doing an adorable crawl.

We lay there, sprawled beside the water, not rapping, not smoking, not doing fuck-all, like a couple of turds. Even the flies started to take an interest. Huge Alsatian blueflies, so well fed that no matter how hard they buzzed they couldn't get off the ground.

Marie, why did you betray us? You slut! What's that big hunk got that we don't? A fatter dick! A longer one? One that vibrates, that swells up inside? One with a tickler at the end? I'd give anything to know! Maybe he got it from his old lady. A knack for fucking, a genius at screwing. But shit, Pierrot and me, we're no slouches at the art. We're crazy about it, we can go all night. Me, forget it, I'm just an average type, but Pierrot, he's a right-on, hard-on fucker! One of the best dicks in France! A samurai! Ditched for that kid who ain't even served his time! 'Cause let's face it: the big con was really kicked out of the clink. He bugged everybody so much with his good conduct that they said, "Listen, buddy, we cut your term. Get the fuck out and don't come back and screw us up!" Nobody dug him anymore. There's only one thing that grabs a guard and that's guarding. Guarding big hoods, toying with privileges and breaks. But Jacques's not a big hood, just a big cock! A well-hung librarian!

You know, Jeanne, your son bores the shit out of us. If we keep our traps shut, it's to do you a favor, because of that debt we owe. He can keep that toothpick—no great loss! Count on us: we won't butt in. Now that we know you, nothing else matters. They don't make them like you anymore. She can holler all her life, she'll never come the way you did, with that tiny cry of yours like a wounded bird. My old

223

lady must have cried out too, in the pillow so she wouldn't wake the kid behind the screen. "Sweetie, don't flush the toilet, he'll have another coughing fit." My cough was her obsession. Every night for five years. "Nothing serious," the doc said, "simple chronic tracheitis. You should take him to the mountains. Do you have any relatives in the mountains?" Out of luck, my ma, she was from the plains. She'd love it here on this canal, with us. There isn't a woman in the world who doesn't dream of sitting in the sun, in an old garden chair, watching her kids horse around. She'd never wash or iron, just bake a few pies, mend a few clothes that really needed it. Marie-Ange would be her only daughter, her favorite, and would tell her everything, her little worries, big heartbreaks, aches and pains, when her periods were late. They'd swap recipes. There'd be two schools of cooking, old and new. We'd compare them. Pierrot would be the kid, the wild younger son, and I the older, sensible one. The only one you could have a little trust in, who'd keep an eye on him. As for that big fucker Jacques, he'd be our buddy from Ensisheim who'd bike over every day, saying, "Just passing by," the faithful suitor, the attentive slob, the one Marie-Ange wouldn't fuck if you paid her. Ma would get a kick out of comforting the reject. She'd take him for a walk. They'd stroll off along the canal, she amused, proud and a little tubby in her housedress that buttoned up the front, with a narrow belt of the same material. We'd watch them disappear, laughing hysterically, stirring our coffee with little silver spoons. "Good riddance," Marie-Ange would say. "Your friend was getting on my nerves!" And she'd fan herself with her skirt, as if to unstick it.

"You're bitchy to him! Shit, you could at least make an effort!"

"I can't help it if I don't go for him! I can't stand the sight of his puss! It just doesn't turn my crank! It bugs me every time I see it!"

"But he's a good-looking dude!"

"I know! He's got everything, but it ain't for me! A guy who never smiles, I can't hack it. Besides, he's weird. He scares me."

224

Hunger pangs finally woke us around three in the afternoon. We dragged our asses up to the house. It was quiet as a church. "They're sleeping, the shits."

On the breakfast table, the butter had melted, the milk had turned, and the birds had pecked the bread to pieces, a real mess.

We barely got inside the kitchen when she started up again. We stared at each other, shocked. She was really going too far this time. We weren't old-fashioned, but this was too much, a slap in the face of our friendship. All those good times down the drain! No kidding, we were on the verge of freaking out, doing something violent, but that would have been dumb, self-ish, even dangerous. Or maybe splitting for good, leaving no address. I'd even gotten out the keys to the Dyane and stared at them, confused, jingling them in the palm of my hand. Just one thing kept us there, a dumb thing, old as the world: the munchies. Thinking about the leftover pot roast going to waste in the pantry. We decided to eat before hitting the road, that would make more sense.

We got out the cold platter, carrots, some red wine, and went outside.

The sun had moved, of course. The world doesn't stop just because one chick gets it on. So we had to push the table into the shade and sweep away the breakfast crumbs to make room for lunch.

We choked down our meal as best we could, our last supper, with background music, which I hate. I like eating in peace. This was like being in a dime store: no way to escape the racket. Damn near barfed at every bite. Don't know what kind of bow the violinist used, but he sure got some far-out sounds out of his fiddle. A gypsy lunch with tremolos in our ears and pizzicato digestion. It felt like the entire band was closing in on us, the singer drooling down our shirt fronts. A strange nightclub on the banks of the canal. The kind of joint where you can't hear yourself think. We rolled the bread into little balls and scarfed as best we could, not rapping, really down, like a couple of cons. With the theme song sounding rotten to us. Not the kind of tune you come away humming.

225

Dig that! Someone blubbering! Must be Marie. Hiccuping like a kid who'd slammed her hand in the door. What was her problem? Was he a sadist? Was he hurting her? Maybe we oughta take a look. "Pierrot, take a peek."

He got up and dragged himself over to the shutters. Luckily she quieted down, blew her nose, and sounded better. Then she started giggling. What the fuck was so funny in there? I jumped up. I'd fix her ass! O.K., good, she cut the laughs. I sat back down. Shit, now it was the moans again! I felt my nerves shatter. Slammed my hand down hard on the table. All the little spoons twitched in the cups. Dig yourself, man. Breathe deep. Have a drink. You could shout yourself silly and they'd never know it, they don't give a shit. They're in another world. Come on, Pierrot! Let's hit the road! We'll eat the fruit in the car!

We split with our mitts full of apricots. Headed for the Dyane, the only thing we owned in the world. We hopped in, the heat was a bitch! Couldn't touch the wheel! Still, with the windows closed, it was one place where we couldn't hear them, our last refuge before the long road ahead. Had to down the apricots fast before they got stewed. There . . . Got any bread? We added it up. Twenty francs in change. No way to get far. We'd have to live off the natives, like ticks.

"What are you waiting for?" he asked.

I pushed the starter. She almost sprang to life, she was so hot. I gunned her three times, eyeing the door of the house.

"Dummy!" Pierrot yelled. "I told you she was deaf!"

Wrong, my friend! Because there she was, coming out! Right then!

There in the kitchen doorway stood a messed-up, bare-assed bitch, wobbling, blinking her spaced-out eyes.

"Will you look at the state she's in!"

A scumbag with a kisser smeared with makeup.

I killed the engine.

She went over to the table, gobbled some fruit, spitting the pits in the canal. Then she finally sat down, all droopy, to have a smoke.

Not the slightest glance at us.

A wreck, a zombie.

226

We got out, ambled over. She didn't even look around! We must have been masochists to want a close-up of our Waterloo.

We sat opposite her, side by side on the bench. She blew smoke in our faces. Mascara was running down her cheeks, watered by tears.

"You shits pigged the whole pot roast!" she said. "I could have used a bite."

Pierrot cooled me out with a firm grip on my arm.

Two tears splashed in her plate.

Pierrot got out his snot rag, dipped it in the water pitcher and wiped Marie-Ange's face gently, dabbing around the eyes. Marie quietly let him, and as the rag got darker she got lighter, becoming the young girl with the transparent eyelids once more.

"Holy shit, what did he do to you?"

"Things . . ."

"What kind of things?"

"Just normal everyday things . . ."

"Nothing special?"

"No . . . Anyway, I was the one who did everything."

"You?"

"Well, yeah . . ."

"You fell for him?"

"No . . . I don't love him . . . But he was so eager . . ."

"How do you mean?"

"Well, he couldn't do anything. He was paralyzed."

"Scared?"

"Yeah. He had the shakes. He was digging my bod and was so jittery. He didn't have the balls to touch me. So I had to do all the work, undress him myself. And then all of a sudden he came in my hands, just like that. He tried to excuse himself. But I thanked him. I said, 'It's a gift you gave me.' I held him close on the bed and whispered, 'Cry if you feel like it. Cry if it'll do you good.' So he did, making love to me at the same time, and he shot right off again, a second later. I asked him if I was the first chick. He said yes, and started at it again. And only then did things get going for me . . ."

"What things?"

"Didn't you hear?"

"No. Why?"

227

"Shhh!" She shushed us and cocked her ear to the shutters. We heard a soft voice calling, "Marie . . ."

"Excuse me," she said, getting up. "He needs me."

Just like all the rest, that little beauty operator! What was her name now? Marie-Ange, yes, that was it, Marie-Ange! Or Marie-Hole, I prefer that, a cute little village nestled in a valley! Marie's ice-cream parlor, dishing come-cones! Marie-on-a-stick! Angel-piss on tap! Where was she while Pierrot and I desperately tried to crash in that big, wrinkled, ravaged, messed-up sack full of crumbs, hairs, come spots, like starch spills, love maps? Four A.M.! Dawn was starting to break! What the fuck was she doing?

She was dancing, no kidding! Madame was at a dance with her stud!

'Cause for the last three days we'd had to live to the rhythm of their passion! In other words, during the day, leave the field clear! The bed, the room, preferably the entire shack, plus the nearby surroundings, so they could give free rein to their affair, come and go bare-assed, get it on wherever they pleased! And especially so she could sound off in comfort, the diva, do her aria without soft-pedaling anything!

Not to say that they turned us off, no! In a way they were really sort of cute, they didn't ask for anything. Didn't pay any attention to us, period. They acted as if the rest of the world didn't exist. Two blind-mutes.

Only unfortunately we were still kicking, even if it was a dog's life, and we weren't deaf, that was the trouble, or blind.

For example, when she tossed her ass around, naturally we didn't touch, since we don't dig leftovers, unlike certain guys fresh out of the slams. Not that we didn't spot her ass passing by under our noses, like it was up for auction. We saw it quite clearly. Not that it was such a rare object, either, but all the same, I don't know why, it was painful, and often just too much to take. We were strung out from watching her butt boogie joyfully from room to room, in this case from the bedroom to the kitchen and from the kitchen to the bedroom with a few detours out to the wooden outhouse which adjoined the cottage and which, needless to say, was the pits in plumbing.

As for the satisfied lover, we never laid eyes on him. He must have pissed in the sink. The water we heard running was certainly that. He never came out of the bedroom. Used to being locked up, I guess. Needed four walls around him.

She, however, showed from time to time, bringing back fond memories. But rarely. Three or four times a day. And not for long. Five minutes, tops. And always bare-assed. Just a matter of making use of her time. It wouldn't have paid for her to get dressed, I agree, in view of her life-style. Bed, pissing, cooking. And always in a rush to slip back between the sheets!

She'd show up in the kitchen, wasted, hairy, polluted, dirty, as if she'd made a whole regiment, then park her ass in front of the stove to chef up a little something for her old man. She'd smoke up the joint with sickening smells: butter, garlic, onions, pork fat.

"You like your kidneys well-done?" she'd shriek to him. "Broiled," he'd answer.

We watched her do her cooking bit, stupefied. Not an ounce of modesty or feminine decency! She bounced her muff under our noses, cool as a cuke! Without a word—not even a hint of a friendly look!

Anyhow, nothing surprised us anymore. Everything seemed perfectly normal. Nothing more normal than for her to serve her Jacquot meals on a tray. No need for him to dirty his feet on the floor, the darling. He stayed horizontal, with just his feet sometimes propped a little higher than his head, a gimmick of Marie-Ange's to increase the circulation to the cock.

We didn't belong in that house. We'd had an earful of their constant sound effects, their whispers behind the wall every time we set foot in the kitchen. It cut our appetites. Had to go picnic in the fields to get away from that squeaking bed, walk a good ten minutes into the wind to escape their chamber music. And even then, sometimes, if the wind happened to change, a moan would come and die at our feet at the end of its course, like a stray bullet. So we'd pick up and go even farther, like two hunted animals. Not to mention that in Alsace, in the haystacks, quite a lot of hanky-panky goes on. Not always easy to find a secluded spot.

We'd bring our fishing lines, just to kill time, and fish,

not really getting into it, while the Valkyrie got her hitch. Obviously, the fish didn't bite much. Our floats just sat there. The fish didn't give a shit about us either. We could see them gliding through the clear water, not a care on their minds. They'd sniff the bait sulkily and move on. Not hungry.

That was when Marie-Ange would come pay us her daily visit. Needing fresh air, no doubt, or out of simple courtesy. In any case, never for longer than a few minutes. Too hot to trot to hang around. We could almost hear her stud champing at the bit.

"Well," she'd ask, "any nibbles?"

"And your mother?" we'd answer.

She'd plop down on the grass beside us, wiped out and contented. A dolce-vita pussycat purring in gratitude because there was a pound of fish on her plate. She'd come to stretch, to lie down and wallow in front of us. She let her happiness hang out in the sunshine like sheets airing in a window. It was always in the morning, by the way, before ten. So we couldn't bitch.

"It's crazy how much I'm getting out of this!" she'd say. "I take my sweet time, real slow. I don't lose a crumb!"

"Good for you!" we'd answer. "It's a pleasure to hear that!"

She'd do a take, not catching it. I still believe she didn't dig the hurt she was causing. She'd show up sweet and innocent, with no intention of provoking us, not the vaguest idea of making assholes of us. She'd lick herself, smooth her fur, fluff her buns, catch a butterfly and let it go. A dumdum, that's all. A sweet dumdum. Smug and dangerously harmless . . .

The crunch was she'd always ask our advice about her conquistador's oddball habits. "Why doesn't he ever smile?" she'd ask us. "Why doesn't he talk? I know he's happy, shit! With all the times I get him off! Only he gets off in total silence! I have to keep the conversation going all by myself! He only says the bare essentials: yes, no, thanks, again! Stand up, sit down, lie down! Swallow, rub, open your legs, your ass, your mouth, your fingers! Slower, faster, in front, behind! I get the feeling I'm fucking a gym teacher! And never a smile! He never opens up!"

"Maybe he hasn't noticed that he's free. You oughta clue him in."

Personally, we tried to avoid the big slob. Not that he scared us—far from it—but we felt uncomfortable with him. I don't know, something in his eyes turned us off. We decided that Marie-Ange was quite gutsy to do all those solos with him.

They'd dress at sundown and get a breath of fresh air for an hour or so down by the canal, have a little aperitif, get their heads straight. Then they'd split in the car, *our* car, looking for a good-time bar, some intimate dive, to cut up a country conga.

Swell of them to split, we could put the joint back together.

Usually we'd find a ten-franc note stuck under a plate, enough to keep us in smokes. Our pocket money for the next day. He probably had some bread stashed . . .

We'd clean up a little. Go into their room and oil the bedsprings so they would squeak less during the day. We'd go back into the kitchen, fix ourselves a quick bite. Because, of course, no more yummy little meals! Madame was dining in town! You kids fix something for yourselves! Peeling potatoes, getting our hands filthy in the coal cellar—that was our scene now.

We'd eat sadly, face to face, not really hungry. We pictured them in a garden, table for two under the Chinese lanterns, gazing like a couple of assholes at the bubbles in a *blanc de blanc*, holding hands on a checked tablecloth, touching knees under the table, exchanging vows, the memories of the afternoon. We zeroed in on them in our thoughts like radar, going to a dance, waltzing for hours, Marie zonked on the stony shoulder, eyes half-closed. Or with their arms around each other on the streets of Colmar, Mulhouse, Strasbourg, coming out of the flicks, strolling through a fair. Or in Germany—why not? No sweat for them to cross the frontier—no one was after *their* asses! Pushing on to Munich, abandoning us forever, no bread, no wheels, alone in the world . . .

We sat next to the fireplace smoking our pipes like two old men who have nothing left to say to each other. We began to feel like we were from another generation. No truck with the young fools of today who only dig having a good time and have no respect for their elders. Two grisly farts without a boob tube, listening to the clock tick. With rheumatism and stiff joints. Nothing left but to mope around, poke the fire every now and then and dream of the good old times, of gorgeous spas with Russian princes and diaphanous dancing girls. Two deadweights. On welfare. Then why didn't they stick us in a comfy rest home, where we could be with other golden oldies?

The first night it turned our stomachs to crash in their filthy sheets, so we decided to drag two blankets outside and sleep under the stars. No luck. It rained. Had to go back in.

We wound up back in their sack, fully dressed, holding our noses. It was some bummer! We didn't dare move, just lay there, stiff as boards, hands folded over our chests. Two corpses. No way we could catch any Zs—our heads were working overtime.

We listened to the silence of the night. We waited for the sound of the Dyane coming back, the doors slamming. We waited for their footsteps in the kitchen, Marie-Ange's laugh. We thought, They're going to open the door, turn on the light, find us in their sack, and we're going to look like dummies.

But the hours passed and they didn't come back.

We still didn't peep and dawn was breaking.

Then things started happening by themselves, just like that, spontaneously. Pierrot had his head on my shoulder, so his cheek wouldn't have to hit the dude's pillow.

"She's a slut!" he said.

"They all are!" I answered. "You'll see when you get to be my age. One no better than the next."

"Then why can't we do without them?"

"Don't ask, man. 'Cause we're fuckheads!"

I felt his hand slide in, timidly. It did us both good to do it.

When we heard the Dyane engine, the doors slamming, Marie-Ange's laugh, we didn't give a shit! We just waited for them, relaxed.

They didn't come in the house. What the fuck were they doing? Not a sound, nothing! We dragged ourselves out of the sack to have a peek through the shutters.

Outside it was getting lighter and lighter. Marie-Ange was

on her knees and there was a cock crowing in the distance. Sexual obsession in all its glory!

We got back in bed so as not to have to watch. But no way to escape the nightmare. They were tuning their bagpipes again for the great overture! A fucking beehive, that Alsatian Philharmonic! They rehearsed and rehearsed till they hit perfection—you could tell that Germany wasn't far off. Too bad they only knew one piece: a wedding march! Too bad it wasn't a transistor. Couldn't just flip the dial. Not to mention that we were always in the front row, lifetime guests of honor. Pierrot was getting to be less and less of a music freak. Even regressing horribly from a cultural point of view. Climbing back up his family tree! A desperate flight to the darkest night of time! A fucking primate, *hominum furiosus!* Capable of anything! Purple with apelike rage! Had to control him to avoid a bloody tragedy! Not having a straitjacket, I dumped him down hard on the bed, blocked him with all my strength. Practically choked him to death! What a great hold! Time it took to count ten, he went limp. Threw in the towel and became my buddy again. Became Pierrot again, always faithful. We wrapped our arms around each other and started in softly, two ugly ducklings dancing to avoid being wallflowers . . . Easy, with the record player right under the window . . . The needle rubbing in the groove, the hushed sounds of the speaker, we caught it all. All we had to do was sway with the music . . .

It couldn't last forever.

One night around seven we were fishing, for a change, when Marie-Ange showed up, looking weird.

"Come in for dinner," she said. "I made beef stew."

No shit! Well, O.K., why not? We'd go and scarf her stew, even if she'd slipped something into it. We let them cool their heels for about fifteen minutes, then showed.

The table was set in the kitchen. Four places. A black pot simmering on the stove. They were waiting for us.

Jovial as always, I held my hand out to the big turkey. "Greetings!" I gave him. "Glad to finally make your acquaintance! Marie's told me so much about you!"

No way to raise a smile on his puss. He shook my paw in

silence. Humor really wasn't his bag. The guy's dimples had been paved over.

The same with Marie-Ange. But Pierrot kissed her on both cheeks. "Sorry to arrive empty-handed," he said. "With this bakery strike, everyone's mobbing the florists, no way to come by a bouquet!"

Another flop. Not a ghost of a grin! Not the same chick at all, our ex-chucklehead. Passion makes you gloomy, eats away at you faster than cancer. Unless we'd bumped into a lovers' quarrel. But then why invite us? There was something I didn't dig about the setup.

We sat down, unfolded our napkins, tested the knives—all this in the atmosphere of a wake. We held our plates out to Marie-Ange, who filled them with stew. His napkin around his neck, Jacques was digging in, while Marie, beside him, just picked at her food like a bird. Not a bad stew. Nothing to write home about, but O.K. Had what it takes.

Pierrot and I scarfed away, waiting for enlightenment. Why the sudden chow? There had to be something they wanted to rap to us about, but what? Or else they were going to lay some bad news on us. I figured they were getting married, for example, and going to live abroad. Or else they were fixing to ask us a favor.

The second case. It never fails. The perfect couple needed us.

It was Marie who tossed the ball out. "Well, that's it," she said. "There's no dessert because our cash just ran out. There's none left, and I mean none. You've just had the last crumbs in the bread box."

"Oh," I answered. "That's a bitch."

I mopped up some gravy with my last hunk of bread. Pierrot, from his smile, must have been flashing the same as me: we were wanted again. We'd have to get out our bag of tricks.

Superstud, for the time being, was just worried about one thing: the way the beef kept disappearing off his plate. He licked it clean.

"We'll have to score some bread," Marie continued. "Can't go on like this, can we?"

234

I turned to Pierrot. "You feel like working?"

"Mmm," he answered. Not exactly enthusiastic.

"You'll just have to give us a hand," Marie added.

I stared at her blankly. "A hand with what?"

At that Jacques, miracle of miracles, snapped out of his silence. "A hundred thou," he announced. "A cinch, no risks. Some old folks."

I snapped back just as cool, "We prefer to make our own decisions when it comes to risks."

Marie, uptight, clutched her sugar by the arm. "See?" she said. "I was sure they'd cop out! And they're right! It's going too far! It's crazy!"

Zap! I gave her a smart slap in the kisser. "Who said anything about copping out?"

Since when do chicks butt into business matters?

You picture retired couples living in little cottages, the roofs loaded with ivy, ivy even growing in the windows, broken-down joints crumbling under greenery, as if the vines were climbing up to strangle them because they refused to croak, the whole scene hidden behind rusty iron fences on peaceful little streets lined with aging sycamores, not to mention the blind cocker spaniels and television antennas on the kitchen porches.

Well, no, that wasn't exactly it. Except for the TV antenna.

It was an enormous antenna, a huge dumb-ass radar pointing at the sky strung between four cables, enthroned on the flat roof of a little doll's house. A white prefab box, no name, no number, like it had fallen from the sky at the end of a dead-end street that trailed off into the most vacant of vacant lots. The last house in Ensisheim. A stretch of road we were supposed to make our getaway from, with an extra hundred thou in our bags.

The night was fantastic. Not a cloud. With the moon and all the stars out for the hit. You could see like broad daylight. The opposite of guaranteed camouflage. And almost nowhere to hide. Three trash cans, a concrete mixer, a few trees as big around as my arm. Even if we split up we'd look suspicious, sure as shit, sort of like commandos. Lucky for us, it was deserted. Like the end of the world, with just a pack of starving cats tracking us with their luminous eyes.

We could hear the boob tube from the street corner. It was blaring some program like "Enter Without Knocking," a

236

boring game show. All they needed was us to make the evening complete. Rest assured. We were on our way.

Jacques took the lead, hands in pockets, walking down the middle of the street. He'd insisted on carrying the gun, saying that it was *his* heist, and he was taking *his* own risks. We'd just come along for the ride, to give him moral support. O.K. by me, but it meant that now he was in command, and I can't say I dug that idea too much. Too late to turn back—besides, it's not my style.

Pierrot and I tracked him, one on each sidewalk, like in some bad dream. With that strange fear you get in dreams, sometimes, not really knowing why. Except that in this case we knew. Our panic was real enough, all right.

Unarmed . . . Jacques claimed that this old couple had no guns! At least that's what his cell mate had told him, the guy who'd hipped him to the operation, asking him to stash half the loot, a little nest egg for when he got out himself two months later, so he'd have something to live on. Classic case of blind trust between cons.

Marie-Ange was waiting by the canal. I pictured her freaking out, poor thing. Pacing around the kitchen, eyes glued to her watch. Or sitting beside the water, watching for the Dyane headlights on the towpath. She'd kicked up quite a fuss to keep us from going.

Ten o'clock . . . We'd asked her to get ready for a fast takeoff. We were supposed to flash by to pick her up and split from there to distant lands—the Alps this time. It was the end of June, so the great rush for the beaches would start soon. We'd figured the best place to escape the vacation crush was in a ski resort. Winter sports, by definition, don't happen in the summer. There wouldn't be so much as a pussycat about, and we could cool it, drop out again. All we'd have to do was move into some empty chalet. And besides, the chick would dig seeing the mountains. She dreamed about touching the ice of a real glacier. Not to mention the change of climate. Just a few formalities and we'd be heading out. We could already see ourselves there among the cows at the foot of the snowy peaks.

The front door was locked. Normal in such a deserted area.

Jacques rang the bell several times, long, repeated rings. Without any noticeable results. Only one thing interested our clients: the boob tube.

Jacques, his nerves in perfect control, stepped to the right and started banging on the shutter. It made a scary echo in the street. Like the Gestapo.

"Why don't you pull the gun?" I asked him.

But the shutter was opening. A head peeped out. A round, soft head, not too ugly, and not really ancient. Let's say sixty, tops. A guy in a beret.

"Pirolle!" he shouted. And a big smile lit up his puss!

Fuck! Pierrot and I could have shit in our pants! Now it turned out he knew this famous retired couple. But why hadn't he said so? What was he hiding?

I wasn't too pleased. Frantic desire to slam into reverse and disappear into the night, leaving him there with his buddies, since they seemed so chummy.

Could it be some kind of gag? I searched my memories of Jacques and couldn't come up with one time he'd ever kidded around. Unless he was suddenly turning out to be a dead-pan artist.

"How nice of you to drop in!" said our host, clearly tickled.

"I got two friends with me."

"Excellent! Be right with you!"

The shutter closed.

I pounced on Jacques. "Just a minute, pal! What the hell's going on?"

The door was already opening. Things were moving too fast for my brain, which was rusty from goofing off. A blast from the tube surrounded us.

"Come on in!" said the voice behind me.

Jacques took me by the arm. He wasn't kidding at all. I even thought he looked sort of sinister.

He pushed me in front of him, made the intros: "Jean-Claude . . . Pierrot . . ."

What an asshole! He really could have found some other names!

The nice man with the pot belly offered us his clammy mitt.

238

"You're in luck—there's some champagne left."

Then he grabbed Jacques by the shoulders, like a papa. "Pirolle! Good to see you!"

An odor of haddock floated through the hall. And the tube boomed out like an organ in a cathedral. The doors were open to the living room and I could see it would be a tight scramble for our hundred thou, since it was packed with people. Shirt sleeves and suspenders, chignons, glasses, three kids sitting on the floor and one baby sucking his mama, plus a grandma in black, knitting and chomping on her dentures. They were all spread out in a circle watching Bellemare. We'd lucked right into the middle of a family reunion. They all turned around, got up, smiled at us. Except Grandma, the baby and the three brats, who were riveted to the screen.

"One of my old protégés," our host said, pushing Jacques in front of him. "They miss me, see? They can't get along without me!"

Jacques shook hands all around. We watched, trying to be as inconspicuous as possible. I'd never seen Pierrot so shy. They asked him to sit down, but he kept standing there. They poured him a drink and he said, "That's enough." But grandma kept on knitting, eyeing us over her specs. Bellemare was still blabbing away with his mystery guest.

"Well," said Grandpa, lifting his glass to Jacques's health, "what are you up to?"

"Same game as before."

Total shock. The face under the beret turned white.

Didn't look like we'd have time to finish our champagne, since Jacques had just whipped out the gun. And he was aiming it straight ahead, right at his old pal's belly button.

The others weren't digging the action because Bellemare was giving out with "I won't say yes and I won't say no," and they were all breaking up.

Gramps managed to come up with a twisted smile. "Jacques, you're joking!" He could hardly speak. Jacques flipped the beret off his head. That cleared the air.

The old guy gave a cry of real terror. "Raymond!"

Raymond looked around. "What's up? You O.K.?"

He stood up. He was a young tough, the judo type. Getting the layout, he grabbed a chair and shouted, "Lucien! Quick!"

Lucien got into the act too. Bony and nervous. He jumped to his feet. His sons, or sons-in-law—what was the diff?

Jacques calmed them down on the spot. "One move and I empty the clip!"

I stepped forward, fixing to speed the action. "Where's the money?" I asked.

"What money?" the old guy asked.

"Hand over the bread!" Jacques ordered.

Total hush! The whole family gawked at us, mouths hanging open, dropping Bellemare like a hot potato. The live news was copping his audience. And the French claim they only like comedy. Like hell! Another rigged poll! A good suspense drama will grab 'em, I'm telling you, especially if it's free.

"I never did you any harm," the retired guy whispered. He wasn't shitting in his pants yet, but his panic meter was at zero. Jacques decided that wasn't good enough and fired a bullet in his foot.

Women shrieked. The baby, its tit snatched away, started howling at the top of its lungs. The brats were still torn between Bellemare and the shooting of Grandpa. Utter confusion—except for Grandma, who just kept knitting.

The old man, struck dumb, didn't even let out a yell. He didn't even look at his foot, which was spouting blood from a hole in his slipper, staining the rug. Probably didn't feel any pain yet. For the moment he was hooked on one thing, the noise the shot had made, rattling the windowpanes. And we figured the same thing he did: Jacques had completely flipped! It was turning into a real nightmare! We stood there paralyzed, unable to move. Pierrot's lower jaw had dropped like he was at the dentist's.

"I got five more here for your fat gut," Jacques snarled between clenched teeth.

Bellemare busted out laughing. The contestant fell right into the trap! He said "yes"!

"Fuck this!" Jacques snapped.

Then the two sons-in-law, or sons, started wailing together.

240

"You sick in the head or what? You're not going to kill him in cold blood? A defenseless old man?"

"Yeah." To Jacques, nothing more obvious.

"You know what you're in for, you little scum?"

"I don't give two shits."

It was getting sort of unbelievable for a moment there. Then Raymond started shooting off his mouth again.

"Well go ahead, then! What're you waiting for, huh? Fire, and I swear you won't get out of here alive! We'll make you eat your revolver! Go on! Do it! Pull the trigger!"

"Please," Grandpa stammered. "Come on, take it easy . . ."

"I advise you all to shut your yaps," said Jacques.

"We're not shutting anything! You're not getting away with this!"

They had to come on strong, those two jerks. Hero's blood running through their veins!

"Quiet," said the old man.

A four-eyes popped up, a stranger, didn't know where he'd come from, a real peacemaker. "Please, gentlemen, let's all calm down. My wife is pregnant. You want money? Good! Fine! We'll empty our pockets!"

"No!" screamed his wife, bolting up in a rage. "I don't agree, don't agree at all!" She hooked herself on Grandpa's arm, making a shield of her swollen belly, six months gone. "What have you got against him? Huh?"

"Christine! Don't flirt with death!"

"I'd like to know why they want to kill my father—you mind?"

Jacques was ticking like a time bomb. His eyes hurled lightning bolts at the old man, who sweated heavily in his shabby vest, knees knocking. He'd just discovered his bloody slipper and was staring at it, horrified.

"You have no right!" screamed the future mama, two shakes from giving birth on the spot. "He's a beautiful man! Sacrificed his whole life for rotten bums like you! And this is how you thank him? Aren't you ashamed? Get the hell out of here! Leave my father alone! He *earned* his retirement. Get out before I call the cops!"

241

Jacques handed her a smart slap. She spun into her husband's arms, who held her close. "Don't be frightened, dear, it'll blow over, it's nothing."

I tried to grab Jacques by the arm and tell him, "Let's split." No way, he shrugged me off like the others, like I wasn't there. In my opinion the jig was up. No one could stop him now. We should have jumped him. But then what? They'd all hit on us! If we got him down, we'd go with him!

"Jacques," murmured the old man. "Shall we telephone the chaplain?" He spoke in a very soft voice, amazingly calm in the crazy scene. "Come on, Jacques, don't do anything foolish. You're at home here! It was me who gave you the address, remember? I said, 'When you get out, you'll have to come see me, come by the house.' No one's going to hurt you. Let's go into my room, O.K.? And have a little talk."

I felt Jacques weakening. The effect of the soft voice, maybe. I saw his finger let up on the trigger. That's all I watched: his finger, the letup.

"Be very careful!" shouted Lucien, whose opinion no one had asked. "Think it over, you little shit! Think of who you're going to kill! Cuttoli, the head correctional officer! A name that's the symbol of warmth and help in time of trouble! All the guys worshiped him!"

Gloomy fuck. Now he was giving a funeral rap!

"And when he left the prison, you weren't there anymore, you dirty shit. You don't know what happened! Well, I'll tell you! The guys all organized a farewell party for him. And the warden O.K.'d it. They read him poems they'd scribbled on old pieces of cardboard. They gave him a memory book with all their signatures in it. Some were even weeping openly!"

The dude had tears in his eyes. And Jacques too. Far out! I thought he was gonna bawl like a baby. He raised the gun to the guard's gut, his hand shook, his finger tensed.

"Don't be an ass!" Pierrot yelled.

Too late.

The shots rang out in the cottage. The little old man fell to his knees, not a whimper, not a flinch, like firing into a pillow.

242

And that was it. He didn't move. End of the line.

There was a long silence. Not even heavy—more like a relieved silence. Everyone stared at the floor, the pile of clothes in the middle of the living room. Only Grandma's knitting moved. Then suddenly the two sons-in-law sprang, two mad dogs. Jacques pistol-whipped them, then kicked them in the balls. Looked like he wanted to hang onto his skin. But I figured his number was up. I really didn't see how he was going to get out of this one.

In the meantime no one paid the slightest attention to us. We split like a couple bats out of hell. Into the lit-up night. The car, quick! Behind the billboard. The keys, shit! Hard as hell fumbling through your pockets while sprinting. Even harder dodging trash cans and streetlights while looking behind you. What you need is a rear-view mirror.

One break in our rotten luck: no one behind us. Just a hundred yards to go to salvation—the good old Dyane, so faithful till now, never letting us down. The last fifty yards, time for a final nightmare: what if all the tires were flat? We raced around the billboard. Mad takeoff, praying the engine would hold up. Tore ass through Ensisheim like an ambulance, I could almost hear the siren. Two dying freaks running red lights! We'd have to change mounts fast, find a couple of fresh horses, 'cause the great chase was on again! Flames up our ass and we didn't even have the gun anymore! Shit, what got into that goon? Doing in such a friendly old man! In my opinion you shouldn't try to figure it out: guys out of jail just have some part of their brain missing.

Pounded down the towpath at top speed. Whoa! A parked car between the canal and the house. A red Mustang with black racing stripes, its lights out, and us screeching up on our hubcaps. My heart pounded, ten years off my life. Fucking skid! Wild slide! Inches from landing in the canal! Not to mention that Pierrot and I don't dig mysterious nocturnal visits. We waited. Our pulses slowed to 70. We got out quietly. Tried to take a peek through the shutters, identify the bastard.

Who could come fuck us up on the sly? We jumped: the door opened. In the lighted rectangle the outlines of a rich dude appeared, snobby cigar, with Marie, the trapped hostess. She did a take in a flash: not all present and accounted for. Her eyes hunted for Jacques in the dark. We all stood around. No one budged. The silence got uncomfortable. Except for the dude, who was grinning to himself like an asshole. Someone would have to break the ice.

Finally Marie made the move. Came up with a short explanation. "The gentleman's here from Mulhouse. About a job. Filling in—one of his girls is sick. Too bad, just as we're about to leave!"

"Yeah," I said, "that's really a shame . . ." Pierrot and I looked at each other. Then we looked at the Mustang. A buggy that could move. Then we looked at the Dyane. No comment. Then we looked at the dude. Another haircurler. In a steel-blue suit. Cut tight. "You single?" I asked, looking like I didn't give a shit. He broke up, the turkey.

"Yes . . . Why?" Listen, sweetie, don't ask. What's more natural than a single guy staying out all night? Gotta take advantage of your freedom! No point going home—nobody there biting their nails! And when they sound the alarm, we'll be long gone. In the Alps! We'll ship you a basket of edelweiss to stick in your chippies' hairdos! It'll be the rage!

I admit that for once this was an O.K. haircurler. Wouldn't go so far as cute—let's just say bearable and leave it at that. He let himself be shoved around, not bitching, just asking that we tie him up on something soft. He was even sort of an ass-kisser. For example, his need to rap: "I've got excellent insurance coverage," he said. "Don't worry about that! You can even crack her up, I've got an all-risk policy! Actually, that would suit me fine. So if you get a chance, smash up the front end a little. I'd like to get it rebuilt, it's all scratched. It's damn tricky trying to make my garage. I'm always denting the fenders."

We didn't give a fuck about his front end. What interests me in a car is the engine. I love a beautiful machine. And this car would spoil me for life. Holy shit, what pickup! A Ford Mach 1, a real mother! Gobbled up the miles! But you gotta watch out for skidding on curves. Tend to oversteer, these

245

American mobiles. No big surprise—all they got is superhighways. And the mileage is pathetic—the needle drops before your eyes. Seven miles to the gallon, tops! We wouldn't get far, I knew, but we'd get there fast. And for me speed was the main thing. Had to cut out of Alsace with its stench of death.

No way, of course, we could stick its red nose in any service stations. Not for lack of bread, no. On that score we were all set—the haircurler had been kind enough to bring five hundred francs along in his pocket. But with a machine like that it would be nuts to show yourself. Check your oil? Water? How about the tires? Lick your windshield? Flashing: Fuck! Three snotty kids in this classy chassis? Might as well call the cops ourselves and tip them on the details: "Presently moving in a south-south-westerly direction, heading for the Alps via Besançon, Poligny, Lons-le-Saunier . . ."

Let's roll while she's still warm, I told myself. Make tracks! When she runs dry, we'll take it from there. Nice and comfy in my bucket seat, I lost myself in the ecstasy of top performance. I drove like a pro, shifting down for curves, hitting them from the outside, flooring it coming out, brights on, beaming light into the sycamores, boring a luminous tunnel of escape through the night at 10,000 rpms. Your luxury getaway. Total comfort inside the air-conditioned cockpit. Supersmooth ride. The green lights of the dash dancing palely below my eyes, thick carpeting, cigarette lighter, adjustable steering wheel, adjustable seats—the only nonadjustable thing was the luck factor people have in relation to each other in life. Why hadn't my ma rigged it so I could become a haircurler, huh? That was a perfect example! She had to have been laid by a haircutter some time or other. At least she could have given a little thought to the problem. All she had to do was rap to him about me a little in the sack, and zap! I would have been an apprentice. For Chrissake, I wouldn't be in this fix! And Marie should have had the opposite happen to her—she should never have gone into haircurling. I eyed her horizontalized on the back seat. No doubt about it, it had come as a shock when we told her about dreamboat's brilliant performance. I got the feeling that nothing, but nothing, would ever grab her again. So I tried to find some words to comfort her. "Don't cry," I said. "One down, ten to go!"

"I'm not crying," she answered. "I don't give two shits!"

"Didn't you love him?"

"I don't know, I didn't have time. He was a good fuck, yes. But you really have to be the king of assholes to shoot a cop when we could have gone on fucking like that for days on end!"

"It wasn't a cop! It was a guard!"

"Even worse."

It made me sick to my stomach, seeing her like that. Poor kid. And to think that all her pa had to do was get his shit together and zap! Marie saved! She could have been a sweet young thing in organdy going to vespers, wearing a big smile and bunny furs for minding the store. Life is fucked up, no one would tell you different. But also, sometimes it's through the shit that man's terrific genius shines most brightly. Dig. Because in a way our hasty retreat had some hidden good in it. And like I always say, you have to look on the bright side. First, we'd gotten our old lady back. Second, it was time for us to shake the shit off our shoes anyhow. We'd been turning into a couple of faggots—in our heads. But now, with panic in the air, I felt the wheels starting to turn again under my hat. My reflexes checked out. My old creativity revived. The proof? I'd found the solution to our refueling worries! Gotta admit that Mulhouse haircurler was a smart kid. A big surprise was waiting for us in the trunk: a twenty-gallon jerrican! Bright yellow, with a little wagon like a shopping cart for rolling it along. Naturally there wasn't a drop of gas in it. So here was the gimmick: when a lit-up gas station flashed ahead, we'd zoom by and, a hundred yards later, screech to a stop. Marie—good old Marie, the only one of us who could still show her face in front of the fuzz—would truck off down the road with the jerrican on the wagon and pop into the station. "Drat!" she'd say to the grease monkey. "Just not my lucky day. I'm not wild about running out of gas in the middle of the night. She'd truck back with twenty gallons and we'd roll for an hour or so, till we hit the next gas station. Marie left a trail of grease monkeys dazzled by this gorgeous nocturnal spirit, dudes pissed that they were on duty, they'd have walked a mile for a piece of her. But nobody could brag they'd seen the red tornado, not even trucks we met, 'cause we whizzed by in a blinding flash. We zoomed up behind them so fast it felt like they were going to hit our laps with their tarpaulins, calves and crates of endives. Then the truck would be behind us, and ahead the road, the black night. We'd flash our ass at them and wink our taillights. Average speed: 80–95. By the time the haircurler got himself untied from the bed, we'd be in fat city.

We saw dawn break over Bourg-en-Bresse. Between Pont-d'Ain and Morestel, Marie dozed off and I slowed on curves so as not to wake her. We hit Grenoble along with all the guys biking to work. And it was there that we switched cars, in a residential parking lot. Basic safety measure.

There were already quite a few dudes in shirt sleeves getting ready for the big trip, strapping stuff onto their luggage racks, cramming the trunk, piling junk up over the rear window—to hell with safety! Kids were chugging back and forth, dragged to the ground by shopping bags. Their old ladies screamed from the window, their hair down, wearing Lycra superstretch bras, ultra-sheer models for the road. We prowled around in low, looking for our chance.

The minute I spotted the dude with grease all over his shirt from cleaning his sparks, I flashed, There's our man. What you call a hunter's instinct. I stopped a little farther on.

In my panoramic rear-view mirror I saw him close his hood and climb behind the wheel. Then I heard the engine catch, and three big guns from the accelerator. Satisfied, the guy got out, leaving the engine idling, and looked up at his apartment house.

"Madeleine!"

Apparition of a bathing suit at a window on the sixth floor. White skin and curlers.

"I'm ready!"

Pops consulted his pocket watch. "Only five more minutes!"

"Look at you!" she answered. "That shirt was clean this morning!"

248

"What? What's the matter with my shirt?" He tucked in all his chins. "Damn! How stupid!"

"Come on up," the wife shouted. "I'll put some K2R on it."

That's it, go get yourself cleaned up, you slob! Meanwhile, Pierrot slipped behind the wheel of the rattletrap that was purring so sweetly. All he had to do was throw her in first and off she went. Yippy-shit for the clean plugs! Beautiful! Quite a bomb, your indigo Renault 16, piled with suitcases, busting with junk!

Pierrot tailed me through Grenoble. I led him out onto the autoroute for Chambéry. When the Ford stopped, tank empty, I jumped into the Renault, dragging our half-awake chick.

U-turn to cover our tracks. Back through Grenoble. I could just hear their coded messages: "Wild Boar calling Blue Omega. Ford found out of gas. Probably continuing Geneva via Annecy. Or Chamonix through Albertville. Establish roadblocks . . ."

So we steered for Briançon on 91. We went through endless valleys, following our noses. Gobbled the couple's picnic, their sandwiches and bananas. They'd thought of everything. Even the gas gauge read full. And their little Renault ran O.K. It was good to be driving French wheels again. The road climbed and wound around, fewer and fewer trees and more and more stones. We crossed a mountain pass in sparkling sunshine. But Marie didn't give two shits about the white peaks above us or the patches of snow beside the road. She was wiped out.

"You asleep?"

"No."

She was bluesed out.

"At least look at the glaciers!" I told her, pissed. "You wanted to see them so much. There they are! Right in front of your nose!"

"Fuck me," she answered. "I've got to know . . ." She was already unbuttoning her dress.

"Yes, Marie. Right away."

There's nothing better after being up all night, after a little violence. We fucked her beside the road, in a grove of whispering pines. We fucked her between her legs methodically, taking turns and not panicking, with trusty cocks that never give an inch, alpenstocks built to last. And we each made her come in turn,

249

once, twice, three times, like a big girl. Marie got off in the dried grass, lost herself in the sheep shit. "If you only knew how good that feels," she murmured hungrily between clenched teeth, "what satisfaction I feel in my cunt! All these mountains around me—what a fantastic place to come!"

It really looked like a super screw to me, and this time she was doing it with *us!* Thanks to *us!*

We hit the road again after eleven, our kneecaps pretty chafed.

We settled on a resort that didn't look too bad. "Ski French at Froide-les-Nivelles," the billboard said. The road ended there anyway, so you sort of had to get out. End of the line.

Not even a chalet. Just three buildings stuck among the rocks, cubes of gray cement, like in Toulouse and Mulhouse, except that this was a high-altitude suburb. And then towers, of the same gray, climbing up the shale, with empty cables, not even a bird sitting on them. And then some cranes, cement mixers. Algerians in yellow hard hats carrying girders. A hellish racket.

Marie was bushed. No question of starting off again, she nixed any idea of travel. Had to leave her in a pea-green snack bar, with all the Arabs munching on their cruddy couscous.

"Don't move," I told her. "Wait for us nice and quiet. Give us time to check out the area, see if we can find a secluded spot on the mountain."

Our dream was a little shepherd's hut lost in the Alps. But all Froide-les-Nivelles had was stones. All the roads that climbed the mountainside came to a dead end in a pile of stones. Not a hut in sight. Nothing. Just a soaring eagle that seemed to be eyeing us. And the car smoking like a steam engine from working too hard in first. Time to ditch it. I pushed it into a ravine. It crashed with a great kaboom that's still echoing back and forth. A spot the fuzz wasn't likely to stumble on: the end of the world, the planet Mars. We went back down on foot, sliding over the stones. The workmen were laying off. We picked up Marie-Ange, hunched near the jukebox. I told her we were moving on. "Fuck me," she answered. "That's the best thing for us to do." Then, just as we were passing by l'Etoile des Alpes, a big co-op-style store, we spotted our mug shots: a copy of

Dauphine taped to the window. Pierrot and I were stars again! And this time we'd made the front page! With Jacques in the middle, in the best spot, a superstar! A fucked-up account, but nothing we could do about it. "The assassins of a model guard!" it blasted in banner headlines. All it needed was the amount of the reward. I decided Marie had been right: the only thing left in the cards for us really was her ass.

We sent her in to buy the crummy rag, so informative, so objective, so juicy for the masses. We sampled its tidbits in a bus full of Algerians that took us back into the valley, to the pollution and the three-star lock-ups. The paper also served as a shield when we caught a beady Arab eye peering at us.

The story was far fucking out! Jacques in the hospital in critical condition. The asshole doctors working miracles so he could get his ass back into the hole fast, instead of letting him sweetly split in his coma. As for us, thanks to the serial number on the gun, we'd copped a rap of "accomplices to murder"! They hadn't taken long to check that out, those crafty dicks! We were desperadoes again, haircurler assaulters, master criminals, public enemies!

"No way you can stay with us," I announced to Marie as we got off in Gap. "We're contagious. You're in luck—you haven't been honored by the press!"

"Not for long," she answered. "That Mulhouse hairdresser must have spilled the beans by now. And talked plenty about me. I'm in it with you."

"You dummy! You didn't come with us to the guard's house. You're not an accomplice to anything. You didn't hurt anyone. You can tell them that you were sexually abused. Now do us a favor and get out of here! Go back to Puy—to your folks!"

"Just when I'm really getting it on?" she shot back. "No way!"

We rang her chimes almost all night long, like fanatics. I really think our panic put new life in our equipment. The more we used it, the less tired we got. We kept digging it, digging it more and more, like we felt the end of the world coming on. We got it up like hanged men. Really went to town on the cracked leather of our latest jalopy, by far the funkiest of the bunch, an antique Citroën 15 CV, the only heap we could cop in a hurry in the dreary parking lots of Gap. A fucked-up choice. The clutch gave out on hills and the shocks ripped your guts out. And the wheel had a first-class case of the shimmy, the pride of the thirties. While I struggled to hold her on the road, Pierrot socked it to Marie on the back seat. Their feet kept kicking my head, till I could hardly handle the curves anymore. So I just pooped along, hanging loose, averaging 45. When I finally heard silence behind me, I pulled over with a sigh of relief. Pierrot got behind the wheel, I took his place in Marie's arms, and we chugged off again. In the back of the 15, waiting for the road-blocks, searchlights and cop cars, I screwed Marie and she got off as we rattled over bumps and potholes. Oncoming headlights flashed on her eyes, her mouth, her dizzy blondness. Fascinated, I stored up pictures for the slams. Marie's thighs, Marie's ass, Marie's waist. Marie satisfied, Marie arched up, Marie spread out. Shoulders bare, hands held out, hair wild, teeth glittering. All things those pawing guards couldn't confiscate, even if they felt up my insides! Even if they opened up my balls! It would be my private picture show, dig? My head stuffed with takes—like a film festival! All the great classics, which I'd project at will! They could beat me up! Throw me in the hole! Who'd give two shits?

Tonight we're showing "The Last Mazurka!" and I don't want to miss it! Tragic love! I eat it up! Baden-Baden, Monte Carlo—all the resorts of Europe starting to crumble. Light the chandeliers! Spin the cartridge chamber, the barrels against your temples! A shot rings out in the dark, the ballerina was lying about her age. Alone on my musty bedroll, I won't need any-body. No packages, no mail, no visitors. So don't come fuck me around, I'll be in my projection room with my silhouetted nude heroines in those maddening shadow shots, my head reeling with soft music. But if I knew that you too, Marie, were rotting in a cage, then all would be lost, my flicks would go dark, I'd be blind and deaf, in hell, with just the spoons and nails and screw-drivers to stab my heart with. Marie, for Chrissake, listen to us! It's Pierrot and Jean-Claude, we're begging you! It would be a real bitch! You're much too pretty. I can't see you in a cell, a number on your back, with no mirror or fake eyelashes or perfume. What a rotten waste. You should always shimmer with warm reflections, dine by candlelight, flirt in front of the fire, curl up on furs, velvet, satin, a pillow behind your head. And who would fuck your ass in the shadow of the damp stones? Who would take care of your ravenous hungers? Who would watch day and night over your recovery, follow up on the treatment, give you the precious drops of life at the right times to prevent a relapse?

I tried to rap to her, reason with her gently. "We'll drop you off . . . Near a station or a hotel . . . It's the parting of the ways, the time for good-byes has come. Now that we've cured you, stretch your wings and fly."

"I'd really appreciate it if you'd shut the hell up," she answered hysterically. "Just shut up, make love, and let whatever happens happen. If we get out of this, we'll have it made. Listen to my feminine instinct! Sometimes I have visions, and I'm hardly ever wrong. We're *not* going to jail!"

We wound up believing in her trip. We'd escape the metal cuffs of the law, the 15 would worm its way out of the trap. We took old forgotten roads, switched to deserted areas where the mail hadn't been delivered in years, and slept in a little grove of dwarfed bushes that smelled of lavender . . .

We took off again around noon, as much in love as ever . . . and ran smack into a traffic jam! Everybody had the same idea— to leave the main highway. Nowhere to hide anymore. Cars were crawling down the road, the great vacation rush, the slow surge to the sea. Go ahead, blow your horns! Pass! We're digging the countryside in case we never see it again. We stalled and dawdled, our top priority was grooving. Don't fuck with the wedding! It's a hush-hush marriage, no flowers or white veil. Excuse the lack of ceremony, but it doesn't keep us from getting it on! The bride couldn't care less. She even drinks in public! A toast to the grooms of the highway! Dig that thigh in the rear-view window! Toss coins at us and wish us luck! Who needs Venice? Our gondola is this Citroën. We're rowing through a flood of tourists, hitch-hiking chicks. Sorry, kids, no time for nookie! The car's in quarantine, you might get bugs! There's sperm crawling all over our leather seats! The first one in would get knocked up! Hey, Pierrot!

Check out the trash feeding at those tables! A double row of cookout freaks melting away beside their overheated hot rods, simmering in the sun, heating up their shorts and staining their girdles in the back, mopping themselves under the arms, eyes and hair, then wiping the baby's chin, who's drooling his whole bottle. While a few yards away a cool hillside awaits them, the pleasures of shade, a carpet of moss and a gurgling brook. No, they'd rather hog the eats by the car on a bed of greasy papers, a soggy warm meal, bologna and hard-boiled eggs. A bus passes. Now they're gagging in fumes, gulping the exhaust, noticing the cheese is spiked with diesel oil. With carbon monoxide on top of that, they'll be stoned out of their minds! When they hit the road again, they'll be bouncing off the trees. Can't hack your scene, you Sunday drivers, we'd rather walk.

"I'm sick of driving," said Marie. "My skin is all sticky and I can't breathe in this heap. What if we took a rest in some breezy spot so I could air my feet?"

We all went for that. Always up for a siesta. We weren't in any great rush, were we? No one was after our ass 'cept the man! We didn't know where the fuck we were heading!

We left the clogged highway. The shady back roads were for us. Two feet from the crunch it was like a desert, the dawn of man! We went in deeper and deeper . . .

"Look! Can you believe it? A D.S.! Plates from up north. Holy shit, a fuel-injected twenty-one! Not bad . . . I might even say tempting . . . Ditched in the woods like that, with no one around. Wait a minute!" I spoke too fast! A family was munching in a clearing close by, with a table, folding chairs, the whole bit. Papa, Mama and their big girl. Cute as a picture, wouldn't hurt a fly. Real nature-lovers. I figured there'd be no sweat.

"Why don't we stop here?" I suggested.

"Dynamite," said Pierrot.

We got out of the car and tipped over to the D.S. like zombies, no self-control. A gorgeous baby, the fine cut of keys glittering from the dashboard.

Pa-Ma gave us the once-over and shrugged their shoulders, obviously not pleased in the least. The kid gave a broad-minded stare while she scarfed a greenish-looking sandwich. Sweet sixteen, with the round eyes of a virgin and a couple of choice, healthy honeydews underneath her yellow shirt.

Then a silent fear put the lid on snack time. We were making them choke on their chow.

"What's the matter with my car?" the guy came on with after a tight gulp.

"It's far fucking out, man," I answered. "Dynamite!"

The chick filled her face, ignoring the scene, while her parents went pale. Then I saw from the spark in her eye that she was getting a real charge out of it.

Ma finally got into it with a certain dignity. "Perhaps you'd like to share our lunch?"

"No thanks," I answered, "no way. But don't get in a huff, if we felt like cutting in on you, we would."

"Then what do you want?"

"It's about that car of yours . . ."

"You have one! Leave us alone!"

"O.K.! O.K.! We're going . . ."

We left the holy family with its jaws working. Trucked back to the good old Citroën, opened the trunk, pulled out the jack, the crank, and returned, all smiles. Hi, it's us again.

They sprang up like jack-in-the-boxes. That did it, they were scared shitless, doing flashbacks on all the front-page coverage they'd read in the news—crime, hippies, delinquency, murderous frenzy. The headlines danced before their eyeballs.

"J-just a m-m-minute," the dude stuttered. "You're not going to do anything stupid?"

The chick thought it was hilarious. "That sure is the impression I get!"

"You think it's funny?" the mama snapped at her.

"Sort of."

"Jacqueline!"

"Well, so what? We'll make the trip in their car!"

Jacqueline . . . Jacqueline . . . A name I'd heard before. But where? When?

"Your daughter has just put the basic element of the problem quite clearly," said Marie, madame ambassador, stepping forward with a smile. "It involves a friendly little exchange—our ball-buster for your limo. A deal?"

"A fifteen!" Pierrot added. "Gotta admit that's funny. You'll still be true to Citroën—just turn back the clock and there you are, at the wheel of an ancestor of your D.S.!"

The dude lunged for his car. I cut him off, demonstrating one of the many uses of the jack.

"Careful!" I explained to him. "It's very hard, and it hurts. Especially in the head . . ."

"I forbid you to touch my D.S.!"

Jacqueline came and took him gently by the arm. "We don't give a damn about your D.S.," she said calmly. "A car is a car! It doesn't matter. Papa, listen to me! It's a beautiful day, it's vacation time, tonight we'll be sleeping at the beach, I flunked my exams, so what? Life is beautiful!"

Whack! That's how he answered. The deranged daddy dealt her a backhand belt, a stinging slap!

Jacqueline didn't dig it much. "You poor old bastard!" she cried. "You piece of shit! You asshole! You animal! Engineer, my ass! You know what your sweet darling daughter has to say to you? Your only child? I've had it! It's over! I'm not going to your cute little cottage in Pyla! You can play your volleyball and tennis, and go shrimping and take walks to Bombard without me! I'm getting out!"

Far out! I never saw folks so stunned or dazed as that pair of fuckers with their mouths hanging open! Not to mention that I was floored by Jackie's style myself! Jacqueline, Pyla, it was starting to click, that funky aroma was coming back to me, that terrific odor, those perfumed bikinis! I couldn't take my eyes off the angry little cuss, especially since she was heading our way, begging us.

"Take me with you," she said. "We'll take the old farts' D.S. and get the hell out of here! I can't hack their trip anymore! I'm being buried alive. I know I'm ready to make the break, or else it's curtains for me! Please, give me a breath of fresh air, I won't be dead weight!"

"We can't," said Marie, all motherly. "It's a shame, but we really can't swing it. It would be a bummer to take you where we're heading."

"You're not going to leave me here with them? It wouldn't work anymore! I've burned all my bridges!"

256

Problem. Responsibility. We all looked at each other, feeling her king-size hopes weighing heavy on us.

"O.K.," said Marie. "We'll give you a lift somewhere, then drop you off with enough scratch to make out."

"They have two thousand francs," Jacqueline added. "In Mama's bag."

Pierrot went over with the crank. The bread rolled out of the purse, no hassle. And we cut out in the D.S., loaded to the gills, the chicks in the back, already heavy soulmates.

"I dig your shirt, it's cute," Marie said. "From Cacharel?"

"No, Mary Quant. I've got a blue one too."

The old farts faded in the rear-view mirror, shoulders bent and arms hanging, then vanished in the green background. Not bad: we'd left them a Citroën. With four flats, of course. I flashed the look on their faces when they got a load of Pierrot's porno art all over the house, a private opening of their new collection . . .

Two o'clock. On the road again. The blinker jammed, horn blaring, I kept on passing. I cut right through the crowd, weaving in and out, grazing bumpers. The pack was barking up my ass. The rear-view mirror was crammed with fists. The cars in the opposite lane flashed their brights right in my puss. Squirm, you lousy cocksuckers! They thought I was playing with death when I really was together, elbow out the window, two fingers on the wheel, a third nudging the gears. The tip of my big toe was doing a boogie on the brakes, thumping the accelerator, I was scratching myself with the other foot. It was total mastery, with a backseat rap session and yackathon.

"How old are you?"

"Sixteen."

"Get laid yet?"

"No . . ."

"Tsk, tsk, you poor thing! For real?"

"Yes."

"Shit. That gets to me. Hey, you guys, we can't let her go like that! Let her loose in such an unnatural state of mind and body?"

"It would be cruel," said Pierrot.

Two thirty. An isolated wood, a siding covered with poppies.

257

We reclined the seats.

"Shall I take everything off?"

"Leave the sandals on."

Some good deeds are really sweeter than others. Giving one-self to others is dynamite once in a while!

"Does it hurt?"

"No . . . Not at all . . . not a bit."

It went off very well. Marie fanned her with a Michelin map. I saw the envy in her eyes: the kid was sprouting a pair of crackerjack tits, nifty knockers—boss boobies, you might say.

Five o'clock. Finished. Pierrot and I had done a number on her. She was pleased as punch. We dressed her, combed her hair, forked over all her folks' bread. She deserved it, it was hers. We told her, "Be cool, the road's a hundred yards away, you'll get picked up easy." We left her sprawled out under a tree, smiling and content.

"I don't know how to thank you . . ."

"Our pleasure."

We cut out fast, keeping it short. Emotion is for assholes. I saw her wave in the rear-view mirror. At least something we'd done wasn't all bad. There was a chick with a good solid foundation.

Six o'clock. Gotta admit, a beautiful sunset, when it's right, is far fucking out. Soon it would be three months that we'd been blazing a tourist trail through our fun-loving country. Soon, too, it would be twenty minutes that we'd been rolling along, accompanied by the kingly red disk, on a narrow country road that was, for the time being, totally deserted. A sneaky little road with no billboards, so they didn't make a cent off it. It snaked easily through the hills, trying in a million roundabout ways not to offend anyone, carefully respecting every inch of the sacred land survey. Instinctively, we slid into low gear, a slow-motion trip, obeying the speed limits, careful of old dogs crossing the road. We drove for pleasure, in the coolness, with no definite purpose.

We'd thought about going through Puy so Marie could say hello to her folks. And talked about hitting Toulouse so I could pop in on my ma. Both ideas were finally scratched. We didn't really see any point in them. For the moment, we'd decided on

Paris. To avoid the main roads, coast along peacefully till we reached the capital. Then melt into the giant city. Hide out with a certain Caroline, former mistress of some dude Marie had put out for, who, after a period of boring jealousy, became one of her best friends through some abortion incident, a pretty cruddy story. We didn't give a shit about the details, all that interested us was that the chick in question lived in a duplex in Montmartre where we could crash as long as we wanted.

No reason to get excited, everything works out sooner or later. No use in sprouting gray hairs at our age. So what if the establishment shot us in the ass—we already had a hole there! We just headed north, in no hurry. Now we were through with fuckups! We drove at a reasonable speed into the horizontal rays of the sinking sun. Like old farts, not rapping. What was the use, since no one felt like it? Why force ourselves? We didn't have to be polite. We'd already said everything we had to say, and were fucking happy with our mutual feelings. I was behind the wheel. On my right, Pierrot was daydreaming, his feet up on the dash. And in back Marie had her arms around our shoulders tenderly. So close—with her breath, hair and end-of-the-day body odors—she seemed to be sitting between us, up front. Inseparable, that's what we were. A tightly knit trio with total understanding. We were all so contented nobody even felt like fucking anymore. Superfulfilled, with nothing to hide from each other, nothing to steal. Marie-Ange, my sister, and Pierrot, my brother, whom I knew by heart. I could recite you both like a poem. I could sculpt you with my fingertips, I could paint you in the dark. You were mine, and I was yours. We were open books. I would've liked to meet the asshole politician with his so-called program who had solutions to our troubles, since we didn't have any, we could do without all that campaign bullshit. He'd do better to concentrate on the fate of hairdressers and defenseless picnickers. Exploited proletarians. Bitter businessmen. No need to get in a sweat about us! We were drifting through life like kings in the comfy D.S. that glided so easily around the blindest, meanest, unbanked curves, playing with the road, thumbing its nose at bumps and jolts and pot holes. Cool. Relaxed. No efforts. Limp pricks. We'd get it up when we felt like it. For the time being, we were just on a peaceful drive, in an amorous, silent understanding. Optimistic. Confident of the future. Nothing could shake me anymore. Even if, suddenly, there was a sinister crunching sound, even if I knew we were going to die in a minute, I'd laugh about it.

ME (*In a calm, cool and collected voice*): I'll never get sick of this buggy. What performance!

MARIE-ANGE (*Stroking the backs of our necks*): And all that crap about how you get seasick in the back seat? Bullshit!

They hadn't heard anything, the lucky stiffs, or seen anything. We were starting down a marvelous hill, straight down for a mile or so, a journey to the center of the earth, stoned out on our scenic tour, a swell curve at the bottom and the sun right in our pusses, a bloody omen.

Then it happened: Pierrot let out a horrible holler.

PIERROT: Hey look! Where'd the wheel come from?

ME: Ours, man.

PIERROT: You're shitting me!

ME: Hell, no.

It did look funny. A few yards from the nose-diving hood, a tire was trucking on ahead of us.

ME: It's the right front wheel.

It was following the same course as us, perfectly aligned. It wouldn't leave the road for anything. It insisted on escorting us to the end. Only, it took the lead, like it wanted to show us the right way so we wouldn't goof up.

ME: We're the assholes that sawed it off! You asked for it—it's your ball's revenge!

PIERROT (*Getting panicky*): Why don't you use the brakes?

ME: I'd be glad to, but at seventy, on three wheels, we'd be part of the landscape. Even in a D.S.

PIERROT: We'll be part of the landscape down there too!

ME: Yeah. Only it gives us a little time.

MARIE-ANGE: I even recognize this rotten jalopy! There, see that spot on the ceiling? Well, I made it! With a bottle of Coke that'd gotten too hot! One day when he took me out to screw in some pine trees!

PIERROT: You might have said so earlier, you dummy!

When I think of all those lucky fuckers who can do whatever they damn well please! Decide, for instance, to cross the courtyard and shoot the breeze with a neighbor. Or slip on a jacket, hit a bar and watch a game with a glass of wine. Or even, if the mood strikes, go down to the riverbank through the park, dodging the hopscotch players, hula hoops and tricycles. For us, those times are gone forever. Have to go through with it, die on that curve whether or not we're up for it. Not that the notion charms us, but in the end, one solution is as good as another, all things considered.

PIERROT: What if we jump?

ME: Yeah . . . sure . . . we could . . .

MARIE-ANGE: I really think you *want* to kick it on wheels!

The chick was right. Why should we always want something better—better than today, better than tomorrow, more and always more? That's how you fuck up, banging your head against a wall, nerves shot to hell. Everyone's gotta croak at the end of the line. So? Wisdom. Stoicism. Stay with what you've got, with the possible, the tangible. It's a groovy set of wheels that doesn't leave the road even with one wheel missing! Two good buddies, tons of memories, youth racing through your veins, perfect health. A beautiful sunset, a swell curve, soft fields beyond for our remains. I could see it already: that loop-the-loop we'd go into, with the red sky for a background! A postcard death! Dare-devil triple somersault! One doll, two puppets, flying away! Great slow-motion effect! Like the flicks, fellas! Except that it's for real, it's tough. The good earth of France coldly breaking your backs. There's no net, no tricks, no camera and no audience. An anonymous crackup, no witnesses. No chills running through the crowd. Not even a peasant leaning on his scythe. I peered all around, couldn't spot a soul. They're all at supper, watching the evening news. We could croak, rot, with steel in our guts, it wouldn't grab anyone. When I think of that faggot haircurler not even bothering to keep his fucking heap! What an asshole! First he gets it swiped, and then he sells it! Chickenshit! No balls! There's another jerk who'll die in bed, nice and comfy. Pass away, as they say, while innocents crack up on the highways, and not just on weekends! I looked at my watch. My watch works fine. I dig it a lot. Never gave me any trouble. Just wanted to check the exact time of my death. Eight o'clock. No need for TV. I could see our great pal the Toulousian kinker from there.

He'd just rolled the steel shutter down on his last customer, was dropping the venetian blinds, flipping out the red lights, and trucking into the wig salon, a grin on his kisser.

MARIE-ANGE: Pierrot! Jean-Claude! We'll never split up!

PIERROT: We'll never split up, Marie. We'll never be apart.

MARIE-ANGE: We really got our rocks off good!

PIERROT: I'm not scared, Marie! I'm not scared!

ME: Let's hold hands.

MARIE-ANGE: Screw death!

PIERROT: I'm giving it the finger.

ME: There you go, cunt! Stick that up your ass!

Time seemed to be dragging. Our tragic end was all fucked up, not even flashy. Like everything else, not especially brilliant. It all started in Toulouse with that fucking haircutter. It only takes running into one bastard. Why did he have to have a gun, the rotten prick? To protect what? His wheels? His so-called trusty D.S.? But we were bringing it back to you, you faggot! If it wasn't for you and your fucking rod, Jeanne would be alive! Without you and your piece, the guard in Ensisheim wouldn't have died! We'd have rolled sweetly along forever. Croaked in our beds too, like haircurlers, surrounded by affection. Maybe found work, who knows? That's what I miss the most: wholesome activity! More than a dozen yards left, I've still got time to get a job! There, I'm rolling up my sleeves! Opening a salon in Puy! Chez Jean-Claude and Pierrot, hairdresser brothers! Wash-and-set at slashed prices! We work our asses off nonstop! Ma handles the cash box, chats up all the customers, listens to all their gripes while we skip around with our combs. One day my watch stops. I show at the corner watchmaker's. Push the door with the jingle bells. Stroll into a forest of clocks that smells of wax and licorice. She tips up shyly: "Sir?" A way of saying "sir" that rips your heart out. While she's checking my watch, an autopsy with a magnifying glass, I get off on her neck, so dainty under her curls. Next day she shows at the salon with lowered eyes, and I'm the one who does her, curls and perfumes her. Under the dryer she flips through a movie mag. Marie-Ange and Jean-Claude! I'll cut the story short, time is running out! A young couple who'd make you jealous. Did you catch them coming out of the church? A gorgeous wedding! Such a well-matched pair! And the two mothers so elegant, beaming with pride! Real fine people!

STRANGE LADY: I heard that you were looking for a maid . . .

MARIE-ANGE: Why, yes. Sit down. Would you like some tea?

STRANGE LADY: I wouldn't want to impose on you . . .

MARIE-ANGE: Do you have references?

STRANGE LADY: No, madame.

MARIE-ANGE: You never held another position?

STRANGE LADY: No, madame.

MARIE-ANGE: Ah . . . That's a bit of a nuisance. What did you do before?

STRANGE LADY: I made boas, madame.

MARIE-ANGE: In Paris?

STRANGE LADY: No, madame. In Rennes. At the Central in Rennes . . . I see you don't understand . . . I'm talking about a prison. I spent ten years there.

MARIE-ANGE: Ah . . .

STRANGE LADY (*Rising*): You probably think I won't do?

MARIE-ANGE: No, no! Not at all! Wait! I must discuss it with my husband!

I insist we take her. On trial. And wind up liking our gray-haired maid. Even digging her style. A few years in the clink knocks some sense into their heads. What a change from all those other girls we've tried, incompetent, dirty, thieving. Our new maid gives us a boa for Christmas. My wife gets off on it. And I dream about Jeanne, up there, celebrating all alone. Our new maid's quite chic, with her white apron tied over her black dress. In the morning I wait impatiently for the moment she comes in, when she knocks softly and appears in our room with the breakfast tray. I catch myself getting a hard-on for her, under the covers. One night, unable to resist anymore, I go and join her under the eaves. Now I'm the one who knocks softly.

"Who is it?"

"Monsieur."

She opens the door wearing gray cotton, a nun's nightie . . .

I see myself arched up, between Jeanne's legs, and it's not pretty. I see my ass in a palace bedroom, beside a dead woman, and it's not pretty. I see Marie dying in a field of daisies, and it's not pretty. I see Pierrot's face on a butcher's block, and I admit it's not pretty.

Life is too complicated. No matter where I look I can't find anything simple. You think you're doing good and it's shit. Always shit.

Don't worry, you hairdressers, we're leaving the stage, it's your show!

The end.

MARIE-ANGE: Pierrot! Jean-Claude! What's happening to me? My mouth is full of excrement!